A

FEATHER

ON THE

WATER

A
FEATHER
ON THE
WATER

A NOVEL

LINDSAY JAYNE ASHFORD

LAKE UNION
PUBLISHING

Published by Lake Union Publishing, Seattle

www.apub.com

Amazon, the Amazon logo, and Lake Union Publishing are trademarks of Amazon.com, Inc., or its affiliates.

ISBN-13: 9781542037952
ISBN-10: 1542037956

Cover design by Faceout Studio, Tim Green

Printed in the United States of America

For Mum
July 30, 1932–November 19, 2021

PART ONE

CHAPTER 1

Williamsburg, Brooklyn: June 1945

Martha sneaked into the hallway in stocking feet and stood for a moment, listening. The snoring had a steady rhythm, like waves breaking on pebbles. So long as he stayed asleep, she was safe. Closing the door as gently as she could, she tiptoed across the cracked linoleum and made her way down the stairs, hugging the suitcase to her body to stop it from catching on the banister. Only when she reached the front door did she slip her feet into her shoes.

The linden trees on South First Street were heavy with blossom, their honey scent tainted by the stink of garbage as she passed the alley that ran alongside the grocery store. Ahead of her, on the corner of Wythe Avenue, a young man in paint-spattered pants was doing pull-ups on a bar of scaffolding. As she passed by, he whistled. She dug her chin into the collar of her blouse, dodging past him.

She headed downhill, toward the welcome black shadow of the Domino sugar refinery. Pausing to catch her breath, she tasted a sweetness mingled with fumes from the factory chimney. From where she stood, she could see the East River. The water was smoky quartz beneath a clear blue sky. Great barges and motorboats glided past. And on the other side, glinting in the morning sunshine, was the towering glory of Manhattan.

It was too early to get the subway to Queens. She set her suitcase down next to a low wall by the river's edge. It was as good a place as any to kill time. He'd never think of coming to look for her here. Reaching into her bag, she pulled out a newspaper cutting and unfolded it. There was a stain over the first couple of paragraphs, from when he'd thrown an empty bottle of Jack Daniel's across the kitchen, and the dregs from the smashed remains had spattered the front page.

She smoothed out the scrap of paper and laid it on her knee. WAR LEAVES 4 MILLION HOMELESS IN EUROPE. Under the headline was a photograph of a hollow-eyed woman standing outside a makeshift shelter, a baby in her arms and a frightened child peeping out from beneath her skirts. It was impossible to look at those faces without something tightening under her ribs—as if some invisible thread were tugging at her heart. She'd read the report so many times, she could almost have repeated it with her eyes closed. And at the end was an appeal for recruits: a few short sentences that had set her mind reeling. "Must be free to travel at short notice. No dependents."

The interview had been easier than she'd expected. She'd felt foolish at first, when they'd asked her if she spoke any foreign languages. How could she not have realized that they'd want that? She'd mumbled something about knowing a little Louisiana French Creole, courtesy of her New Orleans grandmother. To her relief, they'd simply nodded and moved on to what seemed of far more interest to them: the fact that she had run the food distribution section of the Henry Street Settlement on the Lower East Side. *Had*. Until Arnie came back from the war and put a stop to it. Thankfully, they hadn't asked her reason for giving up her volunteer work. Nor had they inquired why, as a married woman, she was applying for a job overseas. To her amazement, she'd been offered the post of assistant director at a camp in southern Germany.

In another compartment of her handbag, concealed inside an empty powder compact, were the two red patches they'd handed her at the end of the interview. She rummaged around until her fingers found the cold metal edge of the compact. Snapping it open, she picked out the patches. Each bore the letters "UNRRA" stitched in white: United Nations Relief and Rehabilitation Administration. She'd been instructed to sew them onto the uniform she would be given when she arrived in Europe: on the cap and at the top of the left sleeve of the jacket.

As she tucked them back inside the compact, she caught her reflection in the mirror. In the bright sunlight her skin looked paler than usual. She hadn't been able to get hold of face powder for months, but in the past few days it had reappeared in Walgreen's. Only one shade was available—and she'd applied it a little too liberally to conceal the scar on her left cheek. Her lipstick was called Tea Rose—nothing too bright, she'd thought, for this first day. The only other makeup was a touch of mascara on her top lashes.

Arnie had once told her that the color of her eyes reminded him of Hershey Kisses. She snapped the compact shut, trying not to remember. In just a few hours' time, she would be far away from him. Her insides flipped at the thought of flying across the Atlantic. She'd never been on a plane. Never traveled outside the USA. The longest journey she'd ever taken was the train from Mobile to New York in the summer of '32. She'd been a different person then. Nineteen years old and brimming with fantasies of the new life Arnie had promised.

She fixed her gaze on a passing coal barge, counting the seconds before it slipped beneath the Williamsburg Bridge. A mindless exercise to block out the images jostling for space in her head: his eyes as they could look, as they used to look; his hands stroking her skin, in the days when she could let him touch her without tensing up at the thought of what might follow; her face in the mirror as she took off her jewelry on their wedding night, winking at her reflection—so elated, so certain, so hopelessly naïve.

She made herself wait until three trains had thundered across the bridge. Then she got to her feet and picked up her suitcase. Clenching her fingers around the handle, she told herself that crossing thousands of miles of open ocean couldn't possibly be worse than the fear she was leaving behind.

Newhaven, England: Two Days Later

Kitty heard the sea in her sleep. The distant smack of waves against a wooden pier. The sound triggered a dream about her old school in Austria. She was in the yard, jumping a rope that slapped the ground as she chanted a rhyme. *"Schifflein, Schifflein, fahr nach Holland. Die Wellen schlugen hoch, hoch . . ."* Little boat, little boat, go to Holland. The waves beat high, high . . .

After she opened her eyes, it took a few befuddled moments to work out where she was. The train compartment was in semidarkness, the curtain shifting in the draft from an open window. Why had they stopped? Moving slowly so as not to disturb the slumbering body beside her, she lifted a corner of the moth-eaten fabric and peered through the dusty glass.

The sky was tinged pink with the coming sunrise. She could see the corner of a building up ahead, and the first four letters of a sign: "NEWH." They must be almost there, then: waiting for some signal to allow the train to enter the station. To her right were metal railings, through which she caught the glimmer of water. Craning her neck, she saw that they were at the mouth of a river, where it met the open sea. The swell, ruffled by the breeze, turned the surface into a silver shoal of ripples. The masts of fishing boats swayed back and forth.

She spotted the hull of a big ship heading slowly into port. Was that her ship? Even from a distance it looked old, battered. But everything that had come through the war looked that way: buildings, bridges, vehicles. People, too. She glanced at the man slumped in the seat opposite. His thinning hair was gray above a face that looked anxious, even in sleep. He'd wished her good evening in an accent that marked him as foreign, as hers had once done. She wondered if, like her, he'd come to England to escape the war. And what he'd be returning to.

Looking back at the view through the window, she watched the climbing sun streak the water with gold. She thought how different the sea looked from the image she'd carried inside her head for so long: a memory of gunmetal waves whipped up by an icy December wind; gulls screaming; children crying; the stink of rotting fish as she'd marched up the gangway, clutching her little suitcase.

She'd been too young then to know the name of the water she was crossing. At twelve years old, all she knew was that the boat was taking her to England. The safe place. *You'll like it there.* Her father's voice echoed down the years. He'd taught her one phrase in English, which she'd repeated over and over as the boat lurched through those angry waves: "I'm hungry—please, may I have some bread?"

Closing her eyes, she tried to remember the faces of her parents. There had been no photograph wrapped in the clothes inside her suitcase, because they'd tried so hard, when they waved goodbye, to pretend that everything was normal. *Just a little while, and we'll all be together again.* Why was it that she could recall her mother's voice—those parting words, whispered in German—but couldn't remember the color of her eyes?

The train jolted back to life, bringing murmurs and movement from the other passengers in Kitty's compartment. As it drew nearer to the station, she caught sight of a man holding a cardboard sign with the letters "UNRRA" scrawled across it. She felt her mouth go dry. It was real. She really *was* going. Those untidy black letters spelled escape from this country that had both saved her and held her captive. Before

7

the sun went down this evening, she would be in France. And after that, she'd be on her way to Germany.

As she reached up to the luggage rack to retrieve her bag, she remembered the words Fred had hissed in the darkness of the theater on her last night in Manchester. He hadn't wanted her to go. In a clumsy sort of way, he'd asked her to marry him. And when she'd said that she couldn't think of settling down until she'd found out about her parents, he'd gone quiet. Then, as the lights went down and the show was about to start, he'd said: "Why can't you just face it? You're an orphan, Kitty."

Orphan. Somehow, the word sounded even lonelier in English than in German. He hadn't meant to be cruel—she was certain of that. He was only saying what any logical, right-thinking person would conclude after reading the harrowing newspaper reports and scanning the lists posted by the Red Cross. Millions had died. How could her parents have been spared? And if, by some miracle, they were alive, why had there been no letter from them in five years?

The queasiness in Martha's stomach hadn't subsided since takeoff. The journey had been every bit as arduous as she had feared—two long flights punctuated by a stopover at Nova Scotia to refuel. The military airplane was so noisy that conversation of any kind during the flight had been impossible. There were five men and one other woman in the UNRRA group, but apart from perfunctory introductions as they'd been about to board, she hadn't had the chance to find out anything about them. The men looked to be late forties or older—past the age limit to have been drafted. The woman was closer to Martha's age. She hadn't smiled when they'd been introduced. And she hadn't looked pleased to be seated next to Martha on the flight. She'd been asleep throughout the second leg of the journey.

Martha peered out at the lightening sky. They were flying above a fluffy blanket of clouds. After a few minutes, holes appeared. It was just possible to see that they were no longer flying over the ocean. She wasn't sure if the land she could see was England.

Arnie's face suddenly superimposed itself on the blur of green below. It occurred to her that he would have seen this same view, just over a year ago, when he went with the army to prepare for the D-Day landings. But he'd never made it to France. He'd gotten into trouble days after he arrived in England—arrested for wounding a man in a drunken fight—and had been shipped back to New York with a dishonorable discharge before the invasion of France had even begun.

Martha wondered what he would do when he realized that she was gone for good. She glanced at her watch, still on East Coast time. Probably he was asleep. Probably there would be an empty bottle on the bedside table. Would he have been smoking in bed? The number of times she'd taken a lit cigarette from his fingers when he was out cold . . . She took in a sharp breath. She mustn't think of him. Mustn't torture herself over what she'd tried—and failed—to change.

The plane started its descent. She caught a sudden glimpse of the dome of Saint Paul's Cathedral, looking like an island in a sea of crumbling, bombed-out houses. The realization that London lay beneath her had hardly registered before the pilot veered away from the city, bringing them down to land in what looked like a farmer's field.

When they juddered to a halt, the woman in the next seat blinked awake and bent to the floor, rummaging for something in her handbag. Martha saw her pull out a set of false teeth and pop them into her mouth. Perhaps that explained her reluctance to smile, Martha thought. But there was no time to find out. They were ushered off the plane and straight into a military truck.

Martha was the only one of the group small enough to fit into the front seat, between the driver and one of the UNRRA men. As the truck bounced along potholed country lanes, Martha tried unsuccessfully to stop her left knee from bumping against the right thigh of her fellow passenger. She turned to apologize, but before she could open her mouth, he asked her where she was from.

"Brooklyn." She gave something near a smile. It felt awkward, being this close, even if he was old enough to be her father. "How about you?"

"New Jersey." He braced himself against the dash as the truck lurched around a bend. "Know where you're headed?" He had the brisk tone of a sergeant major.

"Not exactly. Someplace in the south of Germany: Bavaria." She'd gone to the library to look it up, not sure if it was a town or a city. She'd sat staring at the map for a few minutes before she realized that it was a whole region, like an American state, with rivers and forests and mountains.

The man beside her nodded. "Pretty place—leastways it used to be. Went there in the twenties. Good skiing." A shaft of sunlight caught the white stubble on his jaw. "Hope to make it there for a few days come winter."

"Where will you be working?"

"Up north, near Hanover. The Belsen camp."

She searched his face, wondering if she'd heard right. Images from newsreels flashed into her head. Harrowing scenes of skeletal figures, barely alive, clinging to barbed-wire fences. "Belsen? Wasn't that . . ."

"It's a Displaced Persons Center now," he cut in. "Awful for them, but there's no choice. Too many people with no place to go—and these camps lying empty. Just gotta make the best of it."

Martha stared through the windshield, the trees and fields a blur of green. It was beyond awful. Like a sick joke. People punched senseless by war, forced to live in a place where thousands had been put to death. *Please, God, don't let me be going to a place like that.* Even as the thought entered her mind, she realized how cowardly it sounded.

"Plenty of other places being used as well." His voice was gentler now, as if he was trying to reassure her. "The army's commandeered all kinds of joints—factories, Boy Scout camps—even a zoo up in Hamburg. Guess you'll be . . ." He broke off, shading his eyes with his hand. "Ah! There's the English Channel!"

She craned her neck to catch the glimmer of water on the horizon. The fields gave way to houses as the truck rattled downhill. Soon they were driving past yachts and fishing boats. Farther along the quayside, the bigger boats were anchored. She saw a man standing by a gangway holding up a sign with "UNRRA" handwritten in black letters.

The man beside her had the door open before the driver had cut the engine. He held it for her as they scrambled out. As they waited in line for their papers to be checked, Martha studied the people climbing the gangway. Only one was female. Martha was struck by how young she looked. Her glossy black hair, worn in a long braid, blew out behind her in the breeze. She was wearing bobby socks, and she took the steps two at a time, as if she couldn't wait to get aboard. Could she be the daughter of one of the men boarding the boat? But the recruitment ad had said no dependents.

Half an hour later, Martha was up on deck. She covered her ears as the foghorn signaled their imminent departure, and gazed back toward the land they were leaving, at the town of Newhaven with its jumble of quaint houses, so very different from the skyscrapers and apartment blocks surrounding New York Harbor. She wished she'd had more time in England. Time to explore the countryside they'd sped through—and to see London. Maybe she'd have the chance to visit sometime in the future. The man in the truck had talked about traveling when he had time off, of going skiing in the mountains. But it was hard to square that idea with the images of Europe in the newsreels and the papers. Impossible to imagine taking any kind of vacation on a continent ravaged by war.

She felt the boat shudder as they began to move away from the quayside. When she could no longer make out the people and the buildings, she turned away from the rail and scanned her fellow passengers.

There was no sign of the man she'd talked with in the truck, nor the woman she'd sat next to on the plane. The only person she recognized was the young girl she'd spotted on the gangway. She was standing alone at the bow of the boat, staring out to sea. There were knots of men in army uniform nearby, smoking and chatting. They were casting the odd sly glance at her.

"Hello again!" Martha turned to see the British man who'd checked her papers standing beside her. He was peering at her through thick horn-rimmed spectacles. In his hand was a clipboard. "I'm pairing people up for when we get to the other side," he said. "You're in the American zone: sector twenty-three." He ran his finger down the list of names attached to the clipboard, then took off his glasses, shading his eyes against the sun as he scanned the passengers. "The young lady over there is in the same team." He was looking at the girl with the long black braid. "I wonder if you'd mind introducing yourself?"

"Yes, of course." Martha made her way toward the bow of the boat, one hand clutching her beret to stop the breeze from taking it. She dodged unsteadily past the groups of soldiers, avoiding their eyes. Some of them called out as she passed by, asking her name, offering cigarettes. She didn't look back.

It wasn't until she reached the girl that she realized how tall she was—probably not far short of six feet. Martha had to raise her voice to make herself heard over the noise of the engine. "Good morning!"

A pair of large gray eyes met Martha's. They had a wariness and a hint of something else. Something feral. Like a wildcat about to lash out. Her lips were painted a bold shade of red that instantly dispelled the childlike image conjured by the hairstyle and the bobby socks. She held out her hand to the girl. "I'm Martha Radford. I'm told we're going to be working together."

The girl eyed her for a moment longer. "Kitty. Kitty Bloom." She slid her hand from her jacket pocket. Her grip was hard, like a man's. "You're American?"

Martha nodded. Her free hand went to her head, her fingers tucking a windblown wisp of hair back under her beret. The uncertainty in the girl's voice had made her feel self-conscious. Probably the only American women this girl had seen were Hollywood stars.

"From New York?" Kitty's accent wasn't like the English voices Martha had heard in movies. She made "York" sound more like "Yark."

"Yes. But I grew up in Louisiana."

From the look on her face, Kitty had never heard of it.

"How about you?"

"Manchester."

Martha nodded. She had only a vague idea of the geography of England. "Is that far from here?"

"Far enough," the girl replied. "It took all night to get here. Everything's slower than it used to be because of the bombs they dropped on the rail tracks."

"Was your town bombed?"

Kitty nodded.

"That must have been terrifying."

A slight tightening of the lips was the only response to this. Martha wondered how old Kitty would have been when the war started. It would be tactless to ask. She remembered how it felt to be taken for someone younger than your actual age: if it happened now, she'd be flattered, but back then, it had made her mad.

"Are you hungry?" Kitty cocked her head at the white-railed staircase that led below deck. "There's a place you can buy sandwiches."

Martha followed her down the metal steps. It had been many hours since she'd last eaten. The ordeal of flying had robbed her of her appetite—and now the motion of the waves was making her feel queasy again. But perhaps it would do her good to try to eat something.

She changed her mind when she saw what was being offered. The bread was a grayish color, and there were only two fillings to choose from: Spam or fish paste. The only other food for sale was packets of something called Rich Tea.

"What are these?" Martha picked one up, peering at the tiny writing on the back.

"Biscuits," Kitty replied.

"Do they come with gravy?"

Kitty gave her a blank look. "Gravy? With *biscuits*?"

"I think they're cookies." Martha recognized the voice of the man from the truck. He was standing in line, a couple of places behind her.

"Ah!" She nodded, feeling foolish.

"They're quite nice if you dunk them in tea," Kitty said. She was smiling, and it transformed her face. She had the most unusual eyes—pale gray irises that were almost lilac, with an outer ring of charcoal.

Martha felt even more idiotic when she came to pay for the tea and cookies. The woman behind the counter frowned at the dollar bill she proffered. It hadn't occurred to Martha that she might need British money. The only foreign currency she had in her purse was German reichsmarks.

Kitty pulled coins from her pocket, counting what she had left, when the familiar voice behind them said: "Let me get that."

"Thank you," Martha said when he came over to their table, carrying a plate piled with sandwiches. "I can pay you back in German money if that's okay?"

He waved the offer away. "You hold on to your money—you're gonna need it. The pay's not much to write home about, is it?"

"Well, thank you." It was true. They were getting food and accommodations plus four dollars a week. But she hadn't taken the job for the money.

He sat down, smiling at Martha. "Now," he said, "I know a little about *you*—but what about this young lady?" He turned appraising eyes on Kitty. "Why did you join this outfit?"

"I could ask you the same question." She looked defensive.

"Oh?" He grunted. "Well, I guess I was frustrated at being stuck across the pond. Too old to fight the Nazis. But not too ancient to help clear up the mess they've left behind."

Kitty's expression softened a little. "I've been working in a factory, sewing uniforms. I tried joining the Wrens, but they only wanted typists. They wouldn't let women go to fight."

"Well, you'll be in the thick of it soon," he said. "You won't be fighting, but you'd better be ready for some grim sights." He bit into a sandwich and swallowed it down. "Do you know where you're headed?"

"The south." Kitty looked at her plate. "Somewhere near Dachau."

Martha frowned. This was news to her. She hadn't picked it up when she'd pored over the map of Bavaria in Williamsburgh Library.

Their companion nodded at Kitty. "You know about that place?"

"Yes." She peeled back a corner of bread, examining the pink, mottled slice of processed meat underneath.

Martha couldn't see her face. But the girl's discomfort radiated from her like the smell of the Spam in her sandwich. Kitty had thrown out the name of the German concentration camp like a baited hook. Martha had seen kids at the Henry Street Settlement do a similar thing: let out some morsel of insight into things they shouldn't know about, to make you probe deeper, to make you dig up the story they wouldn't tell you. She wondered what had happened to Kitty in those years of sewing uniforms and dodging bombs to make her want to name such a place.

CHAPTER 2

Cherbourg, France: Later the Same Day

The army tent was in the middle of a field, within sight of the sea. Delphine glanced at the sparkling water as she stood in line, waiting for her new clothes. Hard to believe it was only a year ago that these Normandy beaches were battlegrounds. It felt like a lifetime, so much had changed. A year ago, she had still allowed herself to hope, still believed that life could be normal again. But here she was, surrounded by strangers, in a part of France she had never visited before, her Paris apartment and its contents sold.

It was a kind of freedom, but not what she would ever have wished for. Thinking about the future made her tremble inside. She told herself she mustn't think of it: must focus only on what was happening today, at this moment. But the faces of Claude and Philippe were never far away. She wondered what they would think of her going to Germany—the feared, hated land.

"Espèce de pisseuse!"

Heads turned at the shouted insult, delivered by a man ahead of her in line. The woman handing out the uniforms was glaring at him through narrowed eyes. He had called her a bedwetter. He was pulling at the buttons of a jacket that was clearly too tight for his ample frame. The woman's reply was delivered in an icy American accent.

"How lucky you are, monsieur. You must have been eating foie gras while everyone else in France was subsisting on cabbage soup. I'm so sorry we don't have anything in extra-large."

He frowned and pursed his lips. Delphine suspected his English wasn't good enough to get the sarcasm. He took off the jacket and flung it over his arm, muttering more curses under his breath as he walked away.

Soon it was Delphine's turn. She had the opposite problem. Her waist was smaller now than it had been on her wedding day. The trousers and jacket—in two different shades of gray wool—looked as if they would drown her. Two white cotton shirts, a peaked cap, and a plain black tie were added to the pile, along with a worn-looking leather belt and two patches pierced with a threaded needle. Holding the bundle in outstretched arms to avoid stabbing herself, Delphine was directed to an improvised cubicle on one side of the tent.

She was glad there was no mirror. She could hardly stand to look at her reflection. The loss of weight had done her face no favors. The deep furrows in her forehead and dark circles under her eyes made her look like a ghost of the person she'd once been.

But you're alive.

That was what she had to keep repeating. Even if she wished that she weren't.

As she put on the clothes, her mind slipped back to the day, just a few weeks ago, when she'd been standing in another line. It was at the Lutetia—the vast Paris hotel on the Left Bank that had been commandeered as a resettlement center for returning prisoners of war. She'd gone there day after day, waiting for each new list of survivors to be posted. Desperate by the end of the first week, she'd pinned photographs of her husband and son on the wall, with a plea for information. Two days later a man had come up to her. He'd been in Dachau with Claude and

Philippe. Claude had been his doctor. Despite being offered a transfer to a softer billet to sit out the war, her husband had refused to leave the fellow prisoners he was caring for. And Philippe . . .

Delphine struggled to silence the man's voice, a hoarse whisper in her head. She slid her arms into the jacket. The sleeves were so long they covered her fingers. She could cut them off. Sew the raw edges. She'd never done any tailoring before, but she'd sewn plenty of human flesh in her time at the American Hospital. Fabric couldn't be much different. Less messy, certainly. She wished the uniform weren't gray, which was the color worn by the Helferinnen, the German women sent to Paris to assist the SS after the invasion. God forbid she should look like one of them.

Two hours later Delphine was sitting in the back of a battered army truck, stitching one of the UNRRA patches onto her cap. There was nothing to cut the thread with, so she bit through it. At least her teeth were still in good shape, she thought, as she cast a critical eye over her needlework.

The afternoon sun was beating down on the metal roof of the truck, and although the tarpaulin flaps at the back were pulled open, it was unbearably hot. She fanned herself with the cap, wondering how much longer she would have to wait until the other people on her team arrived. She could see the quartermaster's tent on the other side of the field, the line of people snaking out of the entrance. She'd been told that the others were coming by boat from England. She supposed they would have to stop by the tent to pick up their uniforms, as she had.

There were only a few women in line. Delphine wondered if any of them would be on her team. It was hard to tell, from this distance, what ages they were. Fifty-seven was the upper limit for recruits. She only knew because, at the interview, they'd queried her date of birth.

Apparently, conditions in the camps were considered too hard for anyone over sixty. Realizing that they'd reckoned her to be at least five years older than her true age hadn't helped her state of mind.

She shifted her weight—her buttocks numb from sitting so long on the hard, wooden seat. As she looked up, she caught sight of three people walking toward the truck: an American soldier and two women. He stopped and pointed, then walked off in the direction of the quartermaster's tent. From their gait, both women appeared to be young. Like Delphine, they were wearing mismatched uniforms: the taller one wore what looked like a man's battle-dress jacket that drooped at the shoulders. On her head was the kind of boat-shaped cap the American GIs wore. The shorter woman had a peaked cap and a jacket of a different style that hugged her figure. Delphine wondered how she'd managed to get her hands on enough food to keep such womanly curves.

As they drew closer, she saw that the taller one was no older than Philippe. Delphine swallowed away the lump this brought to her throat. She must stop it: mustn't view every new person she encountered and every new thing she did in terms of what she had lost.

"Good afternoon," she said in her best English accent, as they clambered into the truck. "Delphine Fabius. Pleased to meet you."

———

Kitty could hear Delphine talking to the driver. She'd learned some French at school in Austria, but it wasn't as good as her German or her Polish.

"What's he saying?" Martha asked. "Something about the route we're going to take?"

Kitty nodded. "She's asking him something else now: about when the others are coming, I think." They both listened for the driver's response—but there was none.

Delphine shook her head as she climbed back into the truck. She had sharp, birdlike features. A prominent nose and small, watchful green eyes. Her hair was faded auburn, tinged white at the temples. "No one else is coming." She shrugged. "It's just us until we get to Munich." She sat down, a world-weary look on her face.

After the initial greeting, Delphine had been twitchy and silent. Kitty wondered if the twitchiness was down to being hungry. She certainly looked as if she could do with a good meal. It was bad enough in England—never enough of what you wanted to eat, even though the war was over—but in France it had to be a lot worse. She wished she'd bought something extra on the boat to share.

"Oh well," Martha said, "at least we'll have room to get some sleep tonight." She lifted her feet onto the seat that ran along the side of the truck. She went to lie down, but her hips were too wide. She made a grab for the edge of the bench as she slithered off, landing in a heap on the metal floor.

Her helpless laughter as she rubbed her bruised limbs was contagious and broke the ice. Kitty could see a smile hovering on Delphine's lips as she offered a hand to pull Martha up.

"If you're really intent on injuring yourself, you'd better do it now, while we've still got access to medical equipment." Delphine wagged a finger as Martha settled back on the seat. "It's going to be a long journey."

Martha mirrored Delphine's wry smile. "Your English is very good," she said. "Where'd you learn it?"

"I did my nurse training at the American Hospital in Paris," Delphine replied. "The course was taught in English."

"A whole hospital—just for Americans?" Kitty said.

"It wasn't only Americans. We had British people, too—in this last war and the Great War."

"You must have been nursing for a lot of years," Martha said.

"Yes. My first patients were soldiers wounded in the Battle of the Somme. That was grim: men with burnt flesh, with shattered arms and legs." Delphine blinked, as if the images were imprinted on her mind's eye. "It was mainly Americans, between the wars," she went on. "Some of the patients were quite famous: Ernest Hemingway came in once when a skylight fell on him."

"You met him?" Martha's eyes widened.

Delphine nodded. "I took his stitches out. He told me he was glad he'd had the accident because he'd been struggling to come up with a story for his next book. The pain had reminded him of being wounded during the war, and that had given him an idea." She arched her eyebrows. "I told him it was a hell of a way to get rid of writer's block."

The truck's engine suddenly roared to life, drowning out further conversation. Soon they were rolling through the Normandy countryside. It was hard to see much. The sun was shining through the gap in the tarpaulin that covered the rear of the truck, blinding Kitty and Martha when they craned their necks to catch glimpses of this new, unfamiliar country.

Kitty saw that Delphine had fallen asleep, her head resting against her jacket, which she'd folded into a makeshift cushion. The lines on her forehead seemed to have disappeared. In this relaxed state, her face looked much younger, much softer. Kitty felt an old, familiar ache beneath her ribs. Looking at this woman, wondering how old she was, she couldn't help thinking of her mother. But it was not a face that came to mind when that word entered her head. It was the smoky tang of roasting chestnuts and the aroma of gingerbread, the peal of church bells and the wheeze of an accordion, the feel of fur against her skin and the sting of tiny snowflakes. A family outing to the Christmas market in Am Hof Square—their last time together before they'd put her on the train to Rotterdam. Her mother trying desperately to make everything seem normal. It was as fresh in her mind as if it had happened yesterday: the noise and the smells and the jewel colors of the lanterns strung across the stalls. But the faces of her parents were blurred—as if a flurry of snow hovered persistently around their heads.

Kitty blinked away the image. She had to focus on where she was going, what she needed to do. With every passing mile, she was getting closer to Vienna. She had only a rough idea of the location of the camp they were going to. But she knew that the zone it was in lay less than a hundred miles west of the border with Austria. There must be a way of getting there, of finding people who had the answers to the questions burning in her heart.

A gentle grunt of a snore broke into her thoughts. Both of her traveling companions were asleep now. Delphine's head was lolling forward with the movement of the truck. Her hands were nestled in her lap, the fingers entwined. Kitty could see the glint of a wedding ring. She saw that Martha wore one, too. Where were the husbands of these women who were traveling so far from home, she wondered? Perhaps Martha and Delphine were widows. It was a strange word, *widow*—one that must be as uncomfortable to wear as *orphan*.

Kitty didn't think she'd be able to sleep. As the light began to fade, she lay sideways with her head on the army rucksack that contained her clothes and the few personal items she possessed. She could feel the bristles of her hairbrush poking through the canvas, and she slid farther down on the bench a bit to get comfortable. In England, on those nights when thoughts of home had kept her awake, she would always reach for paper and a pencil. What she drew on sleepless nights was always the same: women in silk dresses—impossibly beautiful and remote, like the models her mother had dressed for fashion shows in Vienna. It always soothed her, drawing imaginary faces and elegant clothes, as if the act of creation brought back a glimmer of what she had lost.

The next thing Kitty was aware of was the sound of men shouting. She couldn't understand the French words the driver was spitting out.

She heard an English voice yelling over his: "Unless you want to swim across, you've got to go south, mate!"

"Sounds like the bridge has gone." Delphine was on her feet. "Think I'll just go and stretch my legs."

Kitty and Martha followed her out.

"Where are we?" Martha glanced at the sentry box ahead of them, then at the dark expanse of water glittering in the moonlight.

"That's the Rhine," Delphine replied. "The border with Germany. But we can't cross." Her hand swept the air, indicating a place out of sight, beyond the sentry box. "The Allies bombed the bridge. So, we have to make a big detour."

The truck swerved dangerously as they pulled away. It was as if the driver held the women personally responsible for lengthening the journey and was determined to make the rest of it as uncomfortable as possible. Martha asked Delphine if she had any idea how long it might take to get to Munich.

"I can't even guess," Delphine replied. "They say the roads in Germany are ruptured. We'll be lucky if we make it before morning."

"Have you ever been to Germany?" Martha asked. "Before the war, I mean."

Delphine shook her head.

The truck took a sharp bend. A shaft of moonlight shot through the tarpaulin flaps, momentarily lighting up the Frenchwoman's face. Kitty saw that her eyes were glassy with tears. Had her husband died fighting the Germans? She looked a little too old for that to be the case, Kitty thought. She wondered what images were running through Delphine's mind. Would it be appropriate to reach out, to take the woman's hand? Would that help? Or would it seem too familiar an action, given that they barely knew one another? Batting these questions around her head, Kitty knew that whatever the answer, she couldn't do it. Touching another person—other than for a handshake—was something quite alien to her. There had been Fred, of course. But that was different. Touching, hugging—to give comfort or to show the kind of love that came from family ties—that had stopped the day she boarded the train out of Vienna.

———

The sun had been up for hours by the time they reached Munich. The driver had stopped somewhere to take a nap, and when they'd set off again, dawn had revealed rolling farmland and quaint villages—not at all what Martha had expected. The houses were like something from a book of fairy tales. There was even a castle, its towers and turrets glinting coral in the sunrise. It was a landscape that seemed untouched by war—until they neared the city.

Munich was a horror of destruction. Whole streets lay in ruins. Glimpses of lives smashed to pieces by falling bombs could be seen inside the skeletons of houses: the charred remains of a double bed, with a smoke-streaked crucifix hanging askew on what was left of the wall behind it; rose-patterned curtains flapping at shattered windows; an armchair, the springs poking through the torn leather upholstery, resting on the splintered boards of what had once been a floor; a child's doll, naked and missing an arm, lying on a heap of broken glass.

The truck came to a stop a short distance from UNRRA's headquarters—a small, squat building in a sea of rubble. The only cheering sight for the women as they picked their way across shattered cobblestones was what appeared to be a doughnut stand, run by the Red Cross.

Martha shaded her eyes against the sunshine, wondering if she might be hallucinating. The smell told her that her eyes were not deceiving her. Kitty and Delphine were already there, holding out money. Standing together, the contrast between the two women was stark: Kitty so young, and almost a foot taller than Delphine, who looked old enough to be the girl's grandmother. The only common feature was their slimness—which, in Delphine's case, was extreme. No wonder they were going wild for doughnuts. They looked as if a strong breeze would fell them like bowling pins.

Martha looked around for the driver, but he had disappeared. Probably he'd gone in search of cigarettes, which he'd complained of having run out of during the night.

"Come and eat!" Delphine waved Martha over to the stall.

When they'd sucked the last crumbs of sugar from their fingers, they stood outside the door of the UNRRA office, waiting for the driver and watching people crossing the square in front of them. A couple of months ago, these people had been the enemy. It gave Martha a frisson of shock to see that they looked so normal. There were women in dresses and hats, some carrying shopping baskets; men in business suits; children in school uniforms. Everyone looked tidy and clean, in sharp contrast to their surroundings. *What were you expecting?* her inner voice reprimanded her. *Ogres wielding hand grenades?*

"I don't think he's coming back." Delphine was peering at her watch. "He was really mad about having to make that detour. I thought he was going to abandon us at the border. I don't think he realized how bad it was going to be."

"How will we get to the camp?" Kitty pushed back a lock of hair that had worked its way free of her braid.

"We'd better go and ask." Martha pressed the button at the side of the pockmarked door. There was no sound—no bell or buzzer. She tried the handle. It wasn't locked. She led the others down a dingy corridor. The smell of new, damp plaster hung in the air, giving the impression that the office had been hastily fashioned from a partially damaged building—probably one of the few still standing in this part of the city. There was a light at the end of the corridor. Martha could see someone sitting in a room, behind a desk.

"Good afternoon."

The man looked up, startled by her greeting. In that brief unguarded moment, he looked confused, overwhelmed. He was a similar age to the male recruits Martha had traveled over from the States with. He scrambled to his feet.

"Good afternoon, ladies." The accent was English. He came around the desk to shake hands. Martha noticed that his left arm ended at the elbow, the sleeve of his jacket pinned up under the armpit.

The introductions over, he checked their names against a list, then told them that the camp they were assigned to was called Seidenmühle. "It's southwest of here, on the Amper River." He went over to a map on the wall, which was peppered with colored thumbtacks. "There won't be any signs, but you'll see a big mill wheel from the road." He stabbed a patch of blue beneath a yellow thumbtack. "Tell the driver that if he hits this lake, he's gone too far."

"I'm not sure we have a driver." Martha exchanged glances with the other women. "He went off when we arrived, and he hasn't come back."

The man nodded, as if unsurprised by this news. "Don't worry. We'll find another."

"When will we meet the rest of the team?" Kitty asked.

This was met with a look of incomprehension.

"We were told in Cherbourg that we'd join up with the others here in Munich," Delphine added.

"There's been a spearhead team out at Seidenmühle for the past few weeks," he said. "You'll meet them when you get there. And the US Army will be providing backup. There's a tank battalion stationed nearby."

"How many people are there in the camp?" Martha asked.

"A couple of thousand at the last count." He shrugged. "Poles, mostly, I think. Not certain about that, though: could be a few Balts there, too."

"Balts?" This was an unfamiliar word to Martha.

"Refugees from the Baltic countries: Latvia, Lithuania, Estonia."

Martha nodded. One of the families she'd delivered food to on the Lower East Side was from Lithuania. Only the father had spoken English—limited to a dozen or so words. They'd arrived in New York with just the clothes on their backs.

"Some of the inmates were brought in as forced labor by the Nazis from occupied countries," the man went on. "The name of the place means 'silk mill' in English. They made artificial silk from wood fiber, chopping down trees to turn into linings for uniforms. When the place was liberated, there were plenty of empty bunkhouses, so we took it over as a DP camp."

"Empty?" Kitty echoed. "Because people had escaped?"

He shook his head. "Because they'd been worked to death. It wasn't only Jews that the Nazis exterminated—the people at Seidenmühle weren't Jewish, but their chances of survival were not much greater. The Nazis fed them starvation rations. They didn't care who they sent out into the forest: anyone, old or young, male or female, was made to chop wood. And in winter, it's freezing cold. They didn't last long."

From the corner of her eye, Martha saw Kitty's head drop. Could someone so young have had any idea what sort of place she was going to when she signed up? Martha wondered if she'd be able to pull her weight on the team—or whether she'd be a liability, as much in need of looking after as the DPs themselves.

⊷

The replacement driver—another Frenchman—seemed to have little idea of where they were going. Eventually he found the river whose course they were supposed to follow upstream to get to the camp. They were making good progress until the road veered away from the river and they found themselves traveling through a pine forest. After half an hour he admitted to Delphine that he was totally lost.

They gathered around as he spread the map out on a tree stump. The sun had gone down and the light was beginning to fade. It was difficult to make out the names of places.

"There are so many rivers," Martha said. "And all these patches of woodland. How on earth do we know which one we're in?"

"I saw a house back there," Kitty said. "Shall I go and ask where we are?"

Martha turned to her. "How would you do that? Take the map and get them to point?"

"No." Kitty smiled. "I'll ask for directions. And if it's really complicated, I'll write them down."

Martha's eyes widened. "You speak German?"

Kitty nodded, gathering up the map. "I learnt it at school."

"You'd better not go alone," Delphine said. She had a brief conversation in French with the driver. "He's going to take the truck as close to the house as he can. I'll stay with him, to make sure he doesn't disappear, like the last one."

The house was set back from the road. Kitty said she'd only spotted it because of the wisps of smoke coming from the chimney. It was a stone cottage with a thick layer of moss on the roof. Walking through the twilight over a carpet of pine needles to reach it, Martha felt a creeping sense of unease. It was so quiet. Too quiet. Not even birdsong in the canopy overhead.

"What's that?" Kitty hissed. She was looking at a dark shape beyond the path, to their left.

Martha's brain took a few seconds to process what she was looking at. "My God," she whispered. "It's a tank."

Branches festooned the roof of the vehicle, as if an attempt had been made to conceal it. A black cross, outlined in white, was just visible on the side facing them. The tank had the look of a crouching beast waiting to pounce.

"What's it doing there?" There was a hint of fear in Kitty's voice.

"It's abandoned, I guess," Martha replied.

"What if there's someone inside?"

The gun turret was pointing straight at them.

"I don't think it's been driven in a while." Martha pointed to the ground. A fallen tree lay in front of the caterpillar tires.

Kitty nodded. "Sorry," she said. "It's just . . ."

"It's okay." Martha put her hand on Kitty's arm. "It's scary as hell—even empty."

They walked on toward the house. The silence was suddenly broken by the crowing of a rooster. They both jumped.

"Stupid bird—it's getting dark!" Martha felt oddly reassured by the sound. Making their way around the corner of the house, they saw a man, bent with age, tossing scraps to a flock of chickens.

"Guten Abend!"

At the sound of Kitty's voice, the old man froze.

Martha was mortified. "Tell him it's okay, we're just lost."

Kitty came out with a string of words. The man turned, lifting a hand to his heart. With his other hand he beckoned Kitty over.

"He wants to know if we're hungry," she called over her shoulder.

"Please tell him no," Martha called back. They'd scared him half to death and now he thought they'd come to raid his larder.

Kitty spoke in a low, soothing voice, and the old man seemed to relax a little. He went inside the house and returned with a paraffin lamp. Kitty unfolded the map and gave Martha one corner so they could hold it up to the light. The man's finger shook as he indicated where they were. He repeated the word "Seidenmühle," glancing up at Kitty. Then he traced a line across the map, talking to her as he did so.

"Looks like we're quite close," Kitty said to Martha. "We've overshot the place. We need to turn back, then take a left, which should lead us to this fork in the river." She pointed to where two blue lines met. "He says the camp's half a mile downstream."

"Danke schön." It was the only German phrase Martha knew. She hadn't realized how useless she would feel, how difficult it would be to communicate with people. Thank goodness Kitty knew the language. *Never make assumptions.* Martha heard her grandmother's voice as they made their way back along the forest path. She'd had Kitty pegged as an overgrown child in lipstick: someone too young and inexperienced for the kind of work she'd been recruited for. *That'll teach you,* Grandma Cecile whispered.

Less than half an hour later, the truck's headlamps picked out an enormous mill wheel. The water tumbling underneath reflected the light, like streams of molten silver in the dark river. A little way farther on, they crossed a wooden bridge and saw the gates of the camp. A brightly lit stone guardhouse stood just beyond them. A young soldier in the familiar uniform of the US Army emerged from the building and waved the truck to a standstill.

Shining a flashlight at a clipboard, he checked the women's names before ushering them into the guardhouse.

"Where are you from?" Martha asked. She thought how young he looked.

"Salem, Oregon, ma'am," the guard replied.

"Long way from home, huh?"

"Sure is." He returned her wry smile.

There was a crunch of tires outside. Through the open door they saw their driver executing a swift three-point turn.

"Au revoir! Merci beaucoup!" Delphine called out. Her words were drowned out by the revving of the engine as he pulled away. Clearly, the man didn't want to hang around a moment longer than he had to.

"Major McMahon will be along shortly," the guard said. "He'll show you to your billet."

Major McMahon reminded Martha of the owner of the grocery store on Wythe Avenue. He had the same shrewd eyes and paunchy stomach. But the voice was more Boston than Brooklyn.

"Good evening, ladies." He gave a deep nod that was almost a bow as he shook each proffered hand. "Boy, am I glad to see you all!" He led them along a tree-lined track lit by electric lampposts. They stopped in front of a trio of wooden cabins that looked like the Cajun fishing shacks she'd seen as a child on the bayous in Louisiana.

"I hope you'll be comfortable in here," he said, as he unlocked the door of one of the cabins. "It used to belong to the officers."

"Officers?" Martha echoed.

"The Nazis who ran the place when it was a labor camp." He smiled at her startled face. "Don't worry, they left it spotless. Hardly lived here, by all accounts. Spent most of their time at the blockhouse where their Polish mistresses were billeted." His hands forked the air. "Sorry, I don't mean to be crude. But in this place . . . well, you kinda get used to telling it like it is."

He led them up a rickety set of stairs to a large mezzanine room with four single beds. "This was going to be for all three of you to share," he said. "But since the others have gone, you can spread out a little. The places on either side are empty, so take your pick." He tossed a bunch of keys onto one of the beds.

"Who's gone?" Martha felt a prickle of apprehension.

"The guys who came last month. There was a Dutch fella in charge. He only stuck it out for a week. Hitched a ride home with a convoy headed up north. The doctor—Belgian guy—went with him." Major McMahon shrugged. "There was a Texan, too; he was running the warehouse, getting in supplies. But he was a drinker: got hooked on the hooch the Poles make. It turned him blind, so he had to go home."

"That's awful." Martha glanced at the others. "So, who's left?"

"Nobody." The major blew out a breath. "Just you three ladies in charge now."

31

CHAPTER 3

The major's words were still echoing in Martha's head as she lay down in bed.

He only stuck it out for a week.

Why had her predecessor run away? And the doctor, too. What had made them abandon the people they had come to help after just days on the job?

She tried to imagine the people lying asleep beyond the trees that screened the cabin from the rest of the camp: hundreds of men, women, and children herded together in a place far from home. She thought of the newspaper image still tucked away in her handbag, of the frightened-looking woman with a baby in her arms and another child clinging to her skirt. How could anyone turn their back on someone in such dire need?

Martha glanced across the room, at the shapes in the other beds. They'd been too exhausted to investigate the neighboring cabins. There was something comforting in them all being in the same room—even though they barely knew each other. She wondered if Delphine and Kitty were already asleep, or if, like her, their minds were racing.

On the other side of the room, Kitty was staring at the dark shadows on the ceiling. She couldn't shake the thought that the bed she was lying in had once belonged to a Nazi. What if her mother and father had ended up in a place like this? The thought of them being sent out in freezing winter weather to chop wood for hours on end made her insides shrivel. How could she close her eyes with that image in her head?

There was a creak of metal springs as Delphine turned to face the window. Like the others, she was imagining what lay beyond the trees. She was trying to picture the camp hospital. Who had been looking after the patients since the doctor disappeared? What was she going to find when she got there tomorrow morning? And there was something else hovering like a specter on the margins of her mind's eye. Just a few miles beyond the boundary of Seidenmühle lay Dachau. What had she been thinking, coming here? She had hoped for a feeling of closeness to Claude and Philippe from being near the place where they died. But all she felt was the horror of it, the unfathomable injustice.

"Are you okay?" It was Martha who called out in the darkness.

"I can't sleep," Delphine replied. "Sorry—did I wake you? These beds are rickety, aren't they?"

"I can't, either." Kitty sat up.

"Shall I make us all a hot drink?" Martha got out of bed and made her way downstairs.

In the kitchen she found a big jar of Nescafé. Coffee had been severely rationed in American grocery stores since Pearl Harbor. *Hooray for the US Army,* she thought. Lying next to it on the counter was a loaf of bread wrapped in waxed cloth. While she waited for the kettle to boil, she investigated the contents of the cupboards. She found canned milk, a jar of raspberry jelly, and a bag of sugar with the Domino logo emblazoned on it. It seemed strange to see something so familiar in a DP camp in the heart of Germany. Had it been only three days since she'd hidden in the shadows of the refinery in Williamsburg? It seemed like a lifetime ago.

She found a tray and some tin mugs and carried the coffee upstairs. But there was no sound when she pushed the door open. In the time it had taken her to make the drinks, the others had fallen asleep.

Major McMahon arrived as they were finishing breakfast the next morning. He took them to the camp office, which was a short walk along a trail through the pine trees. On the way he explained that the army expected to relinquish responsibility for Seidenmühle as soon as possible. "We gotta concentrate on denazification," he said. "Round up the ones that got away before they can regroup and start a partisan war against us."

Martha turned to him, startled.

"That's why we need to pull out of running this place—we gotta hunt 'em down and lock 'em up."

The women exchanged anxious glances. "When will you leave?" Martha asked.

"End of the month," he replied.

"But that's only a few days away!"

"We'll be on hand if you need us," he said. "We're only ten miles from here. And I'll be leaving a couple of guys to guard the place."

"What about a doctor?" Delphine said. "Will the army send a replacement for the one that left?"

"No ma'am," he replied. "But one of the DPs was a surgeon in Kraków—poor guy lost a couple of fingers in a loom before this place was liberated, but he can still use a scalpel. You'll be fine, believe me."

The office was a large, bare room with a single window. The only furniture was a row of filing cabinets and a huge desk with a couple of mismatched wooden chairs behind it. On the desk was a field telephone, and on the wall behind it was a drawing of the layout of the camp.

The major was carrying a short, blunt cane, which he pointed at the symbols on the map. "The black squares are the blockhouses. You got around a hundred and fifty people in each one. These two yellow circles are the kitchens. They bake thirteen hundred pounds of bread every day." He moved the cane across to a green diamond. "This is the mess hall. Lunch is the main meal of the day, served in four sittings, between twelve thirty and two o'clock. Mornings they get bread delivered to the blockhouses, cheese or jelly to go with it, depending on what's available.

"The red cross is the hospital, and this blue triangle is the warehouse. We guard that twenty-four seven, but stuff's always disappearing. They sneak around after dark. Sometimes it's cigarettes they're after, other times it's sugar for their vodka stills. If we catch 'em, they spend a night or two in here." He tapped an orange triangle next to the warehouse. "We confiscated ten stills last week. They'll find a way to make new ones—they're a cunning bunch. You gotta keep that in mind."

Martha's eyes went back to the black squares. She was counting them, multiplying numbers in her head. "So, there are more than two thousand people living here?"

"Close to three thousand at the last count," he replied. "But it's growing all the time: we had twelve babies born this month, and I heard we're expecting about thirty by the end of August."

"Can I see the hospital?" Delphine asked.

"Sure—I'll take you." He glanced at his watch. He turned to Martha, talking faster as he rattled off more facts about the camp. Each of the blockhouses had a leader who made sure everyone had a job to do; that person was also responsible for allocating living spaces and monitoring the basic hygiene of the occupants. He told them about the supply of DDT kept in the guardhouse for delousing new arrivals, and the storeroom full of secondhand clothes and shoes that were available for those who turned up in nothing more than rags.

"The biggest challenge facing you ladies will be getting in enough supplies and firewood to see this place through the winter," he said. "When the snow comes, the roads will be impassable. You might be holed up for a month or more with nothing coming in."

"Won't the army be providing food?" Martha asked. She was thinking of her time at the Henry Street Settlement, where her main job had been organizing the collection of food donations to distribute to sick and needy people in the neighborhood. Back then she had been trying to feed hundreds, not thousands.

"Some of it," he replied. "But all the fresh stuff comes from the local farms. You'll have to negotiate with the Germans for that."

"But . . ." Martha felt a wave of panic rise from her stomach.

"I'll send you the details," he cut in. "For now, everything you need to know about the DPs is in those files." He glanced out the window. "This time of morning they start lining up outside for passes. There's a rubber stamp and ink pad in the desk drawer: no one gets past the gate unless their papers have been stamped. Can't have 'em wandering in and out of the place at will."

"That makes them sound like prisoners." Kitty's eyes narrowed as she spoke.

"Well, until we get the go-ahead to send them home, that's essentially what they are. They don't belong here." He tucked his cane into his belt. "We won't keep them here any longer than we have to, but it's anybody's guess when repatriation's gonna be possible. The Nazis woulda wiped Poland off the map if they'd had their way. Pretty much burned Warsaw to the ground before they were done."

Kitty looked away. Martha saw the muscles in her jaw flex.

"You need to screen the requests carefully," the major went on. "Only give out a pass if it's urgent. If in doubt, ask for verification. You'll hear some real sob stories—you gotta learn to distance yourself, or they'll break your heart. Oh, and watch out for the black marketeers."

Without pausing to explain further, he ushered Delphine out the door.

"How on earth are we going to do this?" Martha went to the window, staring in dismay at the ever-lengthening line forming outside. "Do you think any of them will be able to speak English?"

"It's okay," Kitty said. "I can translate for you."

"You think they'll speak German?"

"I doubt it. But I speak Polish."

"Really? You learned *that* at school?"

"No. From my mother. She lived in Poland before she met my father."

"Oh?" That would explain the reaction to what the major had said. Perhaps there were relatives in Poland. She hesitated, afraid to ask. Kitty turned away, opening a drawer in the filing cabinet and examining the contents. Martha wondered if her mother had tried to stop her from coming to Germany, if Mrs. Bloom was sitting at home in Manchester, worrying about what her daughter had gotten herself into. Before she could ask, the door opened, and a head appeared. It was a woman about the age of Delphine, her face gaunt and her eyes troubled.

"*Czy mogę teraz wejść?*"

"She's asking if she can come in," Kitty said.

Martha nodded to the woman. She came up to the desk, adjusting the scarf knotted over her gray hair. Her cotton blouse was the same spotless white as the scarf, and a black apron was tied around her tiny waist. She rattled off her request, looking from Martha to Kitty with pleading black eyes. Martha understood just one word: *Dachau.*

"She says her daughter is about to give birth in another camp and she must go to help her. The father of the baby died in Dachau, so there's no one else to assist."

"Can you ask her name?" Martha opened a drawer in the desk. There was a ledger inside marked "Passes." Flicking through the pages, she found the latest entry, dated the previous week. "And we'll need the number on her identity card."

Kitty relayed this to the woman. "Her name is Sinaida Sikorsky. But she says she has no identity card."

Before Martha could query this, the woman pulled back the sleeve of her blouse, revealing eight numbers tattooed in purple on withered skin. She murmured something without looking up.

"She says it's the only thing she has." Kitty had gone very pale. She looked as if she was fighting back tears. "It's the number the Nazis gave her in Dachau."

Martha swallowed hard. She'd seen a photograph in *Time* magazine of a mark like this. But the shock of seeing it for real was something else. She reached into the back of the drawer, where her trembling fingers found the rubber stamp and ink pad. "What can we give her as a pass? Is there anything in the filing cabinet?"

Kitty opened one of the drawers, then another. "There are some blank forms here," she said.

Martha wrote down the woman's date of birth and city of origin as Kitty translated. She pressed the stamp down on the paper, imprinting the word "Seidenmühle" in red ink. "Can you ask her how she's going to get to the camp her daughter's in?"

"*Pójdę,*" the woman replied to Kitty's question.

"She's going to walk," Kitty said.

"How far is it?"

The woman told them it was around thirty miles. "Tell her I'll ask the major to arrange transport. And when the baby's born, we'll bring all three of them back here to live. It's inhuman that she was separated from her daughter in the first place."

When Kitty relayed this news, the woman darted around the desk and planted a kiss on Martha's cheek. As she withdrew, Martha felt the wetness of tears on her skin. The woman said something to Kitty, her words punctuated by sobs.

"She says she was told there was no room for her daughter, that the camp's full already."

"Nonsense," Martha replied. "We know for a fact that there are empty cabins next to ours. They can move into one of those."

As Martha handed over the pass, the major's warning rang in her ears. *You gotta learn to distance yourself, or they'll break your heart.* She could imagine him rolling his eyes when he heard what she'd done.

"There's about twenty people in the line now," Kitty called from the doorway.

Martha took a deep breath. Twenty people. Each one carrying a burden of sorrow she could only guess at. And this was just beginning. How on earth were she and the others going to cope? Three women caring for nearly three thousand DPs—in a country where she didn't speak the language and was going to have to find the resources to keep them alive in the coming winter?

She closed her eyes, struggling to quell the rising tide of fear. And she made a silent prayer: *Please let me do right by these people. Help me to be wise.* "Okay," she called to Kitty. "Show the next one in."

—◆—

To reach the hospital, Major McMahon took Delphine along the main cobbled road, past the kitchens, where the smell of freshly baked bread hung in the air. It made her stomach rumble. She hadn't eaten as much as she could have at breakfast—her insides seemed incapable of dealing with the quantity of food she had been used to before the war. She wondered if she would ever be able to manage a substantial meal again.

Past the kitchens was the warehouse, and beyond that the first of the twenty blockhouses where the DPs lived. Delphine was surprised to see ducks and chickens pecking about outside the long wooden buildings. And there were shoots of what looked like lettuce sprouting from earth-filled rubber tires. She asked the major how the camp inmates had managed to get vegetable seedlings and where they'd acquired the poultry.

"You can get pretty much anything on the black market if you've got something to trade," he said. "We turn a blind eye if it's harmless stuff like this. What you have to watch for is the cattle rustling."

"What?" Delphine looked at him, mystified.

"They steal livestock from the local farms. Butcher it in the woods at night, then trade it around the blockhouses. It's caused a lot of bad feeling because the Germans are already obliged to hand over a percentage of what they raise on their farms."

"Have you caught anyone?" It occurred to Delphine that the German farmers might be making it up, that pretending their livestock had been stolen would be a way of holding on to what they were supposed to be handing over.

"Not yet," the major replied. "But we've found plenty of evidence: cow horns and hides don't grow on trees." He stopped and waved his hand toward a square concrete building set on the edge of the camp. "That's the hospital," he said. "The surgeon's name is Ignatz Jankaukas. You can't miss him: he's six foot four."

"Does he speak English?"

"Not much."

"French?"

The major shrugged. "Don't worry, you'll make out fine. The Polacks don't care what language you speak, so long as it's not German." With a grunt he cocked his head back toward the blockhouses. "I have to go now—okay if I leave you to it?"

"Yes, of course." She was aware that the pitch of her voice had risen, that she sounded shrill. The way he spoke about the DPs implied a lack of respect. Perhaps it was unintentional, but it offended her.

He didn't seem aware that her tone had changed. With a nod he turned and walked away.

Delphine heard a commotion coming from the hospital as she made her way along the path to the main entrance. She could hear babies crying and, from somewhere farther away, men's voices yelling words she couldn't understand.

She pushed open the door to the lobby, where a boy was sitting at a table, rolling bandages. He looked no more than twelve or thirteen years old. The sound of the door opening made him look up. She saw a flash of fear in his eyes. It was her uniform. It made her look like a German.

"I'm a nurse." She said the words slowly, in English. She pointed at the red patch on her sleeve, then took a few steps toward him. His face was blank. *"Je suis Française,"* she tried.

"Francuzka?"

Delphine nodded. She jabbed her hand at her chest. "Madame Fabius."

"Wolf." He mimicked her gesture, a shy smile transforming his pale face. He stood up and beckoned her to follow him.

The volume of noise increased as he opened the door. It was a female ward—a mixture of pregnant women and new mothers. The adult voices subsided as Delphine entered the room, but the high-pitched wail of babies went on unabated. There was one in the cot nearest the door, its face red with crying. A woman lying in the bed next to the child was fast asleep—probably drugged after a difficult birth, Delphine thought, for surely no mother could sleep when her newborn was making a racket like that.

She scooped the infant out of the cot and held it to her, rocking on her heels the way she had when Philippe had been this size. The baby stank. She glanced at Wolf, pinching her nose. He nodded, pointing to the cot, where a greenish-brown stain was clearly visible on the mattress. Then he touched her elbow, ushering her across the room to a wooden table, where a pile of cloth diapers lay in an untidy heap. At least they were clean, she thought, as she laid the baby down.

Removing the soiled diaper revealed inflammation on the little boy's skinny bottom and legs. No wonder he was wailing. Delphine motioned to Wolf to come and stand by the baby. This allowed her to open her knapsack and rummage through the supplies she'd helped herself to in the medical tent at the army base back in Cherbourg. There was an emollient cream that would help soothe the rash. But first she needed clean water and something to wipe away the mess. She glanced around the room. There was no sink to be seen—just rows of beds.

"Water?" She mimed raindrops falling from the sky to Wolf, who looked back at her uncomprehendingly for a moment, then motioned with his foot to something under the table. It was a bucket with a tin army plate for a lid. The water inside looked clean enough. There was a chipped enamel jug alongside it, which Delphine examined before dipping it into the bucket.

Wolf helped her pin a fresh diaper around the struggling baby once the cream had been applied. To her surprise, the crying subsided as Wolf hovered above him, making faces and little cooing sounds. With more sign language she asked him to hold the little boy while she went to find Dr. Jankaukas. She couldn't believe there was no one other than this child on hand to assist the new mothers. There must at least be auxiliary staff, even if there were no trained nurses.

She found the doctor in a neighboring ward. This one was full of men. Some had obvious signs of broken bones. Others had bandages over their eyes. Ignatz Jankaukas was bent over a patient with blood oozing from a wound on his neck. Delphine stopped in her tracks, not wanting to interrupt what appeared to be a medical emergency. She watched him stanch the flow of blood, then administer an injection. The missing fingers the major had mentioned were on the hand holding the syringe.

He looked younger than she had expected. Late thirties, perhaps. But even from a distance, she could see exhaustion etched on his face. As he straightened up, he caught sight of her. There was a momentary wariness—not far short of the fear she'd seen in Wolf's eyes. But unlike the boy, the doctor must have recognized the red patch on her cap.

He came toward her, wiping his hands on a surgical coat that was streaked with blood. *"Madame Fabius—bonjour! Excusez-moi—je voudrais embrasser votre main, mais je suis tout sanglant!"*

She was surprised that he knew her name, and amazed that he spoke French so eloquently. He was apologizing for being unable to kiss her hand because he was too bloody. In the next breath he told her she was an angel from heaven, that since the Belgian doctor had taken flight, the hospital had been on its knees. He said he had never in his life been more grateful to see a nurse.

Delphine didn't often blush, but she could feel her throat and cheeks turning pink. In all her years of nursing, she had never received such a flattering welcome. She complimented him on his French and asked him where he had learned it. He told her that he'd studied it in college, alongside medicine, that he'd been offered a post at a hospital in Lille, but the war had prevented him from taking it.

She asked who else was helping at the hospital, explaining that she'd already met Wolf and needed someone to prepare a bottle for the baby she'd left him holding.

"There is a woman from the camp who comes in to wash and feed the men," he replied in French, "but she refuses to care for the women." He cocked his head toward the door to the maternity ward.

"Why?" she asked.

He told her that it was because many of the babies being delivered were fathered by the Nazis who had run Seidenmühle when it was a slave labor camp. The DPs didn't want anything to do with the mothers of German bastards.

Delphine clicked her tongue against her teeth. *"Et le garçon?"* She wanted to know why Wolf was willing to help when others had refused.

Dr. Jankaukas explained that Wolf was an orphan. He spent his days helping at the hospital because he wanted to be a doctor when he grew up. *"Pauvre petit,"* he said, shaking his head. Poor little one. Clearly, he thought this a forlorn hope.

"Montre-moi où tu gardes le lait," she said. Show me where you keep the milk. That was her first priority: to get some nourishment into the

poor thin baby next door. Then she could start working out how on earth to get this place running as it should.

———————

By the end of the morning, Martha felt as if a stone had lodged itself in her throat. It was the effort of suppressing emotion, of swallowing back tears. It was as if she and Kitty had opened the door to a tidal wave of human misery, the wreckage of lives torn apart by war. The people in the camp had washed up in a place far from home, desperate for any comfort, any meaning, they could find. One man, who had been an opera singer before the war, had opened his mouth wide to show the stumps of his teeth, which he said had been smashed by the Nazis. He was asking for a pass to visit a dentist in the town downriver and planning to pay for the treatment by selling his mother's wedding ring. Another man—wild looking, with a mud-spattered shirt and torn trousers—had said he wanted a pass to go to the woods outside the camp. At first, Martha had suspected that he might be one of the black marketeers the major had warned her about, but on further questioning, he had broken down in tears and explained that he had lost his wife and all three of his children in the war. In his previous life he had been a botanist—and all he wanted now was to be allowed to wander the forest, searching for wildflowers. The look he had given Martha when she'd handed over the pass had been utterly heartbreaking.

Some of the people who had lined up outside the office had simply come to beg for help to locate missing relatives. Kitty had once again surprised Martha with a maturity beyond her years when she explained that there were lists published each week by the Red Cross and that she would get them sent to the camp and display them for everyone to see.

"How did you know about those lists?" Martha asked when the last person in line had left the office.

"I heard about them in England." Kitty turned away, opening a drawer in one of the filing cabinets to replace the remaining forms. "Someone I worked with in Manchester was trying to trace family in Germany."

Martha nodded, staring at the rubber stamp on the desk in front of her. She knew that she was going to have to put everything she had seen and heard out of her mind if she was going to get through what needed to be done: there were the blockhouses to inspect, the supplies in the warehouse to check out—and she wanted to talk to the people who worked in the kitchens to find out how the food was distributed to the DPs.

Talk. The word mocked her. How was she going to run this place if she couldn't even communicate with the inhabitants of the camp? She could hardly expect Kitty to follow her around like a dog on a leash, always on hand to translate.

"I want you to have the time to help people find their relatives," Martha said. "Apart from food and shelter, it's the single most important thing we can do for them. But this morning has shown me how little I can do without a translator." She gave Kitty a wry look. "How long would it take for you to teach me Polish? Just the basics . . ."

"That depends," Kitty replied.

"On what?"

"On how many hours a day you put in. And if you have an ear for languages. But there must be people here who speak some English."

Martha nodded. "We just have to find them." She picked up the receiver of the field telephone—a strange-looking contraption like a large battery with bells on top. She turned one switch, then another, before she heard a crackly voice say: "Command post."

"Hello . . . it's Assistant Director Radford here. Can you put me through to Major McMahon?"

"I'm sorry, ma'am; he's on his way to Munich."

"Oh." She hesitated. "Who am I speaking to?"

"It's Sergeant Lewis, ma'am."

"I wonder if you can help me, Sergeant? Do any of the DPs in the camp speak English?"

There was a moment of silence at the other end of the phone.

"No one?"

The line crackled. Then she heard the sergeant clear his throat. "Sorry, ma'am, got a supply truck wanting to come through the gate. You could try the DP they call Chance; he speaks English."

The line went dead.

"Chance?" Martha turned to Kitty. "Is that a Polish name?"

"Not one I've ever heard," Kitty said.

"He said, 'Try the DP they call Chance'—would it be a nickname?"

Kitty frowned. "Hmm. I wonder if . . ."

"What?"

"*Ksiądz.* Sounds like *chance*. It means 'priest' in Polish."

"Really?" Martha frowned. "A priest who speaks English? How would someone like that wind up in a place like this?"

Kitty shrugged. "Want me to find him?" She grabbed her bag and headed for the door.

⬥

A woman in the camp kitchen, who was tossing shredded cabbage leaves into an enormous pan of soup, told Kitty that there was a little chapel in the woods, built by the DPs themselves, where she might find the priest.

Kitty nodded. The smell of the soup was making her salivate. She wondered how many of these gigantic pans it took to provide enough for almost three thousand hungry people. She listened as the woman told her the way to the chapel—the description punctuated by slurps and the shaking of salt into the bubbling liquid.

The route took Kitty along the river, past the huge weaving shed where the Nazis' slave laborers had worked day and night, producing artificial silk. Some of the windows had been smashed in. She peered through a gap in the glass. The shadowy shapes of the looms were like rows of giants standing guard over the place. The thought of someone losing fingers in one of the machines was horrific. To make silk.

For Kitty, that word carried bittersweet memories. Silk had been her parents' livelihood, the business that had sustained them until the fateful night in November 1938 when—like the broken panes she was looking through now—the windows of Blumenthal's had been shattered by flying bricks.

Her parents hadn't been there because it had happened after dark. If her father had been in the shop, he would surely have been dragged out and beaten, as so many of Vienna's businessmen had been that night. Clara, who lived in the upstairs apartment and helped with the tailoring, had described it to them the next day. Kitty remembered her mother asking Clara if she had been afraid. And she could still recall Clara's mumbled, hesitant reply: "Not really, Mrs. Blumenthal . . . because I'm not . . ."

Not a Jew. Kitty's father had finished Clara's sentence. And just five weeks later, Kitty had boarded the train that would take her away from everything and everyone she'd ever known.

The memory of her father's words brought something else to mind—something that had been troubling her ever since she and the others had left Munich. The UNRRA officer had said that the people working as slave laborers at the artificial silk mill had not been Jews. But surely there would be Jewish refugees among those who had been brought to the camp since the war ended. Kitty had assumed that every DP camp in Germany would house Jews, that there would be people she could talk to from Vienna or who might have met her parents during the war. But what if she'd been wrong about that? What if there was no one here to help her in her search?

She took in a deep breath, stepping back from the derelict weaving shed. She could smell the wildflowers that grew along the banks of the river. The sun was high in the sky, making it hard to tell which direction she was facing. But she remembered from studying the map that the river ran from south to north. So, she must be looking east—toward the border with Austria. She thought of Sinaida Sikorsky, the woman who had been prepared to walk thirty miles to get to her pregnant daughter. Vienna was at least four times farther than that. How would she get there?

Be patient. She heard her mother's voice—words she'd spoken so often when the two of them had been sewing together in the workroom at the back of the shop. Kitty had struggled with stitching silk; she'd never really believed she could be as proficient as her mother. For Kitty, drawing the clothes, coming up with new creations, had been the attraction of the business. Her mother had told her she should go to college to study textile design. That poor dream had ended the day she'd left Austria. What would her mother have made of her toiling over a machine in the factory in Manchester, her fingers coarsened from the daily grind of fashioning clothes for men to fight in?

"Where are you, Mama?" she whispered. The slap of water on stones was the only reply.

Listening to all those people in the office asking for help to find loved ones had left her feeling raw. She'd wanted to tell them she felt their pain, that she would do whatever it took to help, that every time a new list arrived she would be scouring the names as eagerly as them. But she had kept silent. Because revealing that pain would be like taking a bandage off an open wound.

Walking on, she passed the giant mill wheel that had once powered the looms. It was still now, the water splashing over the paddles, some of which had been smashed, like the windows of the weaving shed. Ahead of her was a thicket of trees: the start of the forest that surrounded the camp. The little chapel was in a clearing a few yards from the path. It was built of wood, painted white, with a metal cross mounted on the roof. As Kitty drew closer she could hear a low, rhythmic chanting.

The door was ajar. Through the gap she saw a gray-haired man in a white robe overlaid with a shimmering pale green garment edged with silver braid. He was kneeling in front of a table covered with an embroidered cloth that reminded Kitty of the linen her mother had kept for special occasions—part of the trousseau she'd brought from Poland for her marriage.

On the table were three objects: the largest, in the center, was a wooden cross with a sculpted figure of the crucified Jesus. To the right was a picture of a woman with a crown and to the left was a silver bowl. On either side of the table, in blue enamel jugs, was a profusion of wildflowers: purple foxgloves, oxeye daisies, honeysuckle, and forget-me-nots.

Kitty had never been inside a church. As a child she'd watched the Easter processions across the square outside Saint Stephen's Cathedral, fascinated by the opulent outfits worn by the Christian holy men and the intricately embroidered symbols that embellished them. Her mother had told her that real gold was woven into the thread.

As the priest made the sign of the cross, the braid on his sleeve glinted in a beam of sunlight. The garment was pristine, expensive looking—in stark contrast to the drab secondhand clothing everyone else seemed to be wearing. Kitty wondered where the fabric to make such a thing had come from.

He rose from his knees, reaching for the edge of the table for support, when a young woman came out of the shadows to the left of the altar. In her arms was a sleeping baby.

The priest took the child from the woman. He dipped his hand into the silver bowl. An arc of droplets flew into the air as he withdrew it. Then he touched the baby's head, sweeping his fingers back and forth. To Kitty's surprise, the baby remained silent throughout the ritual. It was only when the priest handed the child back that it let out a wail.

The woman put her finger in its mouth and began to rock back and forth. Angling her body away from the altar table, she caught sight of

Kitty. The look in her eyes changed to one of absolute dread, and she backed away, clutching the baby to her chest.

"Proszę, nie bój się." Please don't be afraid. Kitty took a step forward. She pointed to the patch on her arm.

The priest turned to the woman, saying something Kitty didn't catch. The woman glanced at Kitty, still fearful, then back at him. The priest came toward Kitty, limping slightly as he closed the distance between them. His face was tight with emotion, as if he was struggling not to break down.

"Przyszłaś zabrać dziecko?"

She shook her head, horrified. He was asking her if she'd come to take the baby away.

There was a small room behind the altar, accessed by a near-invisible door in the wooden wall. In one corner was a pile of sacks with a blanket laid on top.

"That's where she's been sleeping." The priest was speaking in English now. His whole demeanor had changed when Kitty had explained who she was and why she'd come to the chapel.

"She's been hiding?" Kitty glanced back through the doorway at the woman, who was sitting on a chair, the baby at her breast.

He nodded. "She couldn't go back to the blockhouse where she was living. There's too much bad feeling from the other DPs. She came to me yesterday, begging for help. She wanted the baby baptized before it was taken away."

"Taken where?"

"I don't know. Someone in the camp arranged it." He shook his head. "There's a black market in babies. Childless couples will pay for a baby fathered by a German."

"She's going to *sell* her baby?"

"That was her plan. She was going to use the money to start a new life somewhere." He spread his hands, the movement making the heavy fabric of his outer garment rustle. "I could see it wasn't what she wanted. So, I offered her a place to hide while she worked out what to do."

"Will you wait here while I fetch Mrs. Radford?" Kitty said. "She's running the camp now. I'm sure she'll come up with a solution. I'm sorry, I . . ." She hesitated. "May I know your name?"

"I'm Josef," he replied.

"And the name of the mother?" She looked again at the woman, who was stroking the baby's head.

"Bożena."

"You won't leave her, will you?"

"No." His lips turned up at the edges. It was almost a smile—as if his mouth were too weary to do what he wanted it to do. Kitty wondered if he'd been in the chapel all night, guarding Bożena and her baby.

"I'll be back as soon as I can," she said.

CHAPTER 4

Delphine crept out of the bedroom and shut the door as silently as she could. Mother and baby were both asleep and would, hopefully, remain so until everyone else in the house had had a chance to get something to eat.

"Is the baby okay?" Kitty looked up from the table as Delphine came to join them.

"She's perfect," Delphine replied. "Does she have a name?"

"I don't know," Kitty replied. "Bożena didn't say. I'm not sure she trusts us, not yet." She looked at the priest, who was sharing the meal of cabbage soup, bread, and sausages. "Did she tell you, Josef? Sorry— *Father* Josef."

He looked different without the clerical robes. His corduroy jacket was patched at the elbows and had moth holes in the collar. "Bożena didn't want to give the baby a name," he said. "I think she was afraid to because she couldn't see a way of keeping her. But you can't baptize a child without a name, so she asked me to pick one. I called her Anny— after the saint our chapel is dedicated to."

"What about the others?" Delphine turned to Martha. "There are three other newborns in the hospital and two mothers due any day. The surgeon's working flat out with hardly any help because the DPs refuse to have anything to do with these women."

"We need to accommodate them in a separate section of the camp, away from the blockhouses," Martha said. "I suggest turning the cabins on either side of this one into mother-and-baby units. Bożena and her little girl can move next door tomorrow and we'll bring the other new mothers to join her when they're well enough to leave the hospital." She glanced at Kitty, then back at Delphine. "It'll mean the three of us sharing in here for a while. I hope you won't mind."

"Of course not," Kitty said.

"I think it's a good idea." Delphine nodded.

"They'll be safe up here." The priest laid down his spoon and dipped a chunk of bread into his soup. "But I think it will only work in the short term. There's no future for them in a place where everyone knows their past."

"That's true," Martha replied. "I wonder if it would be possible to get them transferred to other camps? In a different zone if necessary—somewhere they can make a fresh start."

"It makes me shudder to think of that little soul asleep up there being traded like a piece of meat," Delphine said.

The priest shook his head. "In a place like this, you learn quickly that everything has a price. But you also have to remember that life has been hard—very hard—for these people. And it still is."

I know. Delphine didn't say the words out loud. It would have sounded like a competition in hardship if she'd launched into a description of what had happened to Claude and Philippe.

"It's so important for us to be able to understand," Martha said. "Our problem is that only Kitty speaks Polish. We need people to work as translators—that's why I asked her to find you. But it seems you've got more than enough to deal with already."

"Of course, I'll help you in any way I can," he replied. "But sometimes it will be impossible. There are a lot of troubled souls here, Mrs. Radford."

"We got a glimpse of it this morning." Martha nodded.

"There is someone else who could be of use to you. He speaks some English and a little German, too. He was a timber merchant in Warsaw before the war."

"What's his name?"

"Stefan Dombrowski. He lives in the same blockhouse as me: number fifteen."

"Sergeant Lewis didn't mention him." Martha glanced at Kitty. "I wonder why not?"

"He's a quiet man," the priest said. "Like many people here, he doesn't like to talk about the past. He built our little chapel. He spends his days felling trees for firewood—ironic for a man who used to buy and sell timber."

"I imagine there are plenty of others capable of chopping wood," Martha said. "Could you ask him if he'll come and work with us?"

Stefan Dombrowski arrived at the office the next morning. He filled the doorway—his blond hair brushing the lintel as he stepped over the threshold. Martha couldn't help noticing the well-muscled arms beneath the thin fabric of a shirt whose collar was frayed at the edges. He looked older than her, but not much.

"Miss Radford?" His eyes were very blue, very alert.

"It's Mrs. Radford." She held out her hand, wondering if his English was good enough to know the difference.

"Sorry." He looked uncomfortable. She wondered if the priest had had to work hard to persuade him to come.

"That's okay. Please sit down." She gestured to the chair she'd placed on the opposite side of the desk.

"Now, Mr. Dombrowski . . ." She hesitated. If they were going to work together, she needed to know a little about him. But she was wary of appearing nosy about his past. "Father Josef tells me you speak English and German."

He nodded. "I learnt English for my business in Poland. I traded with Britain before the war." He looked at his hands, the fingers interlaced, resting on the desk. They were tanned from summer days spent outdoors, the knuckles rough and the cuticles ingrained with dirt. "The German, I picked up in Rathenow—near Berlin. I worked in a factory, making Heinkel bomber planes."

"How long were you there?"

"Three years."

It was hard to respond without sounding trite. "That must have been tough," she said.

He looked up, his eyes meeting hers momentarily before he bent his head again. "I survived. Many did not. I learnt German—it helped me to live."

"Will you help me?" she asked. "If I'm going to run this place, I have to understand the people who are living here, and I have to deal with the Germans, to organize supplies for the camp." She waited for him to respond. When he remained silent, she said: "It's a position of some responsibility, and that would be recognized. You would receive an extra allowance of cigarettes." She had no idea if he smoked, but she knew that cigarettes were like currency in the camp. He could trade them for whatever else he needed or wanted.

"Yes, I can translate for you," he said without looking up. "But cigarettes I do not want. To chop trees is harder, no? You give me more, I cannot look those guys in the face."

"I understand," she said. "But when we get started, you might change your mind. If so, you must tell me." Martha stood up. "First of all, I'd like to see where everyone lives. Will you show me around the blockhouses?"

Kitty had taken over the job of giving out passes while Martha went to inspect the camp. She was glad she'd been able to watch Martha handling the people who'd come the previous morning: it would have been terrifying to be thrown into that kind of work without some knowledge of what to expect.

There was one person she suspected of trying to deceive her: a man who said he wanted to go to the nearby village to buy strawberries for his child, who was recovering from pneumonia. He held up a small cup made of silver, the kind of thing a baby might receive as a gift. He said he was going to trade it for the fruit.

It was a request that would melt any heart. But some indefinable aspect of his body language made Kitty wary of saying yes. But how could she tell if he was lying?

In a flash of inspiration, she asked him the name and age of his child. The momentary hesitation confirmed her suspicions. There *was* no child.

The man had slunk out of the office, muttering words she didn't understand—obscene Polish curses, she guessed. He'd been the last in line for passes, and she'd grabbed a coffee when the door closed, thankful for a few minutes' peace. But as soon as she'd drunk it, she was riffling through the filing cabinets. There was something she'd been wanting to do since she'd first set foot in the office. The files contained the details of every person in the camp. Somewhere in those drawers there must be a list of names—a document that would reveal in a matter of minutes whether there were any Jewish DPs in Seidenmühle.

It didn't take Kitty long to find what she was looking for. The names were not in alphabetical order; the list had a randomness that suggested people had been added as they'd arrived. The columns were dominated by common Polish surnames: there were dozens of Kowalskis, Nowaks, and Wozniaks. She searched for the familiar names of her childhood. For a Klein, a Bergmann, or an Adler. But no such names jumped out of the rows of black type. She read through the list a second time, just to be certain, then sat down heavily in the chair. It seemed impossible. Poland was a place that many Jewish people called home—her mother had been born there—so why were there none in this camp?

Kitty picked up the phone. Sergeant Lewis—the officer Martha had spoken to the day before—answered in the guardhouse that doubled as the camp switchboard.

"I need to put through a call to the Red Cross office in Munich," she said.

"I can look up the number and get back to you when I have them on the line," he said. "By the way, did you manage to track down that guy yesterday?"

"Yes, thank you," Kitty replied. "It took us a while to work out that he was a priest."

"Sorry—I should have explained. Things were going a bit crazy down here when your boss called."

"I found him in the chapel." Kitty hesitated. She wasn't sure if she should reveal that they were concealing Bożena and her child in their billet house, and were about to convert the other two cabins into a mother-and-baby home.

"Did he tell you he was in Dachau?"

"No." The flesh on the back of Kitty's neck prickled. "He didn't say anything about his past. We did wonder, though, how he came to be here."

"He didn't like what the Nazis were doing and wasn't afraid to speak out in public," the sergeant replied. "He was lucky: they sent hundreds of guys like him to Dachau—only a handful survived."

"H . . . have you been there?" Kitty felt the tremble at the back of her throat. "Is that how you know?"

"We liberated the place." His voice betrayed no emotion. "Around a quarter of the men in this camp were prisoners there. The rest were slave laborers—either here or in factories across Germany."

A host of questions filled Kitty's head. All she knew about Dachau was what she'd read in British newspapers. The reports had contained horrific images but precious little detail about the prisoners. Had there been women survivors? How many of those liberated were Jewish? Were any of them from Austria? And—most important of all—where were they now?

"Hello? Are you still there?" Sergeant Lewis broke the silence.

"I . . . I'm sorry. Someone's just arrived. Have to go." She replaced the receiver, her hand shaking, cursing herself for not having the nerve to come out with what she wanted so desperately to know.

A light drizzle was falling as Martha followed Stefan Dombrowski along the cobbled main street to the blockhouses. The first thing she noticed as he opened the door was the smell. It was a mixture of damp wool and woodsmoke, with a hint of something unsavory—the sort of sour odor that wafted out of the entrance to the Marcy Avenue subway station in Brooklyn.

There was a list inside the door of everyone who lived there—145 names. At first sight, the interior of the blockhouse resembled a fabric warehouse. Dombrowski explained that the DPs had divided what was basically a large barn into minuscule apartments, using nothing but suitcases, piled on top of one another, and blankets suspended by ropes from the wooden rafters.

It reminded her of something she'd seen in New Orleans as a teenager. The Mississippi River had flooded, and hundreds of homeless families had been brought to warehouses near the docks. She and her grandmother had gone to take food donated by the neighbors. Climbing up to where the grain and cotton were stored, she'd been mesmerized by the faces peering over walls made from piles of sacks.

"This place is for families and married people." Dombrowski paused in front of a blanket that had been tied back with what looked like a dressing gown cord. A wizened old woman in black clothes and a white headscarf sat on a three-legged stool, guarding her little domain with a look as ferocious as a mountain lion. From inside the dark interior space, Martha could hear children's voices.

Dombrowski had a brief conversation with the woman. Although Martha understood none of it, she saw a look of alarm cross the woman's face before her expression softened a little.

"She thought we came to bring more people to live here," he said. "She said: 'No room!' I told her we are just looking around—we haven't come for that."

"How many in her family?" Martha asked.

"Six people in here," he replied. "She is the grandmother. There is also her daughter, her daughter's husband, and three children. The daughter works in the laundry. The husband is in the kitchen. He bakes bread." He cocked his head toward the old woman. "She looks after the children."

Martha frowned. "Is there no school in the camp?"

"Some days they have school. Not today. The teacher is sick."

"Just one teacher? For . . . how many children?"

"Maybe two hundred," he replied. "It grows each week—we get more families. Trains come to Fürstenfeldbruck, full of DPs. The army brings them here." He swept his hand over the rows of makeshift cubicles. "They are happy to see new people because maybe some might be from their village in Poland, have news of family they have not seen for years. But they are afraid, too, because there is not enough room for more people."

Martha nodded. "I understand." As she followed him along the central passageway toward the back of the blockhouse, the hot, fusty air made her feel faint. The idea of cramming still more people into this place was out of the question. What on earth was she going to do if the army brought another trainload?

At the far end of the building, a single potbellied stove sat in a space festooned with washing that hung on lines strung from one wall to another. On the stove was a steaming pot, which smelled revolting. It was being stirred by a woman who could have been the twin of the one they'd just seen. Her clothes were identical and her expression grew equally fierce when she saw them coming.

After another exchange in Polish, Martha's guide explained that the pot contained not food but soiled diapers. "She's boiling them to make them clean. She says she doesn't have enough to send to the laundry: it's too long to wait to get them back."

Martha shot a sympathetic glance at the woman. She'd witnessed similar scenes in the tenements on the Lower East Side: families so poor they had nothing but rags to bind around their babies—rags that were boiled on a stove every day until they fell apart.

"Where do the people go to wash themselves?" she asked.

"Out there." He pointed to a door to the left of the stove. "They get water from a pump. And there are lavatories."

"Can I see?"

He went over to the door and opened it, stepping back to allow her inside. Martha tried not to gag as she counted the cubicles—just six for the 145 occupants of the blockhouse. They were screened from each other by shoulder-height walls of plywood. The water pump separated the cubicles from a concrete gully that appeared to be the men's urinal.

"Are all the houses like this?" she asked, as she came out, shutting the door behind her.

He nodded. "Some are for men only. Some for women. One is for children with no mother or father."

"How many children like that?"

"Thirty. Forty." He shook his head. "Really, I don't know."

"Who takes care of them?"

For a moment he didn't answer. She heard him clear his throat. Then he said: "The ones who . . ." He hesitated. "They have lost a child." His eyes seemed to change color—from the clear blue of a summer sky to the burning blue at the heart of a flame.

Martha remembered what Father Josef had said the previous evening, *He lives in the same blockhouse as me: number fifteen.* That would be for single men if a priest lived there. She wondered if, like so many others in the camp, her new translator had been separated from his family and longed for news of them.

"Come," he said. "I will take you to another place."

⊰——⊱

Delphine arrived at the office as Kitty was speaking on the phone.

"Danke schön," Kitty said, replacing the receiver.

"Who was that?" Delphine plonked down in the chair on the other side of the desk.

"The Red Cross woman in Munich. She said they update the information on DPs in all the camps in the occupied territories once a month. They have motorcycle couriers who drop off the lists. We should get one by the end of next week."

"That's good," Delphine said. Kitty thought how tired she looked. She'd volunteered to sleep in the same room as Bożena and the baby last night, while Kitty and Martha had spent the night in the cabin next door.

"Would you like some coffee? I think it's still warm." Kitty went over to the filing cabinets, on top of which a pot sat, swathed in a cloth to keep in the heat. Next to it were three tin mugs and a brown paper bag containing sugar.

"How did the transfer go?" Kitty asked, as she placed the mug in front of Delphine.

"Okay," Delphine replied. "Father Josef helped. He borrowed an army jeep. Wolf helped, too—he's the young boy I told you about: the one who wants to be a doctor. He looked after the babies while the mothers settled into the cabin. There are three of them now, including Bożena." She took a sip of coffee. "Father Josef's going to christen the other two babies this afternoon."

"In the chapel?"

Delphine nodded. "He said he'd do it at lunchtime when no one was likely to notice them going over there."

"It's a beautiful little place," Kitty said, "considering it's made of trees cut from the forest."

"Is it?" Delphine's eyebrows arched. "He wanted to know if we'd be coming to the service on Sunday. I didn't like to tell him that I haven't been to Mass since . . . well, it's been more than a year, I think."

"Oh?" Kitty took in a breath. "Actually, my family don't go to church."

Why can't you just say it? Her mother's voice hissed inside her head. *Are you ashamed of being Jewish?*

Before Delphine could make any comment, Kitty told her what Sergeant Lewis had said about the priest being a prisoner in Dachau.

"He didn't mention that." Delphine cradled the tin mug in both hands, looking down at what was left of the coffee. The name of the prison camp seemed to have made her shrink back into herself, like a snail when salt is thrown into its path. Kitty was reminded of the moment on the journey from France when she'd asked Delphine if she'd ever visited Germany, and the moonlight had caught tears in the nurse's eyes. Now, as then, Kitty felt paralyzed—incapable of reaching out for fear of exposing what she'd kept inside for so long.

A knock made them both look up.

"Someone wanting a pass?" Delphine said.

Kitty glanced at the clock on the wall. "They're not supposed to come in the afternoon." She went to open the door. Standing in the rain was a girl about her age, her blond hair plastered to her head. When Kitty stood aside to let her in, the girl shook herself like a wet dog. She put her hand in the pocket of her coat and pulled out a folded piece of paper, which she thrust at Kitty.

"Muszę wyjść z obozu." I need to go out of the camp. Her voice was high pitched, agitated.

Kitty unfolded the paper. It bore the insignia of the United States Third Army, Tank Battalion. A scribbled note in English read: "Dear Jadzia, Frank has been shipped out stateside. He asked me to pass on his best regards." The message was simply signed "Jimmy."

"Muszę znaleźć Franka." The woman looked from Kitty to Delphine, as if she expected the older one to take charge of the situation.

"What is it? What does she say?"

"She wants to go and find an American soldier." Kitty frowned. "Sounds like it's her boyfriend, and he's gone."

In the exchange that followed, the woman became visibly distressed.

"She says there must be a mistake," Kitty said. "She says he can't have gone back to America—they were due to be married next month."

"Can we phone the major? What's her name?"

"Jadzia," Kitty replied. "We can't phone the major; he's on his way back from Munich."

Delphine went over to the woman, repeating her name as she put a hand on her shoulder, and offered her a handkerchief. This had the opposite effect of what was intended: Jadzia began to weep hysterically.

"Ask her which blockhouse she's in." Delphine raised her voice above the wailing. "I'll take her back. Give her something to calm her down."

———

At the dinner table that evening, Delphine told Martha and Kitty what she'd discovered when she'd helped Jadzia remove her coat back at the blockhouse.

"She's about seven or eight months pregnant. I'll need to do a proper examination to know exactly how far on she is; she was too distressed for that this afternoon."

Kitty blew out a breath. "If it's not the goddam Nazis fathering babies on these women, it's the GIs. I wonder if he ever intended to marry her? Pretty cowardly, getting his friend to send that note—and hard to believe he wouldn't have had the chance to write to her himself."

"I wonder if the major could do something to help her when he gets back," Martha said. "There's been a lot of talk in the US newspapers about getting foreign wives of servicemen over to the States. If Jadzia's boyfriend was serious about marrying her, it might be possible to get her on a boat."

The talk turned to the women who had moved in next door. Martha asked Delphine if she'd discovered who was responsible for trying to sell Bożena's baby on the black market.

"She won't say," Delphine replied. "Father Josef tried to find out, but she's too afraid to name the man."

Martha pushed her plate away. They'd been living in the camp less than forty-eight hours, but the list of what needed tackling seemed insurmountable. And she hadn't even started on the urgent tasks—like checking how much food there was in the warehouse and working out how much more would be needed to see them through the winter. The major had warned them not to allow the personal tragedies they would encounter to engulf them. But it was impossible to wave away what had happened to Bożena and Jadzia. These women were going to need far more than food and shelter to rebuild their lives.

"You look worn out." Delphine was on her feet. "I think we all deserve a little treat." She went upstairs and returned with a bottle, which she set down on the table.

"What is it?" Martha peered at the label.

"The best cognac." Delphine smiled. "Rémy Martin—Louis XIII, 1938. One of the few things I brought with me from Paris." She fetched three glasses and trickled a little of the golden-brown liquid into each one. *"Santé,"* she said.

"Bottoms up!" Kitty smiled as she raised her glass. "It's what they say in Britain, goodness knows why."

"Cheers!" Martha held up her glass, but she didn't lift it to her mouth when the others did.

"Oh, don't you like it?" Delphine said.

"I . . ." Martha hesitated. "I do—I mean, I used to really enjoy a drink. But . . ." Should she tell them the truth? She was supposed to be in charge. Was it okay to reveal something so personal about herself?

"You've given up alcohol?" Delphine's expression was a mixture of surprise and concern.

Martha shook her head. "I haven't given it up—it's just that the smell of spirits brings back bad memories. My husband's an alcoholic. Drinking made him violent." There. It was out.

"That must have been a nightmare," Delphine murmured.

"Is that why you left New York?" Kitty asked. "To get away from him?"

"Partly," Martha replied. "I really wanted this job. I didn't tell Arnie about it. He would never have agreed to me going overseas. On the morning I was due to catch the plane, I just walked out while he was still asleep." She cradled the glass in her hand, watching the liquid glint amber as it caught the light. "It was cowardly, I know. He has no idea where I am. I will write to him. But not yet."

"You shouldn't feel bad about it," Delphine said. "No one would blame you for doing what you did."

"I can't help feeling guilty, though, because now he has nothing. He went off to fight in the war—really wanted to do his bit—but it all went wrong. He drank too much and ended up fighting someone on his own side." Martha let out a sigh. "I'm sorry. I shouldn't be going on about it." She looked at the others. "I can't imagine what the past few years must have been like for you, Delphine, living under Nazi rule—nor for you, Kitty, with all the bombing."

Delphine took a sip of brandy. Martha saw that as she set down her glass, there was a slight tremble in her fingers. Kitty was staring at the table, her face tight, as if she couldn't trust herself to speak.

A sudden wail from outside made all three women turn their heads to the door. There was a single knock, then it opened to reveal one of the trio of mothers from next door, a crying baby cradled in her arms.

"Potrzebuję mleka w puszce."

"She's asking for more of that canned milk," Kitty said.

"I'll go and get some." Delphine disappeared into the kitchen.

As Martha watched her go, she wondered what memories had caused Delphine's hand to shake like that. And Kitty—who was now chatting with the mother in Polish so fluent, it could have been her first language—what had been going through her mind in the seconds before they were interrupted?

She sensed that each of them had buried something of the past when they had pulled on those ill-fitting gray uniforms and sewn on their UNRRA patches, that like her, they were wary of revealing the twists of fate that had brought them to this place.

Wary? Or plain scared? It *was* scary, Martha thought, to peel off your shell and expose what lay beneath. Now they knew that she was a runaway, a poor judge of character, a failure as a wife. Would that knowledge diminish her in their eyes? She hoped not.

CHAPTER 5

When Martha woke the next morning, her heart was pounding. She'd been in a deep sleep, dreaming about Arnie. In the dream, he'd come to Germany to find her. He was standing outside the gates of Seidenmühle, shouting to the guard to let him in.

She took in a long breath and let it out slowly. The sight of the other women, still fast asleep, was comforting. Delphine, in the bed opposite hers, was gently snoring. The lines on her face seemed to disappear when she was asleep, making her look younger. Kitty slept on the other side of the room. Her hair covered the pillow. Each night she undid the braid she wore and spent a few minutes brushing the shiny black waist-length locks. Usually, she braided it again before getting into bed, but last night—probably due to the effects of the cognac—she hadn't.

The beam of sunlight penetrating the gap in the bedroom curtains told Martha that the rain of the previous day had cleared. Very quietly she slid out of bed, took her clothes from the bedside chair, and made her way downstairs, trying to avoid the places on the treads that creaked. Sneaking out of the house like this, she couldn't help being reminded of running out on Arnie. The dream had rattled her. She couldn't ignore the guilt it stirred up. She tried to picture what he'd be doing at this moment. Probably he was still awake, sitting up late with a bottle for company, or playing cards in his favorite bar on Wythe

Avenue. She wondered if he really had tried to find her, if he'd gone to the homes of any of her friends, banging on doors and demanding answers. She hoped not. She hadn't told anyone she was leaving, just in case. It had hurt, not being able to say goodbye to them. In a week or so, when the dust had settled, she would write letters.

Making her way along the path through the trees, Martha headed for the entrance to the camp, struggling to banish images of Arnie and focus on the day ahead. She hadn't had a chance to explore the place properly. Getting up before everyone else was the only way to make the time to do it. When the gates came into view, she swerved left, away from the main route through the camp, taking a track that led down to the river.

She knew from the map on the wall of the office that the Amper River formed the eastern boundary of the camp. She'd glimpsed it from the road when they'd arrived at Seidenmühle, but the view from the opposite bank was very different. Fingers of mist hung over the water, lit by the early morning sunshine. A heron stood, still and elegant, in the shallows. Swallows flitted over her head, diving so low they skimmed the surface. To her left was the mill wheel, strewn with weeds that hung like tangled hair from the splintered paddles. Beyond it she could see two figures, standing up to their thighs in the water. Fishermen. Up and about their business even earlier than she was. She wondered if they were from the camp or were local men from one of the farms. They looked innocent enough, but she couldn't help remembering what the major had said about Nazis on the run. The thought of them hiding out in the woods outside the camp sent a shiver down her spine.

As she watched, one of the men started to pull vigorously on the rod he was holding. She saw the silvery body of a sizeable fish flapping about in the water. A joyful shouting erupted as the man landed his catch. German words—or Polish? She wondered how long it would be before she could tell the difference.

She followed the river until she came to the edge of the forest that formed the southern boundary of the camp. Through the trees she caught the glint of something metal, high up. Stepping off the path she saw that it was the cross on the roof of the chapel Kitty had found when she'd gone looking for the priest.

She hesitated a moment, tempted to go and see if the door was unlocked. It reminded her of the little church near her uncle's farm in Louisiana. She glanced at her watch. *Not now,* she thought. She'd planned an inspection of the kitchens, and she wanted to be there while the baking of the daily bread ration was in full swing.

<hr />

It was a little after eight o'clock when Martha made her way to the huge concrete bunker that served as the camp's warehouse. Her cheeks were pink from the heat in the kitchens—and her stomach a little bloated from the loaf she'd been pressed into sampling. The bakers had clearly been working flat out to produce the thirteen hundred pounds of bread needed to feed close to three thousand hungry mouths. She'd felt bad about eating any of it, knowing that a loaf would be delivered to her cabin that morning. But she sensed that to refuse would offend them.

There was a GI on duty in a stone outbuilding attached to the bunker. She recognized him as the soldier who'd been at the gate when they'd arrived at Seidenmühle. She recalled that he came from Oregon.

He smiled when she asked him if he'd had any news from home lately. "You have a good memory, ma'am."

"Not that good," she replied. "I'm afraid I can't remember your name."

"Corporal John Brody, ma'am."

"Well, Corporal, I'd like to see inside the warehouse."

The door was secured with the biggest padlock Martha had ever seen. Corporal Brody led her through a maze of stacked boxes.

"Everything on this side comes from the States," he said. "You got sugar in this pile; coffee's over there; salt, pepper, oil, and vinegar over by the wall." He waved his hand to the left, where wooden racks were piled with potatoes, cabbages, and onions. "The stuff on that side comes from the farms around here. We got meat in the cold storage through that door. Fresh milk, too, though we've got plenty of cans of it if we run out."

Martha was jotting it all down in a notebook. "What's the meat allowance for the DPs?"

"Twelve ounces per adult per week. Six ounces for children under fourteen years old."

"Hmm. That doesn't sound too bad." She added the figure to her notes. "But I've heard there's an illicit trade in meat in the camp, with DPs stealing livestock from the farms."

He nodded. "Problem is what we get is often substandard. The Germans hate that we make them give to the DPs, so they give us the lousy stuff—more bone than meat, sometimes."

Martha recorded this comment and marked it with an asterisk. Something else that would need tackling, she thought. "What's in these boxes?" She walked over to a stack near the door. "Oh—I can see—it says soap powder."

"Cigarettes, actually," the corporal replied. "We put them in those boxes to keep them from walking out of here."

"But the place is padlocked . . ."

"Not all the time: when we get a big delivery, it's all hands on deck—everyone but the patients in the hospital comes to help unload. You have to have eyes in the back of your head."

Martha clicked her tongue against her teeth. "Okay, I think I've seen enough. Thank you, Corporal."

When she came outside, she saw Stefan Dombrowski waiting for her. He was leaning against a car whose bodywork gleamed in the sunshine. As she drew closer, she saw that there were holes in the rear door, and tape across the window above it.

"*Dzień dobry.*" She hoped she'd pronounced the words properly. Kitty had written out a list of basic Polish phrases, with a phonetic version beside each one. Martha had been practicing them during her walk around the camp.

"Good morning." Dombrowski smiled. "I have a car for you." He held out keys on a leather fob.

"For me?" Martha's eyes widened. "Where'd you get it?"

"It was left here by the Germans," he replied. "Bullet holes here, see? From when they tried to get away. But I will fix that. Opel Kapitän—good car."

"It runs okay?"

He nodded. "Some damage to the electrics. But I can get new parts."

"How?"

"In the forest are tanks, also left by the Germans. I will find what I need." He opened the door. "You want to drive?"

"I . . ." Martha hesitated. It had been a long while since she'd driven a car. Arnie had sold the Model T Ford he'd owned when they met to raise the money for the deposit on their apartment in Brooklyn. Would she even remember what to do?

"I will start the engine for you," Dombrowski said. "You can drive around the camp. Then we will go on the road. Yes?"

She smiled as he climbed into the car, realizing that he would probably have been more than happy to drive it himself. But he had figured out how important it was going to be for her to get around the local area, and he wasn't going to let her chicken out. When the engine chugged to life, he jumped out and stood aside for her to get behind the wheel. She could feel the warmth where his hands had been. It triggered an odd sensation, almost like a memory: something from long ago and far away, when she had still been in love with Arnie.

⊸—⊷

After breakfast, Delphine went to blockhouse number nineteen, where Wolf lived. Martha had told her what she'd seen when she'd visited the place. The younger orphaned children had been absorbed into family groups, with one or two adults caring for up to six boys and girls. But the older ones had formed a family of their own. Ranging in age from eleven to fourteen, they occupied their own section of the blockhouse and, from what Martha had found out, pretty much took care of themselves.

Delphine could see curls of smoke drifting across the roof of number nineteen. She wondered if the older children had to heat their own water for washing and bathing on the potbellied stove Martha had described. Wolf was a very capable boy—watching what he did in the hospital had filled her with admiration—but he was still a child. It pained her to think of him and the others having no one to provide the most basic home comforts.

The door to the place was open. Two girls, about the same age as Wolf, were sitting on the step, one braiding the other's hair.

"Dzień dobry." Delphine couldn't remember any of the other phrases Kitty had given her. "Wolf?" She pointed through the doorway.

One of the girls said something back in Polish. She finished the braid, tied it with colored string, then jumped to her feet and disappeared inside.

Moments later Wolf appeared, grinning. Delphine couldn't tell if he was embarrassed or proud to have been summoned by the camp nurse. She thought his friends must know that he spent his days in the hospital. It had occurred to her that some of them might be interested in joining him. With no parents to prejudice them against the women in the maternity ward, they might be willing to work as auxiliary nurses. She could offer certificates for when they eventually left the camp, give them a better chance of employment. It was something she needed to talk over with Martha.

As they walked across to the hospital, Wolf pulled something out of his pocket. It was a faded black-and-white photograph of a man and a woman, very smartly dressed, the woman cradling a baby in her arms. Wolf pointed to the baby, then at himself.

Delphine nodded. "Mama and Papa?"

Wolf nodded back. His face betrayed no emotion.

"Dobrze." It sounded pathetically inadequate, to say "good" in response to him showing her something so intensely personal. But she felt that to say nothing at all would have been worse. She longed to be able to ask him about his parents: to find out how old he had been when they had died and how he had survived the war without them. But she didn't have the words. Fishing in her bag she pulled out the piece of paper Kitty had given her and scanned the phrases. There was just one that would serve. *"Przykro mi,"* she said. I am sorry.

Wolf said nothing in response. He peered at the list, a curious expression on his face. Following Kitty's handwriting with his finger, he said: "I . . . am . . . a . . . nurse!" The way he pronounced the last word was quite comical—it sounded like "nursie"—but Delphine was impressed that he could read the English.

"Dobrze!" She patted him on the shoulder.

Wolf clapped his hands, triumphant. Then he tried another one: "Have . . . you . . . opened . . . your . . ." He turned to her, clearly perplexed by the word that followed.

"Bowels. Bow-els." Delphine felt the corners of her mouth turning up. She mimed lowering herself onto a toilet seat and jabbed her thumb at her behind.

"Bowels," he repeated. At which point they both burst out laughing.

By the time they reached the hospital, Delphine was wiping tears from her eyes. It seemed like years since she had laughed like this. How was it that this child, with whom she couldn't even hold a conversation, had the ability to take her out of herself? She wanted to give him a hug, but she held back, remembering how reticent and self-conscious Philippe had been as an adolescent. Instead, she rummaged in her bag for a chunk of Bavarian smoked cheese, wrapped in waxed paper. It had been part of last night's meal, but it had been too much for her, so she'd saved it to eat for lunch. She held it out to him.

"Thank you for making me laugh again." She knew he couldn't understand, but it felt good to hear herself say it.

———

Martha couldn't quite believe that it had come back to her so easily. She was driving along the road that followed the river, the windows down, breathing in the scent of the pine trees.

"You are doing very well." Stefan smiled as she glanced sideways. "But watch out for holes."

She nodded. "The roads are bad; we hit quite a few potholes on the way from France."

"How did you get from America? By ship?"

"Plane," she replied. "I'd never flown before; I was quite scared, but it was fine."

"I have never done that," he replied. "I went on many ships: to England, Holland, other countries. Where do you live in America?"

"New York. But I grew up in the South—Louisiana."

"You like New York?"

She hesitated. "I like some things. But it's not an easy place to live." She realized as the words came out how flippant that must sound to someone who had spent the past three years as a slave laborer in a German factory. "What I mean is, it's a good place to be if you have money, but if you don't . . ."

"It is the same in all the world, I think. In Warsaw, where I live, just the same. But when the Germans came, it made no difference how much money you had."

Martha tried to picture him as he would have been before the war: a man running an international export business—probably wealthy. What would have happened to that business when the Germans took over? Would there be anything to go back to, if and when DPs were able to return to their homelands? And what about his family? Had there been a wife? Children?

Before she could frame any question that might prompt him to open up about his past, she saw something that made her slam on the brakes. A wagon pulled by a pair of oxen was blocking the way ahead. It was piled high with cabbages, a couple of which had tumbled off and lay in the road. A few yards away, on the riverbank, a man was shouting at a couple of other men, both of whom carried the kind of makeshift wooden fishing rods she'd seen earlier.

"*Verdammte Ausländer!*" The man shook his fist at the fishermen. They were backing away, but with the river behind them, there was nowhere to go.

"What's going on?" She turned to Stefan. "What's he saying?"

"He called them dirty foreigners." Stefan's hand was on the door. In a moment he was out of the car. Martha watched, alarmed, as he strode right into the middle of the confrontation. He put his arm up, holding the German at bay while he spoke to the fishermen. She saw him jerk his head downriver, in the direction of Seidenmühle. Then he turned to the German. There was a brief exchange before the man climbed back onto the cabbage wagon and urged his oxen forward.

"What did you say?" Martha asked, as he climbed back into the car.

"I told them to go fishing in a different place."

"And the German—what did you say to him?"

"I told him they won't take his fish anymore."

"*His* fish? Does he own this land?"

"No. He comes from Fürstenfeldbruck." He shrugged. "Germany is his country. So, *his* fish, that's what he says."

Martha drew in a breath as she put the car in gear again. She wondered how he'd managed to remain so calm, so controlled. He must hate the Germans for what he'd suffered during the war, and for reducing him to the status of a penniless refugee in a foreign land. It was incredible that he hadn't lashed out at the man.

As if reading her thoughts, he said: "He hates us because Germany lost the war. If he sees people from the camp, it reminds him. But, for now, we must live here. So, it's not worth making trouble."

She jabbed the horn as they overtook the cabbage wagon. In the rearview mirror she saw the German raise his arm in an obscene salute.

Martha wondered how she was going to find a way to work with people like him. If the local farmers resented the DPs so much, it was going to be a nightmare of a task to get them to provide enough food to lay in for the winter.

"Not all Germans are bad like him. Some hate what the Nazis did."

Martha kept her eyes on the road ahead, wondering if he'd say more. In the silence that followed, her mind turned to the girl, Bożena, who had been on the verge of selling her baby to a German couple. It was hard to square the resentment she had just witnessed with the idea of local people paying to adopt a DP's child.

It occurred to her that in a small community like Seidenmühle, news like that would travel fast. Dombrowski might even know the identity of the DP who had arranged the shady transaction.

"I heard that some Germans offered to buy a Polish woman's baby," she said.

"Yes," he replied. "The father was a Nazi."

"I know there's a black market in the camp—that things are traded—but to sell a *baby* . . ."

"Yes, it is very bad."

"If I knew who had set up a deal like that, I'd have him locked up."

There was a moment of silence. She heard him take a long breath.

"I am happy to do translation," he said. "I want to help you. But, please, do not ask me to be your spy."

CHAPTER 6

Kitty was working through the list of tasks that Martha had left for her. The Polish mothers who had moved in next door had taken up most of her morning. She was only supposed to be making a note of what they needed from the warehouse—but she quickly realized that what they really wanted was to find out what the future held for them. Were they going to be sent to another camp? Where would it be? Would they stay together? And what about their friends, still in the hospital waiting to give birth? Would they be going to the same place? And how long would it be before they went back to Poland?

Kitty couldn't answer any of these questions. All she could do was reassure them that Martha had their best interests at heart and that arrangements would be made with the army as soon as possible.

"Gdzie się nauczyłaś polskiego?" Where did you learn Polish? It was Bożena who asked, smiling shyly as she looked up from feeding her little girl.

"My mother's Polish," Kitty replied. "She was born in Łódź."

One of the other women said she had an aunt who came from Łódź. Then Bożena wanted to know where Kitty had grown up.

"W Anglii." In England. It wasn't really a lie: she had been a child when she'd arrived there. She hoped this short answer would satisfy them, but it didn't. They wanted to know how her mother had come

to be living in England, whether her father was English, what the food was like there—and why she had chosen to come to a terrible place like Germany.

To Kitty's relief, Father Josef appeared as this volley of questions was being fired. He'd brought another of the new mothers, who had given birth to a baby boy the previous night. The attention of the other women immediately shifted to this new arrival. Kitty and the priest were able to leave them to help her settle in.

"Would you like coffee?" Kitty asked, as they stepped outside.

"That would be very welcome."

As she followed him along the path to her cabin, Kitty noticed that his limp was more pronounced than it had been that first day, in the chapel. She wondered whether he'd been injured while he was a prisoner in Dachau. Would it be okay to let on that she knew he'd been held there? There was so much she wanted to know. Would it be unfeeling to ask him about it?

"Your English is very good," she said, as she put the kettle on the stove. "Where did you learn it?" That was a good way to start, she thought.

"In Warsaw," he replied. "I taught English at the university before I went into the Church."

"Is that where you were living when the war started?"

"Yes. I was at the cathedral there—Saint Anny. We gave our little chapel the same name."

She spooned coffee into two tin mugs. Without looking at him, she said: "I hope you won't be offended, but one of the GIs told me that the Nazis arrested you for speaking out against them."

"That's right." He exhaled. "My sermons were my weapon, my only way of defying them."

"That was brave of you."

"Not really. I had Jewish friends. I couldn't keep quiet when I realized what was happening."

Kitty's hand hovered over the sugar bowl. It would have been the most natural thing in the world to tell him that she, too, was Jewish. But she'd been bottling it up for so long that the thought of it made her tongue stick to the roof of her mouth.

"It didn't help, anyway," he went on. "To the Nazis I was simply a loud-mouthed nuisance. They sent me to Dachau—did the American tell you that?"

Kitty nodded. She went back to the stove, lifted the kettle even though it wasn't boiling yet, then replaced it. She didn't trust herself to look at him in case her face gave her away. Swallowing hard, she managed to say: "I thought that was a place they sent Jews to."

"It was," he replied. "There were thousands of Jews there, from many different countries. But mostly it was for political prisoners, which included people like me. At one time there were nearly as many clergy in Dachau as there are DPs in this place—Catholics, Protestants, Greek Orthodox—but . . ."

Kitty heard the chair creak as he shifted his weight.

"I'm sorry," he said. "I have to stand for a moment. My leg . . ."

She turned around. Pain was etched on his face. "Did that happen in Dachau?" She hadn't intended to ask. But there—it was out.

He nodded. "They used us for experiments. For some reason they chose the Polish priests, not those from their own country. What they did to me wasn't as bad as what they did to others."

"What did they do?"

"Injections of bacteria." He bent to rub his leg, then sat down heavily. "Dr. Jankaukas says the bone is affected. But it won't get any worse, so I count myself lucky."

Lucky? He'd given her a glimpse of hell. How could she have gone blundering in, thinking it would be all right to probe into the nightmare world he'd inhabited?

The kettle began to whistle, startling Kitty out of her state of shock. With a trembling hand she took it off the stove and poured water into the mugs. When she added the milk, it slopped over the sides. She wiped up the mess, then set the coffee down on the table. "I'm sorry," she said. "I shouldn't have brought it up—it must be terrible for you, remembering."

"It is painful," he replied. "More painful than the leg, actually. But sometimes, you need to feel pain. It reminds you that you are alive." He lifted the mug, a curl of steam misting his chin. "As a priest, I shouldn't say it, but with survival comes guilt. Sometimes I can't bear waking up, seeing a new day, knowing that so many people have died."

Kitty felt as though he'd shone a flashlight through her eyes and looked inside her head. He had described it exactly—the darkness that so often enveloped her when she emerged from sleep. The guilt had begun that first winter in England, when she had tried and failed to get the work visas that would have allowed her parents to get out of Austria. The sense of powerlessness—that no one would listen to a child—had overwhelmed her. And then, eighteen months on, when the letters from home had stopped coming . . .

"I light a candle in the chapel each morning," he went on. "I look into the flame and I see them; they talk to me." He took a sip of coffee. "That makes me sound a little crazy. But it helps."

"It doesn't sound crazy to me," Kitty murmured. She was gazing at the liquid in her mug, willing the faces of her parents to appear.

Tell him. It was her mother's voice. *Go on. He's a priest. He won't mind.*

"I'm looking for my family. They're Jewish—from Vienna. I went to England. It's nearly seven years since I've seen them." It all came out in a rush.

He was silent. Had she really let it out? Or just imagined it? Then he said: "Tell me about them."

"My mother's name is Elsa. She was born in Poland. My father is Hermann. He's Austrian. They had a business—a shop in the city— importing silk and making clothes."

He nodded. "They sent you on the Kindertransport?"

"Yes. I thought they'd be coming after me. But I . . ." Suddenly there were tears running down her face, dripping into her coffee. "I . . . I'm sorry." She dragged the back of her hand across her face.

"Here, have this." He offered her a square of pale blue cotton, frayed at the edges. "It's clean," he added.

She took it, mumbling her thanks.

"Do the others know?" he asked when she'd blown her nose. "Are they helping you?"

She shook her head. "Please don't say anything. If they knew, they might send me back."

"I'm sure they wouldn't. You're far too useful," he replied. "But I understand. I won't breathe a word if you don't want me to." He took a mouthful of coffee. "There are Austrians in this camp, but none of them are Jews. The Jewish survivors of Dachau were sent to a different place—Feldafing—south of here."

"Oh?" The idea of DPs being segregated hadn't occurred to her. "Why?"

"It's what they wanted—to form their own community, to support one another."

"How far is it from here?"

"I'm not sure. But there are other ways of getting information. The Red Cross . . ."

"Yes. I know about the lists."

"I think they're the best way of tracing missing relatives," he said. "There are more than twenty Jewish DP camps in Germany alone, and I don't know how many others in Austria. Think how long it would take to visit them all, to talk to everyone."

Kitty sucked in a breath. Her instinct was to get up and run all the way to Feldafing, however far it was. But she had no solid reason for thinking that her parents had been in Dachau. They could have been taken anywhere. There was no arguing with the sense of the priest's advice. "There are new lists coming soon," she said.

He nodded. "If you'd like me to, I can write to the bishop of Vienna. There's sure to be a way of finding someone in the city who could help you."

"Thank you." She dabbed her eyes with his handkerchief. The relief was overwhelming: finally, someone was going to help her.

He swallowed what remained of his coffee. "And I'll talk to the Austrians in the camp, find out if anyone knew your parents. Don't worry, I won't let on that it's you. Just make a note for me of the details you can remember: the location of the shop, what the business was called, the names of any employees, any close friends." He stood up, holding on to the table for support. "And please, Kitty, come and find me if you want to talk."

It was late afternoon when Martha returned from her drive. She'd seen the village upriver whose elegant castle was pockmarked from shell fire. In the ruins of what had once been a market hall, cages of live rabbits were on sale next to a stall piled with baskets of black cherries. She'd stopped to buy some of the fruit before heading north to the town of Fürstenfeldbruck. Now she knew where the train station was located— and the mayor's office, where she would need to go to meet the official representing the local farmers to negotiate food supplies for the coming weeks.

Stefan Dombrowski had been a great help throughout the journey. He was reserved and polite but conveyed a quiet sense of authority when answering her many questions about Germany. She couldn't help comparing him to Arnie, who had been a terrible passenger in the days when they had owned a car: he'd only allowed her to drive when he was too drunk to do it himself—and if he wasn't asleep, he'd be criticizing her for going too slowly, or not being aggressive enough to pass.

As she turned into the entrance to the camp, Major McMahon pulled up behind her. In the rearview mirror Martha saw him jump out of the jeep. She rolled down the window and he leaned in.

"This is Mr. Dombrowski," she said in answer to the major's raised eyebrow. "He's helping with translation."

The shrewd eyes narrowed. "I need a few minutes with you, Mrs. Radford. See you outside the warehouse in five."

He followed them for a short distance, then veered off onto the track that led to the forest. When Martha reached the warehouse, she passed the car keys to Dombrowski. "Thank you for giving me the confidence to drive again," she said.

With a nod he climbed out of the car and got into the seat she'd vacated. As he pulled away, she heard the jeep coming around the corner.

"Don't look so worried." Major McMahon gave her a broad smile as he walked toward her. "I just wanted to check what's in the warehouse and talk you through the ordering process." He paused, cocking his head to one side as he reached her. "Sergeant Lewis tells me things have been running pretty smoothly since you arrived."

"Not exactly." Martha took a breath, wondering where to begin. "We have a problem with accommodations. Every blockhouse is at full capacity. I keep hearing that more DPs are likely to arrive any day, and I don't know where we can put them." She tilted her head in the direction of the cabins. "I've already had to turn the place next door to ours into a mother-and-baby home for the women whose children were fathered by Germans."

"You did what?" Major McMahon rolled his eyes. "Those Nazi mistresses don't deserve any special treatment. You should have just turned them out of the hospital and let them get on with it."

"I don't imagine they had much choice about sleeping with the enemy." Martha bristled. "What do you think would have happened to them if they'd turned a German down? They were hardly mistresses—not in the conventional sense—more likely they were victims of rape."

The major pursed his lips. Clearly, he wasn't going to change his opinion.

"What shocked me most of all was that someone in the camp had arranged to sell one of the babies," Martha went on. "The mother was hiding in the chapel, at her wits' end."

"Doesn't surprise me." He shrugged. "You can sell anything on the black market in this place."

"I've been trying to find out who it was," Martha said. "We have to put a stop to this."

"The only way you can stop it is to get these people out of here. That's the plan: get them on a train back to Poland as soon as possible. But that's not likely to happen before winter: Stalin's got Warsaw in his paws right now, and it doesn't look as if he'll let go anytime soon."

Martha had read enough about the situation in Poland to know that the country was on its knees. But she hadn't grasped that a power struggle was going on. "How long will it be, then? Until people can start going home?"

He rolled his eyes again. "Your guess is as good as mine. You're gonna have to sit tight here for a while. Problem is, no other country wants these refugees. I guess plenty of them would give their right arm to be let into the States or Britain. But those doors are shut, and there's no sign of things changing anytime soon." He huffed out a breath. "Come spring, there might be some movement. Just gotta keep them all fed and watered until then."

"So, what do we do if more people arrive in the meantime?"

"There's an old stable block—back there." He jerked his head at the warehouse. "They kept horses to haul logs for the mill before the

Nazis brought Polacks in to do it. Wouldn't take long to convert it into accommodations. You could fit a couple of hundred in there, easy."

"Is there a water supply? What about heating?"

"There's a tap," he replied. "Get the DPs on it: there's sure to be some guy who knows how to fix plumbing. Cut a hole in the roof for a stove—piece of cake." He glanced at his watch. "Now, if there's nothing else, we need to get a move on."

"There *is* something else. We had a Polish woman who came to the office yesterday: she's trying to locate a GI who got her pregnant and promised to marry her."

The major rubbed his chin with his knuckles as Martha repeated what Jadzia had told Kitty and Delphine.

"If he was serious about marrying her, I thought there might be a chance of getting her over to the States," she said.

He shook his head. "There's no right to immigration to the US for these foreign women."

"But there must be thousands like her across Europe."

"I don't doubt it. It's a massive headache for the army. There's pressure on the government to change the rules. Who knows—things could open up soon."

"How soon?"

"End of this year, maybe."

"But her baby's due in a couple of months."

He forked the air with his hands. "Nothing anyone can do. You'll look after her, I'm sure."

"But you'll chase down the boyfriend?"

He frowned. "I'll make inquiries. We had a batch of men leave last week. Course, it would help if we had a surname." He punctuated the sentence with a click of his tongue. "We gotta start winding things up now: once you take charge, I'll get a roster organized to have someone watching this place twenty-four seven. And there'll always be someone in the guardhouse. The main difference after today is that the kitchens and the forestry detail will be unsupervised. But the DPs have been doing it for long enough now to run things themselves."

Martha watched him disappear into the stone building attached to the warehouse. The realization that she would soon be responsible for running everything was terrifying. What had she been thinking, coming to this place, believing she could help these people? She barely knew how she was going to house them all and provide enough food for the coming winter—let alone give them any kind of hope for the future.

"It will be okay. Don't worry." The voice made her jump.

"Mr. Dombrowski. I didn't see you."

"I waited in the car," he said. "And please, call me Stefan. Mr. Dombrowski sounds like . . ." He mimed someone standing to attention.

"Okay." She smiled. She would have liked to add that he could call her Martha. But she was afraid it would sound too familiar. If she was going to run this place, she needed to maintain a distance—however awkward that might feel.

CHAPTER 7

The three women were eating breakfast together. It was the first time in almost a week that they'd all sat around the table at the same time.

In the immediate aftermath of the army pulling out, things had been chaotic. The men in the forestry detail had stopped working two days after Martha had taken charge. They had marched to the office, axes in their hands, and sat down on the cobblestones, refusing to budge.

It was only after Stefan had been summoned that Martha had grasped what the problem was. He explained that the GIs who had been supervising the work had given out extra packets of cigarettes as an incentive to the men. Without this inducement, the DPs didn't see why they should have to do a job that was much more physically demanding than any other work in the camp.

Martha wondered why Major McMahon hadn't told her about this. Possibly he hadn't known. The situation was easily remedied, but it had left her feeling even more anxious about what she was taking on. To forestall further trouble, she had called the leaders of all the blockhouses to a meeting. With both Stefan and Kitty translating, she had listened to their concerns about the day-to-day business of camp life and made a list of what needed addressing.

Aside from practical issues, one of the main problems was the lack of education and training for the young people in the camp. Martha had welcomed Delphine's suggestion of recruiting and teaching auxiliary nurses to help in the hospital. Kitty had offered to organize English lessons, and she'd also come up with the idea of a sewing school. She'd discovered that a couple of elderly women had made the robes that Father Josef wore to conduct services. They'd fashioned them from garments they'd found in the clothing storeroom, cutting them up and expertly remodeling the fabric. They'd also embroidered the delicate altar cloth Kitty had seen in the chapel. Her idea was to persuade them to pass on these skills, producing items that could be sold outside the camp.

"I'll be at the stable block if you need me for anything," Martha said, as she got up from the table. "Stefan says it shouldn't take more than a few days to make it habitable."

"He's very handsome, isn't he?" Delphine gave her a sideways look as she got up from the table.

"Is he?" Martha could feel herself blushing. "I hadn't noticed." She turned away, reaching for her jacket. "He's certainly very useful. We couldn't have sorted out that trouble with the forestry detail without him."

"And he got you a *car*." Kitty's voice was full of admiration.

"Yes." Martha concentrated on doing up the buttons of her jacket, afraid to catch the eye of either of the women. She wondered if they'd been talking about her. She *had* been spending a lot of time with Stefan. It hadn't occurred to her that Kitty and Delphine might read something into that. "It's his way of showing his gratitude for what we're all trying to do here." Was she telling them or herself? She couldn't deny that she liked being in his company. Did the way she acted around him give the impression that she was attracted to him?

"He does seem to have a better grasp than most of the DPs of what we're up against," Delphine said. "When are the new people coming?"

Martha looked up, relieved that the conversation had changed direction. "I'm not certain which day it'll be—the major just said next week." She turned to Kitty. "Will you keep a lookout for Mrs. Sikorsky? I had a message from the camp at Augsburg that she and her daughter and the baby would be coming back today."

"Will they be going next door?" Kitty pursed her lips. "There's not much room in either of the cabins now the other mothers have moved in."

"They'll have to, at least until the stables are ready."

"Hmm. I hope that won't cause trouble."

"Will you talk to her? Explain that it's just for a few days?" Martha reached for her bag, guiltily aware that this was a big ask: something *she* should do, if only she had the language skills. Sinaida had said that the baby's father had died in Dachau. How on earth were she and her daughter going to react when they learned they'd be sharing a house with women whose babies had been fathered by Nazis?

⊰—⊱

Kitty made a detour on her way to the office. The women running the sewing school were having to scavenge thread from old garments in order to sew new ones. It had occurred to her that there might be a ready supply of it in the abandoned weaving shed, but the place was locked up. Kitty thought she might be able to break in through one of the smashed windows, but before she tried that, she dropped by the guardhouse at the entrance to the camp to see if there was a key.

The man on duty was closing the gates as she approached. A cloud of dust billowed around him, thrown up by the wheels of a departing jeep.

"Good morning!" He smiled when he saw her. "What can I do for you, ma'am?"

"Sergeant Lewis?" She recognized his voice from the conversations they'd had on the phone. She was surprised by how tall he was. Most of the men in the camp were several inches shorter than herself. She'd formed a mental image of him when they'd talked, but he was not at all how she'd imagined him. He looked different from the GIs she'd encountered in England and on the boat to France. His eyes reminded her of people she'd glimpsed from the bus on her way to the factory in Manchester, in the part of the city they called Chinatown.

"And you're Miss Bloom, right?" he said.

"Yes." She smiled back. "I've come to ask a favor." She explained about the key.

"There's a bunch on top of the cupboard in there," he said. "I don't know what they're for—never had to use them. Guess it could be one of those."

"Can I take them all?"

"Sure. I hope the place is safe to go into. I'd offer to come and help you, but . . ." He trailed off, cocking his head at the gates.

"Don't worry, I'll be fine."

He went inside the guardhouse and came back with a set of keys of assorted shapes and sizes attached to a rusty metal ring. "Forgive me for asking," he said, as he handed them over. "Are you English?"

"Why do you ask?" She tried to make it sound casual. But her antennae were up. She wondered if Father Josef had broken his word to her, had said something to the sergeant.

"Just curious. I figured you're not American, but I'm not very good with accents. And I've heard you speaking German."

"You have?"

"When I put through that call from the Red Cross."

"Ah." She wondered how long he'd stayed on the line, listening in. "Do you speak German?"

"Only a few words. But you're fluent, aren't you?"

"Not really. I learnt it at school, that's all." She weighed the bunch of keys in her hand. "I'd better find out if any of these will work. I'll bring them back when I'm done." She headed down the path that led to the river, glad to have gotten away without having to tell the man an outright lie. Hopefully, by the time she returned, he'd have forgotten asking her if she was English.

When she reached the weaving shed, she saw immediately that only one of the keys in the bunch was likely to fit the hole in the door. It took some effort to turn the lock, but soon she was inside, standing in a beam of dancing dust motes. The enormous looms looked as if they'd been abandoned in great haste: half-finished sheets of artificial silk still adorned them, the fabric frayed in places where mice or squirrels had nibbled at it. On the workbenches that ran along two sides of the shed were the spools of thread Kitty had come looking for. She picked one up and blew the dust off it. The color was still bright: a vivid scarlet. Further inspection revealed greens, blues, and yellows. And in a basket, she found half a dozen pairs of scissors wrapped in oilcloth.

As she was locking the door, she heard the sound of an engine above the murmur of the river. It wasn't until she got farther along the path that she realized it was a motorbike. The driver was passing something to Sergeant Lewis through the metal bars of the gate. She glimpsed an armband with a red cross on it.

"For you," the sergeant said, holding out the thick envelope as she handed back the bunch of keys.

"Oh?" The words "Tracing Service" stamped on the front set off a pulse of excitement. "Thank you."

This was what she'd been waiting for: the updated lists from all the DP camps. It was all she could do not to break into a run as she turned away.

As soon as Kitty reached the office, she prized open the envelope and spread out the contents on the desk. There were dozens of typed sheets, each bearing the name of one of the various camps in the zones the Allies now occupied. The lists contained details of new arrivals in the month of June. As well as last names and initials, the age of a person was recorded and their place of origin.

A quick scan revealed those with Jewish names. She separated them from the rest, then sat down to study each one carefully. Her heart leapt when, near the bottom of the second sheet, she spotted a Blumenthal. The person was female—and the initial was right, too: *E*. The place of origin was Poland, not Austria. Could it mean the place where someone was born rather than where they'd been living at the start of the war?

As she ran her finger along the line of type, her spirits dived. The age was wrong. This woman was fifty-six. She'd never been sure of her mother's exact age, other than knowing that she was younger than Kitty's father, who had celebrated his fortieth birthday a few weeks before Kitty left for England. Back in Manchester, when she'd written to the Red Cross asking for information about her parents, Kitty had estimated her mother's current age as forty-five.

The next list was no good—not a single name beginning with the letter *B*. She'd just begun working her way down another when the telephone rang.

"Miss Bloom?" It was Sergeant Lewis. "I have two women here. And a baby. They want to come in. Could you come and speak to them?"

⟨⟩

Sinaida Sikorsky beamed when she saw Kitty. She introduced her daughter, Magdalena, and her grandson, Jacoub, who was fast asleep in his mother's arms. Then she launched into a description of the little boy's entry into the world, sparing none of the gory details. Kitty glanced at Sergeant Lewis, who was looking on, bemused. Just as well he couldn't understand any of it, she thought.

"Mamo, proszę . . ." The younger woman tugged at her mother's arm, clearly embarrassed at having such intimate facts broadcast to a couple of strangers. Kitty wondered how she had the strength to hold her child—she looked transparent, with dark circles under her eyes.

"Chodź ze mną." Come with me. Kitty led them along the tree-lined path to the cabins. She hadn't worked out how she was going to explain the presence of the two other mothers already occupying the one assigned to Sinaida and her family.

When Sinaida walked through the door, she let out a little gasp of amazement. *"Pięknie!"* It's beautiful!

Magdalena nodded her agreement. Jacoub opened his eyes and began to wail.

A voice called from above them: *"Kto tu jest?"* Who is here?

Kitty was about to launch into an explanation, when the owner of the voice, a woman named Anka, came down the stairs. Sinaida's reaction to the sight of her was explosive. She called her a German whore, followed by a volley of words Kitty couldn't comprehend.

At the sound of his grandmother's shouting, Jacoub's cries increased. But Sinaida was shaking her fist at Anka, seemingly oblivious to the distress she was causing.

"Mamo, przestań!" Mama, stop! Magdalena put herself between Sinaida and the other woman, her hand protecting the baby's head.

Kitty was horrified. She'd anticipated some hostility, but not physical violence. She moved quickly, ushering Sinaida toward the door. Being head and shoulders taller than the older woman helped; it gave her an authority that belied her lack of experience.

Once they were outside, she told Sinaida that if she wanted to remain in the camp, she was going to have to calm down and be prepared to get along with the other women in the cabin. She added that it would only be for a few nights, until the new accommodations were ready.

"Wolałabym spać w lesie!" I would rather sleep in the forest! The look Sinaida gave her was murderous.

"Dobrze." Good. Kitty called her bluff, jerking her head toward the trees. Watching the woman's face, she felt as if she could hear the cogs going around in her head. For Magdalena and the baby to sleep outdoors would be out of the question. If Sinaida persisted with this defiance, she would be spending the night alone on a bed of pine needles with wild animals for company.

Sinaida glanced back toward the cabin. For a moment Kitty thought she was going to turn around and walk back inside. But the woman suddenly dropped to her knees. She hunched over, her shawl covering her head like a tent, and her shoulders shook with silent sobs.

Kitty didn't know what to do. She stood there, frozen, appalled at what her ill-judged words had triggered. If only Martha were here—or Delphine. Either one of them would have been beside Sinaida in a flash, crouching down beside her and putting an arm around her shoulders. But not Kitty. Invisible strings held her limbs like the wooden marionette that had hung on the wall of her bedroom in Vienna.

The door of the cabin opened, and Magdalena appeared. The baby had calmed down and was lying peacefully in her arms. She glanced at her mother, then darted an apologetic look at Kitty. Sinking down beside Sinaida, she spoke in a soft, low voice. Watching them, it was as if the roles had been reversed—the daughter had become her mother's mother.

Kitty couldn't catch all of it. But she did hear Magdalena say that Anka had a little boy that she loved just as they loved Jacoub, in spite of what his father had been.

After a moment of silence, Sinaida got to her feet, gave a loud sniff, then took the baby from Magdalena's arms and went inside.

"Please forgive her." Magdalena spoke slowly, as if she'd forgotten how well Kitty understood Polish. "She can't forget what the Nazis did to us."

"I'm sorry—I . . . I didn't know what to say to her. It's . . ." Kitty trailed off. Magdalena's words stung her eyes. She mustn't cry. She swallowed hard. "You think there'll be more trouble?"

Magdalena shook her head. "I talked with Anka. She told me that she doesn't know who her baby's father was. None of the women do. She said the Germans came to them night after night. All the men—with all the women."

Kitty felt as if the tears in the corners of her eyes had frozen solid. Did men do that? She dropped her head, unable to look at Magdalena. This was far worse than any of them had guessed. Pain heaped on pain. "You told your mother that?" Her voice came out croaky and gruff, as though it belonged to someone else.

"Yes. She understands," Magdalena replied. "She won't make trouble now."

⟹

Kitty poured herself a mug of coffee when she got back to the office. The lists were lying on the desk where she'd left them, but she needed something to revive her before she started poring over the names again.

Settling into the chair, she picked up the one she'd been about to read when the phone call had interrupted her. To her surprise, there were three Blumenthals listed. But, once again, her hopes were raised only to be dashed when she ran her finger across to the columns giving the age and place of origin.

More than an hour later she slumped onto the desk, her head resting on her arms. She'd gone over all the lists from the Jewish camps—twice. And just in case, she'd also read through the names of every DP in all the other camps. Thousands and thousands of people, and not one that could possibly be her mother or her father.

After a while she made herself get up. It was a good thing it was a Saturday, she thought, and there was no one standing outside the office wanting a pass. It would have been humiliating if anyone had peered through the window and seen her like that. But just because there was no one outside didn't mean she could hide away in here. The people in the camp would be as desperate to see the new lists as she had been. She must keep her promise and post them on the wall of the mess hall, then go around the blockhouses and spread the word.

To her surprise, there was already a crowd assembled when she arrived. Someone must have spotted the dispatch rider at the gates, she thought. When they saw what she was carrying, a hush fell. She was afraid they might press in on her and try to snatch the lists before she'd had the chance to get inside, but they kept a respectful distance. As she passed through the crowd, she spotted several of the blockhouse leaders. It was because of them, she guessed, that calm prevailed.

Only when she had pinned the last sheet of paper to the wall did the DPs come running in. Watching their eager, anxious faces as they scanned the lists was torture. She would rather have left them to it, but she realized that if anyone found the name of a relative, they would be desperate for help to contact them.

"Hello." It was Father Josef. In the scramble of people, she hadn't spotted him. "Nothing there for you?" He must have seen it in her face.

She shook her head.

"I wish I had better news." He pulled out one of the rickety metal dining chairs and sat down beside her. "I didn't want to say anything until I'd had the chance to speak to all of the Austrians in the camp."

She stared at a greasy stain on the surface of the table, unable to meet his eye.

"There are only three from Vienna. One of them recognized the name of your parents' shop, but he'd never been inside, and he didn't know anyone who lived on that street. The others were from the outskirts of the city. They said they'd never had reason to go into the Jewish quarter."

"Thank you for trying." Her eyes were still fixed on the table.

"I've written to the bishop," he went on. "I haven't had a reply yet; I'll let you know as soon as I do."

Kitty nodded. "You're very kind. But . . ." She couldn't put it into words. If she tried, she feared she would lose control of herself. Seeing the lists, allowing herself to hope—how long could she go on doing this to herself? Wouldn't it have been less painful if she'd listened to Fred that night in the theater in Manchester? Faced up to the fact that she was an orphan?

A sudden cry from the other side of the room brought Kitty back to the here and now. An old woman was clutching her chest, looking as if she might collapse. Another, younger woman grabbed her arm, holding her up, while a man—one of the blockhouse leaders—jabbed a finger at the list on the wall in front of them.

"Jej syn! Jest w Hamburgu!" The man's voice boomed out across the room. Her son! He's in Hamburg!

Father Josef reached across the table and placed his hand on Kitty's. "This is hard for you," he whispered. "But please, don't give up hope."

CHAPTER 8

Delphine peeped around the door of the women's ward to watch the trainees as they went about changing bed linens. She had recruited three girls and a boy from among the orphans. With Wolf's help, she was teaching them the basics of hospital hygiene. They didn't seem to mind taking orders from him, even though he was younger than all of them.

This morning, though, Wolf had not appeared at the door of the blockhouse when she had called for the children. She had tried, in her limited Polish, to ask the others where he was. Worried that he might be unwell, she'd said his name and mimed illness, pulling a face and clutching her stomach. One of the girls had shaken her head. She'd looked at the others, who had simply shrugged. Delphine told herself that he must have gone off on some errand—probably involving food, as he always seemed to be ravenous. His name was very fitting in that regard.

"Madame Fabius!" The voice startled her. She turned to see Wolf, clutching a bunch of wild roses, a mischievous grin on his face. "For you, madame." He held out the flowers.

"Thank you." She brought them up to her face, breathing in the delicate perfume. She wondered where he'd found them growing. He'd picked up an astonishing number of English phrases in a very short time, but she doubted he'd understand a question like that.

"You like?" he said.

She nodded. "*Piękne*. Beautiful." This was something she'd learned from Dr. Jankaukas. He said it every time he finished stitching up a wound or plastering a broken limb.

Wolf repeated the word, breaking it up into syllables. The earnest expression in his big dark eyes melted her heart. She had to fight the urge to gather him up in a bear hug.

She found a temporary home for the flowers in a specimen bottle. As she was filling it with water, she spotted Father Josef coming through the door to the ward. He nodded a greeting as he made his way through to the men's ward. After a few minutes he emerged and came over to where she was weighing a baby girl who had been born the previous night.

"Madame Fabius, would you mind if I speak to the ladies in here?"

She looked at him, surprised. "No, I don't mind—although some of them may be a little tired." She wondered if he'd come to invite them to Mass. Perhaps he was hoping to increase attendance at the chapel by catching people who couldn't get away when he came to speak to them.

"The Red Cross lists have arrived," he said. "I know the patients here aren't able to go and read them for themselves, so I thought I might ask if there's anyone they're trying to trace."

"That would be a great kindness." Delphine glanced around the ward, unable to look him in the eye. She felt guilty for misjudging the motive for his visit.

"Your young assistants might like to see the lists," he went on. "They are orphans, I know, but there may be other family members . . ."

"Of course. Will you explain to them if I go and round them up?"

He nodded. "Whatever is easiest for you."

The faces of the auxiliaries lit up with hope as they listened to Father Josef. She gave them permission to go and look at the lists, and they dashed off to the mess hall. The only one who seemed uninterested was Wolf. He hovered on the edge of the group as the priest was speaking, then disappeared into the side room. Reappearing with a pile of clean laundry, he proceeded to strip one of the beds on the far side of the ward.

"I don't understand," Delphine said to Father Josef. "Why didn't Wolf want to talk to you?"

"Because there is nobody," the priest replied. "When he arrived here, he told me that his mother had died before the war. From the way he described it, I think she probably had tuberculosis. After that it was just him and his father. The Germans left them alone at first. But when Wolf was ten, they sent them both to work in a factory making V-2 rockets."

"Ten? That can't be, surely . . ."

"It's hard to believe, I know, but it's true. The Nazis were so desperate for workers to turn out their bombs and tanks and planes, they took children as slave labor. There are others in this camp—boys of fifteen, sixteen—who worked five years in German factories."

"What about Wolf's father? What happened to him?"

"The factory was bombed by the Allies. His father was killed. Wolf only survived because that day, he was too sick to work." The priest shook his head. "It's little short of a miracle that he made it to the end of the war."

Wolf was busying himself at the other end of the ward, oblivious of what Father Josef was telling her. The thought of him heading off this morning to pick roses for her brought a lump to her throat. She had wanted to hug him when he'd presented them to her. Now, more than ever, she felt like gathering him up in her arms.

"Madame Fabius!" It was the doctor's voice, loud and urgent, calling her from the room next door.

With a murmured apology to the priest, Delphine hurried to the male ward. A young man was flailing about, half in, half out of the bed. Dr. Jankaukas had a syringe in his hand and was trying to restrain him.

"*Il délire,*" the doctor said, as Delphine ran to his aid.

This patient had been admitted the previous day with a head injury caused by an accident in the forest. It was no surprise that he had become delirious. *"Maintenez-le,"* she said. *"Donnez-moi la seringue."* You hold him down. Give me the syringe.

Moments later the man lay still. His eyes remained open, but the frantic, frightened look had disappeared. He cast a puzzled glance at Dr. Jankaukas, then at Delphine, as if he couldn't work out who they were or why they were standing by his bed.

The doctor asked her to stay with the patient until the drug took full effect. Delphine reached for the patient's hand, stroking it gently. Watching his face, she saw the eyelids begin to droop. He wasn't very old—barely into his twenties, she guessed. She wondered what the past few years of war had been like for him, what his life had been like before he was taken from his homeland. There was no tattoo on his forearm. Perhaps he had labored here at Seidenmühle before the place had been liberated. Or maybe, like Wolf, he had survived some other death factory.

As he began to lose consciousness, he murmured a string of words. She had no idea what he was saying. But the shapes his mouth made reminded her of Philippe, as a little boy, talking in his sleep. He'd done it often, usually when he dropped off before she'd finished reading him a story. She closed her eyes tight, willing the memory away. She mustn't think of it, mustn't let it in—not here.

The man suddenly gripped her hand tight. His face puckered, like someone about to burst into tears. Then he uttered a single word: "Mama!"

—◆—

Martha was standing inside the stable block, staring up at a large hole in the roof.

"How did that happen?"

"A tree fell on it," Stefan replied. "They didn't see it until they started to clear the place out." He pointed to the pile of straw lying on the floor. Part of the building had been used as a hayloft, and when the men had gone to pull it down, the damage to the roof had been revealed.

Martha followed Stefan outside. The stables had been built right on the edge of the forest. The fallen pine wasn't visible until they went around the back, into the trees.

"Can they move it?" Martha craned her neck. It was impossible to see how far across the roof the tree had fallen.

"With rope, I think, yes," he replied.

"What about the hole? Can they fix it?" It was an old building, constructed long before the blockhouses. The roof was covered in so much moss that it was hard to tell what lay beneath.

"If we get tiles," Stefan replied. "They are very old, made of clay."

Martha raked her hair with her fingers. The sick feeling of panic— never far away since she'd taken charge of Seidenmühle—churned her stomach. The new DPs were due in a matter of days. How on earth was she going to get hold of replacement tiles in time to make the place fit to sleep in?

"There is an old house." He cocked his head to where the trees grew closer together. "No one lives there now. We can take some tiles. I will show you."

He led her through the forest. There was no path, but he seemed sure of the way. The trees formed a canopy above their heads, blocking out the sun. The only sound was the crunch of their feet on the carpet of pine needles. There was no rustling in the branches, no birdsong. Martha wondered if all the wild creatures had been driven away by the tanks that had rampaged through this place. The lack of life gave it a creepy feel. It occurred to her that she had followed Stefan unquestioningly, had put her trust in him, despite having known him for only a short period of time.

"Over there." He motioned with his arm, then glanced back over his shoulder. "You see it?"

She stopped and tried to spot what he was looking at. There was a gap in the trees, but all she could make out was a tangle of bushes. She took a few steps forward.

"There is the gate," he said.

She followed where his finger pointed. Suddenly her brain made sense of the pattern of shadows. She saw the gate, green with moss, hanging askew from one hinge. The low walls on either side of it had been engulfed by brambles.

"Come." Stefan led her through the rotting gate. She saw that among the waist-high thorns there were wild roses, creamy white and pale pink, tumbling over the wall. More of them grew around the door to the stone cottage. It reminded her of the place where she and Kitty had stopped to ask directions when they'd gotten lost on the way to the camp. But this house was no longer a home: the windows had fallen out, and the corner of one wall had crumbled away. A pile of stones lay beneath the scarred facade.

Stefan nudged the front door with his foot. It creaked open, letting out a smell of damp and decay. She followed him in. To her surprise, the interior was pierced with shafts of sunlight. The ceiling had caved in, leaving a clear view of the roof. The light was coming in through the gaps where tiles had come away.

"You see?" He shaded his eyes as he looked up. "Same as the roof of the stable."

"But how would we get them back?"

"The road is there." He swept a hand toward the back of the house. "It would be easy. We have the car. I can bring men with a ladder."

She nodded. It was the perfect solution—and one she could never have achieved without his help. "Thank you, Stefan." She stepped sideways, in the direction of the door. But her shoe caught on a nail sticking out of one of the fallen ceiling beams. With a cry of alarm, she lost her balance. Suddenly his arm was under her, catching her before she hit the ground. For an instant she was unable to move. He was cradling her in the crook of his elbow. She could smell the earthy scent of his skin through his shirt. She felt him exhale as he raised her up.

"I . . . I'm so sorry." She bent down, brushing dust off her leg. The nail had laddered her stocking. She glanced up, embarrassed at her clumsiness.

"Last time I came here, a bird's nest fell on my head." He gave a wry smile. "I looked like a crazy man." The warmth in his eyes set something off inside her. It felt as though their bodies were still touching. The sensation frightened her. It reminded her of the way Arnie used to look at her, what seemed like a hundred years ago.

"We'd better be getting back." She turned away from him, stepping carefully across the floor and through the door. "You go ahead of me," she said, as he came out behind her. "I don't think I'll remember the way."

He said nothing as he made for the gate. She waited until there was a safe distance between them before following. *Safe?* Was it him she didn't trust—or herself?

Delphine had to get out of the ward. She didn't want Dr. Jankaukas nor Wolf nor Father Josef nor anyone else in the hospital seeing her crying. She managed to hold it inside long enough to tell the doctor that the patient with the head injury was comfortable now. Then she made an excuse about needing to check on the stock of milk in the warehouse.

As soon as she got outside, the tears came flooding out. She jabbed at her face with her handkerchief, muttering to herself as she walked up the path that skirted the forest. It had taken just one word to make her crumble: How could she have allowed it to affect her like that? She, who had nursed hundreds of patients over the years and had held the hands of dozens of men who had cried out for their mothers. What was different about this man? How had she lost control so utterly and completely?

The answer came in the faces that hovered, never far away, in her mind's eye. Claude. Philippe. They were with her in everything she said and did. Washing a patient too ill to wash himself, she would think, *This is for you, Philippe;* stitching up a wound she would whisper, "This is what you would have done, Claude." She had believed that they would protect her, would be her armor and her shield in the battleground of emotions she must face each day at the hospital. But she should have realized how illusory that protection was.

Mama. It could have been Philippe's voice. Calling for her when his life was taken. And she hadn't been there. That would haunt her forever.

She stopped walking, stood for a moment, took in a lungful of air. She had to get hold of herself, put on a smiling face and get back inside. As she stood there, eyes shut tight to dam up the tears, she heard the crunch of footsteps. Opening her eyes, she saw two figures coming through the trees. Stefan Dombrowski and Martha following behind him. Ordinarily, she would have called out to her, waved a greeting. But she didn't want either of them to see her like this.

They were walking toward the blockhouses, away from where she was standing, so they didn't spot her. When they reached the place where the trees gave way to the path, they both stopped. Delphine couldn't see their faces. But there was something about the way their heads moved together, then moved apart . . .

Delphine blinked, rubbed her eyes. She watched them walk on, talking as they went, before they disappeared around a bend in the path. She must have imagined it, that thing she thought she'd seen.

You're not yourself. It was Claude's voice she heard.

No, she wasn't. But she must try to be. She thought of Wolf. To lose both parents and survive a Nazi slave labor camp—and yet dream of becoming a doctor . . . His fortitude shamed her. Somehow, he had found the resilience to go on. If she was going to be of any use to the people in this place, she must find it, too.

CHAPTER 9

The sun was low in the sky when Martha left the stable block. It was amazing what the DPs had achieved in such a short time. The roof was repaired, the floor swept and scrubbed, and there were 150 straw-filled mattresses stacked up and ready to be distributed. If the new batch of refugees arrived tonight, it wouldn't be a disaster.

She passed the mess hall, where Kitty was supervising an English class. Her pupils ranged from children as young as six or seven to adult men and women. All were copying sentences Kitty had written on the blackboard she'd set up in a corner of the room. Martha waved from the doorway and Kitty came to say hello.

"I didn't realize you had so many," Martha whispered.

"I think I'm going to have to divide them into two groups—do a couple of evenings instead of just one." Kitty shrugged. "They're very keen. They all want to go to America."

Martha glanced around the room. She saw the intense concentration on the faces of Kitty's pupils as they copied down the phrases on the board. It pained her to remember the major's words about the United States closing its borders to foreign refugees.

"You're doing a great job," she said. "See you back at the house."

As she walked on, past the warehouse, she heard someone calling out to her.

"Mrs. Radford!" It was Corporal Brody. "I've had a call from the guardhouse, ma'am," he said. "There's a German guy at the gates, shouting his mouth off. Says someone from here has stolen two of his pigs."

"What?" Martha looked at him, incredulous.

"He says they were taken from his farm—the other side of the river."

"Whoa . . ." Martha took a breath. "He's saying that our DPs rounded up two pigs and brought them into the camp without anyone noticing? That's ridiculous!"

"I know, ma'am." Brody nodded. "What shall I say to Sergeant Lewis?"

"I guess we'll have to search the camp, just to be certain. Ask him to tell the farmer that's what we're going to do."

"Yes ma'am," Brody replied.

"Tell me, Corporal," she said. "If you had to hide a couple of pigs in this place, where would you choose?"

He pursed his lips. "I guess that would depend," he said.

"On what?"

"On whether they were dead or alive."

She nodded, feeling stupid for not having thought of that. Of course, the obvious thing would be to slaughter the animals in the woods, out of sight and sound, then carry them into the camp. But even then, the risk of being spotted would be huge. It seemed highly unlikely that the farmer's accusation was true. But they were going to have to go through the motions of a search.

"There's a basement under blockhouse five," Brody said. "It's where they put the ducks and chickens at nighttime. You could hide a carcass in there—butcher it and all—without anyone knowing what you were up to."

"Okay, that's where we'll start. Is it safe for you to leave the warehouse unguarded for an hour or so?" She could have gone to find Stefan to help her. But on balance, that didn't seem wise. He'd already told her he wouldn't be her spy. To expect him to help rumble suspected pig rustlers wouldn't exactly endear him to his fellow DPs.

"The next detail's due in half an hour," Brody said. "Shall I ask Sergeant Lewis if it's okay for us to stay on a while and search the place?"

Martha nodded. "I'll meet you at blockhouse five. If there's nothing there, we'll split up and search the other houses. I doubt anyone could hide a whole pig under a bed, but if the carcasses have already been butchered, I guess there could be joints of meat just about anywhere." She realized that she was now talking as if the farmer's accusation were true. In the blink of an eye, she'd switched from refusing to believe the DPs could be capable of such a crime to visualizing how they might conceal their ill-gotten gains. As she walked away from the warehouse, she made a fervent, silent prayer that it wouldn't be true.

The beam of Sergeant Lewis's flashlight picked up a pair of glowing eyes. The duck gave a startled quack, which set off a flurry of movement in the basement. Spooked by the sudden intrusion, the poultry made a racket that echoed off the bare walls. The squawks were punctuated by high-pitched squeals, which the flashlight revealed were made by a trio of frightened guinea pigs penned up alongside half a dozen rabbits.

The sergeant directed the beam around the room. There was nothing much else to be seen. Just a few gardening implements and a pile of hay.

"What's that? In the middle of the floor?" Martha had spotted a glint of something as the beam of light swept across it.

Sergeant Lewis angled the light down. "A wet patch—like someone's been cleaning up, maybe?"

"Could just be they spilled water when they fed the animals." Corporal Brody pointed to a half-full bucket beside the pile of hay.

"We'd better go and search upstairs," Martha said, hoping Brody was right.

She trailed behind the men as they pulled back the blankets dividing families' living quarters. Watching them open suitcases and poke around under beds made her very uneasy.

"What about the latrines?" Brody said when they'd worked their way from one end of the blockhouse to the other.

"We'd better check, I suppose," Martha replied. It was a revolting thought, concealing fresh meat in such a place. But if someone were desperate enough . . .

"Nothing in here," Sergeant Lewis called when he opened the door.

"What about those cubicles—two of the doors are shut." Brody pushed past him.

"Wait!" Martha shouted. "There might be . . ."

But Brody was already kicking the doors open. "Jeez! Pardon me, ladies!" He came rushing out, red-faced. "Two old girls in there," he spluttered. "Sorry, Mrs. Radford, I just thought . . ."

"Okay, Corporal." Martha pulled the door shut behind him. "You two go look in the other blockhouses. I'll wait here and apologize."

Martha stood outside the latrines, summoning the few Polish phrases she had mastered. It was bad enough that the people in this place had had soldiers rifling through their meager belongings, but for elderly DPs to have been disturbed while on the toilet was an indignity too far. She wished Kitty were with her to say something more than a simple "I am sorry."

Five minutes passed. Then ten. When there was still no sign of anyone emerging, Martha opened the door and peered inside. There was no one to be seen. The doors of the two cubicles were still shut. They must both be ill, she thought, to still be in there after all this time. She made her way past the urinals and the water pump and knocked softly on one of the doors.

"Źle się czujesz?" Are you unwell? It was one of the phrases she'd picked up from Delphine.

There was no reply. No sound at all from either of the cubicles. Martha racked her brains for more words. *"Potrzebujesz pomocy?"* Do you need help?

Still nothing. Could Corporal Brody have been mistaken, she wondered? Had he imagined seeing the two old ladies? Gingerly, she pushed open the door. She gasped at the sight of a hunched seated figure with a shawl pulled over the head.

"Oh my God!" Martha's first thought was that the poor woman had died of shock when Brody's boot had forced the door. Instinctively she reached out, pulling back the shawl. But what she revealed was not a woman's face. What she was staring at was the whiskery snout of a pig.

***

"That's unbelievable!" Delphine listened, open-mouthed, as Martha related the story.

"Quite brilliant, really," Martha said. "Honestly, they were so life-like. Whoever did it had put long skirts on the carcasses to cover the trotters, then swathed them in shawls so the heads were in shadow. You should have seen Corporal Brody's face—I don't think I've ever seen a man blush like that."

"What did he say when he found out it was the pigs in disguise?"

"I haven't told him. I'm going to keep it quiet for now. The fewer people that know, the better. It's such a battle getting the food quota from the local farmers—if word got around that our DPs were stealing . . ."

"I see what you mean." Delphine nodded. "In some ways, you can't blame them for it; the meat we've been getting is all bone and gristle. But what about the farmer who made the complaint? What will you say to him?"

"I'm going to send Corporal Brody around to tell him we searched the place but found nothing. That's not a lie, as far as Brody's concerned. He'll take a couple of hundred cigarettes from the warehouse as a peace offering. Hopefully, that'll calm things down."

"And the pigs?"

"They're in the kitchens, being cooked as we speak. It would be wicked to waste that meat—but only the women and children will get to eat it. You see, I don't know for sure who stole the animals. It was the only retribution I could think of, apart from cutting the cigarette ration to blockhouse five to allow for what we're giving the farmer."

"How will you stop it from happening again?"

"I don't know. That pork would have been worth a lot on the black market. I just hope the fact that the carcasses have been confiscated will put off whoever was responsible. They took a big risk, sneaking onto the farm. If the farmer had spotted them, they could have been shot."

"It's like the war's still going on," Delphine said. "Germans versus Poles, but now it's food they're fighting for. And we're stuck in the middle."

"It's so hard, trying to be fair to everybody." Martha shook her head. "I guess we're just making it up as we go along, and it isn't easy to know if you're getting it right."

Making it up as we go along. Her words echoed in her head as she made her way to the clothing storeroom. She had to start sorting through the piles of coats, trousers, skirts, and sweaters the army had dumped there, work out if there was enough of everything to clothe the influx of new DPs who would be arriving any day.

The smell of stale sweat greeted her as she pushed open the door. Everything was going to need washing, and what couldn't be washed was going to have to be hung out to air. It was going to be a mammoth task. The women in the laundry had enough to do, trying to keep up with the washing created by the people already in the camp. She was going to have to work out some way of getting hundreds of garments clean and dry before they ran out of time.

She leaned back against the wall, suddenly defeated. It wasn't just the clothes. How were they going to stretch their meat supplies, which were already so pathetically inadequate, to feed yet more hungry DPs? What had she been thinking, coming here? Believing that she could help these people?

She'd come to Germany because she wanted to run away from home—from a life she could no longer tolerate. What would the families in the camp make of that? This was their reality: the cast-off clothes, the lack of decent food, the overcrowded blockhouses. It had been one thing to read about the war in the papers, quite another to find herself face-to-face with the men, women, and children who had suffered unimaginable horrors and had no home to return to.

She felt a powerful urge to cut and run: to pack her bags and leave. Now she understood why the spearhead team had deserted the place. It was too much. An impossible task. The realization made her legs crumple under her. She slid down the wall and slumped onto the cold concrete floor. She felt paralyzed. Tears blurred her vision. She tried to blink them away. A sea of brown met her eyes. She saw that it wasn't clothes, but boots. Dozens and dozens of pairs of army boots, stacked beneath the tables. Most were caked in desiccated mud. And some were smeared and spattered with something else. As she stared, she realized the dark stains were dried blood.

It dawned on her that these boots had almost certainly belonged to the Allied troops who had fought their way up through France and Germany and had died in battle.

And you're going to run away. Again.

It was Arnie's voice. It might have been cowardly, running out on him. But how much more cowardly would it be to run away from the people the owners of these boots had given their lives to save?

CHAPTER 10

Two days later, the phone in the office rang to announce that a trainload of DPs was on its way.

"That was Major McMahon," Kitty said, as Martha came through the door of the office. "He says four hundred people are coming to us. They're due to arrive at Fürstenfeldbruck this afternoon."

"*Four* hundred," Martha gasped. "But we can't fit more than two hundred in the stables!"

"What can we do?" Kitty shook her head. "He wants us there by three o'clock to meet them off the train."

Martha blew out a breath. "We'll have to talk to the blockhouse leaders. Tell them they'll have to make room for more people."

"But there's already . . ."

"I know," Martha cut in. "Hardly any space in any of them. But we're going to have to persuade them."

"How?"

"I don't know. Extra cigarettes? We'll have to squeeze at least ten more people in each house." Martha burned with anger at the thought of the major ladening them with so many more DPs than they had been expecting. It was as if he were setting her up to fail.

"You want me to go and talk to them now?"

"I'm sorry, Kitty—you always end up having to do my dirty work. It'd be mostly sign language if I tried to do it. If you could go to blocks one to eight, I'll ask Stefan to do the rest."

Stefan appeared ten minutes after Kitty had left the office. Despite her agitation, Martha felt a tingle at the sight of him. She hoped it didn't show on her face. This was *not* what she'd come to Germany for—to get involved with another man. She had to snuff out this feeling before it took hold of her.

No sooner had she explained to him about the coming influx of DPs than a loud rap at the door announced the arrival of a delegation of blockhouse leaders. The news had spread through the camp like wildfire.

"Nie mamy miejsca!" We have no room! The oldest of them, a bearded man in a long military coat with several buttons missing, came striding up to the desk, hands spread in front of him.

Stefan asked him what sounded like a question. A heated exchange followed. Martha was reminded of the time Stefan had broken up the spat between the fishermen and the German farmer.

A few minutes later the three leaders left the office. Martha was alarmed by their scared, bewildered expressions as they turned to go.

"What did you say to them?"

He shrugged. "I told them that if they didn't make room, the army would come and do it—then put them in jail."

"Stefan!"

"You think I told a lie?" There was fire in his eyes. "It happened before you came. How do you think all the DPs live this way without fighting?"

Martha sank into the chair. She'd tried so hard to manage things without resorting to the army. The thought of threatening these people with jail after what they'd suffered at the hands of the Nazis was anathema to her. And yet Stefan was saying it was the only way things could be run. The chasm in her understanding gaped before her. And now four hundred more were coming.

Martha went to warn the cooks that there would be many more mouths to feed that evening. Then she went to tell the guard at the warehouse that more supplies would need to be sent down to the kitchens. After that she hurried to find Delphine.

It was Wolf who met Martha when she got to the hospital. "Madame Fabius go see woman." He mimed a big belly. "Number six house."

Martha ran all the way to the blockhouse. She found Delphine examining Jadzia—the young woman who was still waiting for news of her GI fiancé.

"I'm sorry to interrupt," Martha said, "but we're about to get four hundred new arrivals. I'm going to need you to come with me."

"I'll go and tell Wolf to get extra beds ready." Delphine put her stethoscope away. "There are bound to be some sick ones. And we'll need DDT to dust them down at the gates."

Martha nodded. Stefan had told her how he'd been herded into a tent on arrival at Seidenmühle to be covered from head to feet with vile-smelling powder. It was the army's method of killing the body lice that bore typhus. "I'll ask Sergeant Lewis to set that up," she said. "We'd better get some food sent to the gatehouse to hand out while they're waiting."

Delphine nodded. "Canned milk, too—for the babies and children." She glanced at her watch. "What time are we leaving?"

"No later than two."

"Is someone coming to collect us?"

"No, I can drive. I know the way."

"Will it be all right? All of us going?"

"I'm leaving Stefan in the office," Martha replied. "He won't stand for any nonsense."

"I'm sure he won't." Delphine smiled. "He's what my husband would have called the strong, silent type."

Delphine had never mentioned her husband before. Since that evening when Martha had told the others about Arnie, there had been no time to learn more about her. Martha would have liked nothing more than to sit down with Delphine now, over a coffee, and find out more about her husband. But there was no time.

"I'll pick you up by the warehouse in half an hour."

The station at Fürstenfeldbruck was eerily silent when the women arrived. Kitty spotted a couple of men shoveling coal into a wagon and went to ask them when the next train was expected.

"They have no idea." She shrugged.

"Is that Major McMahon?" Delphine shaded her eyes against the sun. There was a man in uniform striding along the platform.

"Good afternoon, ladies." He didn't look pleased to see them. "There's a problem, I'm afraid. Something wrong with the engine."

"Should we come back later?" Martha hadn't meant it to sound sarcastic. But she was struggling to suppress the anger she felt inside. There had been no apology for the panic this morning's phone call had triggered. There was not a shred of empathy in the way he behaved.

His eyes narrowed. "Better not—they shouldn't be too long." There was a glimmer of surprise in the way he looked at her.

"Where are they coming from?" Martha held his gaze. She wasn't going to be pacified. She wanted details.

"Czechoslovakia," the major replied. "A place called Pilsen, about fifty miles west of Prague."

"But they're Polish, aren't they?" Kitty said.

"With a few Balts in the mix." He nodded. "Most of 'em worked at the Skoda plant. Czechs used to make cars there; Germans turned it into a tank factory."

"How long will they have been traveling when they get here?" Delphine asked.

"Four days. Should've taken two—would've, if *we'd* been running the show." He shook his head. "Can't run the damn railroad without Germans, and don't they just hate doing anything to help these folks."

"I hope they've at least had food and been able to get some sleep," Delphine said.

"Food, probably," the major said. "There are Red Cross outfits at most of the big stations. As for sleep—well, I guess those stock cars aren't too comfortable."

"Stock cars?" Martha echoed. "You mean cattle wagons? Surely they . . ."

"No choice, ma'am." He cut her short. "Listen, I gotta go make a call; no point in the trucks getting here until there are people to transport. I'll catch you ladies when the train comes in."

"Major McMahon, wait just a moment, would you?" Martha followed him along the platform. "Is there any news on the fiancé of the girl at the camp? You were going to find out where he'd gone."

"Yeah, I did that," he called over his shoulder. "The engagement was a fantasy. Frank has a wife in Boise, Idaho."

Martha stopped dead. *A wife.* How on earth was Jadzia going to take that?

***

While they waited for the train, the women tried to work out how to break the news of Jadzia's betrayal.

Delphine was worried about the effect such a shock could have on a pregnant woman. "It could bring on premature labor," she said. "The baby might not survive."

"But what are we going to tell her?" Martha frowned. "She's bound to come asking if we've had any news from the base."

117

"We'll have to make up some story about them having trouble locating Frank since he got back to America," Kitty said. "Play for time."

"But wouldn't it be worse to wait until she's had the baby?" Martha replied. "Imagine how much more vulnerable she'll be feeling then."

The debate was still going on when a piercing whistle came down the tracks. A plume of steam shot into the sky before the engine chugged into view. Then they saw the cattle cars.

Kitty watched, mesmerized, as they glided along the tracks toward the platform. They were exactly like the photographs she'd seen in the British newspapers. Huge wooden containers with no windows. The only difference from those harrowing shots of the concentration camp transports was that the doors of these wagons were open. Faces stared out. There were no smiles, no waves of greeting. Even the youngest looked weary.

When the train came to a stop, people began to jump onto the platform. Young men and women, some carrying children, were the first out. Then Kitty saw older people—women, mostly—being helped off the train by the younger ones. Gigantic bundles were passed down to waiting hands and set down on the platform for the children and old ladies to sit on.

An American soldier stumbled out of the front of the train. When he reached them, he looked as if he barely had the energy to raise his hand in a salute to the major. "Three hundred and ninety-four passengers, sir." His unshaved face was haggard. "We lost five along the way: one climbed onto power lines and was electrocuted, four disappeared when we stopped at the border." He dragged the back of his hand across his forehead. "We delivered a baby boy last night, and there's a woman about to pop in car four. Have you got a doctor?"

Kitty and Delphine followed the GI down the row of boxcars. They found the mother of the newborn baby sitting on a suitcase, her son at her breast.

"I think they're both okay," Delphine said when she'd checked them over. "I don't know how she's managing to feed him, though—she looks half-starved."

"We ran out of food the day before yesterday," the GI said. He took them farther down the train to where a girl who looked like a child was crouched on the straw-covered floor of the wagon. Beside her was a young man who, like her, was probably only in his teens.

Delphine crouched down beside the girl. "Ask her how often the contractions are coming," she said to Kitty.

The girl opened her mouth to reply to the question, but no words came out. Her face contorted in pain.

"We can't wait for the trucks to arrive," Delphine said. "We need to get her back to the camp now. Can you get Martha?"

Five minutes later, the girl was being carried to the car by her scared-looking young man. She sat in the back of the Opel with Delphine beside her. Delphine had her hand over the girl's belly, trying to time the contractions.

Martha rolled down the window as she pulled away. "I'll meet you at the gate," she called to Kitty. "But if I'm not there, don't let anyone through until they've been dusted down."

The little boy was born in the back of the car, half a mile from Seidenmühle. Delphine had delivered several babies during her nursing career—but never in circumstances like this. The baby's head had started to emerge when they were still some distance away from the camp. The girl was screaming out in pain, and Martha had pulled over to the side of the road. But Delphine had urged her to drive on. Luckily, the back seat was big enough for the girl to lie down on.

Martha drove right up to the entrance of the hospital. She and the baby's father helped the girl through the doors into the ward while

Delphine carried the baby. Wolf was there, making beds with one of the trainee auxiliaries. He ran to fetch Dr. Jankaukas.

"You don't mind if I leave you?" Martha put her hand on Delphine's arm. "I'd better get over to the gate."

"No, we'll be fine now." Delphine glanced up as she wiped blood from the baby's face. "Oh—are you all right?" There were tears in Martha's eyes.

"Sorry." Martha rubbed her face with her knuckles. "It's just . . . I've never seen a baby being born before."

"I'd ask if you'd like to hold him." Delphine smiled. "But there isn't time now. Maybe tomorrow."

As Martha took a parting glance at the child, Delphine glimpsed something she'd never seen in someone looking at a newborn baby. If she'd been asked to describe the expression, she would have conveyed it with just one word: *grief.* What had caused that look? Had the failed marriage to a violent husband held more misery than Martha had let on?

Delphine stared at the door of the ward as it swung shut, wondering if the others ever thought about her the way she was thinking about Martha. She had tried—and failed—to control her own tears when the patient with the head injury had called out to his mother. Had there been other times, unguarded moments, when her secrets had shown on her face?

Martha was the only one of them who had confessed to unhappiness in her past—and to that unhappiness being part of her reason for coming here. That kind of honesty took courage. Delphine couldn't imagine opening up the way Martha had. To let it all out would be to risk losing the fragile hold she had on her sanity.

—◆—

The protests from the blockhouse leaders about there being no room for the new arrivals seemed to be forgotten when the DPs saw the procession of people winding along the road from the gates. Excitement ran like an electric current through the camp, bringing everyone outside to see who was coming: whether there was an aunt or an uncle, a distant cousin or a neighbor from their own village in Poland—anyone who might have news of those they had lost.

The men, women, and children from the train had a strange ghostly appearance; the DDT powder that had been squirted down collars and trousers and up skirts had settled on their hair and their faces.

Stefan, who had come to help Martha manage the transfer of people from the army trucks, led the procession. As they neared the cobbled street where the other DPs had assembled, he held up his hands and shouted something.

Martha could see that the crowd was already surging forward, about to engulf the weary travelers in the frantic search for a familiar face. But whatever Stefan said, it worked. They parted like the Red Sea, allowing the newcomers to pass through.

"What did you threaten them with this time?" she asked when the new arrivals were safely settled in the mess hall, tucking into their first proper meal in days.

"Nothing bad," he said, returning her wry smile. "I told them the new people have chocolate—and they will get some if they are patient."

"Chocolate?" Martha stared at him. "But we don't have any! What are they going to do when they find out you lied to them?"

"We do have it," he replied. "The Red Cross came when you went to Fürstenfeldbruck. They had boxes with all kinds of things: fish, beef, ham—maybe five, six hundred tins—and many, many bars of chocolate." He jerked his head toward the blockhouses. "But they don't know what was in the boxes."

"Thank you, God," Martha murmured under her breath. This really was the answer to her prayers. By the sound of it, they now had more than enough protein to eke out the meat quota from the farmers, even with four hundred extra mouths to feed. She smiled at Stefan. "You're a magician—did anyone ever tell you that?"

"Ma-ji-shen?" He repeated it slowly, as if trying the word on for size. "That is a good person, yes?"

"*Can* be good."

"Also bad?"

"Could be. A magician makes people believe things. He has power." As she said it, she sensed that, without realizing it, she'd stumbled upon the trait that most defined Stefan. He had a quiet power, a magnetism, that emerged whenever there was a crisis. In exercising it, he conjured up consequences that would scare or thrill his audience.

Like Arnie? It was Grandma Cecile's voice that whispered back at her.

No, she thought. *Not like him.* But there was no denying the memories triggered by his name: the spell he'd cast on her when he'd walked into the diner on Frenchman Street where she'd waited tables, the way he'd made her laugh. In those early days, when she was grieving for her grandmother and all alone, he'd created a sparkling new world full of promise. Her mistake had been to believe in the illusion.

"You think *I* have power?" Stefan's voice broke into her thoughts. His face had changed. The smile had given way to a blank, unfathomable expression. His eyes were the pale blue of a winter sky.

<hr />

Martha and Kitty were exhausted by the time the new arrivals were settled in. As they headed along the path from the stables, they spotted Delphine hurrying toward them. Even though the light was fading, there was no mistaking the troubled look on her face.

"What is it?" Martha asked. "What's happened?"

"It's Jadzia. She knows about Frank being married."

"What? How?"

"I don't know. She wouldn't say. My guess is she's been hanging around the guardhouse, asking every GI who comes in and out. I only found out because the leader of her blockhouse came running to the hospital. She said Jadzia had gone crazy. She was storming through the place, tearing down blankets, knocking over piles of suitcases. I've had to give her something to calm her down."

Martha's hand went to her forehead. "I hope to God she hasn't hurt herself."

"What about the baby?" Kitty said.

"Nothing's happened—yet. Jadzia's blood pressure is okay and the baby's heartbeat is normal."

"Well, that's a blessing," Martha breathed. She glanced at Kitty. "I'd like to have a word with the blockhouse leader, ask if someone can keep an eye on her. We're going to have to work out how we can support her when the baby's born."

Kitty nodded. "Could she move into one of the cabins next to us? It might help if she was with other single mothers."

"We could suggest that. It'd be a tight squeeze—although there'll be more room if we can get Bożena and a couple of others transferred to a camp in the British zone."

Number six was one of the all-female blockhouses. After a brief word with the leader, Martha and Kitty went to look in on Jadzia. She occupied an area no bigger than a cupboard, screened off by upturned boxes and a blanket. American paraphernalia was strung like a garland across the entrance: Hershey bar wrappers, gum packets, and empty Lucky Strike cartons. When Martha pushed the blanket aside, they saw Jadzia lying perfectly still on her straw-filled mattress.

"You wouldn't believe it, would you," Kitty whispered.

Martha shook her head. The tranquil expression on Jadzia's sleeping face belied the frantic incident the blockhouse leader had described. And in a few weeks' time, her baby would enter the world—yet another child born to a woman used by a man, then discarded. What kind of life could a baby have with a start like that? Could she and the others make any difference when the magnitude of the problem was so great? All they could do, when the baby came, was offer some sort of hope. But if what the major had said was true—if the Russians were tightening their grip on Poland and no other country would take the refugees—the future looked very distant and very uncertain.

CHAPTER 11

Delphine monitored Jadzia carefully for the next forty-eight hours. On the second morning, she found her sitting on the bed, fully dressed and with her hair tied back. She was eating the Red Cross–issue chocolate that had been distributed with last night's evening meal. She hardly spoke during the examination, other than to decline the sleeping pill Delphine offered. There was a strange sort of calm about her. Perhaps now the truth about Frank had sunk in, and she'd found an inner strength to face the future.

With a nod to the blockhouse leader, Delphine set off on her next visit. The baby boy born in the back of the car was only days old, but his parents wanted him to be christened. The mother, Aleksandra, was still in the hospital, getting bed rest and treatment for anemia. Marek, her young man, was so shy that he lacked the confidence to approach Father Josef—especially as the pair were not married. As slave workers in Germany, Poles could only marry if their Nazi masters granted them a special permit. He'd told Dr. Jankaukas that he was afraid his little son might be refused baptism because he was born out of wedlock, so Delphine had offered to speak to the priest for them.

When she reached the blockhouse where Father Josef lived, she spotted Stefan coming through the door.

"He is not here," Stefan replied in answer to her question. "He went to the chapel—to prepare for Mass."

Delphine had forgotten it was Sunday. Since coming to Seidenmühle, weekends had ceased to exist.

She'd walked past the chapel many times, but she'd never been inside. She hesitated on the threshold. The idea of entering a holy place—however humble—felt uncomfortable. The last time she had entered one had been the day she'd discovered that Claude and Philippe were never coming home.

She'd wandered into an empty church near the Hotel Lutetia. Half-blind from crying, she'd slumped down in one of the pews. Sitting with her eyes closed, breathing in the smell of wax polish and incense, she'd prayed for a sign. For something, anything, to let her know that they were still there. But there had been nothing in that hallowed building that spoke to her. Looking about her, she had an overwhelming feeling that the beauty of the architecture and the objects that adorned it were for the glory of man, not God. And the silence was unbearable. There was no comfort to be had in that place.

"Madame Fabius!" Father Josef must have spotted her loitering in the doorway. She hardly recognized him in his priest's robes. He was standing at the far end of the chapel, beckoning her inside.

With a deep breath, she walked down the narrow aisle. It felt different from what she'd expected. The wooden walls gave off a warmth that had been sadly lacking in the Parisian church. And it smelled different. No beeswax here, nor incense. The single candle on the altar table gave off no discernible odor. There was a faint scent of something that reminded her of the florist's shop on Avenue Foch that she used to visit before the war. She spotted the vases of wildflowers on either side of the altar: roses, like the ones Wolf had given her, and trailing swathes of honeysuckle.

"I'm sorry to disturb you," she said.

"Don't be." He smiled. "It's a pleasure to see you. You're a little early, but it doesn't matter."

"Oh." She looked at her feet, embarrassed that he'd thought she'd come for Mass. "I'm afraid I can't stay; I have to get back to the hospital. There's a woman there—one of the new arrivals—who would like her baby baptized."

"Of course. I understand," he said when she explained about the parents not being married. "Tell them I can marry them at the same time as I christen the baby, if that's what they want."

Delphine's eyes were drawn to a crucifix on the table behind him. She had always thought it a gruesome aspect of the Catholic Church, to have an effigy of that broken body on display. In her opinion, the cross on its own was enough to convey the message. But suddenly she saw it in a new way, as if she were looking through the eyes of the DPs who would soon be arriving for Mass. It struck her that such an image would have a particular poignancy for people who had survived the horrors of Nazi labor camps.

"Kitty told me you were in Dachau." The words came out unbidden. Something about this place had drawn them out of her.

"Yes, I was," he replied.

"My husband died there. And my son." It was as if someone had invaded her body, taken control of her mouth. The realization that she had uttered the words that she had feared letting out for so long made her feel faint.

"What are their names?"

Are? He'd used the present tense. As if they were still alive.

"M . . . my husband's name is C . . . Claude," she stuttered. "M . . . my son's is Philippe." It was the first time she'd said their names out loud since that terrible day in the Hotel Lutetia. Her legs gave way. She sank down onto one of the wooden benches.

"Can you tell me about them?" Father Josef sat down beside her.

Delphine took a breath. Then it all came tumbling out. "Claude was a doctor at the American Hospital in Paris. He used to hide people on the wards—Allied airmen on the run from the Germans. If we had a visit from the Nazis, Claude would pretend that the men were unconscious, so they wouldn't give themselves away if a German spoke to them." She pressed her lips together, aware that her jaw was trembling. "Philippe was in the Resistance. He helped the men get out of France—organized a safe house and an escape route via Spain."

"And they were arrested?"

"Yes." The word caught in her throat. "I . . . I'm sorry," she mumbled. "I . . . haven't . . . I've never . . ."

"It's all right. Take your time."

She nodded, swallowing hard. Now that it was out, she needed to tell him all of it. "By the spring of '44, too many people knew the secret. Someone told the Germans about the safe house. Claude was there with Philippe when the place was raided."

"They took them to Dachau?"

"I didn't know where they were. Not at first. Then I got a postcard. It was months after they were arrested. Claude had smuggled it out via someone in the camp who had a sister in Switzerland—that was where it was posted from. It said that he and Philippe were alive and that they were together." She paused. Her mouth was so dry she had to swallow again. "That was at the end of August '44. The Allies had already invaded, and Paris was liberated. I kept hoping, praying that my boys would come walking through the door."

She told him about the daily vigil at the Hotel Lutetia, and the man who had spotted the photographs she'd pinned up on the wall. "He was in the Resistance—running a safe house in another part of Paris," she said. "He was arrested the same day as my husband and son. When he told me what had happened, I realized that by the time I'd received that postcard, Claude and Philippe were already dead." She grasped the hard wooden edge of the bench, the thin skin on the backs of her hands as tight as a drum. "They were together, at least," she murmured. "That's what I cling to."

"Do you have their photographs?" The priest's eyes had a wistful, faraway look. "May I see them?"

"Of course." Delphine bent to retrieve a leather wallet from her nurse's bag. "I take them everywhere." She tried to smile, but the edges of her mouth felt numb, as if the muscles had been anesthetized. She passed him a picture of Claude with his arm around Philippe's shoulders. It was a snap that had been taken on vacation in Brittany before the war. She tried not to look as she took it out of the wallet—it was impossible to catch sight of their faces without welling up.

Father Josef angled the image to the light. "I wish I could say I knew them. I would have been there when they arrived. But there were so many of us. Thousands from Poland alone. There was a whole section of Dachau reserved for French political prisoners. We were on the other side of the camp. We rarely saw them."

"I was afraid of telling anyone," Delphine whispered, as she took back the photograph and slipped it into the wallet. "The other day, at the hospital, there was a young man who so reminded me of Philippe. I had to go outside. I wandered about, crying, talking to myself, telling myself that if I couldn't keep these feelings hidden, I was in danger of falling over the edge . . ."

He nodded. "I feel like that sometimes. It would be easier to shut away the memories. But there are other men in this camp who were at Dachau. They say it helps them to talk to someone who lived through it, as they did."

"I wonder if any of them would remember Claude or Philippe?"

"It's possible, of course—although, like me, they are all Polish. The Nazis seemed to have an especial hatred of our country. They liked to keep us separate from all the other prisoners." He raised his hand to his chin, rubbing the knuckles against his beard. "Tell me, did you come to Seidenmühle to be close to the place where your husband and son died?"

"Partly," Delphine replied. "I'd already decided that I had to leave Paris. For me it was a place full of ghosts. Not just Claude and Philippe. So many others were gone—and there was so much destruction. When I applied to work for the refugee organization, they asked me if I had any preference as to where I would be sent. I knew that Dachau was in Bavaria . . ." She trailed off, taken aback by the matter-of-fact tone of her own voice. She sounded as if she were talking about picking a vacation destination.

"Have you been there?"

She shook her head. "I don't know where it is, only that it's somewhere near Munich."

"It's not far from here, just a few miles to the north. It's been taken over by the Allies as a prison camp for SS officers."

Delphine closed her eyes. It took a moment to process this. All she could think was that if only the Allies had come sooner—if they had reached Dachau a few months earlier—Claude and Philippe would have been saved. They would still be alive.

"Would it help you if you went there?"

"I . . . I don't know." She'd thought of it many times. Part of her longed to see the place where they had died. There would never be graves to visit. If she could lay flowers at the place where they had spent their last days, that would be something, wouldn't it? But another part of her recoiled at the idea. Wouldn't it be better to remember them as they were, to not have their memory defiled by allowing the death camp to burn its image into her brain?

"Is it even possible?" She was staring at her hand, still gripping the bench, at the blue veins showing through the thin, translucent skin.

"You can drive up to the gates," he replied. "You can't go in, of course. But you can stand by the fence and look through the barbed wire."

"You've been back there?" She glanced up at him. *"Why?"* She couldn't conceal the astonishment in her voice.

"I didn't want to." He let out a long, slow breath. "After I'd been here for a while, I realized that I needed to. I had many friends there—men who didn't survive. I never got the chance to say goodbye to them."

She nodded. "That's how I feel. But I don't know if I could face it. The thought of seeing a place like that, of actually knowing it was real . . ."

"Think about it," he said. "If you decide you want to go, I'll take you there."

"Thank you." She could hear people outside. Any minute they would be coming through the door. "I must be getting back." She stood up. Her legs still felt shaky. As she made her way out, she thought about what it would be like to make that journey. She'd been there many times in her nightmares. Always she had gone there alone. Would it be less traumatic with someone by her side?

She nodded and smiled at the people going past as she walked back toward the hospital. The mask was firmly back in place. But she felt as if a little of the weight had shifted off her heart.

Kitty stared at the pile of paper on the desk in front of her. She was making files for all the new arrivals, translating details from dog-eared documents that had barely survived the long train journey from Czechoslovakia. Some had been lost, which meant visiting each block-house to search for the people on the transport list for whom no identity papers existed.

She pushed back the chair and went to pour herself some coffee. It was lukewarm, but the caffeine gave her the boost she needed. She stood by the window while she drank it, watching people going past outside.

Most were heading for the path that led to the chapel. She glanced at her watch. Nearly nine o'clock. They must be on their way to Mass.

She thought of Father Josef, dressed in his priest's robes, waiting for them. She hadn't spoken to him since the day the Red Cross lists arrived. She was sure he would have come to find her if he'd had any response to the letter he'd sent to the bishop of Vienna. With a long sigh she put down her mug and went back to the desk. It had been kind of the priest to write that letter, but it seemed a slim hope. Kitty longed to go to Vienna herself. It would be grim, seeing the places she had known and loved. The search for news would be daunting and could well be fruitless. But it would be better than this endless not-knowing.

She picked up the document on the top of the pile and tried to focus on the smeared, near-illegible writing. How could she even think of leaving the camp to make a trip to Vienna? If any one of them disappeared for more than half a day, there would be chaos.

The sound of someone tapping on the window made her look up. She saw a spiky-haired boy, not tall enough for his chin to appear above the sill. Kitty went to the door and unlocked it. No passes were handed out on Sundays. Probably the boy was just up to mischief. She peered around the corner of the building to where the boy was standing.

"Czy mogę z panią porozmawiać?" Please, miss, can I talk to you?

He came toward her, his eyes round and earnest. He didn't look as if he had mischief on his mind. She let him in and pointed to the chair on the other side of the desk. When he sat back in it, his legs didn't reach the floor.

His face was unfamiliar. There were dozens of children coming to her English classes—but she didn't recognize this boy. She asked him his name.

"Edek Dijak," he replied.

"O czym chcesz ze mną porozmawiać?" What do you want to talk to me about?

"Muszę znaleźć mojego ojca." I have to find my father.

Kitty listened as Edek told her about the conversation he'd had with one of the new arrivals. He said that this man—who came from the same village as his family—had seen his father. He'd spotted him when the train had been held up in Munich and the passengers had been allowed out to stretch their legs.

Kitty asked the boy how he could be sure the man was right. He replied that his father had a distinctive scar on his face, below the left eye, from an accident on the farm where he'd worked before the war. Then he took something from the pocket of his trousers—a folded slip of paper, which he pushed across the desk.

Kitty saw the words "Zone Français" stamped in red across one corner. The document was a record of the transfer to Seidenmühle of two women from a DP camp in the French zone of Germany. It was dated June 18, 1945—the week before Kitty and the others had arrived at the camp. Under "Reason for Transfer," it said, "Request from Edek Dijak, son/brother of above."

Kitty looked up, puzzled. *"Znalazłeś ich?"* You found them?

He nodded. *"Na rowerze."* On my bicycle.

Kitty listened, incredulous, as he described how he had traded a gun he found in the woods for a pedal bike. He'd tracked down his mother and sister by riding from camp to camp, living on carrots and strawberries stolen from German farms. He struck his chest with the flat of his hand, saying that he'd often felt tired and hungry, but he'd made himself keep going because he knew in his heart that his family was not dead.

He pulled something else from his pocket and handed it across to her. It was a photo of his father, smiling out from a sunny field stacked with bales of hay. Tears pricked Kitty's eyes as the boy described how he used to help his dad with the harvest. He said the picture had been taken just a few weeks before the Germans invaded. Having found his mother and sister, he was convinced he could now find his father.

"Ile masz lat, Edek?" How old are you, Edek?

He hesitated. She told him that he must tell her the truth—that she could look in the files and check his age if she wanted to.

"*Dwanaście.*" Twelve.

It took every ounce of self-control for Kitty to tell him that she would have to check before a pass could be issued, that she couldn't allow him to set off on his bicycle this time. She told him she would arrange for him to travel by army transport to Munich and organize help from the Red Cross when he reached the city.

When he'd gone, she locked the office door behind her and went in search of Martha. She wasn't sure where she'd be. Most mornings she was up and off before Kitty and Delphine were awake. The stable block was the likeliest place.

But Martha wasn't at the stables. No one Kitty asked had seen Martha since the previous day.

As Kitty made her way back past the warehouse, she spotted Delphine. She had her head down and her shoulders were hunched. She looked as if she were trying to make herself invisible.

"Delphine!"

At the sound of her name, Delphine looked up. There was a bewildered expression on her face, like someone disturbed in the middle of a daydream.

"Kitty." A smile transformed her face. "Sorry. I didn't see you."

"Have you seen Martha?"

"Not this morning. Have you been to the stables?"

Kitty nodded. "I forgot it's Sunday—there's no one working."

"Hmm." Delphine pursed her lips. "What did you want her for?"

"A boy came to the office. He's only twelve. He wanted to go to Munich on a bicycle to find his father. He showed me a photo of . . ." Suddenly she couldn't see. Tears blurred her eyes. She heard herself utter a strangled sort of sound, like someone fighting for breath.

"Kitty! What is it? What's wrong?" Delphine's arms were around her. She felt the warmth of her hands through the fabric of her shirt. Being hugged made the tears come faster.

"I . . . it's . . ." The words wouldn't come. It was as if a dam had broken inside her.

"Come on," Delphine said. "Let's get you back to the cabin."

Martha was in the kitchen when Kitty stumbled through the door, guided by Delphine.

"Hi," Martha called, without looking up. "I'm making coffee—want some?"

The chair scraped against the floor as Kitty sat down.

"Hey, what's wrong?" Martha came across to the dining table, the Nescafé jar in her hand.

"She's going to tell us, aren't you, Kitty?" Delphine's voice was soft and low. "And she might need something a little stronger to go with that coffee: I think there's some of my cognac left in the cupboard."

CHAPTER 12

Martha thought how different Kitty looked now from the girl she'd first glimpsed on the boat to France. The bold red lipstick and the feisty, defiant manner had masked a grief she couldn't acknowledge—not even to herself.

"It was the photograph, I think," Kitty was saying. "When he took it out and passed it to me, all I could think was that he was so lucky to have that image of his father—because I can hardly even remember my parents' faces. And I hated myself for even thinking it: this poor kid had cycled halfway across Germany, searching for his mother and sister, and here I was, sitting feeling sorry for myself." Her head dropped into her hands. "It made me feel so ashamed," she murmured. "I should have done what he did. I should have come to Europe back in May, as soon as the fighting stopped. I probably could have got the money—if I'd really tried. But I didn't have the guts to do it on my own."

"You mustn't blame yourself for that." Delphine put her hand on Kitty's shoulder. "You said you were just a child when you last saw your parents."

Kitty raised her head, shrugging off Delphine's hand. "I was the same age as Edek—twelve."

"But to be on your own, in a foreign country . . ." Martha clicked her tongue against her teeth. "I can't imagine how awful that must have been."

"It was. Sometimes I think the reason why I can't clearly remember what my parents looked like is because during that first year in England, just thinking of them made me cry. I used to try to remember things we did together—the happy times. But nothing came. It was as if all the pictures in my head had been erased and the only one left was of that moment, at the station in Vienna, when I saw them for the last time. And reliving it was so painful—I didn't *want* to remember it."

Martha nodded. She knew what that felt like: on the one hand, struggling to recapture memories, while on the other, trying to suppress them. She wondered if it would help Kitty to tell her that she had lost her own parents at a young age, that their wedding photograph, placed on her bedside table by Grandma Cecile, had caused her more sorrow than comfort. But she kept silent. It would be tactless to mention it—because for Kitty, there was no proof that her parents were dead, however likely it seemed.

"I felt like a ghost girl in England," Kitty whispered. "It was as if I'd left part of myself behind in Vienna."

"Who looked after you?" Delphine asked.

"When I arrived on the train, I went to a sort of camp," Kitty replied. "Not like here—it was the sort of place British people went for their holidays. We lived in chalets. It was freezing cold because they were meant to be used in summer and it was December." She reached for her mug of coffee, draining what was left. Then she took a sip of the cognac Delphine had put beside it. "People would come round choosing children. I was taken by a couple who were much older than my parents. I remember he was wearing a bowler hat. And she was very stern. They took me to live with them in London. They both went out to work. I was supposed to go to school, but I didn't speak English and the other kids teased me for being foreign. My foster parents didn't seem to care whether I went. I was basically a maid, hoovering and polishing and washing up, a young pair of legs for going shopping. I can't ever remember them hugging me or giving me a kiss." She shrugged.

"Maybe they just weren't the type of people who would do that—but I think it was probably that they didn't like me."

"Why do you think that?" Martha asked.

"Because I kept asking them to give my parents a job. It was the only way they could get out of Austria. People they knew in Vienna were being taken on as cooks or gardeners in British houses. All you needed was a written offer from England—then you could get a visa to travel. But the couple I was living with said they didn't need any paid staff. I said they wouldn't have to pay them, just pretend they were giving them a job. I knew if my parents could just get to England, we'd survive somehow. But they kept saying no. And then the war started, and it was too late."

Kitty was staring at the table, wisps of hair hanging down around her face. "Then the woman got ill and had to go into hospital. They couldn't keep me after that, so I went to live with two old ladies. They were nice to me. I'd brought a book with me from Austria, called *Gone with the Wind*—it was the only book I had. They bought me the English version. That was how I learnt the language, really. I taught myself to read and write English by copying out a chapter every night." She pushed her hair back from her face. "I was desperate to fit in, to be normal. I thought that if I could learn to speak without an accent, other kids would start liking me.

"My father used to tell me that knowledge was a precious, everlasting possession. He was pleased when I wrote to tell them I was fluent in English. He said: 'Always remember, Kitty, the riches of the mind do not rust.' He put that in the last letter I had from them. I knew that if I tried hard enough, I could master almost anything. It gave me the sense of being in control—it was the one thing I *could* control." She paused, fingering the cognac glass, her finger tracing the rim. "I liked it, living with the old ladies, even though I was scared of the air raids. But then the house was bombed."

Delphine's hand went to her mouth. "Were you hurt?"

"No. I was out when it happened—and so were they, thank goodness. But we had nowhere to live. I was sent to Manchester after that. The people I went to live with said I was too old to go to school."

"Is that when you started the job you told me about?" Martha said.

Kitty nodded. "I knew how to use a sewing machine. My mother was a seamstress and I used to help her. I liked earning money. When I was seventeen, I left my foster parents and took lodgings with one of my workmates from the factory."

"How long is it since you heard from your parents?" Delphine whispered the question, leaning in close to Kitty.

"The last letter I had was in August 1940, when I was still living in London. There was nothing after I moved to Manchester."

"But would they have known where you were?" Delphine frowned.

"I sent my new address each time I moved. And when the war ended, I went to the Red Cross office in Manchester. They had lists, like the ones they deliver to us. But after a few weeks, I was getting desperate. I thought if I could just find a way to get to Europe . . ."

Delphine nodded. "You want to go to Vienna."

"That was my plan." Kitty shook her head. "I was so naïve. I had no idea what it was going to be like here in Germany. I thought I'd be able to hop on a train and be there in a couple of hours."

"It'd take a day or two, I should think," Martha said, "but we could arrange it. The army would help, I'm sure."

"But how could I possibly leave the two of you to cope with all this? And anyway," she added, "Father Josef has written to the bishop of Vienna, asking if someone in the Church can make inquiries."

"That's good. He's such a kind man."

Something in the tone of Delphine's voice made both Kitty and Martha turn her way. She was staring at the table, her eyes glassy.

"Delphine? What is it?" Martha said.

A tear ran down Delphine's cheek. "He's offered to take me to Dachau. But I don't know if I can bear it."

"Dachau?" Kitty gasped. "Why?"

"M . . . my husband died there. My son, too. Claude and Philippe. They . . ." The words were lost in a choking sob.

Martha gathered her up. Her body felt so slight, Martha could feel her ribs through the fabric of her shirt.

Kitty held a glass of cognac up to Delphine's trembling lips, and she shuddered as the liquid went down. She closed her eyes, tears oozing out from under pale lashes. Then she took a long breath.

"They worked for the Resistance in Paris." She was staring at the wall beyond the table now, as if the faces of her lost family were projected onto it. She repeated what she had told Father Josef a little more than an hour earlier—words that had been locked inside until today.

"That was so brave," Martha said. "Risking their lives for those men."

Delphine nodded. "I didn't know the full story at the time. They kept most of it from me—to protect me, I think. But someone in the hospital betrayed them. The Nazis arrested them, and I . . ." She trailed off, glancing at Kitty. "I'm like you. I had a hidden reason for coming here. I just wanted to be close to them." She turned to Martha. "I thought it would help, seeing where they . . . ," she faltered, her voice threatening to break again. "But when I think about it . . . that awful place, just a few miles beyond these woods, I feel as if the sight of it would tip me over the edge."

Martha and Kitty exchanged worried glances. Martha opened her mouth, but before she could say anything, Delphine was on her feet. "I need to get back to the hospital," she said.

"Are you sure?" Martha whispered. "Please don't go if you don't feel up to it. I can go and tell Dr. Jankaukas you're not well."

Delphine shook her head. "I'll be fine. I'd be far worse, sitting here doing nothing."

"Why didn't she tell us before?" Martha said, as she unlocked the door of the office. "How could she have lived with it all this time, not saying anything?"

"For the same reason as me, I suppose," Kitty said. "If no one knows, they can't remind you of it. Putting it into words makes it . . . *real*."

"But bottling it up—that's just as hard, isn't it?"

"Yes, but telling someone doesn't take away what you feel. She said she came to Seidenmühle to be close to her husband and her son. But wherever she is, she carries the grief with her. Whatever happens— whether she goes to Dachau or not—it won't bring them back."

There was an edge to Kitty's voice; she sounded almost angry. She plonked down on the chair and grabbed a sheet of paper from one of the piles on the desk.

"Why don't you take a break," Martha said. "You've had one hell of a morning. This stuff can wait."

"And do what?" Kitty huffed out a breath. "Go for a walk around the camp? Paddle my feet in the river? Pick wildflowers? Don't you see? I'm the same as Delphine—I don't *want* time to think! I just . . ." She broke off, burying her face in her hands. "God, I'm sorry," she mumbled. "That was so rude of me. Unforgivable."

Martha pulled the other chair around the desk and sat down beside her. "You've got nothing to be sorry for. You've worked so hard and handled an impossible situation so bravely. I don't know how you've managed to keep a lid on your feelings all this time. Every day, you're dealing with people who are desperate for news of their families—that must be torture."

"I thought I could do it." Kitty nodded. "It was that kid this morning. It made me feel so ashamed."

"Ashamed? Of what?"

"Of not doing enough. I've felt that for years. Ever since the war started. If I'd tried harder, learned English quicker, I could've got my parents to Britain. I used to dream about writing to the prime minister. I'd fall asleep composing letters in my head."

"You were so young," Martha murmured. "It must have been terrifying, arriving in a foreign country, not knowing anyone, not speaking the language."

"I was scared at the beginning," Kitty replied. "By the end I felt angry—and guilty. I knew how lucky I was to have survived when so many people hadn't, but the thought of what had probably happened to my parents . . ." She clenched her hands into fists. "I had a boyfriend in Manchester. He asked me to marry him. I told him I couldn't do that until I'd found out about my mother and father. He thought I was a fool, to carry on hoping. He said I should just accept the fact that I was an orphan."

"I guess he had his reasons," Martha said. "But that's a pretty cruel thing to say to someone you love."

"That's how he was," Kitty said. "If I ever mentioned how hard it was, growing up in England without my family, he'd say something like 'Everyone had a lousy childhood.'"

"It sounds to me as if he didn't want to understand you." Martha felt as if she were talking to her younger self. Kitty's description of her boyfriend reminded her of Arnie. "Will you go back to him?"

"He didn't come to the station to see me off. I think he'll find someone else."

Martha thought she'd probably had a lucky escape. But Kitty didn't need to hear that—she already had more than enough heartache to deal with.

"Who's that?" Someone was tapping at the window. Kitty got up. "It's Mrs. Grabowska from the sewing school."

Martha went to open the door. Mrs. Grabowska came in, beaming. Kitty chattered away with her for a few minutes, then, with a little bow to Martha, the woman left.

Kitty was smiling. "She wanted to know where she could get fabric to make a wedding dress. The couple whose baby was born in the back of your car are getting married."

"Oh, how lovely!"

"It's going to be next Saturday—the mother should be out of hospital by then. Father Josef's going to baptize the baby at the same time. And you'll never guess what . . ."

"What?" Martha shook her head.

"They want you and Delphine to be godparents."

CHAPTER 13

That evening, Martha went to the hospital. Aleksandra was lying down, her face as white as the pillow. In a cot beside the bed, her baby, wide awake but making no sound, was opening and closing his little mouth. Martha leaned in to look at him, watching a bubble form between his lips. He was so perfect. It seemed incredible that this tiny new person had started life on the back seat of her car.

Aleksandra opened her eyes, smiling when she caught sight of Martha. She murmured something in Polish.

"May I pick him up?" Martha mimed cradling with her arms.

The girl nodded.

Martha's hands trembled as she went to lift him out of the cot. He was so light in her arms, his skin so delicate and transparent that she could see the blue veins at his temples. She'd held babies before when she'd visited families on the Lower East Side. But he was so much smaller—probably because his mother hadn't had enough to eat when she was carrying him.

She turned away, not wanting Aleksandra to see the tears prickling her eyes. His pale fragility brought back agonizing memories—images she'd shut away in a dark, silent corner of her mind. She swallowed hard. She could see through her tears that his eyes were fixed on her face. There was a curious depth to those eyes, as if he knew what she was thinking. His mouth turned up at the edges. Was that a smile? Surely he was too young for that. And yet . . . Martha felt a surge of something she couldn't name as she gazed down at him. And when she laid him back in his cot and walked away, she felt different. Lighter.

———

Martha was nervous about the christening.

"Why?" Stefan said when she told him.

"I'm worried I'll get the words wrong," she said. It was true—there were a lot of responses she would have to make, in Polish. It was a big responsibility. But there was another reason why Martha felt uncomfortable. She hadn't been in a church since she was a teenager. Grandma Cecile had gone every Sunday, but that had been as much about business as spirituality. Her grandmother had earned a living making cassocks and surplices for choristers, and it was her close connection with the church that had secured a place for Martha at the best school in the neighborhood. As soon as that was accomplished, Grandma Cecile stopped making a fuss if Martha said she didn't want to go to Mass.

"I can help you." Stefan opened the door for her to get into the car. "We can practice what you have to say."

They were going to the army base to pick up medical supplies for the hospital. Martha had planned to drive there alone, but when she read through the list Delphine had given her, she realized she was going to need help.

It was fun, rehearsing with Stefan. She hadn't brought the written responses with her—Stefan seemed to know them by heart. When she asked him how he knew all the words, he told her that, before the war, he'd stood as godfather to his niece and nephew.

Martha longed to ask him about where these children and their parents were now. Had they survived the war? Had he been searching for them in the Red Cross lists? But she and Stefan had established an unspoken pact. Martha never asked him about his family and he never asked about her life before the camp. He'd never commented on the fact that she was *Mrs.* Radford—nor had he questioned why she was living half a world away from her home. If he ever wondered if she was a wife or a widow, he didn't let on.

"There's going to be a party after the church service." She slowed down as she drove over a bridge with chunks missing from its walls.

"Yes, I know." He grunted. "Have you been to a Polish wedding?"

She shook her head.

"You like to dance?"

"Well . . . yes. I suppose so." She couldn't remember the last time she'd danced.

"You like vodka?" There was a smile in Stefan's voice. "At a Polish wedding, there is plenty of dancing—and plenty of vodka."

Martha didn't want to ask where the vodka was likely to be coming from. She'd heard rumors that new stills had been made to replace the ones the army had confiscated. So far, she hadn't done anything about it—given the circumstances, the DPs deserved whatever enjoyment they could get—but she worried about the consequences if they overdid the hooch. She didn't want the GIs on guard duty going back to base with tales of wild behavior at the camp. No doubt Major McMahon would respond with a very heavy hand.

"Will you come to the party?" She tried to make it sound casual. But the truth was that she wanted him to come. She couldn't shake the memory of the way he'd looked at her in the old house in the forest. Replaying it had become addictive. She knew she shouldn't be thinking about him that way. But telling herself that didn't seem to help.

He shrugged. "If they ask me. They will want people they know, people who came on the train with them."

"You could come as my guest," she said. "To translate for me," she added, in case that sounded too forward.

When he didn't reply, she glanced across at him. He was looking out the passenger window, at the trees whizzing by. She caught his face momentarily reflected in the glass. If she'd asked him to go and empty one of the cesspits, he couldn't have looked more unhappy. Had she stirred up painful memories? She shouldn't have pressed him like that. She wished she could think of some way of apologizing—but she sensed that anything she said would only make things worse.

Martha brought the car to a stop outside the gates of the army base. Stefan nodded to the soldier who emerged from the guardhouse. His mask was back on now—a poker face, revealing nothing. He hadn't said if he would come to the wedding. Whatever memories the invitation had triggered had been locked away. She wondered if, like Kitty and Delphine, there would be a breaking point: a time when whatever he was holding inside would have to come out.

———

Kitty locked the office door when the last of the morning's passes had been issued and made her way to the guardhouse. She wanted to get into the weaving shed to find some fabric suitable for making a wedding dress.

Sergeant Lewis was on duty at the guardhouse. His smile at the sight of her lit up his face. When she explained what she'd come for, and the reason why, he said it was a shame he'd be stuck in the guardhouse on the day of the wedding. "Take a picture," he said. "I'd like to see what you're planning to make."

"I would—if I had a camera," she replied.

"I've got one. You can borrow it if you like." He said he'd drop it off at the office next time he was on duty.

As she took the keys from him, their fingers touched. It was only for a fraction of a second, but she felt the warmth of his skin. Walking away, she couldn't help thinking of Fred, whose hands had been cold and clammy. The first time he had touched her, she had flinched at the feel of them. She'd struggled to overcome the disagreeable sensation, telling herself that all men's hands must be like that when they got excited about touching a girl.

Once she was inside the weaving shed, she got to work. After poking around the dusty shelves, she noticed a roll of silvery material protruding from a high shelf. She looked around for a ladder. There was a contraption on wheels in the far corner—the sort of thing she'd seen in the lending library in Manchester. It took all her strength to push it over to the shelf where the silvery fabric lay. She tested the treads, hoping they weren't rotten. When she'd convinced herself that the ladder was safe, she climbed up to inspect the roll she wanted. But she couldn't shift it. It was wedged in, and she risked falling if she tugged too hard. She huffed out a breath, frustrated. She was going to have to fetch one of the men from the camp to help her. She hated the idea of asking for help from anyone. In England, her physical strength was the only thing that had given her the edge over the playground bullies. It was one of the few things she liked about herself.

"Miss Bloom!" The voice from outside almost made her lose her balance. She turned to see Sergeant Lewis silhouetted in the doorway. "Hope I didn't startle you," he said, as he walked toward the ladder. "I was just curious—never been inside this place."

"I thought you weren't supposed to leave the guardhouse?" She climbed down to where he stood, glad that she was wearing trousers.

"The relief detail just arrived," he replied. "The driver has a thing for one of the ladies in the kitchen. He likes to go see her before we head back to base."

"Well, since you're here, I wonder if you could give me a hand?" She explained the problem with the roll of fabric.

"Well, sure I can." He was looking at her in a strange way, the corner of his mouth flexing, as if he was trying not to smile.

"What? What is it?"

"You have a cobweb on your head."

"Ugh!" She raked her fingers through her hair. As she lowered her arm, she saw that the sleeve of her jacket was covered in dust.

"No—you missed it." Sergeant Lewis leaned forward. "Can I . . ." She felt his hand brush her head, gentle but firm. "There. It's gone." He held out his hand. A wisp of gossamer floated out in the draft coming through the door. He rubbed it off and started climbing the ladder. Moments later the roll of artificial silk was on the workbench. He helped her roll out a little of it, to check its condition.

"Will it do?"

"Yes, I think so. It's hard to tell in this light. But there's yards and yards of it, so even if I find some damage, there's sure to be enough to make a dress."

He cocked his head to one side. "I can just about sew on a button—wouldn't have a clue how to make anything."

"Well, I won't actually be making it; the ladies at the sewing class will do that. I'm just going to work out the design."

"Where'd you learn to do that?"

"I . . ." She hesitated, not wanting to say anything that would prompt further questions about her past. But the look in his eyes was disarming. There was a warmth in them that made her feel . . . what? She couldn't put her finger on it. Comfortable? Safe? It was both of those, but something else as well: something she couldn't name. "My mother taught me," she said. Then, before he could probe any deeper, she glanced at her watch. "Goodness! Is that the time? I'd better be getting back."

"Can I help you carry it?"

"No—thank you. I'll be fine now." Bending her knees to brace herself, she hoisted the roll onto her shoulder. It was heavier than she'd expected, but she was determined not to admit defeat a second time. With a wave of her free hand, she made her way out, blinking in the dazzling light of the midday sun.

Kitty stayed downstairs when the others went to bed that evening. She got out the sketch pad she'd brought with her from England and the pencils she kept wrapped in a scarf that had once belonged to her mother. When she took them out, she held the silk square up to her face. It still carried a faint trace of her mother's perfume.

It was the first time Kitty had attempted to draw since arriving at Seidenmühle. In truth, there hadn't been time. But it wasn't just that: what had been her solace on long, lonely evenings in England seemed entirely frivolous in a place like this. Now, however, there was a reason for it.

She was looking forward to designing the wedding dress for Aleksandra, the girl from the train. A girl who, it turned out, was the same age as she was. Like Kitty, she had left her place of birth far behind and arrived somewhere new and strange. There were many similarities between them; they even looked alike, with long dark hair and gray eyes. It would be fun to design a dress for her—a sort of fantasy of what Kitty might one day wear herself.

She tried to imagine what it would be like to be a bride. But the picture that came into her head was incomplete. The man beside her had no face. Was that because Fred was fading from her memory now that she was far away from him? She didn't like to admit it to herself, but she had known the instant he had made that ham-fisted proposal in the middle of a crowded theater that she could never marry him. What she'd said about not being able to settle down until she found out what had happened to her parents had been absolutely true. But, to her shame, she had used it as an excuse to brush Fred off.

Her thoughts turned to Sergeant Lewis. Fred would have made fun of her for getting herself all covered in dust and cobwebs to retrieve something that was destined to be worn by someone else. But the sergeant hadn't raised an eyebrow when she'd told him what she wanted to do. She wondered if he'd remember his promise to lend her his camera for the wedding.

With a sigh that turned into a yawn, she laid down her pencil. The sketch was finished now. The next stage would be to turn the design into a paper pattern. She was glad that Mrs. Grabowska was going to make the dress. Sewing it herself would have brought back painful memories of sewing back in the workshop at Blumenthal's with her mother close by, checking her seams and darts.

As she cast a critical eye over what she'd drawn, she thought of what it would be like to go back to Vienna. For all she knew, the shop was no longer there. The city had been bombed, just as Munich had—and the sight of those ruined streets had been horrific. If only Father Josef's letter to the bishop would bring some news, some fragment of hope to make the journey back home bearable. It was a little easier now that the others knew. Martha had made it clear she would do everything in her power to allow Kitty to make that journey. But Kitty was still terrified of what she might find when she got there.

CHAPTER 14

The chapel in the woods took on a fairy tale look for the day of the wedding and baptism. Trails of foliage and ivy had been arranged around the door. Wild roses and honeysuckle had been woven into the leaves, forming a fragrant archway for the bride and groom as they stepped outside. The bride wore a garland studded with cornflowers and forget-me-nots. Her hair had been intricately braided, and the dress Kitty had designed shimmered like moonlight on water as she walked.

They had named their baby Rodek. Martha was holding him as she followed the couple out. The baptism part of the ceremony had gone without a hitch. Despite their worries about tripping up over the Polish words, she and Delphine had delivered their responses without a single mistake. Rodek hadn't made a sound during the ceremony, even when Father Josef had doused his forehead with water. The only sign that anything had disturbed him was his little hand opening, the fingers splaying out then closing, like a sea anemone. Now he was fast asleep, his cheek very white against Martha's fuchsia-colored dress.

She glanced across to where Delphine and Kitty were standing. Delphine was showering the newlyweds with handfuls of rice, and Kitty was taking a photograph. Kitty looked lovely in a yellow polka-dot frock that swung out as she moved. Delphine was wearing a black shift dress trimmed with white—the very essence of Parisian chic. For weeks now, the three of them had only been out of uniform when they were getting ready to go to bed. They'd had fun, getting ready for the wedding— putting on lipstick and making corsages from sprigs of lily of the valley picked in the woods.

"You want me to hold him?" Stefan suddenly appeared at Martha's side. She hadn't seen him in the chapel. He must have crept in after the ceremony had started.

"I'm okay, thanks." She was surprised how normal her voice sounded. She *was* okay. Holding Rodek seemed to have a magical effect—like a soothing balm.

"I will take him when your arms fall off."

Martha smiled. Stefan leaned in closer, stroking the baby's cheek with his finger. She could smell the forest on him—a faint scent of pine. She knew that he'd been decorating the mess hall for the wedding reception.

"Lucky boy," Stefan murmured.

"Yes," she said. "He is lucky—if he'd been born on the train, he might not have survived."

Stefan darted a curious half smile at Martha. "That is a nice dress," he said. "I hope the baby does not . . . how do you say it in English?" He touched the corners of his mouth with his finger and thumb and ran them down his chin.

"Drool?" Martha laughed.

A cheer went up from the wedding guests. Aleksandra and Marek were having their first kiss as husband and wife. Then they began to move off, and the guests formed a procession behind them.

There were audible gasps when people entered the mess hall. It looked as if the forest had come inside. The boughs of pine softened the ugly concrete walls and gave the room a fragrance that masked the usual smell of boiled cabbage. The tables had been arranged in a horseshoe shape around three sides of the room, so that everyone could see the bride and groom at the far end.

"You did a great job," Martha said, as Stefan pulled out a chair for her.

"Watch now," Stefan said. "This is a special thing in a Polish wedding."

One of the guests was walking past the tables, carrying a big loaf of bread. He held it out as he walked, so that everyone could see that it was decorated with the initials of the bride and groom, made from interlaced strips of dough. Then he presented it to the couple. They each broke off a piece, then dipped it into a bowl.

"What's that?" Martha whispered.

"Salt," Stefan replied. "When they eat this, it means they will never go hungry."

An ironic custom, Martha thought, in view of what they'd come through. The bride was still painfully thin. Incredible to think that she gave birth just days ago. As she watched, the bread was replaced with two small glasses.

"Now vodka," Stefan said.

The bride and groom raised the glasses, drained them, then threw them over their shoulders. A cheer went up. Martha turned to Stefan, bewildered. "What are they doing?" The guests on either side of the couple were scrabbling about on the floor.

"They will find the glass. If it is broken, they will live together a long time and be happy."

The cheering turned to shrieks of triumph as broken shards were held aloft. Martha glanced at the baby in her arms, amazed that the noise hadn't woken him. Then trays of glasses appeared, along with plates piled with bread and small chunks of the corned beef and Spam that had come in the Red Cross delivery. Each guest was given a bite to eat and a slug of vodka to wash it down with.

"You like it?" Stefan grinned at Martha's face as she took a sip of the colorless liquid.

"It's very strong." She coughed as she put the glass down. She could feel the vodka burning its way to her stomach. She glanced over to where Kitty and Delphine were sitting. They clinked glasses with Dr.

Jankaukas, who was sitting between them. Then all three downed the vodka shots in one go.

She turned to Stefan. "I don't think I can drink the whole thing." She was going to offer him the rest of hers. Then she remembered what the major had said about the UNRRA man who had been sent back to Texas after going blind from drinking the hooch the DPs made.

"This is good," Stefan said, as he took a drink. "Not like what they make under the bed. It comes from Russia."

Martha thought she'd better not ask how a consignment of Russian vodka had found its way into Seidenmühle.

"We found it in the forest."

She looked at him, mystified.

"In that place where we got the tiles for the roof," he said. "There were steps going under the house. I think maybe Russian soldiers hid there." He shrugged. "They left many bottles of vodka."

Martha took another sip. It didn't taste quite as bad as the first mouthful. She heard a shout from the other end of the room. An accordion struck up, accompanied by a violin. The groom led his bride to the middle of the floor. They danced a few bars, then others crowded around. Everyone was clapping in time to the music. As they joined in the dancing, whoops of delight filled the room.

The bridegroom darted across to where Kitty was sitting, grasping her hand and pulling her out of her chair. The bride was grabbed by another man, who whirled her around, making her braids come loose and fly out behind her.

"Poor girl," Martha said. "I hope she'll be all right. She only left the hospital two days ago."

"All the men at the wedding must dance with her," Stefan said.

"Another Polish tradition?"

He nodded. "I will take the baby now, yes?" The wry look on his face told her this was his strategy to avoid this part of the proceedings. "Someone wants to dance with you."

Martha turned to see Dr. Jankaukas standing behind her chair. He smiled and raised his eyebrows in lieu of an invitation. She'd only met him a handful of times—and attempts at conversation had made her realize just how rusty her French was. But the good thing about dancing, she thought, as she took his hand, was that you didn't need to talk.

Martha hadn't anticipated the consequences of partnering with someone so tall. Her feet left the floor every time he spun her around. She felt giddy when the music stopped and clutched his arm, afraid of embarrassing herself by falling over. She was laughing, trying to remember how to apologize in French. He gave her a courtly bow, then passed her to another man—one of the DPs who had helped renovate the stable block. Dr. Jankaukas was swapping her for Kitty. A much better partner for him, Martha thought, as Kitty was only a couple of inches shorter than he was.

Martha's new partner was already a little the worse for wear from the vodka, judging by the way he kept tripping over her feet. Kitty shot her a sympathetic smile as she swept past with the doctor. She looked happy, Martha thought, as if the burden of anxiety had been lifted from her shoulders. It was good to see her enjoying herself—a temporary escape from reality was what she needed, like most of the people in this room.

By the time the dance came to an end, Martha was desperate for a drink. It was water, not vodka, she wanted. As she made her way back across the floor, she saw that Delphine had moved to sit by Stefan.

"Sorry." Delphine got up when Martha reached her. "I've just come to take Rodek. I promised his mother I'd give him a bottle."

"You want me to fetch it for you?" Stefan stood up.

"No." Delphine smiled. "I don't mind—honestly. It's a bit noisy for me, and I really need to get back to the hospital, so I'll take him with me."

Martha could understand how difficult such a celebration must be for Delphine. A wedding was bound to bring back memories—as well as reminding her of what might have been if her son had lived.

"Would you like me to come with you?" Martha asked.

Delphine shook her head. "Absolutely not. You haven't stopped since we took over this place; it's about time you had a chance to enjoy yourself."

Martha watched her take the sleeping Rodek from Stefan's arms. He looked almost reluctant to hand the baby over. Perhaps the wedding celebration was as much of an ordeal for him as it was for Delphine. Martha hoped he hadn't come just because she'd asked him to—as a duty he felt he couldn't avoid.

"I could do with a glass of water," she said when Delphine had gone. "I can't see any, can you?"

He looked along the table. "Only vodka, I think. I can get some from the kitchen."

"I'll come with you." She fanned her face with her hand. "It's getting pretty warm in here."

She waited outside while he went into the kitchen. The sun was still high in the sky, blindingly bright. There was no one about. Those who were not at the wedding had gone indoors to escape the heat.

Stefan came out with a jug in his hand. "No glasses. All taken for the wedding." He offered her the jug. "You mind drinking from this?"

"No, I don't mind." She smiled as she took it from him. If he hadn't been there, she would have poured some of the water on her head.

"It's hot out here," he said. "We can sit under the trees if you want."

She followed him to a log pile at the edge of the forest boundary. Beneath the canopy of branches, it felt much cooler. "Sorry," she said, looking at the half-empty jug. "You haven't had any." She wiped the rim with the sleeve of her dress.

"You are funny." He grinned as he took it from her.

"Why?"

"You wiped the jug. Like you have a bad disease."

She huffed out a chuckle. "I hope not!"

He set the empty jug down on the ground. "Why did you come here?" he asked. "Why did you want to leave a nice place like America?"

She saw that he was looking at her hand, at the ring glinting in the dappled light that penetrated the trees. She thought that perhaps the vodka had melted his reserve. He'd never asked her why she wore it, but he must have wondered. What would he say if she told him she'd walked out on her husband? She didn't like the idea of him knowing that about her. And the realization that she cared so much what he thought sent a frisson of something through her, like a nettle sting or a mild electric shock.

"Why do you ask?" It was all she could say—a delaying tactic to give her time to think.

"If *I* lived in America, I would never leave." He kicked at a loose chunk of bark on a log that had fallen from the pile.

"I came here because I wanted to do something to help. There was a report in the newspaper; it said they needed people to work in the camps. There was nothing to stop me from coming, so . . ." She ended the sentence with a shrug. *Nothing to stop me.* It wasn't really a lie—just not the whole truth.

"Not easy for you, to come to a place like this." His eyes searched her face. She wondered if he could see the thin scar on her cheek beneath the dusting of powder. "You are a good person."

His words shamed her. She couldn't look at him. It felt as though the trees were closing in on them, wrapping them in a cocoon of branches. She could smell his skin, warm and earthy, overlaid with the scent of the forest. All she could think of was how it would feel to lay her head on his shoulder and trace the hollow of his neck with her lips.

Are you insane? Grandma Cecile was hissing in her ear. But Martha didn't want to listen. All she wanted was to lose herself—to forget, just for a moment, that she was the boss of this place, that Stefan was one of her charges, and that she was still married to somebody else.

"Mrs. Radford!"

Someone was shouting her name—someone real. She leapt off the log pile. Sergeant Lewis was running down the path toward them.

"Mrs. Radford." He paused, catching his breath. "They've found something in the river. Can you come?"

—✦—

The two fishermen on the riverbank were among the men who had gone on strike when the army left the camp, depriving them of the extra cigarette ration. Now they stood awkwardly, hands thrust in their pockets, next to a small bundle wrapped in a scrap of blue checked cloth.

"I told them to leave her there until you came, but he's wrapped her in his neckerchief." Sergeant Lewis glanced at the taller of the two men. "He found her in the weeds by the mill wheel. The other one came running to tell me. I couldn't understand what he was saying. I followed him down here and saw her—just lying there on the grass." Sergeant Lewis shook his head. "I think she must have been there for a while."

Martha didn't trust herself to speak. The cloth covered everything, giving no clue to what lay beneath the folds of fabric. It could have been a hunk of cheese wrapped up against the melting rays of the sun, or a trout destined for the dinner table. But it was a baby. A little girl. And she was dead.

Stefan knelt down on the grass. He looked at her as she crouched on the other side of the tiny shrouded body. She nodded, relieved that he had the guts to do what she could not. Very gently, he peeled back the cloth, revealing a face so white and perfect it looked like a china doll. As more of the fabric came away, she saw faint purple marks on the baby's neck.

Stefan turned to the two men and said something in Polish. They shrugged and shook their heads.

"They say they did not make these marks," Stefan said. "The baby had them when they found her."

Martha's stomach turned to ice. She pictured a woman giving birth in the woods, alone and desperate—so desperate that she had taken her baby's life when it had barely drawn breath.

159

"We'll take her to the hospital." Martha struggled to keep her voice level as she addressed the sergeant. "She'll be properly examined there. I'll notify the major."

Stefan carried the baby through the camp. Neither of them said anything as they walked. It felt like a funeral procession. When they reached the hospital, they found Delphine sitting with Wolf at the entrance to the maternity ward. He had Rodek in his arms, singing a lullaby to the little boy in Polish. It was a heartbreaking sight. Martha could barely speak, she was so choked up. Delphine quickly took command of the situation, ushering Martha and Stefan into a side room.

"She couldn't have been more than a few hours old when she went into the water," Delphine said, as she examined the tiny body. "The cord had only just been cut."

"Are there any babies missing from the ward?" Martha asked. "Could one of the new mothers have done this?"

Delphine shook her head. "I doubt this child was born in this hospital or any other. My guess would be that the mother gave birth in secret and disposed of her baby before anyone knew what had happened."

"Do you think it was someone from the camp?"

"Possibly. But it could just as easily have been a local German girl. We don't know where the baby was put in the river, do we? The body could have traveled some way downstream before the fishermen found it."

"How many pregnant women are there in the camp?"

"Twenty or so that I know of," Delphine replied. "I have a list of those I've examined, if you want to see it. But there could be others, of course, who haven't come to me. I haven't had time, yet, to find out how many pregnancies there are among the new arrivals."

Martha glanced at Stefan. He was standing next to the baby, but his head was turned away. He was staring at the floor. His hands were clasped together, the knuckles showing white. She saw the muscles of his jaw tighten. She wondered what was going through his mind. Did he know something that Delphine didn't?

CHAPTER 15

It didn't take long for news of the grim discovery to spread throughout the camp. The wedding party fizzled out as word of what had happened passed around the tables.

Kitty came over to the hospital, her face flushed from dancing. Dr. Jankaukas was with her. He carried out a second examination of the baby, confirming Delphine's opinion that the child had been killed before the body entered the river.

It was getting dark when the three women made their way back to the cabin. Martha had summoned a hasty meeting of the blockhouse leaders, but none of them had been able to cast any light on what had happened.

"What would make someone do that?" Kitty said.

"Could be all kinds of reasons," Delphine replied. "If she'd been raped—like the women next door were. It wouldn't have surprised me if any one of them had done something like this."

"But they didn't, did they?"

Delphine shook her head. "There could be others we don't know about carrying babies fathered by Nazis. It's not difficult to conceal a pregnancy if you wear the right clothes."

"But like you said before, it could have been a German woman's baby," Martha said. "God knows what went on around here in the last few months of the war. I've read reports of soldiers raping every woman in sight when the Allies took control of a place."

"That's true." Delphine nodded. "I saw it in Paris. There were some who thought they had a God-given right to sleep with any woman they fancied—whether she wanted it or not."

"Someone from the military is coming here tomorrow," Martha said. "Major McMahon says there has to be an official investigation. If they find out who the mother is, she could face a jail sentence."

"That's appalling." Delphine huffed out a breath. "Whoever she is, she must be in a terrible state, psychologically. What she did will haunt her for the rest of her life. Don't they realize that's punishment enough?"

"What about Jadzia?" Kitty said suddenly. "Has anyone seen her?"

Martha and Delphine looked at her, then at each other.

"Oh my God," Martha whispered. "Why didn't I think of her?"

"But the leader of her blockhouse was at the meeting," Delphine said. "Surely someone would have noticed if she'd disappeared?"

"Not if it happened during the night," Martha said. "She could have gone off into the woods and given birth and come back before anyone realized she was missing."

Delphine nodded. "I suppose we'd better go and find out."

———◆———

The leader of blockhouse six was surprised when Martha and the others came knocking on the door. She was a woman of about the same age as Delphine, dressed in a long cotton nightgown, with an embroidered shawl draped around her shoulders.

"Wszyscy śpią." Everybody is in bed, she said when Kitty explained why they were there. She said she hadn't seen Jadzia since lunchtime, that she'd been resting and was probably asleep by now.

"Tell her we won't disturb anybody," Martha said. "But we need to check that Jadzia is okay."

The woman nodded when Kitty relayed the message. She put her finger to her lips as they filed past.

The American paraphernalia that Jadzia had strung up was still there. Martha pulled back the blanket that screened off the bed. There was no light inside—but the dim glow from an oil lamp in the neighboring compartment revealed the shape of someone lying down.

"I think only one of us should go in," Martha whispered. "We don't want to frighten her."

"I'll go," Kitty whispered back. "I'll just say Delphine's come to see how she is, shall I?"

Martha nodded.

Kitty tiptoed inside and crouched down beside the bed. *"Jadzia, śpisz?"* Are you awake?

Martha saw the covers shift slightly.

"Pielęgniarka jest tutaj—ona właśnie . . ." The nurse is here—she just . . . Kitty never got the chance to finish the sentence. Jadzia gave a strangled sort of cry and scrambled out of the bed. She crouched in the corner, between the wall and the suitcases, her arms bent over her head, as if she expected a bomb to drop at any moment.

⎯⎯◆⎯⎯

Martha and Kitty were waiting inside the entrance of the hospital.

"Will she be all right?" Martha stood up as Delphine emerged from the women's ward.

Delphine nodded. "It's a good thing we found out when we did: her temperature was a hundred and four. She has postpartum sepsis. A few days of penicillin and she should be okay."

"What'll happen then?" Kitty asked.

"I'll call the major in the morning," Martha said. "Ask him to hold off sending anyone until she's had time to recover."

"Will she go to jail?" Kitty whispered.

"Not if I can help it," Martha replied. "Jadzia wasn't in her right mind. They have to see that." She was thinking about a case that had been in the newspapers when she'd worked at the Henry Street Settlement. A young girl who had been abused by her own father had given birth in a public restroom and left the baby in a garbage can. When the case came to court, the lawyer had invoked a clause about the girl's mental state when the crime was committed, and she had been exonerated.

Martha wondered where she could get the legal advice she needed to support Jadzia. Perhaps someone at UNRRA headquarters in Munich would be able to help. It was too late to call now—but she'd have to get hold of someone before the army investigator arrived.

———

Martha lay awake most of the night. Every time she closed her eyes, she relived the scene on the riverbank. The little girl had been so perfect. She should have lived. They should have realized what a devastating effect the news about Frank being married would have on Jadzia. They should have moved her into one of the cabins immediately. Then they could have kept a closer watch on her and . . .

"Can't sleep?" Delphine's voice whispered to her across the gap between the beds. "Neither can I. Shall I make us both a hot drink?"

Downstairs, the women went over it all again. "She seemed so calm last time I examined her," Delphine said. "No one could possibly have guessed what she was planning to do. We can't blame ourselves for what happened."

"But I *feel* guilty," Martha replied. "If I live to be a hundred, I think I'll always feel there was something more I could have done."

"I feel that way about my husband and my son." Delphine cradled her coffee, a curl of steam rising from the mug. "I go over and over it in my head. The day they were arrested, I was in the hospital. I overheard one of the porters talking about Claude. I didn't catch it all—just his name. I was busy with a patient, so I didn't stop to ask questions. I found out later that someone on the ward had told the Germans that Claude was sheltering Allied airmen in the hospital. I kept thinking that if I'd called him after overhearing that conversation, he and Philippe might not have gone to the safe house. They wouldn't have been arrested—and they might both have lived."

Martha put her hand on Delphine's arm. Whatever she said would be inadequate. Delphine would always carry that guilt, no matter how anyone tried to rationalize it.

"I talk to them all the time," Delphine went on. "In the hospital, usually. Sometimes, I hear their voices, telling me what to do. I worry that I'm . . . you know . . ."

"Going a little crazy?" Martha gave a wry smile. "You're not the only one. I often hear my grandma's voice—usually when I'm about to do something stupid. She raised me after my parents died. We were very close."

"How old were you? When they died?"

"Three," Martha replied. "My mother died after giving birth to a baby—a little brother—who only lived a day longer than she did. My dad couldn't take it; he shot himself."

"My God," Delphine murmured.

"I don't really remember them. There was a photo by my bed, so I knew what they looked like, but I guess I never really felt they belonged to me." Martha took a sip of coffee. "It was strange, the other day—when Kitty said she thought her mind had blanked out her parents' faces because remembering would bring back the pain of that last glimpse she had of them—it made me think of how I used to turn that photograph of Mom and Dad around so I couldn't see them. It felt like a bad thing to do, but I couldn't bear them looking at me, because that would start me thinking about why they'd gone and died and left me behind."

Delphine glanced up at the ceiling. "I worry about how Kitty's going to cope if she gets bad news about her parents. In some ways she's so tough—but it's like she's built a wall around her heart. She won't let anyone in. Even when she was spilling it all out, she shied away when I tried to put my arm around her. Did you notice that?"

Martha nodded. "She seemed to let herself go a bit at the wedding though. She looked really happy when she was dancing, especially with Dr. Jankaukas."

"Do you think there's something going on there?" Delphine arched her eyebrows. "I thought he was getting rather fond of one of our new mothers next door: Anka—she's very pretty."

"Well, that shows how much I know." Martha shrugged. "Kitty told me she had a boy back in England who wanted to marry her. I hope she doesn't go back to him; he didn't sound too nice."

"She's a lovely girl. She deserves someone special. Someone who understands what she's suffered, and what she's still got to contend with."

"And in the meantime, she'll have to make do with us." Martha smiled as she said it, but the words had a hollow ring. She was thinking about Jadzia—her mind still reeling with the tragic outcome that could have been averted. She couldn't escape the conclusion that it all came back to her own lack of awareness. Was she so wrapped up in herself that she failed to recognize the struggles of those around her? If the answer to that question was yes, then she shouldn't have come here—these people would be better off without her.

"Is it worth trying to get some sleep, do you think?" Delphine walked over to the window and lifted a corner of the curtain. It was beginning to get light outside.

"I don't think I could." Martha laid her head on her arms. "You go up. I'll have another coffee. I need to go to the office first thing, make some phone calls." She heard the creak of the floorboards as Delphine came back across the room. Then she felt Delphine's hand on her head, stroking her hair.

"It's Sunday," Delphine whispered. "There won't be much you can do. Try not to be so hard on yourself. You're doing your best. That's all any of us can do."

CHAPTER 16

When Kitty woke the next morning, the others had both gone. She dragged herself out of bed, wondering why her legs felt so stiff. Then she remembered the dancing. It had been quite wild—unlike anything she'd ever experienced in England. She'd been amazed at the strength of the men. Even the short ones had had no trouble lifting her off her feet. And a couple of them had thrown her into the air with such gusto she'd almost hit the ceiling.

She smiled at the memory of it, wondering what Fred would have said if he could have seen her. He would be absolutely livid at the idea of her dancing with any other man—let alone a whole roomful. She was still smiling as she made her way to the bathroom. Then she remembered. Jadzia's baby. Like a thundercloud blotting out the sun, the lightness vanished.

As she got dressed, she thought of Delphine, who was probably already at Jadzia's bedside in the hospital. The drugs had knocked her out pretty quickly, but Delphine would want to be there before they wore off, to prevent a repeat of what had happened last night. It had been terrible, seeing Jadzia crouched on the floor, whimpering like a cornered animal. Martha—usually so calm and in control—had looked completely bewildered.

Kitty found a note from Martha on the table when she went downstairs. She wanted Kitty to go to blockhouse six and talk to the women who lived there in a bid to get evidence that might help Martha plead Jadzia's case with the military.

Kitty glanced at the clock on the wall. It was quite early. And it was Sunday, so the DPs wouldn't be up and about yet. She decided to take a walk to the gates first. She needed to return Sergeant Lewis's camera.

It was unusually quiet outside. The curtains of the cabins on either side were still drawn, and no sound came from either house—not even the faintest cry from any of the seven babies who now lived there. It was as if the whole camp was in mourning for the child found in the river.

As Kitty neared the gates, she saw that they were open. It looked as if the guards were changing shifts. She spotted Sergeant Lewis handing over the keys to the jeep parked next to the guardhouse. A cloud of dust obscured his face as the departing officer revved up the engine and pulled away.

"Good morning," she called. "I've brought back your camera."

He smiled when she gave it to him. "Thanks. I wasn't expecting it back so soon. Hope you got some good pictures." He raked his short black hair with his fingers. She thought he looked tired. Martha had told her he was on duty when the baby's body was discovered. She wondered if he'd been able to sleep after witnessing something like that.

"You must let me know how much I owe you for the film," she said.

"Oh, nothing," he said. "I can get another roll back at base. I can get your photos developed if you want. They have a darkroom."

"Really? That would be great. I was wondering how to do that—thought I might have to scrounge a lift to Fürstenfeldbruck and go searching for a chemist's shop."

"You mean a pharmacy?" He grinned. "You *are* from England. I thought so."

"Well, actually, I'm not. I went to live there a few years back—but I was born in Austria." She was surprised at how liberating it felt, being able to drop that into a casual conversation, no longer having to keep up the pretense about where she came from.

"That's east of Germany, right?"

Kitty nodded. "I lived in the capital, Vienna."

"Do they speak German there? Is that how you know it?"

Kitty nodded.

"But you speak Polish, too—how come?"

Kitty wondered how he knew. She found it a little disconcerting to think that she had been talked about by the GIs who came in and out of the camp. "My mother was born in Poland," she said.

"Guess you're a mongrel, then, like me." He swept his hands in front of his face. "But in my case, it's a bit more obvious."

"Are you Chinese?"

"My grandfather was from Hong Kong. He came to the US to build the railroad."

"Hmm." Kitty tilted her head as she looked back at him. "Lewis doesn't sound Chinese."

"It's Welsh. My dad's side of the family were miners from the South Wales Valleys."

"Where does your family live now?"

"San Francisco." He put his hand inside his jacket and took out a wallet. Opening it up, he held it out to her. Encased in the left-hand section was a black-and-white shot of a smiling, fair-haired man who towered over the petite woman he had his arm around. In the background was a bridge that looked as if it were floating on a cloud.

Kitty felt a familiar lump form in her throat as she looked at it. "It's . . . a lovely photo," she said.

"Where's home for you now?" he said, as he slid the wallet back into his pocket.

She glanced down at the dusty ground. "Here, I suppose." She looked up, saw the confusion on his face. "It's a long story," she murmured.

"There's coffee in there." He tipped his head toward the guard-house. "You want some?"

———————

At the hospital, Jadzia was sleeping.

"She needs to rest until the infection subsides," Delphine said to Martha. "I gave her another dose of the tranquilizer half an hour ago."

"How long will she sleep for?"

"She should be out until well into the afternoon. Father Josef's going to look in on her later. I'm hoping he might be able to talk to her—calm her down a bit."

Martha nodded. "He's been good with the other women in here. He seems to understand what they're going through, despite . . ." She trailed off, not wanting to sound disrespectful.

"Being a man?" Delphine finished the sentence for her. "And an unmarried one, at that."

"He's not a bit like the priests at the church I used to go to as a child—they always seemed so remote."

"He doesn't judge people; that's what I like about him," Delphine said. "I wonder if he was always like that or whether the war changed him?"

"His faith must be mighty strong to have survived what he went through." Martha didn't know if Kitty had told Delphine what Father Josef had said about the Nazis using him for medical experiments. She hoped not. It would be a terrible thing for Delphine to know. Bad enough that her husband and son had died in Dachau, without imagining what they might have suffered while they were prisoners there.

"He's going to bury the baby tomorrow," Delphine said. "He said no one needs to be there but him."

"I think that's best," Martha replied. "I don't suppose it would help Jadzia if we waited till she was well enough to be there."

Delphine shook her head. "He must have known she was pregnant, mustn't he?"

"Who?" Martha frowned.

"The boyfriend. I wonder if he ever thinks about her, now he's back in America with his wife and family? If he has any idea of the misery he's caused?"

"I doubt it," Martha said. "You can imagine him boasting about it to his pals in a bar somewhere, can't you?"

"And there must be hundreds like Jadzia across Germany. I suppose not all the men were so uncaring; some of them really would marry the girls if they were allowed to."

"They have to see that, don't they—the US government, I mean? The major said things might change by the end of the year."

"I hope so." Delphine glanced at the sleeping figure in the bed. "But whatever happens, it's not going to help her, is it?"

—————

Sergeant Lewis was leaning against the desk in the guardhouse, a mug of coffee in his hand. Kitty was sitting in the only chair. Despite the basic furnishings and the bare wooden walls, it was cozy. She wasn't sure why, but she'd found herself telling him things that she'd never felt able to say to Fred.

The sergeant's name was Charles, but he said he preferred Charlie. She'd smiled when he'd said that—and told him that her real name was Katya, but she'd always liked Kitty better.

"The old ladies I lived with in London gave me that name," she said. "They said it would be safer if my name sounded English. There was so much anti-German feeling in England. Telling people that I *wasn't* German didn't seem to make any difference. So, that first year in London, I went from being Katya Blumenthal to Kitty Bloom."

"It must have been so hard," he said, "being all on your own, not speaking the language."

"It was," she replied. "But the worst thing was the guilt. I was safe in England, but my parents were stuck in Austria. I'd tried—and failed—to get them work permits. If only they . . ." She couldn't finish the sentence.

"Father Josef says he feels like that," Charlie said. "He stops by here sometimes when I'm on duty. He once told me there are days he wakes up and wishes he'd died, because he feels so bad for surviving when so many didn't make it."

"I remember when you were telling me on the phone about Father Josef being in Dachau. You said you were there when Dachau was liberated." Kitty looked at him over the rim of her coffee mug. She felt as if she were standing on the edge of an abyss. She didn't want to hear what horrors Charlie had seen—and yet she felt compelled to find out what he knew about the place.

Charlie nodded. "I don't talk about it much. Only to Father Josef—I think he talks to me because I saw Dachau, but I wasn't a prisoner." The desk creaked as he shifted his weight. "I can't imagine how awful it must be for you, wondering if your parents wound up in a hellhole like that."

"He told me there were Jews at Dachau, but they were kept in a separate section, so he never got to see them. I know there were people from Vienna in the camp, so my parents could have been sent there." She felt her throat constricting with emotion. Talking about them was like swallowing broken glass.

"There *were* Jewish survivors—men and women." Charlie was looking at the floor. Kitty could only guess what images had come into his mind's eye. "They were taken to other camps. I don't know where they would be now." He glanced up. "I'm sorry. I wish I could help you."

"It's okay," she said. "You have helped, just by letting me talk. I didn't mean to rattle on—it's just that I've been keeping it in for so long . . ."

He shook his head. "You don't have to apologize. It helps me, too. The guys at the base, you know, they don't like it if you go on about things you've seen. They say: 'We all had a lousy war—what makes you so special?'"

Kitty gave him a rueful smile. How strange, she thought, that those men sounded just like Fred.

The next morning, Martha was on the phone to Munich for more than half an hour. She was eventually put through to a lawyer who acted on behalf of UNRRA—and who, thankfully, spoke good English. After listening to Martha's description of what had happened to Jadzia, the lawyer told her there was a statement she could enter on the incident report that would result in the military taking no further action: she was to say that Jadzia had ended her baby's life due to temporary derangement caused by the agony of giving birth.

After she'd put the phone down, Martha stared at what she'd jotted down—just a handful of words that would, hopefully, change the course of Jadzia's life. The lawyer had promised she would not be arrested or imprisoned. Once she had recovered physically, she could make a fresh start. Quite how that could be achieved was another matter. Perhaps, like the mothers of the babies fathered by Nazi officers, the best thing would be for Jadzia to be transferred to another camp where no one knew what had happened in the past. It remained to be seen whether she would be mentally strong enough to cope with such a move. Meanwhile, Martha thought, all they could do was keep a close eye on her.

When she left the office, Martha went to look for Stefan. She found him in the woods behind the chapel. He was carving something from a tree branch. A spade was stuck into the ground a few yards from where he was sitting.

"It's a cross," he said when she asked him what he was doing. He tilted his head toward the spade. She saw the pile of earth and pine needles beside it. "And then I will make . . . a box—how do you call it in English?"

"A coffin." She stared at the place where the grave would be. The image of the baby, so pale and still on the hospital table, was etched inside her head. It would remain there always, paired with the memory of that other tiny body, Cecile—the baby girl she had named after her grandmother—who had come into the world too soon.

"Coffin," Stefan repeated. He gave a broken sort of sigh.

"Stefan?" Martha caught her own pain reflected in his eyes, as if, somehow, he'd read her mind and understood her sorrow.

"It's a terrible thing, no? To make this for a baby?"

"Yes," she breathed. "The *most* terrible thing."

"Don't cry."

She rubbed her hand across her face, ashamed of the tears that had escaped and given her away.

"Come, sit here." He put his arm around her shoulder, guiding her to the woodpile in the trees.

"I . . . I'm sorry," she mumbled. "I . . . it's just . . ."

"A baby died—that is a sad thing." She felt the warmth of him as he held her close.

"Yesterday, when we saw her, lying there on the riverbank . . . it brought back memories for me." Martha had never talked about it to anyone. Not even Arnie. For him, the death of their child had been a taboo subject. "I had a baby," she whispered. "A little girl. But she died."

"You have this." He took a piece of cloth from his pocket—white cotton with ragged edges. It felt soft against her skin. When she looked up, she saw that he was crying, too. Instinctively she hugged him to her, cradling his head against her shoulder, stroking his hair. For a moment they clung to each other. It was as if they were frozen in time. He murmured something she couldn't make out.

"What is it?" She cupped his face in her hands.

"I feel the same way—like you." His voice was husky with grief. "I have a little girl. I think she is dead." He gazed at the trees above her head as he told her about his daughter, Lubya, who had been three years old when he was arrested by the Nazis and transported to Germany.

"And your wife . . . ?" The word felt uncomfortable, like gristle in a piece of meat.

"I wrote letters when I worked at the airplane factory," he said, "but nothing came from Poland." He closed his eyes. "I made a mark on the wall for every day that passed. It grew—like a child grows. Sometimes when I looked, it broke my heart."

Martha felt something thicken in her throat at the thought of what he must have suffered all this time. How had he remained so calm, so stoic, in the weeks she had known him? How could he have kept it all inside for so long? She should have had the courage to ask, should have admitted to herself that tiptoeing around the subject of his past was as much for her sake as for his. The truth was, she hadn't *wanted* to know.

"You'll go back? When the border opens?" She lowered her hands. Their skin was no longer touching.

"Yes. It's what I'm waiting for. To find where they have gone."

❦

Martha stumbled through the door of the cabin. She needed to be alone for a while. But as she stepped inside, she heard a noise in the kitchen.

"I couldn't eat breakfast," Delphine called, "but I'm really hungry now." Her head appeared around the door. "Have you had anything? Oh, Martha, you look terrible!"

Martha slumped onto one of the dining chairs. "It's just . . . I . . . I saw the grave—for the baby. Stefan was making a cross."

Delphine came to sit beside her. "You're bound to be upset. Seeing him doing that—it makes it so real, so . . . final."

"I started crying." Martha stared at a ring on the surface of the table where something hot had marked it. "Then he got upset, too. He told me he had a daughter in Warsaw who was three years old when he last saw her. He doesn't know if she's still alive."

Delphine put her hand on Martha's. "What else did he tell you?"

"That he hasn't heard from his wife since he was taken by the Germans. He wrote letters but . . ." She couldn't finish the sentence. She blinked at the mark on the table, trying to hold back tears.

"He'll be going through hell." Delphine's voice was level, but it had an intensity that made Martha look up.

"I'm sorry," Martha whispered. "I shouldn't have spoken about it. You of all people must know how it feels."

Delphine nodded. "The not-knowing is like slow torture. But for him, there's an extra dimension."

"Why?"

"His heart is split in two," Delphine replied. "Forgive me, but I've seen the way he looks at you."

Martha stared, wordless, through blurred eyes.

"I thought I was imagining it at first," Delphine went on. "But then, at the wedding . . . You looked so lovely in that dress—he couldn't take his eyes off you." She sighed softly. "I was so afraid for you. I thought there must be someone. I mean, everyone in this place has lost family, haven't they? I wanted to say something to you. Warn you about . . ." She closed her eyes, shaking her head. "About . . . getting too close to him. But I just didn't know how to say it."

Martha tried to speak, but her voice caught in her throat.

"Let me get you some water." Delphine shifted in her chair.

Martha shook her head. "I'm okay." Her voice was croaky. She coughed and tried again. "I was always afraid to ask him about his life before the war. And as time went on, I guess I pushed it to the back of my mind." She squeezed Delphine's hand, as if holding on for dear life. "It could never have come to anything, could it? Even if we were both free. Can you imagine what they would have said in Munich? The woman running the camp getting involved with a DP?"

Delphine's face was unreadable. "That's what you're going to have to keep telling yourself for now. But we don't know what he's going to find when he goes back. And you won't be running the camp forever. One day, there'll be no need for this place."

PART TWO

CHAPTER 17

September 1945

As the nights lengthened in Bavaria, the mornings turned colder. Sometimes a mist crept over the river during the night, giving the entrance to the camp a ghostly look—as if, in passing through the gates, you were leaving one dimension and entering another. Martha was no longer certain which one felt more real to her now: the camp or the world outside.

Much had happened in the last weeks of summer. To everyone's amazement and delight, the young boy Edek Dijak had found his father in Munich and brought him back to Seidenmühle for a joyful reunion with the rest of the family.

That same week, the Japanese had surrendered, which had triggered wild celebrations at the military base down the road. A group of single women from the camp had been invited to the Victory Dance, chaperoned by Kitty. When they returned, Kitty had had a look in her eyes that Martha hadn't seen before—a look that had persisted long after the effects of half a dozen bottles of Budweiser had worn off. Despite the weight of worry about her missing parents, she had a radiance about her. But subtle questions about who might be the cause of it had yielded nothing. If Kitty had fallen for someone, she was keeping it to herself.

After V-J Day, movement in the American zone had become a little easier. Most of the mothers and babies in the cabins next door had been transferred to a camp in the British zone. And Jadzia had moved to Frankfurt, due to another small miracle worked by Father Josef. He had contacted a fellow survivor of Dachau—a German priest—who had offered Jadzia a job as a housekeeper.

On the day she left the camp, Jadzia had looked very different from the young woman who had burst into the office demanding a translation of the note from the army base. She had cut off her beautiful blond hair. The short spiky style made her look more like a child than a woman—especially as she had lost so much weight after giving birth. But, thanks to the care given to her by Delphine and Father Josef, she was well enough—both physically and mentally—to start a new life. She would never forget what she had done, but they had given her the strength to cope with the guilt and the grief.

Not all the single mothers had left the camp. Dr. Jankaukas had married Anka in the chapel in the woods and was planning to adopt Mikolaj, her little boy. They were living in one of the vacant cabins, while Wolf had moved into the other, sharing the place with the other young medical auxiliaries. It was easier for Delphine to have them close by, and she looked after them the way a mother would.

Having the children next door had helped Martha learn some Polish. In the evenings, they all sat outside together. Sometimes Aleksandra would come by with little Rodek, and Martha would bounce him on her knee or give him his bottle. These nights reminded her of her grandma's house in New Orleans, when all the neighbors gathered on their stoops until darkness fell.

Her new language skills meant she relied less on Stefan's assistance in the day-to-day running of the camp. She hated distancing herself from him, but it was the only way to keep her feelings in check.

Martha's days never had much of a routine—life in the camp was far too unpredictable for that. The one constant was going to collect the mail, which arrived at eleven o'clock each weekday morning. This morning, a bigger pile than usual had been dropped off at the guard-house. She riffled through the letters as she made her way back, hoping to see Arnie's familiar scrawl. She had written to ask him for a divorce.

"Anything interesting?" Kitty looked up as Martha stepped into the office.

"Just the same old same old." Martha dropped the mail onto the desk. "And a few letters for the DPs."

Kitty began to sort them into piles. "There's one here for Father Josef." She picked up the envelope, studying the postmark. "It's from Vienna."

"What?" Martha went to see.

"Can I take it to him?" Kitty was already on her feet.

⸺

Kitty found Father Josef in the hospital. He was sitting at the bedside of a man whose leg was plastered up to the thigh.

"He won't be much longer, I don't think," Delphine said. "They've been chatting for ages—about football, of all things. Can you believe a man can spend his days chopping down trees but breaks his leg kicking a ball around a field?"

"I just need to ask him what's in this." Kitty held out the letter. "I know I should have waited for him to have picked it up himself, but . . ."

Delphine nodded. "You must be on pins. I'll go and get him."

Father Josef stood up before Delphine reached him. He grasped the edge of the bed for support, then made his way slowly across the ward.

"Come," he said when Kitty showed him the envelope. "Let's go and open it outside."

They sat on the low wall in front of the hospital. The priest tore open the flap and slid the letter out. Kitty could see the insignia of the bishop's palace embossed in the top right-hand corner of the paper—but she could only guess at what the few lines of black type contained.

"I'm afraid the apartment block where your parents lived was destroyed in a bombing raid in 1943." He turned to her. "They might not have been living there, though. It says that many of the apartments were empty when it happened." He turned the paper over. "They've located a person who might have information. They have a name, that's all. Someone called Clara Schmidt—a former employee at your parents' business."

"Yes," Kitty breathed. "I remember Clara; she wasn't called Schmidt, but I suppose she must have got married. She would have been about sixteen or seventeen when I left. She lived above the shop."

"Well, she doesn't live there now. I'm afraid the shop was destroyed, too."

"Do they know where she is? Can I write to her?"

Father Josef handed the letter to Kitty. It said that a woman from a church in the Vienna suburb of Floridsdorf had responded to an appeal made from the pulpit for information about the Blumenthals. She knew nothing of their whereabouts, but gave the name of Clara, who had lived with her for a while in 1941 after the apartment was destroyed. Unfortunately, the letter went on, the forwarding address the woman had given was of no use: Clara must have moved on again. But further attempts would be made to trace her.

The words blurred on the page as Kitty stared at them. "Clara," she whispered. "Where are you?"

"There has to be a way to find her," Father Josef said. "If the Church draws a blank, we could try placing an advertisement in one of the newspapers."

"But what if she died? What if the next place she went to was bombed?"

"I know it's hard, but try to be patient." He took the letter and folded it back into the envelope. "Is there anything else you remember about her? Did she have relatives in another part of the city?"

"Her mother lived with her—I don't know of anyone else. And they went to a church called Saint Leopold's in Alexander-Poch-Platz; I remember that."

"I'll let them know," he said. "I think we should wait at least a few more weeks before we try the newspapers—I imagine they're being inundated with requests like yours. And in the meantime, there's another Red Cross list due soon, isn't there?"

"It should come this weekend." There had been two more lists since the first one Kitty had pored over. They got shorter each time because fewer people were arriving at the camps. She wasn't very hopeful of what the latest list would contain.

As she made her way back to the office, Clara was in her mind's eye. She remembered envying Clara's auburn hair, wishing hers were that color. And she'd watched, fascinated, as Clara applied scarlet lipstick in the mirror that had hung in the showroom. That was something Kitty had copied as soon as she started earning her own money.

Knowing that Clara could hold the key to what had happened to her parents—that she could be living somewhere in the city, probably not far from where the shop had once stood—was so tantalizing. It made the compulsion to go to Vienna even stronger. It occurred to Kitty that she could go to Saint Leopold's herself—question every member of the congregation if necessary. She wondered why no one there had responded to the appeal from the pulpit, which surely must have been made, as it was at the church in Floridsdorf. Perhaps no one there knew where Clara had gone. Perhaps going there would be a waste of time. And that was the only lead she had. Father Josef was right: she was just going to have to try to be patient.

On the first day of October, Martha received a phone call that sent shockwaves through the camp. She was informed by UNRRA headquarters in Munich that an agreement had been reached by the Allied countries to recognize the provisional government of national unity in Poland, which meant that DPs could now start to be repatriated. Martha was instructed to ask for volunteers to take the first train, which needed to depart before the snows arrived in Bavaria.

Kitty stared, open-mouthed, as Martha relayed the news. "But I thought the major said it wouldn't happen before the spring?"

"He did." Martha nodded. "But somehow it's all been sped up."

There was a crowd of people waiting outside the mess hall when Martha and Kitty went to pin the notice of repatriation to the wall. A map of the newly divided Poland, showing the region now held by the Russians, caused consternation among the DPs.

"Some of them are saying they can't go back," Kitty whispered. "They say their villages are on the wrong side of the line."

Martha glanced around. The fear on the faces of some of the DPs was unmistakable. One old man was weeping. But others had the fire of hope in their eyes.

It's what I'm waiting for. To find out where they have gone. Stefan's words came back to her with stinging clarity.

⸻

The next day, Martha called a meeting of the blockhouse leaders. Stefan and Father Josef were there, too. Martha had deliberately avoided Stefan since the news of the impending repatriation had broken, knowing how desperate he was to get back to Warsaw. Why would he not want to be on the first available train? As the leaders filed in for the meeting, he took a seat on the opposite side of the room. His head was bowed, as if he couldn't bear to meet her eyes.

Martha began by asking each of the leaders to report how many in their blockhouse had volunteered for repatriation. She jotted down the numbers and added them up. Two hundred and six in all—just half a dozen more than the minimum number the army had requested. She had thought there would be more.

"There's a lot of uncertainty," Father Josef said. "It seems Stalin got his way in creating a puppet government in Poland. Our country is the sacrifice he demanded for what the Red Army did to defeat the Nazis. It doesn't matter which side of the line you're on—his men already control everything. There have been stories going around about what the Russians are doing to people who return from the West."

"What sort of stories?" Martha asked.

"That men are being sent to labor camps in Siberia," the priest replied.

"Why?"

"Because the Russians think they will have become infected with dangerous ideas. They have to be rehabilitated, as they put it, before they can fit in to society."

"Is it true?"

"No one really knows. That's the trouble—until people get there, they can't know."

One of the leaders began to speak. Martha caught a couple of words she understood, but he was going too fast for her to make sense of it.

"He says he has nothing left to lose by going back," Father Josef said. "He buried his wife and son after their house was blitzed. All he wants now is to help others get home—to find their families if they can."

Martha nodded. Clearly, for some DPs, that need was driving fear out the window. "What about you?" she asked the priest.

"It was a difficult decision. I prayed for many hours last night. They say the churches in Warsaw have nearly all been destroyed, that the Germans almost razed the city to the ground. I could go back and try to help rebuild—but I believe God wants me to wait, to be here for those left behind."

Martha glanced at Stefan, who had remained silent up till now. "Will you go, Stefan?" She could feel her heart thudding. She had thought it would be less painful to ask him in front of other people, but as he lifted his head, her hands began to tremble. She clasped them together under the table.

He didn't look at her. He just tilted his head toward the leader of his blockhouse. "My name is on the list," he said.

———

A week of frenzied activity followed. Documents had to be prepared for every person leaving the camp, winter coats and boots had to be sourced, and they would need enough food to see them through the ten-day journey.

"They're sending a military escort with the train," Martha said, as Kitty came into the office with water to make more coffee. "They want a female officer on board, too."

"You want to send me?" Kitty stopped short of the desk, slopping water over the side of the jug.

"They need someone who speaks good Polish. You won't have to go the whole way—just as far as the first station over the Czech border."

"Well . . . I . . . ," Kitty faltered. "If you want me to go, of course I will. But won't it make things hard here, with just the two of you doing everything?"

"It's only for a few days," Martha said. "And we'll have two hundred and six less mouths to feed." She got up and took the jug from Kitty. As she spooned Nescafé into the mugs, her words rang in her ears. *Two hundred and six less mouths to feed.* And one of them was Stefan. She hadn't seen him since the meeting with the DP leaders. Throwing herself into the preparations for the departure, she'd tried to block out the painful reality that, in a matter of days, he would be gone. But his face was always there, on the margins of her mind's eye, slipping into full view as she lay down in bed at night, invading her dreams, appearing again in the no-man's-land between sleeping and waking.

On the morning before Kitty was due to board the train, a letter came from Vienna. She ran to find Father Josef.

"They have a new address for Clara Schmidt," he said, handing over the letter for her to see.

"Oh! I remember this street; it's near my old school." Kitty stared at the few lines of type. Her brain was going at a hundred miles an hour. "I must write to her—straightaway. I'll have to get it posted before tonight." Kitty turned to the priest, thinking aloud. "There's so much still to do before we leave. Do you think I could post it at Fürstenfeldbruck in the morning? But it'd be too early, wouldn't it?" She blew out a breath. "If I could just jump on a magic carpet and fly there . . ."

"Well, you could, in a way—if that's what you really want."

"What do you mean?"

"You could go to Vienna on the way back from Poland."

Kitty stared at him, open-mouthed. "How?"

"The route you'll be following takes you close to the Austrian border. Once you've handed the passengers over, you could make a detour south, to Vienna."

"Is that really possible?"

He nodded. "There used to be a direct line to Vienna from a place called Brno. I don't know if the route is still operating—you'd have to check."

"You think I could do it? That they'd let me?"

"You'd have to get permission, of course—and some sort of pass from the military, I imagine. Would you like me to come and talk to Mrs. Radford?"

"No, it's okay, but thank you for offering." As she walked away, Kitty hoped she hadn't sounded ungrateful. But she'd been fighting her own battles since she was twelve years old. She didn't need anyone to make a case for her—she was perfectly capable of doing it for herself.

Martha had mixed feelings when the plan was explained to her. She could see how eager Kitty was. She'd waited so long for a chance like this. But Martha couldn't help worrying how Kitty would cope if Clara had bad news about Kitty's parents. Would it be better to find out by mail that your parents were dead? Kitty had to find out one way or the other. At least meeting Clara face-to-face would allow her to ask questions.

"You'd have to have an escort," Martha said. "I wouldn't want you traveling alone. But I think we could arrange for one of the GIs to go with you; after all, they won't have much to do once the DPs have been handed over."

Kitty nodded.

"Let me make a phone call," Martha said. "You go and carry on with getting the food organized—I'll come find you."

It was late afternoon before Martha managed to get an answer from Major McMahon. He said that he was reluctant to allow any of his men to go off on what he described as a "jaunt" to Vienna. But one of the officers assigned to escort the train had leave accumulated and had volunteered to accompany Kitty.

Martha found her loading boxes of canned milk into the truck that would form part of the convoy leaving the camp at first light the following day.

"Good news." Martha was a little breathless from running all the way from the office. "They've agreed to provide an escort—and you can stay overnight at the army HQ in Vienna if you need to."

"Thank you!" Kitty looked close to tears. She put down the box she was carrying and sank down on the tailgate of the truck.

"You're clearly popular at the base." Martha smiled. "One of the GIs volunteered to take some leave to go with you."

"Really? Do you know who it is?"

"Sergeant Lewis."

"Oh? That's kind of him." Kitty's face gave no hint of what she was thinking, but Martha wondered whether he was the one who had sent her back from the Victory Dance with that twinkle in her eye. She hoped so. Because Kitty was going to need someone who cared about her when she got to Vienna.

⊰⊱

The sun had sunk below the trees by the time Martha left the office. As she passed by blockhouse fifteen, the urge to go inside was overwhelming. All day she'd been thinking of Stefan, marking the hours as they ebbed away. This time tomorrow he would be hundreds of miles from her.

Delphine had tactfully offered to vacate the cabin for a couple of hours to allow them some time together on this last evening. But Martha had declined. It would have been unbearable to sit over a meal with him, to raise a glass to the future. She had decided it would be better for them both if their goodbyes were said in public, at the station. That way, she would be forced to keep her feelings under control.

But as she made her way along the darkening path, a figure emerged from the shadows.

"Can I walk with you?"

She could see his breath in the cool evening air. Her heart raced as he took her arm, guiding her away from the path, into the forest. "Stefan . . . I . . ."

"Please . . ." He drew her closer. She could feel that his body was shaking. "I have to see you," he whispered. "I cannot go away without saying this to you."

His lips were almost brushing her forehead. She longed to wrap her arms around his neck, to find his mouth with hers.

"I don't want to leave, but I have to. You understand?"

She nodded, not trusting herself to speak. She felt his arms encircle her. He held her tight. The warmth of his skin, the musky scent of him, triggered an agonizing surge of longing. It was unbearable—to feel like this when she had to let him go. In the short time they had known one another, he had rekindled what Arnie had snuffed out. He'd given her hope. And now he was leaving. And she didn't know if she would ever see him again.

CHAPTER 18

The departing DPs sat next to their piles of luggage in the chilly morning air, waiting for the trucks to come. Their faces were alive in a way that marked them out from the others in the camp who had turned out to wave them off. The taunts from those staying behind about Russians waiting over the border to pack DPs off to Siberia fell on deaf ears. These people were returning to where their hearts were.

Martha was glad that Aleksandra and Marek were not among those leaving the camp. Last night she had hugged little Rodek to her as they had all sat outside the cabin. His parents were unaware of just how much comfort that gave her. It wasn't just about the baby she had lost. Holding Rodek close had helped—just for a moment—to blot out the pain of Stefan's imminent departure.

When the trucks were all loaded, Martha got into the car and Kitty jumped in beside her. They were bringing up the rear of the convoy, driving behind the supply vehicle, which was packed with food to be loaded onto the train: sacks of loaves, great wheels of Bavarian cheese, crates of tinned meat and milk.

"Have you got your identity card? And your rail pass?" Martha realized she sounded like a mother sending a child off to college. But she was more worried about Kitty's side trip to Vienna than she was letting on.

"Yes." There was a lightness in Kitty's voice. If she was afraid of what she would discover, she was doing a good job of hiding it.

"Promise me one thing," Martha said. "Whatever happens, just let me know. You can wire a message from the base."

"I promise," Kitty replied. "Please don't worry. I know the odds are stacked against me. I just need to know the truth."

Martha nodded. Just like Stefan. But unlike him, whether she found her parents or not, Kitty was free to return to the camp. But the military had made it clear that that was not an option for the DPs who were about to board the train. Once they left Seidenmühle, they were barred from readmission, whatever lay in store for them when they reached their homeland.

Major McMahon was waiting at the station when they arrived, along with a contingent of five GIs. Martha couldn't help feeling a stab of envy when she saw the look that passed between Kitty and Sergeant Lewis.

The major went along the platform, positioning a man in front of each carriage to check paperwork. As the DPs clambered aboard, Martha went from car to car, blowing kisses to the families, clasping the outstretched hands of the men who stood in the doorways.

Stefan was one of the last to board the train. He stood within grasping distance of the carriage furthest from the engine, waiting for her. She couldn't give him a last hug—not with so many people watching. The formal handshake made her insides turn to ice.

"Do widzenia," he murmured. Till we meet again.

Like a prayer, Martha whispered it back. But in her heart, she knew that it wouldn't—*couldn't*—ever be.

As he hauled himself up by the handle of the door, Stefan let his free hand swing down and brushed her cheek with his fingers. He stood in the doorway and followed her with his eyes as the train began to move.

"And they're off!" The major came striding up to where she stood. "Let's hope the Russkies don't eat them for breakfast . . ."

A great cheer went up from the carriages as the train gathered momentum. The DPs were waving flags made of scraps of red and white fabric—the colors of Poland. The cheering was a cry of hope. Everyone on board wanted desperately to believe that their country would really be free, as promised.

Martha stood on the empty platform, looking down the track, watching the plume of smoke rise to meet clouds tinged pink and gold with the rising sun.

"You should smile," the major said. "This is what you came here for: to get them home."

⊰⊱

It was a lonely drive back to the camp. The roads were deserted. Even the fields looked bleak, stripped of their grain crops and vegetables. Martha wondered where the train would be now. The first stop was Nuremberg, where more cars would be added. Then on to two more German stations before crossing into Czechoslovakia. It would be almost halfway through October by the time the train reached Poland. According to the army, it was already snowing there. An image flashed in front of her: Stefan searching for his wife and child in an icy wasteland of bombed-out buildings. What would he do if he couldn't find them? What if the Russians arrested him and took him away before he'd even had the chance to start looking? What if . . . She braked sharply at the gates of Seidenmühle. She had to stop thinking about it—about him. But the way her insides surged at the memory of him kissing her goodbye in the darkness of the trees made that next to impossible. The image of his face as the train had pulled away was etched inside her head. She knew that look would come back to haunt her whenever she closed her eyes.

She couldn't face going back to the office. Not yet. Instead, she pulled up a few yards beyond the gates and wandered down to the river. The early morning mist had melted away. Dew sparkled on the grass along the bank. She sank down, feeling the cold wetness on the palms of her hands, not caring if the moisture seeped into her clothes. The water flowed past her, smooth and silent. In the distance she could hear the people left behind going about their daily business. It was impossible to think of Stefan not being among them.

She thought of the day, nearly four months ago, when she had sat beside a different river, halfway across the world. That morning in New York, she had been scared and excited in equal measure: scared of Arnie finding her and dragging her back, scared of the flight across the ocean—but excited at the prospect of the new, unknown life that lay ahead. What would she have done if she could have seen into the future? If she could have felt the heartbreak of standing on that platform as the train pulled away?

As she gazed across the water, she saw a feather, white and perfect, drifting past her. Her eyes followed it as it moved gently with the current. It looked so delicate, so fragile—and yet it glided down the river with all the strength and balance of a boat. It was not struggling to escape. It was simply allowing itself to go where time and the water would take it.

She watched it disappear around the bend that would carry it to the faster stretch by the mill wheel. No way to know if it would stay afloat in that choppy water. Perhaps it would go under for a while. Perhaps it would emerge a few yards downstream, bedraggled but intact.

Martha stood up, wiping her wet hands against the sides of her jacket. As she walked back to the car, she felt a curious sense of calm. This was the path she had chosen. She couldn't fight against the direction it had taken. Accepting this was a kind of surrender. But it was the only way to find peace.

As she drove into the main part of the camp, she caught sight of a figure coming toward her, waving. It was Aleksandra. She was carrying Rodek on her hip, and she gave a shy smile when Martha got out of the car.

"I make special breakfast for you." Aleksandra had mastered English quicker than Martha had picked up Polish. "You like take him? I bring it to cabin."

Martha took her godson in her arms. He didn't make a sound. As she walked down the path, she bent her head, breathing in the scent of his hair. She whispered his name, stroking the soft skin of his cheek. He gazed up at her, his eyes impossibly wise, as if he could see beyond this moment, this place, to a future she couldn't even contemplate.

CHAPTER 19

Kitty could hear people singing in the boxcars on either side of her. She wasn't surprised that they sounded so happy. She thought that the countryside they had passed through on the journey was the most beautiful she had ever seen. Although winter was not far away, the trees in the valleys were still cloaked in red and gold. Jewel-colored pheasants darted across the fields as horse-drawn plows made slow, dark lines through the pale stubble left behind by the harvest. Once, when the train had stopped early in the morning, she'd seen a hare, just yards away, its nose twitching as it sniffed the air. She'd pulled out her sketch-book in a bid to capture it before it darted off across the fields. Charlie had seen it, too. He'd brought half a loaf for their breakfast, and they'd eaten it together, sitting on the cinder path between the tracks.

The town of Ostrava was the last one on the Czech side, before the train crossed the border into Poland. There was a last flurry of trading at the station. Cigarettes were swapped for finger-licking pastries and bottles of plum brandy.

Then the train began the final few miles of its journey east. The first village inside Poland was called Zebrzydowice. As they approached, the DPs began singing the Polish national anthem, which Kitty recognized because her mother used to hum it sometimes in the workshop—usually when she was tackling a particularly tricky piece of sewing.

Soldiers boarded the train when it stopped. They weren't checking papers—that would come when they reached the bigger town of Dziedzice. But they climbed into each car and took a good look at the people inside. Kitty noticed the hammer-and-sickle badge on the cap of the man who came into her car. It was the first time she had encountered a Russian soldier.

Once the train began to move again, the singing resumed. The DPs were in high spirits now, some of them, no doubt, fueled by the Czech brandy. By the time they reached the final stop, people were leaning out of the open doors, waving the homemade flags they'd brought all the way from Bavaria.

As the DPs began to unload their belongings to transfer to the train to Warsaw, Charlie took photographs. Kitty saw Stefan shouldering a bundle belonging to one of the elderly women who had helped run the sewing class. She hadn't seen much of him on the journey. He hadn't sat outside or stood around on the tracks with the other men, who seemed to take every possible opportunity to get out for a smoke.

She saw Charlie walking over to him, preparing to get a shot. But Stefan waved him away. Head down, he sped up as he made for the Warsaw train, the old lady trailing in his wake.

When all the goodbyes had been said, Kitty went to buy a bottle of Polish vodka. This had been Martha's suggestion—to bring back to the camp something that would prove that she had entered the country and come back without any problem. On a board outside the shop, the prices of various items were written in chalk. Kitty spent a few minutes studying them, trying to remember how many zlotys Charlie had said you could get for one American dollar. She began to jot a few of the prices down in her notebook, figuring it would be useful for the people back at the camp to know how much things would cost if they decided to go back. Then she had a better idea: she could get Charlie to take a photo of the board.

Out of the corner of her eye, she became aware of someone watching her. It was a man in uniform. He wore the high-topped boots of the Russian military she had seen at the border. As she stood there, he began to move closer. She caught sight of the pistol holster strapped around her waist.

"What you do?" The question was delivered in English, which surprised her. The tone of his voice echoed the mean look in his eyes.

"Nothing." She groped in her bag for the vodka she had bought. "Just shopping." She pulled out the bottle.

His fingers went to the handle of his pistol. "You come with me!"

Kitty froze. What had she done? Was it possible that buying alcohol was illegal here? In desperation, she tried speaking to him in Polish. *"Jestem z ONZ."* I'm with the United Nations. She pointed to the patch on her cap.

His hand was still on the pistol. "You come—now!"

"It's okay, bud, she's with me." Suddenly Charlie was beside her. He put his arm around her waist. The soldier scowled at them, his hand clenching on the handle of the gun. Then he glanced at the train and gave a sharp, dismissive nod.

"Jeez," Charlie whispered, as he steered her away. "What were you doing?"

She tried to reply but her mouth had gone so dry she could barely speak. When they were safely back on the train, she told him that all she had been doing was copying down the price list outside the shop.

"He probably thought you were a spy."

"What? But I'm in uniform!"

"Makes no difference." Charlie shrugged. "You're from the West— that's all that matters." He glanced out the open door of the empty boxcar. "The sooner we get out of this place, the better."

On the way out of Poland, they were waved across the border without anyone climbing on board. But as she watched the Russian soldiers at the station recede into the distance, Kitty couldn't help worrying about the DPs now heading toward Warsaw. What if the rumors were true? What if, in leaving Seidenmühle, they were going out of the frying pan and into the fire? For some of them, she thought, it would be a price worth paying: those who were lucky enough to find their loved ones would no doubt be prepared to put up with any amount of hardship, as long as they remained reunited. She thought of what might lie ahead on her own journey. She was going back to a city she remembered as a series of snapshots—a city she would barely recognize if the destruction she'd witnessed in Munich was anything to go by. And yet, if by some miracle her parents were there somewhere . . . She would sacrifice just about anything to be with them again.

Kitty and Charlie left the train at Brno. His fellow GIs whistled and cheered as they waved them off. Kitty felt her cheeks burning. She and Charlie had done nothing to suggest that there was anything going on between them. And yet the others clearly thought there was. Perhaps it was because he had been so attentive during the trip—always looking out for her, bringing her things to eat and drink. At the Victory Dance back in August, he'd held her very close during the last waltz, but nothing else had happened. She hoped he hadn't been bragging about her to his friends. Or that he was hoping for something more now that they were going off alone together. Because however much she liked him, she couldn't think about that right now. And if he really cared about her, he ought to understand why.

They had a long wait for the train to Vienna. There was no regular service—all departures were controlled by the military. They sat on the platform, drinking something that looked like coffee but tasted of nothing Kitty could identify. The drink was just about bearable if she dunked one of the sweet Czech pastries into it.

"What time do you think we'll get there?" She glanced at Charlie, who was brushing crumbs off the lapel of his uniform.

"Probably not until this evening."

"Will it be too late to go looking for Clara?"

"It could be difficult after dark. The problem is the whole city is divided into military zones. I was looking at a map before we left Bavaria: the district the train takes us to—and the area where Clara lives—is in the Russian zone. It wouldn't be a good idea to go wandering about there at night."

Kitty's cup was halfway between the saucer and her mouth. The bite of pastry she'd just swallowed felt like a lump in her gullet.

"Don't worry," he said. "It'll be okay as long as we wait until morning. We just have to get across to the American zone and check into the hotel."

She nodded. He'd told her they could get rooms at the Hotel Regina—the place the US Army had taken over as their headquarters in Vienna. The name of the street was familiar to her. She remembered her father pointing out the big Bank of Austria building as they'd traveled through that part of the city by tram.

It was hard to imagine the Vienna she'd grown up in now divided among the Americans, the Russians, the British, and the French. If Clara's address was in the Russian zone, that meant Kitty's old neighborhood probably was, too. The thought of having to get past men like the one who'd tried to arrest her at the station in Poland made her stomach flip over.

"We won't be able to get right into the city on the train," Charlie went on. "The station at the end of the line was bombed, so we have to get off somewhere on the outskirts. I guess there'll be taxis around."

"There used to be trams," Kitty said. "I wonder if they're still running?" It seemed a forlorn hope. The bombs that had ruined so many buildings had no doubt ruptured tramlines, too. The train station where they should have gotten off was just a short walk to the place where her parents' shop had been—and to the street where Clara now lived. It was both tantalizing and utterly frustrating that she couldn't go there tonight. She told herself she would just have to be patient. What was one more day when she'd waited so many years? But right now, sitting on this dreary platform, watching—hoping—for a train to come, it seemed like an eternity.

It was nearly six o'clock when they crossed the border from Czechoslovakia into Austria. Seeing the name of her homeland triggered a surge of adrenaline. As the light faded, she had a sense of hurtling toward a place where nothing would be as it was supposed to be—a city of shadows and half-remembered dreams.

"How long is it since you left Vienna?" Charlie was sitting beside her. Close enough for her to feel the warmth of his body—but not touching her. He seemed to sense that this wasn't the right time to try to kiss her, or even take her hand.

"It's been almost seven years," she replied. "The Germans had already taken control—but the real trouble started in November '38, when people went round one night throwing bricks through the windows of Jewish shops. My father had to put up a sign above the shop saying it was a Jewish business. We used to have customers from all over the city, but non-Jews weren't allowed through the doors after that. I even overheard our neighbors saying there were not enough lampposts in Vienna to hang all the Jews. I got the feeling they said it deliberately loud so I could hear."

Charlie shook his head. "That must have been terrifying."

"It was. Soon after, curfews were imposed. Jews were not allowed on the streets at night or in the movie theaters, concert halls . . . most public places, I think. At school, I wasn't allowed to talk to my non-Jewish friends."

"How did you feel when your parents said they were sending you to England?"

"I was a little bit afraid—but not like it was the end of the world, because I thought they'd be coming after me. I thought it would be straightforward for them to get jobs and visas. If I'd known . . ."

"Do you think they knew the odds were against that? That they didn't tell you in case you wouldn't go?"

"I don't know."

"They were incredibly brave. I can't imagine what it must have been like, putting you on that train."

Kitty closed her eyes. No matter how many times she tried—it must be thousands—she couldn't retrieve that memory. It was as if grief had burned a hole in her mind's eye. "They *were* brave. I used to say that to myself. I know it sounds awful, but sometimes, when I was in England, I felt angry with them for letting me go. I always felt like an imposter when I lived there. No matter how hard I tried, I was never really accepted."

"My grandma used to say that." Charlie nodded. "When they came to America, she learned English, wore Western clothes, but she couldn't change how she looked. White people looked down on the Chinese. Some still do."

Kitty thought about Mrs. Ho, the Chinese lady her mother had made dresses for. She had been beautiful, elegant. It was hard to imagine that any Viennese citizen had looked down on her. But then, she had been a diplomat's wife, which brought wealth and status—very different from the position Charlie's grandmother would have been in as the wife of an immigrant laborer.

"When I changed my name, I felt guilty about it," she said, "like I was betraying my parents—but it made life more bearable. I worked really hard to lose my accent, which was the other giveaway."

"You did a good job." He smiled. "I had you down as either British or Canadian when we met."

"It's funny," she said. "The camp is the first place I've ever really felt I fitted in. I think it's because in Britain, I was living in a country where it seemed like everyone belonged except me. But at Seidenmühle I'm living alongside people like myself—people in a land that's not their own."

Charlie glanced out the window. Kitty wondered what he was thinking, whether he was worried about how she would feel when she stepped off the train—and how she would react to whatever news Clara might have. Just thinking of that meeting made her sick with anticipation.

"We're slowing down." He turned back, searching her face. "Are you ready?"

"Yes," she breathed. "I'm ready."

The first person they encountered when they got off the train was a Russian soldier who wanted to know why they had come to Vienna. Kitty explained, in German, that they were in the city on official business after accompanying DPs to Poland. It was easier—and safer—than trying to explain the real reason.

She didn't recognize the district they'd arrived in. There were no streetlamps working, which made it very dark. They walked for a while until they spotted a taxi parked on the road ahead.

"Do you think we can afford it?" Kitty said.

"I've got dollars," Charlie replied. "I reckon they'll go a long way in a place like this."

The driver simply nodded when Kitty gave their destination. Charlie didn't need to wave money under his nose—apparently his uniform was proof enough of their ability to pay.

The streets they drove through were very empty. In the glare of the headlights, she saw that Vienna was a smashed, ruined city. Steel rods hung like stalactites from the nonexistent roofs of houses; rusty girders were thrusting like bones through the piles of rubble that lay on almost every street.

The taxi came to a stop at a roadblock.

"This must be where we cross into the American zone," Charlie whispered.

Kitty could just about make out the Stars and Stripes badge on the cap of the man who leaned down to peer into the taxi. They didn't have to show their passes. A few minutes later, the headlights glanced off something she recognized: a huge, prancing horse—one of the great statues that graced the ring of avenues surrounding the inner city. As the taxi wound its way toward the hotel, she spotted the chariots and the eagles, followed by the Titans—the towering, muscled figures supporting the corners of the Hofburg palace. It gave her a glimmer of comfort to see that not everything had been destroyed.

The Hotel Regina was in a street that had sustained less damage than most. An American GI stood on sentry duty outside the entrance. Kitty felt self-conscious as she showed her papers. She could tell by the look on the guard's face that he thought she was a girl Charlie had picked up for the night.

The hotel was a building that would once have been the residence of one of Vienna's wealthier families. The elegant baroque interior was at odds with the military personnel who now occupied the place. Kitty waited in the lobby while Charlie went to speak to more uniformed men. He returned with two keys.

"How about we drop our bags and go find something to eat?" He rubbed the heel of his hand against his jaw. "Guess I could use a shave. Shall we meet back here in, say, half an hour?"

Their rooms were on the top floor—where servants would have resided in the building's glory days. The furnishings were basic, but to Kitty it was unimaginable luxury to have a room all to herself.

She pictured Charlie, probably stripped to the waist, shaving in the small square of mirror above the basin in the corner of the room.

There was no denying the worm of desire that image brought to the surface. She wondered if he was thinking about her. It had occurred to Kitty that he might try to pull some stunt—tell her there was only one room available that they would have to share. Now she felt ashamed for having thought it. Whatever else was on his mind, it was clear that he cared enough to not try to manipulate the situation to his advantage.

———

In the morning, Kitty got dressed quickly. It had been hard to sleep, knowing what lay ahead. Charlie had advised her to wear her uniform rather than the civilian clothes she'd put on for dinner last night—he said it would make it easier to get through the checkpoints.

"Ready to go?" He squeezed her arm as he emerged from his room. "Got your papers?"

She nodded. She had everything, including the laissez-passer of the four powers, which Charlie had obtained for her when they checked into the hotel—a document that allowed nonmilitary personnel to move freely through all the zones of Vienna.

It was a good half hour's walk from the Hotel Regina to the rim of the Russian zone, and it would take at least another half hour to reach the street where Clara lived.

"Are you hungry?" Charlie said, as they stepped around a pile of shattered bricks and broken glass that spilled across the pavement into the road.

"Not really." Kitty had been waiting so long for this day. All she could think about was finding Clara—and what news she might have for her. Charlie had managed to get hamburgers for them last night, but she'd been too worked up to eat more than a few bites.

"I think you should try and get something down," he said. "You can't walk miles on an empty stomach."

"You get something. I'll have a bite of it."

"Promise?"

She raised her hand in a mock salute. "Yes, Sergeant, I promise."

As they turned the corner, she let out a gasp of dismay.

"What is it?"

"Over there." She pointed to the enormous blackened spire of Saint Stephen's, stretching across the sky like a scar. Tears pricked her eyes as she took in the damage the war had inflicted on the once-beautiful cathedral.

"I remember standing right over there, with my mother, watching the Easter procession," she said. "And that street—the Kärntner Strasse—was where she used to take me to buy shoes." It was hard to imagine anyone going shopping there now. Most of the elegant facades were smashed to pieces, as if a giant fist had come and punched through the windows and the walls. Outside one of the few that had survived, a line of people snaked out along the street. Above the door hung a cardboard sign with the German word for *bread* chalked across it.

They walked on, heading east, away from the inner city. Charlie stopped to buy strudel from a man selling pastries from a tray strung around his neck. He offered it to Kitty before biting into it. She took a corner of it, just to please him.

When they neared the canal, she caught sight of the great black skeleton of the Prater Wheel, towering still and silent above the ruined houses. It brought back memories of summer afternoons spent at the amusement park. The ride on the big wheel had been the ultimate treat of those days out with her parents. She had sat between them, terrified, as the car began to sway and climb, almost sick with fear when it reached the top and the whole thing stopped dead for two eternal minutes for the passengers to admire the city spread out below.

"That must have been pretty spectacular." Charlie seemed to have read her thoughts. "I wonder if they'll be able to get it going again?"

"I hope so." It was impossible to imagine children laughing and playing on fairground rides in this desolate landscape. Maybe, one day, this place—this whole city—would rise from the ashes. Would she be there to see it? The question echoed around her head as they walked on.

They crossed a makeshift military bridge into Leopoldstadt, the district where Blumenthal's had once sold silk finery to the wealthy women of Vienna. A noticeboard told them that they were entering the Russian zone. Kitty tensed as they paused at a checkpoint to show their papers, but the guard waved them through.

They walked along a wide, rubble-strewn avenue that ran down to the Prater Platz. The shell damage looked even worse on this side of the canal. Kitty had been afraid of encountering Russian soldiers on every street corner—but there were no signs of occupation.

Kitty spotted the street where Clara used to go to church. The entrance to it was blocked by a tangle of metal girders. Peering through it, she saw there was not one building still standing. The church was gone. No wonder no one from the congregation had responded to the appeal for information.

A few streets farther on, Kitty slipped her arm through Charlie's. Soon they would be passing the place where her parents' shop had been.

"You okay?" He put his free hand on her forearm, squeezing it gently.

"I think so. It's just down there."

"Are you sure you want to see it?"

She nodded. "I have to, or I won't believe it's gone."

All that remained of the shop was a section of the front wall. Her family name had been obliterated—but the sign that the Nazis had made her father put up was still there, hanging by a single rusty nail. *"Jüdisches Geschäft."* Jewish Business. She remembered he'd gone back to the shop at night to hammer it in place because he was afraid of being arrested if he did anything to draw attention to himself. A swastika and graffiti had been painted across the wall beneath the sign. *Du Judenschwein, mögen deine Hände abfaulen!* You Jewish pig, may your hands rot off!

Kitty looked away. She knew she had to suppress the incandescent rage the ugly scrawl had triggered if she was going to carry on. How quiet and dead the whole street looked—utterly at odds with the firestorm of emotion in her heart.

They walked on in silence. She pictured herself in the back room that no longer existed, sitting at the sewing machine, her mother a few yards away, the two of them working in concentrated silence. She remembered how, when she was alone in that room, she would imagine that the treadle of the machine was the pedal of a car, that she was about to set off on a journey and would no longer be stuck inside sewing seams and buttonholes. That dream of escape had haunted her through the years in England. As if by wishing it, she had conjured all the darkness that had engulfed her family.

She thought she knew the way to the street where Clara was now living, but the bomb damage made everything look different. Signs had disappeared and some of the roads were impassable. Eventually she found her way to her old school, which was still standing. Clara's apartment was just around the corner.

"I'll go for a walk around the block." Charlie released her arm. "I won't go far. I'll be waiting outside once you're done."

Kitty nodded. She needed to do this alone.

The door of the apartment block was scruffy, its green paint peeling. But the building was otherwise unscathed. Kitty's hand was shaking as she went to press the bell. She wished she hadn't had to wear her gray UNRRA uniform, which made her look like a Nazi. She could only imagine what effect the sight of it would have on Clara when she opened the door.

At first, the ringing of the bell brought no response. Clara might not be there; she could be out at work, or off on some errand. If that were the case, Kitty would come back in the evening—no matter how difficult or dangerous that might be. But she tried again, just in case.

This time she heard footsteps coming along the hall and a child's voice calling, "Mama!" Then a woman calling back, *"Ich komme jetzt!"* I'm coming now!

Clara looked different from the beautiful teenager Kitty remembered. She was pale and thin. There was no scarlet lipstick now. Clinging to her skirts was a little boy of about three years old. Clara's eyes narrowed at the sight of Kitty. There was no flicker of recognition in them.

"Was willst du?" What do you want? Clara was staring at the UNRRA badge on Kitty's cap.

"Ich bin es—Katya," Kitty breathed. It's me—Katya.

"Katya?" Clara's hand went to her mouth. "Katya Blumenthal?" She looked as if she might faint from shock. The little boy began to wail. "Come," she said in German. "Come upstairs."

The little dark hall smelled of cigarette smoke. They went up winding stairs to a threadbare-looking room. A pair of men's boots sat on a sheet of newspaper on top of a table, a crumpled cloth, smeared black, beside them. At the other end of the table was a sewing machine. In a corner of the room, an old woman sat knitting. The little boy ran to climb on her lap. As she turned to set her needles aside, Kitty saw that it was Clara's mother.

"Oh, Katya—we thought you were dead!" Clara clasped both of Kitty's hands in hers. There were tears in her eyes. "How did you get back here? How did you find us?"

"I'm living in Germany now," Kitty explained. "I work for the United Nations, in a refugee camp." She paused, not wanting to embark on a lengthy explanation of how she'd tracked them down. "I'm sorry if I frightened you." She searched Clara's face. "Why did you think I was dead?"

"Your mother said the house in London where you were living had been bombed. The last letter she sent there was returned, marked 'Undeliverable.'" Clara bit her lip. "She was sobbing her heart out when she showed it to me."

"But I wasn't there when the bomb fell—I wrote with my new address: to the apartment and to the shop."

"They must have gone by then," Clara whispered.

"Gone where?" Kitty could hear the blood pulsing inside her ears, like waves scouring the shore.

"I don't know. They just disappeared. It was in 1940, September or October—I don't remember the exact date. I think they had visas for China. But I don't know if they got there."

"China?" Kitty gazed back at her, incredulous.

"Do you remember Mrs. Ho? She used to come to the shop before the war. She said your mother was the best seamstress in Vienna."

Kitty frowned, bewildered by the mention of the woman whose name had floated into her mind when Charlie had been telling her about his grandma. "Yes, I remember her. Mama used to take me to the embassy sometimes—when she was measuring Mrs. Ho for a new dress. I used to play with her little boy, Monto."

"Well, a couple of years after you left, her husband helped a lot of Jewish people get out of Austria. He gave them visas when no one else would. Your mother waited in line for days on end outside the other embassies, but Britain, America, and Australia all refused them entry." Clara glanced at her little boy, who was peeping at them over the edge of his grandmother's shawl.

"I came down to the workroom one morning. The Nazis had closed the shop by that time, but I'd heard a noise and went down to investigate. Your mother was copying something from the ledger in which the accounts were kept. She told me she and your father were leaving Vienna, but she wouldn't say where they were going, for fear of putting me and my mother at risk."

"But you think they had visas for China?"

Clara nodded. "She was copying an address from a page of silk suppliers. I saw her underline it before she closed the book. And then she said that if, by some miracle, you were alive and sent a letter, I was to open the book and I would know where to send it on to."

"But you never got my letters . . ." Kitty felt panic rise like bile in her throat. The shop was gone and, presumably, the book with it.

"The building was bombed less than a month after they left. But I took down the address the minute your mother was out the door." Clara went over to the table where the sewing machine sat and opened a drawer. She pulled out a small notebook, thumbing through the pages until she found what she was looking for. "There it is."

Kitty had trouble controlling the pen as she copied it down: Ezra Medavoy Silks, 118 Nanking Road, Shanghai, China. Could her parents really have cheated death and found sanctuary in this unknown, faraway place?

"I wanted to write to them—but I was afraid to," Clara said. "When the Japanese entered the war, Günther, my husband, said it might put them in danger, sending something through the post."

"Why?"

"Because the Japanese were in control of China. They were already there when the war started."

Kitty's stomach lurched. How terrible for her parents, to have escaped Austria only to be confronted by Hitler's allies on the other side of the world. Had the Japanese hated Jews as much as the Nazis did? Would they have hunted them down in their new home?

As she handed the notebook back, her head was bursting with questions that Clara couldn't possibly answer. "They . . ." Kitty faltered, her voice threatening to break as she opened her mouth. "They never wrote to you?"

"They might have tried to—I don't know. But they wouldn't have known about the shop and our apartment being destroyed. They wouldn't have known where I'd gone." She put the notebook back in the drawer. "What will you do now?"

"I . . . I'm not sure. I need to talk to someone." She was thinking aloud. "The Red Cross might be able to help. I don't know if they operate in China, but I can find out."

"Good luck," Clara whispered. "I wish I could have helped you more."

When she caught sight of Charlie waiting across the road, she ran into his arms. Tears streamed down her face as she tried to tell him, in a stuttered jumble of words, what Clara had revealed.

"They got away! That's fantastic news!" He hugged her to him, stroking her hair.

"I . . . kn . . . know," she mumbled into his jacket. "B . . . but I . . ." She knew she should be laughing, dancing for joy at the news of their escape. But all she could feel was numb despair at the thought of their chances of surviving in that distant, war-torn land.

"We'll go to the Chinese embassy," Charlie said. "Can you remember where it is?"

She nodded, gulping back tears. "Y . . . you think they might be able to tell me something?"

"I don't know. It's worth a try."

They tried, without success, to find a taxi. After traipsing across the city for two hours, they reached the Chinese embassy, only to find that the doors were padlocked. A sign said that no ambassadorial services were available at present. The lettering looked faded. Mr. and Mrs. Ho, it seemed, were long gone.

Back at the hotel, Charlie asked if they could put a call through to the Red Cross. But the person Kitty spoke to said there was no branch in China. Relief work there was only just getting underway.

That evening they went to an ice-cream parlor near the hotel. It was full of GIs with their Viennese girlfriends, their laughter spilling out into the street. They found an empty table in a dingy corner, away from the hubbub at the entrance. There was no menu—it was vanilla or nothing. Kitty spooned it into her mouth, not really wanting to eat. But the cold sweetness had a strangely soothing effect on her frazzled nerves.

"Do you think the silk merchant might have a telephone?" she said between mouthfuls. "Is there a way of finding out numbers for people in China?"

"I doubt it." Charlie put down his spoon. "Listen, Kitty, I don't want to sound negative, but it's been four years since the Japs came into the war. I imagine Shanghai will be very much like this place: not like it used to be."

"Did America bomb it?"

"Probably. It's a major seaport."

She closed her eyes. It was unbearable to think of her parents being caught up in raids by the very people who were trying to defeat Hitler.

Charlie reached for her hand. "Why don't you try sending a wire? But maybe not from Vienna—from what I've heard, the service isn't very reliable. Messages get lost or scrambled. Better to wait till we get back."

When they returned to the hotel, Charlie walked her to her room. She fished in her bag for the key. It wasn't in the inner compartment where she'd put it. She fumbled around, unable to locate it. Had she dropped it somewhere? She slumped against the wall of the corridor, utterly defeated. Fresh tears spilled from her eyes and coursed down her cheeks.

"Kitty! What is it?" Charlie cupped her face in his hands.

She shook her head, groping in her pocket for her handkerchief. The key tumbled onto the carpet as she pulled it out.

Charlie bent to retrieve it. "Come on," he said. "Let's get you inside." He stood on the threshold, holding the door open, as she stumbled into the room. "Can I get you anything? A whiskey? Something to help you sleep?"

She shook her head. "Would you stay with me?" She sat down on the bed.

"Course I will." He came and sat beside her.

"I don't mean . . ."

"I know," he whispered.

"Would you just hold me?" she whispered. "It's just that I . . ."

"It's okay—you don't have to explain."

They both kicked off their shoes and lay down together. He pulled the cover over them and slid his arm around her.

Kitty nestled into the hollow of his shoulder. "It was seeing Clara and her family," she murmured. "And the shop. It made me realize just how much I miss *belonging* somewhere."

<hr />

The next morning, they woke up late. In the hazy space between sleeping and waking, it dawned on Kitty that something warm was touching the base of her neck. She turned to see Charlie, still fast asleep, his head half off the pillow, as if he had burrowed under the sheets in the night. It must have been his lips she had felt on her skin. He was still wearing the shirt he'd had on yesterday. She ran her hands down her body to reassure herself that her clothes were still on, too.

"Charlie!" She tugged his shoulder. "Wake up! It's nearly half past nine!"

He opened one eye. Seeing her, he reached out, his hand finding hers. "Kitty," he murmured. "We don't have to get up yet, do we?"

"Yes, we do!" She pulled back the sheets. "Our train's due to leave at ten forty—we have to get to the station."

He leapt out of bed and stuck his feet into his shoes. Then he remembered he was in the wrong room. "I'll be five minutes," he said, as he headed for the door. "Meet you in the lobby."

They made it onto the train by the skin of their teeth, not helped by the Russian official at the barrier who insisted on seeing every document they possessed before waving them through.

"Thank goodness," Kitty breathed, as they sank into their seats. "We'd have been stuck here for another night if we'd missed it."

"That might not have been so bad." Charlie gave her a teasing smile.

She dug the heel of her hand into his arm. "Don't get any ideas, buster."

He grunted a laugh, but she saw that her words, even though spoken in jest, had hit home. There was a despondent look on his face that hadn't been there before.

"Thank you for staying with me last night—it was kind of you." Too late, she realized she'd made things even worse. It sounded as if she wouldn't have wanted him anywhere near her unless she'd been desperate. It wasn't that she didn't want him—sometimes the strength of the attraction overwhelmed her. But if she told him that, he'd take it as a signal that she was ready to go further.

"You don't have to thank me," he murmured. "I'd do anything for you, Kitty. I . . ." He fixed her with his beautiful pale brown eyes. "I love you."

She stared back at him, taken by surprise, unable to find a response. Leaning forward, she took his head in her hands and kissed the tip of his nose.

CHAPTER 20

The snow came early to Bavaria that year. On the day Kitty returned to Seidenmühle, a light dusting of flakes covered the roofs of the blockhouses. By the time the three women gathered for their evening meal, the snow was deep enough for their shoes to leave imprints on the path outside the cabin.

"Thank goodness you got back when you did," Delphine said. "Imagine if you'd got stuck somewhere!" She ladled some of the steaming contents of a saucepan into a bowl and passed it to Kitty.

"Mmm . . . Cabbage and meatball—my favorite!" Kitty gave her a wry look. "Although, I have to say our DPs get better food than people in Vienna."

"What was it like there?" Martha pulled out a chair and sat down beside her.

"It was grim," Kitty replied. "The only people with full stomachs were the soldiers. Ordinary people have to stand in line for hours to get a loaf of bread. From what Clara told me, the black market there is much worse than what goes on here. I wanted to give her something as a thank-you, and she said a couple of packs of Lucky Strike would get her enough to feed the family for a week."

"And *they're* supposed to be the lucky ones," Delphine said. "The ones who still have somewhere to call home."

Kitty nodded. "Clara said she was just grateful that her family survived the war. I think she felt terribly guilty that she hadn't been able to help my parents."

"I'll call the major in the morning," Martha said. "Ask him about sending a wire from the base."

Kitty nodded. "I've sent a letter, but it could take weeks to get there." She stared at the solitary meatball floating in the bowl of soup. "I wish I knew if they really did make it to China. It seems . . ." She trailed off, unable to say the words that had been echoing around in her head since Clara had shown her the address in the notebook. It was such a long, long way. Was it possible to have successfully reached their destination when every country they traveled through was at war?

"I can only imagine how you must have felt, hearing that," Martha said. "It must be torture, knowing that they got away, but not having any clue what happened after they left."

"It is," Kitty murmured. "And I can't bear the thought that when they escaped from Vienna, they believed I was dead." She took in a long breath. "I was terrified of going to find Clara. I was expecting her to tell me what I'd been dreading—that they'd been rounded up by the Nazis and never seen again. I thought that because they couldn't get visas for Britain, they'd have been trapped in Austria. It never occurred to me that there might be some other place they could go." She picked up her spoon and dipped it into the bowl, moving it around but not bringing it up to her mouth. "Before, when I was going through the Red Cross lists, finding nothing, Father Josef told me not to give up hope. I thought he was just trying to comfort me—that there was no real chance of them being alive." She submerged the meatball in the watery soup and watched it pop up again. "I *do* have hope, now. But I'm almost as afraid as when I first came here. I guess I'm scared to allow myself that hope because the odds against them having survived seem so enormous."

Martha and Delphine exchanged glances. There was nothing either of them could say that would not sound hollow.

"It's good to have you back." Delphine stood up. "We should drink to that. I think there's a little of the cognac left."

Kitty looked up. "We could have vodka. I bought a bottle in Poland. I'll go and fetch it."

When she disappeared upstairs, Delphine said: "Do you think there's any chance of the army helping her?"

"I don't know," Martha replied. "I didn't know what else to suggest. It could be months before the Red Cross starts putting lists together."

"Found it!" Kitty called from the bedroom. She came down the stairs, holding it out for them to see the Polish writing on the label. "I nearly got arrested when I bought it."

"What?" Martha glanced at her, perplexed.

Kitty told them about the incident with the Russian soldier. By the end of the story, Martha's stomach was in knots. Kitty's experience gave credence to the ugly rumors that had been circulating since the Russians had taken control of Poland. If this was how they treated an aid worker, what fate awaited men like Stefan if they stepped out of line?

⊷

The next day, it had stopped snowing, but the temperature had dropped below freezing in the night. Martha crunched her way to the office. The air smelled of woodsmoke. The potbellied stoves in the blockhouses were being stoked up. Thank goodness she had been forewarned about stockpiling logs for the winter. If the weather continued like this, the camp might be snowed in before Thanksgiving.

Thanksgiving. After all these months in Germany, she was still thinking like an American. These people had probably never heard of it. She thought of Arnie. Would one of his drinking buddies invite him

220

over for turkey and pumpkin pie? Or would he spend the holiday alone, with a bottle of Jack Daniel's for company?

There had been no reply to the letters she'd sent. Either he didn't care about getting a divorce, or he was no longer living at the apartment. The familiar pang of guilt went through her as she imagined him being unceremoniously evicted. But that might have happened even if she'd stayed. He wouldn't let her get a job, and the work he'd been getting on construction sites after he came back from the war was sporadic. She'd had to pawn her winter coat to pay the rent the month before she left.

Delphine had asked her why she still wore her wedding ring. When Martha had first arrived in Germany, it had been something to hide behind. She wasn't sure if she could get it off now, even if she wanted to.

She remembered how the gold had caught the sunlight the first time she had touched Stefan's face. She had wanted him so much. The glint of it had magnified the guilt that desire had caused. Where was he now? It was the first thing she thought of every morning when she opened her eyes. She pictured him wandering along streets full of rubble, searching, always searching. What would he do if there was no one to be found?

She tried to put him out of her mind as she unlocked the door to the office. There were people waiting for passes. Kitty would be along to take over later, but the poor girl was still unconscious—hardly surprising after that long journey back from Austria. It wasn't only the passes Martha needed to attend to: there were supply lists to be drawn up, and she must find time to call the major about the possibility of sending a wire to China.

When the ledger was open on the desk and the rubber stamp ready to be inked, she went to the door. *"Dzień dobry, kto pierwszy?"* Good morning, who is first? Her Polish was improving. She could go about the camp on her own now, able to greet people and hold basic conversations. But how she longed to turn back the clock, to those early days at the camp when Stefan had been her shadow.

Delphine followed Wolf and the others along the path to the hospital. The trees looked like images from a Christmas card, their branches dusted with snow. One of the girls stopped to make a snowball, but the missile disintegrated before it reached its target. Then they all joined in, grabbing handfuls of snow and stuffing them down the backs of coats or rubbing them into each other's hair.

It was good to see them laughing. Sometimes—usually in the evenings when they were together—one of them would give a glimpse of what their lives had been like before Seidenmühle. They would mention a parent or the name of a sibling, the place where they had grown up, some favorite food they remembered eating. Delphine had learned from her years of nursing that someone who had suffered an emotional trauma needed to be allowed time to reveal it. Trying to get them to talk about it before they were ready was likely to make them retreat still further into silence.

One thing that had surprised her was the way they had responded to Kitty. She'd brought her sketchbook to show them one evening and had offered them paper and pencils to have a go themselves. Each one of the children had soon become engrossed in drawing. What they produced had been harrowing to look at: pictures of houses on fire with stick figures fleeing in all directions, skies full of planes with bombs dropping out of them, and the one Wolf had drawn: black swastikas sprouting like stalks of wheat from a field scattered with bodies oozing blood.

Disturbing as these images were, the children were clearly eager to take part in what soon became Kitty's regular art sessions. It was obviously a form of therapy, a way of expressing what they couldn't bring themselves to talk about.

Her own attempt at therapy was the visit to Dachau she had arranged—she'd go in a few days, on what would have been her thirtieth wedding anniversary. She had kept putting it off, but it was time. The mental image of it constantly hovered like a specter on the edge of her consciousness. She dreaded what it would feel like to stand outside the barbed-wire fence, looking in. And yet it was something she had to do. If Claude had died of natural causes and had been buried in one of the Paris cemeteries, she would visit his grave. So, she had fixed the date with Father Josef. They would borrow Martha's car and he would drive her there—so long as there was no more snow in the meantime.

As she trailed behind the laughing children, she thought about how she would feel if the trip had to be put off because of the weather. It would be like being told that the surgery you needed on a painful joint—an operation that offered only limited prospects of success—had been postponed, that you wouldn't have to endure the ordeal you had been building yourself up for . . . yet. But you would have to face it sometime soon. Because if you didn't, the pain would overwhelm you.

Martha couldn't get through to Major McMahon. The officer on duty told her that he was away from the base, assessing conditions for another transport of DPs to Poland before winter set in in earnest. Her whole body tensed at these words. *Another* transport. It had been hard enough getting volunteers for the first one. She didn't want to try to persuade people to go back to live under a regime that sounded harsh and potentially dangerous.

"I wonder if you can help me." She struggled to make her voice sound matter-of-fact. "I just need to send a wire."

"Sure. Where to, ma'am?"

"Shanghai."

"Is that in Japan?"

"No—China. It's for one of my colleagues, Miss Bloom. She has Jewish relatives who may have gone to Shanghai to escape the Nazis. She has an address, but she doesn't know if they got there."

There was silence at the end of the phone. "Sorry, ma'am, I'm just checking . . ." After a long pause, he said: "I'm afraid there's no wire service available at present. The US military has a presence there, but it's early days. Maybe in a month or so . . ." He trailed off, sounding genuinely sorry.

A few minutes later the phone rang. It was the same officer. "I thought of someone who might be able to help you," he said. "Have you heard of the Joint?"

"No, I haven't," she replied. "What is it?"

"It's a relief organization for Jewish people. They operate in some of the camps in the American zone. But it's international. If anyone knows anything about Jewish refugees in China, they will."

As Martha scribbled the details down, she realized that she had come across it. Its full name was the American Jewish Joint Distribution Committee. She'd met one of its representatives during her time at the Henry Street Settlement in New York.

"I can reroute the call via central command if you want," the officer said.

"We'll put a call through later, if that's okay. Thanks for your help." Martha replaced the receiver. Kitty would want to make the call herself.

When Kitty arrived at the office, Martha stayed just long enough to make sure that she had gotten through to someone from the Joint. Then she went to deliver the list of supplies to the warehouse, returning when she judged enough time had elapsed.

Kitty was sitting at the desk, staring into space. She looked like someone in a trance.

"What is it?" Martha frowned. "What did they say?"

Kitty shook her head slowly, as if she was trying to make sense of something confusing. "That my parents might not have gone to China. They could be in Palestine. Or the Dominican Republic. Or Cuba."

"What?"

"The woman I spoke to said that the visas for Shanghai were just transit visas. A Jewish person had to have a visa to get out of Austria, but once you were over the border, there were a few other countries you could go to that didn't have a ban on letting people in."

"But that address Clara gave you—why would your mother have asked her to send letters there if they didn't intend on going to China?"

"That's what I'm hanging on to," Kitty said. "But the woman said travel to China would have been difficult by the end of 1940—which is when my parents left Vienna. They would have had to go all the way across Russia by train to Vladivostok, which was the only place you could get a boat for Shanghai by then. The Russians were still on the side of Germany at that stage, so traveling through the country with Jewish papers could have been dangerous."

"But those other countries you mentioned—Cuba and Palestine and . . . where was the other place?"

"The Dominican Republic."

"Wouldn't it have been just as difficult to get to any of those?"

"Not according to what she told me. There was a Jewish underground organization running boats from the Black Sea to Palestine. Or you could go west, via Portugal, across the Atlantic. She said people who managed to get out of Austria and Germany went to Romania or Hungary and were hidden in safe houses until a boat was available." Kitty spread her hands on the desk, palms up. "It's not all that far from Vienna to the Black Sea coast—we used to go there for summer holidays. But it's thousands of miles from Moscow to Vladivostok."

Martha didn't know what to say. Kitty had a stony, defeated look in her eyes. Hardly surprising. She'd come back from Vienna with a glimmer of hope, only to have it all but snuffed out by this latest news.

"Did the woman you spoke to have any suggestions? Do they have immigration lists for the countries she told you about?"

Kitty shook her head. "She gave me the address of someone who was in Shanghai during the war—an aid worker who's based in Belgium now. She said it might be worth writing to her."

"Well, that sounds . . ."

Kitty didn't allow her to finish the sentence. "She also told me that thousands of European Jews emigrated to Shanghai before the war broke out. The chances of that person remembering my parents—*if* they went there—would be pretty slim."

"But you're going to write?"

"Yes, I will."

Martha caught the flash of tears in her eyes. She longed to give her a hug. But she remembered how Kitty had shrugged Delphine away when she'd tried to do the same. It had been a while since then—and there were chinks in the armor Kitty wore around her heart—but Martha sensed that what she wanted right now was to be left alone to think things through.

"I know it's easy for me to say," Martha murmured, "but try not to lose heart. They got away from Vienna: that's the important thing. Just keep telling yourself that."

Kitty nodded. "I just wish I knew that they'd made it, that they're alive, somewhere—anywhere. If I knew that, I'd write a thousand letters if I had to."

CHAPTER 21

Delphine didn't usually wake before the others. It wasn't properly light when she sat up in bed and peeled back a corner of the curtain. But she could see enough of the gray landscape beyond the window to know that it hadn't snowed in the night. The roads would be clear.

She lay back on the pillow, thinking about what this day might have been like. Claude would probably have planned a trip away for them. They might have gone to a hotel on the Cote d'Azur—maybe to the Negresco in Nice, where they'd spent their first-ever vacation together.

She thought of the time when Philippe had tried to surprise them with breakfast in bed on one wedding anniversary. He'd only been eight years old—barely old enough to know how to make coffee. He'd gotten everything ready while they were still asleep and brought it up on a tray. But instead of putting it down when he reached the bedroom, he'd tried to balance it in one hand as he opened the door. The coffee pot had flown off the tray, spraying its contents over the walls, and two of her best china cups had been smashed to pieces. But the worst thing had been seeing him so upset. He'd wanted so much to make the day special.

Remembering it brought tears to her eyes. She blinked them back, trying to steel herself for what lay ahead.

———◆———

The landscape had a stark beauty in the weak sunshine. A thin layer of snow still covered the fields, shimmering like diamonds where the sun's rays caught it. As he drove along the road to Dachau, Father Josef was asking her about how she and Claude had met. She wasn't sure if he really wanted to know or was just trying to take her mind off the coming ordeal.

"We were working at the same hospital," she replied. "On the same ward, actually. We had our first kiss in the linen closet." She glanced at him, wondering if she'd embarrassed him. But he was smiling. "We got married two months later. It wasn't a big wedding—just our parents and a few friends from the hospital. We were one year into the First War, so you couldn't have a proper celebration. We were back on the ward in the afternoon—no chance of a honeymoon." She paused, remembering their first night together, in the spare bedroom of her parents' apartment, trying not to make noise in a bed that creaked every time they moved. "Claude took me on holiday to the South of France as soon as the war ended to make up for it. We stayed in some fabulous hotels— in Nice and Antibes—but it wasn't quite like a honeymoon, because Philippe was on the way by then and I had terrible morning sickness."

"The photograph you showed me—was that taken in the South of France?"

"No, that was Brittany. One of the surgeons at the American Hospital had a house in Saint-Malo and we used to go there most summers. They had a boat—a little dinghy. They'd just been out fishing when that photo was taken." She had a sudden flash of Philippe coming up the path grinning, holding out a bucket of freshly caught sardines for her to see. She heard something—a gulping, choking sort of sound. It had risen from her throat without her even realizing. "I . . . I'm sorry," she mumbled.

"Please, don't apologize," he said.

"Losing them was the worst moment of my life. That photograph was the one I put up on the wall of the Hotel Lutetia, where all the prisoners of war were brought. That was how I found out what happened to them—when someone recognized them and came to find me. I spent days after that just wandering around Paris in a fog of despair."

"When did you decide to come to Germany?"

"It was about a month later. The heartache was so . . ." She faltered, unable to find a word to convey the intensity of the pain. "I knew it could never heal. But I was alive, and I had to find a way to go on living. I left my job at the hospital when Claude and Philippe were arrested, and I couldn't face going back there. But it came to me one day that I could help myself best by healing others—if not in Paris, then somewhere else. Then I went for the interview for UNRRA. I could have gone anywhere in Germany, but I deliberately chose the camp nearest Dachau. I had to feel that I was close to them, even though the very name of the place set off this scream inside my head."

"We're almost there," he said. "Are you ready?"

She nodded. As they turned off the main road, she caught a glimpse of a high fence topped with razor wire.

"This is it." The tires crunched frozen snow as Father Josef pulled onto the grass verge. "We'd better leave the car here."

As they walked toward the fence, Delphine could hear voices from inside the camp: a shouted command in what sounded like German, a snatch of conversation in American-accented English. She couldn't see anyone beyond the low-roofed buildings that fringed the perimeter of the camp. She remembered what Father Josef had said about the place being used as a prison for SS officers awaiting trial. A bitter irony, she thought, especially for those who had been the masters of Dachau during the war. Did it help to know that the men who had murdered Claude and Philippe were likely facing a death sentence themselves? It should have. But strangely, the thought of it left her numb.

In her hand she carried a wreath that Wolf and his friends had made for her. There were no flowers to be had at this time of year, so he had gone into the woods and picked holly, bright with berries, and gathered cones lying on the carpet of pine needles. It was as good as any creation she might have bought from the florist on the Avenue Foch—the sort of thing she would have hung on the door of the apartment for the Christmases between the wars.

"Will it be okay to tie it to the fence?" She glanced at the wire, wondering if it was electrified.

Father Josef nodded. "Would you like me to help you?"

"No—thank you. I can manage." Her fingers trembled as she looped the string through the wire. A holly leaf pricked her thumb as she tightened the knot. A bead of blood oozed out. She sucked it. A tang of metal on her tongue. It was as if just touching this place made bad things happen, that the tentacles of evil snaked out through the gaps in the fence.

"You've hurt yourself." Father Josef offered her his handkerchief.

"It's nothing." She waved it away. The sight of it made her suddenly, inexplicably angry, as if he were responsible for what had happened here. Or—more precisely—that the supreme being he represented had failed to prevent it from happening. "Tell me, Father," she said. "Why did God ignore the cries of the people who died in this place?"

She saw his breath, a cloud of white in the frosty air. "I used to ask myself that question," he said. "Every day there would be one more terrible act in the litany of cruelty. There was one particular morning, when we were all standing outside for roll call. It always took hours, and we were all weak with hunger. But you had to stand there until it was over. On this morning, a couple of men keeled over, and the guards beat them with the butts of their rifles. These men were being killed in front of my eyes, and there was nothing I could do to save them." He glanced up at the razor wire running along the top of the fence. "When the screaming stopped, I was aware of another sound. It was like music:

a beautiful, piping melody, somewhere above the camp. I looked up and realized it was skylarks, flying overhead. In that moment I sensed that God was there, above it all—crying for the wickedness that he was looking down on—and that he would always be there, and nothing the Nazis did could ever change that."

"So, why didn't he intervene? Why didn't he save those men?"

"That I can't answer. Except to say that when we suffer, he suffers with us. He didn't create the evil that was done here. He gave us free will—the choice to love and nurture or to hate and destroy one another. Mankind has been getting it wrong since the dawn of time."

"There must have been times when there were no skylarks," Delphine murmured. "Did you never come to a point when you thought faith was just an illusion?"

"Of course." He lowered his head, his eyes on hers. "To exist in a place like this is like one long dark night of the soul. But always, at my lowest ebb, something would nudge me back from the brink of despair. Sometimes it was a small act of kindness from a fellow prisoner—like the time I found a scrap of bread hidden in my bedding after I'd been starved for one of the medical experiments. Other times, like the bird-song, it was nature that spoke to me. Once I caught a glimpse of a ghostly moon in a blue sky and thought of the stars that were up there, too, day and night, even though I wouldn't see them until it got dark. It felt like God saying, 'I'm here, I'm always here—even when you think I'm not.'"

Delphine held his gaze. "You told me before that you felt guilty for having survived when so many others died. But don't you ever feel angry? If you could get past this fence and come face-to-face with one of those SS men, wouldn't you want to kill him? *I* would."

He nodded. "I understand that. Becoming a priest didn't take away those instinctive emotions. But my faith forbids me from acting on them."

"You would forgive them?"

"I would."

"How? Why?"

"Because if I didn't, I would be the worst kind of hypocrite. I believe in a God who, twice a day, washes all the sands on all the shores of all the world. He makes every mark disappear—from the gaping hole dug by a spade to the footprints left by a gull."

"You're saying that you're as bad as them?" Delphine frowned, tilting her head toward the fence.

"What I'm saying is we all need forgiveness."

"How can I forgive someone who stole my husband and my son from me? They might as well have ripped my heart out of my chest."

"But no one can steal the memory of your love for them."

Delphine's eyes ranged over the buildings beyond the fence, at the watchtower with guards lolling against a wooden balustrade, at the soot-blackened chimney in the far distance. "That's true," she whispered. "But it doesn't mean they deserve to be forgiven."

"It's a strange word, *forgiveness*," he said. "I never really understood it until I studied Greek at the seminary. The Greek word in the Bible—*aphiemi*—means 'to set free.' When I heard that, I suddenly grasped what it was all about: forgiving is about freedom. It's not just about pardoning the wrongdoer—it's about releasing yourself from the power of what they did to you. Forgiving someone sets you free."

"Do you really believe that's possible?" She searched his face.

"I wouldn't have said it if I didn't."

For a while, she went silent. Then she said: "I don't think I'm strong enough to do that. But I am glad I came here. Just standing here makes me feel closer to Claude and Philippe: it makes me believe that I *will* see them again."

He nodded. "You're stronger than you think. You've already shown how strong you are."

"Have I?"

"You could have stayed in Paris, hidden away, nursing your grief. But you didn't." He was looking at the wreath tied to the fence, at the holly berries, vivid red against the twisted foliage. "It's what defines a person, the way they deal with life's unfairness. And when you see your husband and your son again, you'll be able to tell them all about Seidenmühle, about what you do, every single day, to make their lives count."

CHAPTER 22

It was snowing again when Martha went to pick up the mail. For a whole week, the temperature hadn't risen much above freezing. In the Frankfurt area, there had been a big dump of snow. The major had called to say that there would be no more transports to Poland this side of Christmas. Martha was glad. She hated the thought of her DPs heading off to a place where life was likely to be harder, not easier, than at Seidenmühle. *Her* DPs. She rolled her eyes. She was doing exactly what the major had warned her against. Identifying with them, thinking of them as family. But how could she help it? She had been living alongside these people every day for more than four months. She had witnessed their pain, their grief, and—occasionally—their joy. She had become godmother to a Polish baby, and she had fallen in love with a man whose language she could barely speak.

On her way back to the office, she sifted through the letters. It was something she always did as she walked. If, by some remote chance, there was a letter from Stefan, she needed to know before she reached the office. She couldn't face making that discovery in front of anyone else.

That last night in the camp, they hadn't talked about keeping in touch. In the brief snatched moment under the trees, she hadn't thought to ask if he would write. But she longed to know that he was safe, that he hadn't been marched off to some terrible prison camp in Siberia for the crime of having lived in the West. She was riven with guilt every time she thought about him searching the ruined city of Warsaw for his missing wife and child. It had been more than a month since he'd gone, but her feelings for him refused to subside. She hated herself for wanting him to be free, for imagining him writing to tell her that his search had been in vain. She told herself that if she truly loved him, she would be happy to receive news of a reunion with his wife. But the voice inside her head hissed that she was incapable of such selflessness.

There was no letter from Poland. Martha drew in a breath and blew it out. Nor was there anything from America. She had addressed her most recent letter to the bar that had been Arnie's second home—but there had still been no response. As she shuffled the envelopes in her hand, she saw one addressed to Kitty that was postmarked "Bruxelles." Martha started walking faster. She prayed that it contained good news.

Kitty ripped open the envelope and pulled out the letter. Martha could see that it was handwritten, not typed. And there looked to be at least three sheets of paper. Whatever this person had to tell Kitty, she'd clearly taken a lot of time and effort over it.

"Would you like me to leave you alone?"

"No—it's okay." Kitty was scanning the first page, her expression unreadable. Soon she was on to the second sheet.

When Kitty laid the last sheet down on top of the others, the only change in her face was a narrowing of the eyes, as if she were pondering the answer to something unfathomable. "What does she say?"

"I'll read it to you." Kitty's voice gave no hint of what she was feeling.

"'Dear Miss Bloom,'" she began, "'I read your letter with great interest and enormous sympathy for the situation in which you find yourself. The information you were given is quite correct: I was the representative of the American Jewish Joint Distribution Committee in China for two and a half years—from May 1941 to December 1943. I lived in Shanghai at the organization's headquarters and oversaw the aid program to the Jewish refugees who had sought sanctuary in the city.

"'What you are longing to know, of course, is whether I encountered your parents during that period. I have to tell you that their names are not familiar to me. But you should not be disheartened by that—there were approximately eighteen thousand Jewish refugees resident in Shanghai during my time there, so you will understand, I'm sure, that I could not have known everyone by name.'"

Kitty looked up. "If only I'd had a photograph of them. She might have recognized their faces."

"What else does she say?"

"She says that Shanghai was a safe place for Jewish immigrants from Europe until the attack on Pearl Harbor in December 1941." She began reading again: "'I was placed under house arrest for a time, but it was still possible to operate the soup kitchens our organization ran for the refugees. By March 1943, all Jews had been moved by the Japanese into what was known as the "Shanghai Ghetto"—a section of the city from which movement in and out was forbidden. This, I know, will sound alarming to you. But conditions there were nowhere near as bad as in the Jewish ghettoes in places like Warsaw. The Japanese had no antipathy to the Jewish people—in confining the refugees to a designated area, they were merely bowing to pressure from their Nazi allies.

"'Many people were forced to leave their homes and businesses around the city and move to Hongkew, where the ghetto was, so it is unlikely that you will receive a reply to any letter sent to the address of the silk merchant. I know the name of the business, but not what happened to the Medavoy family. It is possible they may have gone into hiding—as some people did—rather than move into the ghetto.'"

Kitty laid down the paper and picked up the final sheet.

"Does she have any suggestions?" Martha asked. "Is there *anything* you can do?"

"She says that the Joint hopes to reopen their Shanghai office in December, and that lists of Jewish refugees will be issued via the Red Cross as soon as possible. This is the last paragraph: 'I will forward your name and address to our representative in Shanghai, along with the details you supplied. Meanwhile, the only other suggestion I can offer is that you write to Rabbi Meir Ashkenazi at the Ohel Moshe Synagogue in Hongkew. If your parents worshipped there during the war, their names will have been recorded. My sincere good wishes in your search for your family. Laura Margolis.'"

"Well, that's a good idea—writing to the rabbi," Martha said.

"*If* they went to the synagogue." Kitty folded the letter and slipped it back into the envelope. "We weren't a particularly religious family—not what you'd call observant. Being Jewish was more about our heritage and our culture than anything spiritual. We hardly ever went to the synagogue in Vienna."

"But that might have changed when they moved to a foreign country," Martha said. "It might have helped them get to know people."

"I suppose it would." Kitty nodded. "Do you think I should try writing to synagogues in the other countries they might have gone to as well?"

"It's worth a try. But how would you get the addresses?"

"I'd just have to put 'Chief Rabbi' and the name of the capital city of the country."

"That would probably work for Cuba and the Dominican Republic," Martha said. "But what about Palestine? There must be hundreds of them." She glanced at the envelope lying on the desk. "If the Joint has an office in Shanghai, it's quite likely there are representatives in these other countries, too—especially Palestine, I should think. Why don't you write back to Laura Margolis and ask her if she'd forward your parents' details to her colleagues in the other places they might have gone to?"

"That's a much better idea—why didn't I think of it?" Kitty shook her head. "Since I got back, I feel as if my brain's turned to mush."

"Don't be so hard on yourself." Martha shot her a wry smile. "You've been on an emotional roller coaster since you were twelve years old— and in the past few weeks you've been hanging on by your fingernails."

"It does feel like that sometimes." Kitty glanced at the window. "I wouldn't mind if I knew they were there, waiting for me, at the other end. I could put up with anything if I knew that."

⚬

Within a week the road outside the camp was impassable. A night of heavy snow and high winds had left drifts six feet deep against the gates. Martha couldn't open the door of the cabin. She went to wake the others. Kitty decided the only solution was to get out through the bedroom window.

"Please tell me you're not going to jump," Delphine said. "You could break your leg."

"The snow looks deep enough to give me a soft landing—but if it makes you happy, I'll use a sheet. You two can hold one end and I'll lower myself down."

When Kitty finally managed to prize the front door open, she looked like an Arctic explorer, her clothes and her hair encrusted with snow and her cheeks rosy from the effort of digging her way through the drift.

"We'd better get the children out." Martha glanced at the neighboring cabin. "What about Dr. Jankaukas?"

"He was on duty at the hospital last night," Delphine said. "I suppose it'll be as bad down there as it is here."

"I'll go round up some help. Can I leave you two to get the others out?"

It wasn't easy, getting through the snow. It had settled unevenly, making every footstep tricky. At one point, Martha sunk up to her thighs in it and had trouble extricating herself. When she reached the first of the blockhouses, she saw that people were already outside, using yard brushes, rakes, and their bare hands to clear the snow.

The same thing was happening across the camp. Once the doors were freed up, the leaders of each blockhouse organized teams to clear the paths. Within a couple of hours, the hospital and the kitchens were accessible. By lunchtime it was possible to get from one building to another with relative ease.

Kitty went to find Charlie, who had been on duty at the warehouse during the night. She took him a pan of soup swathed in cloths to keep it warm.

"Boy, are you a sight for sore eyes!" He grinned as she came through the door.

"Me? Or the soup?" She arched one eyebrow as she laid the pan on the desk-cum-table in the corner of the cell-like room where he'd spent the night. "Does this snow mean I'm going to have to put up with you being here all the time?" she teased him.

"I guess so." He shrugged. "Doesn't look like I'll be going back to base anytime soon."

"What on earth will you do, cooped up here, all on your own?" She sidled up to him and nuzzled his cheek. He slid his arms around her waist. There was no need to worry about being seen; the window was covered with snowflakes. They'd become much closer since the trip to Vienna. He hadn't been pushy—she had been the one who'd taken the initiative. Their first proper kiss had been a revelation: she'd never felt that way with Fred.

"Hey! Your soup's going cold!" She broke away, laughing.

"That's not fair," he murmured. "Making me choose between hunger and . . ." He trailed off, pulling her back.

"I can't stay—I've got to go and help get more logs from the woodshed."

"I'll come with you," Charlie said. "I don't think anyone's going to be trying to break into this place anytime soon."

She waited while he padlocked the door, then let him lead the way along the path—on purpose, because she couldn't resist the temptation to throw a snowball at him. She made a direct hit in the middle of his back. In a flash he threw one back. It caught her right in the solar plexus, which made her cough and laugh at the same time. She chased after him. Soon they were rolling around in the snow.

"We'd better go," she panted. "They'll be wondering where I've got to."

He almost fell over as he got to his feet. He held out his hands to pull her up. "Will you come back tonight and keep me company?"

"I have the English class at seven," she said, batting away the white clumps that clung to her coat and scarf. "And I've promised an art session afterwards."

"Come after that, then. I'll build us a campfire." He tilted his head toward the warehouse. "We have twelve hundred tins of Spam in there. We can break open a can and barbecue it."

"Mmm! Charred Spam! You really know how to treat a girl, don't you? What will it be for dessert? Toasted fir cones?" She took a handful of snow and stuffed it inside his collar. He got his revenge by grabbing her ankles and dangling her upside down so her hair swept the ground like a mop.

"Put . . . me . . . down!" Kitty could hardly get the words out, she was laughing so hard.

He fell back onto the snow, pulling her on top of him. Neither of them noticed Martha coming down the path that led to the warehouse. She stopped dead when she saw them. It wasn't a surprise—she'd seen the look that had passed between them when they were waiting to board the train to Poland. But it didn't stop her from feeling as though an icicle had pierced her chest.

She was glad for them—of course she was: if anyone deserved a bit of happiness, Kitty did—but it was a bittersweet feeling because of the startling clarity of the memories it triggered. No matter how much she tried to push those intimate moments with Stefan to the back of her mind, the pain she felt at losing him was as raw as the day when he'd stepped onto that train.

<hr />

Kitty was walking around the mess hall, looking at the images forming on the sheets of paper. She'd managed to beg paint and brushes from the army base, so now the children could put color into their artwork. There was a lot of red being used, she noticed. All the pictures had a vivid, alarming quality about them: not one child was painting anything that could be described as pastoral, tranquil, or pretty.

She stopped by Wolf's chair, leaning over his shoulder. "I like the way you've drawn that. Is it a real place?" She asked the question in English. As the art session followed the English class, she thought it would help to get them to put what they'd learned into conversation.

"Yes, miss," Wolf replied. "I live here with my father." He dipped his brush into a pot of yellow paint and mixed it with red. Then he smeared it across the top of the paper, above the building he had drawn. "This is fire," he said. "When bomb fall on it."

"And who are these two people?" She pointed to a stick figure wearing a hat with a red cross on it, holding a protective arm around a smaller figure.

"This Madame Fabius—and this one, me." He jabbed the brush toward his chest. "She not there when this happen. But she love me now."

She love me now. The words played back on a loop as Kitty moved silently around the room. The bond that had developed between Delphine and Wolf was plain to see. He was helping to heal the gaping wound that losing her husband and son had inflicted, and she was doing the same for the boy.

She thought of Charlie, who, at this moment, was making a fire outside in the snow and preparing a meal for her. She'd worked out what she was going to say to extricate herself when they'd finished eating, how she was going to stop things from going too far. On the train back from Vienna, when he told her that he loved her, it had frightened her. To say that she loved him, too, would have been a step too far. It would have felt as if she'd split open the shell that she'd inhabited for so long.

She glanced across at Wolf. He had finished his painting and was chatting to the boy in the seat next to his. He looked like someone who didn't have a care in the world. And yet he'd lost both his parents. There were no ifs, buts, or maybes. They were dead.

She love me now.

Suddenly she grasped it: in those four words lay the secret to happiness.

Charlie's face was lit up by the glow from the fire. Stars as bright and sharp as nails pierced the velvety blackness of the sky.

Looking up, Kitty saw a strange glimmer. Over the tops of the trees, there was a faint, greenish light that seemed to move as she looked at it. "What's that?" She pointed. "It looks like headlights or something—but there can't be anything on the road: not with all this snow."

"I think it could be the northern lights."

"Really? I've heard of them—but I thought you had to be up in the Arctic to see them."

"Usually, you do. But sometimes you get a glimpse of them farther south. It depends on the weather, I think. It probably has something to do with all this snow—reflecting stuff back into the atmosphere."

"Have you seen them before?"

"A couple of times. Last winter, when we were lying in wait for the Germans in a forest up near the Belgian border, we were sitting in a dugout in the dark, keeping watch, and I saw a flash above the trees. We thought it was tanks coming our way. But there was no sound, nothing at all. One of my buddies—a Canadian guy—said it was the northern lights. He said where he came from, folks call them the ghost riders."

"I can see why." Kitty could see that the green glow was swirling and changing color. The patch of sky was shot with streaks of yellow and orange. Then shapes began to form in front of her eyes. Spectral riders with flaming hair appeared on crimson horses. They raced across the sky like a wildfire. "It's magical," she whispered. "Like something from another world." She watched the figures dissolve into a faint, misty halo of golden light. "You said you'd seen them more than once—when was the other time?"

"It was the night before we liberated Dachau. We were camped about a mile away, but you could smell the incinerators, even though the Nazis had cut and run by then. And when we saw the lights in the sky, I swear, it looked like some great green-eyed demon was hovering over the place."

"You've never spoken about it," Kitty said. "Not since that time on the phone, when you told me you were there."

"I wouldn't have mentioned it then if I'd known you were searching for your parents."

"It must have been horrific, going in there."

"I can't even describe it. Things get bad in war, I know, but this was beyond anything you could imagine." He looked into the fire, the light casting deep shadows across his face. "I threw up when I saw the state of some of the prisoners. They were like living skeletons." As he moved his head, Kitty caught the glint of tears in his eyes.

She moved closer, reaching out to draw him to her. "I've been very selfish," she whispered. "Always going on about myself and my parents—never thinking about what you must have been concealing for the sake of my feelings."

"I wouldn't want you carrying those pictures around in your head. There are some things best kept inside."

"Do you ever talk to your friends about it?"

He shook his head. "We don't have what you might call deep conversations. It's mostly stupid stuff. If you let on about what's bugging you, they think you're weak."

"People in England could be like that," she said. "There was a boy I went out with. His name was Fred. He hated me talking about my parents. If I ever mentioned how terrible it felt, not knowing what had become of them, he'd tell me to toughen up and just accept that I was on my own in the world."

"I think when guys say things like that, it's because they're bottling something up. Maybe he had bad parents who didn't care about him."

"I didn't think of that."

"In a weird kind of way, he might have envied you—being part of a family that loved you so much they went through the hell of putting you on that train."

She kissed the skin above the collar of his jacket. "You're so different from him. Before I met you, I thought all boys were like that." She traced a path with her lips, up to his ear. "I love you, Charlie." She felt him twist in her arms, his mouth finding hers. "Come on," she whispered, as she broke away. "Let's go inside."

CHAPTER 23

Major McMahon's warning about the camp being cut off from the outside world had been no exaggeration. Four weeks after the first big dump, they were still snowed in. There could be no deliveries of food, and it was impossible to transport felled trees out of the forest for firewood. Martha thought the stocks they had built up over the past few months should just about see them through. But Christmas was coming. It would be the first one since the end of the war, and the DPs were keen to celebrate. Father Josef had told her that in Poland it was a three-day holiday—and there would be plenty of drinking and dancing.

In the week preceding Christmas, groups of people from each blockhouse ventured into the woods to collect greenery. If logging was impossible, cutting down branches was not. They returned with great bundles of fir, which they made into garlands and trimmed with clusters of holly berries and all manner of man-made objects—even using a few empty sardine cans. Martha didn't realize what they were until she examined one up close and spotted "Rockport, Maine" written on the dangling metal.

One of the many strange things about this very different Christmas was not getting cards in the mail. There had been no mail delivery since the first big snowfall, but even if there had, Martha reflected, she was unlikely to have received many cards. Her cousins in New Orleans might have sent something. Certainly not Arnie, who remained as elusive as ever and was probably wishing her the worst possible Christmas. And Stefan . . . She wondered what sort of Christmas he would be having, whether people would even be allowed to celebrate it with Stalin's henchmen lurking everywhere. Part of her was relieved that no mail was coming through. She would only have fretted about the lack of communication from him, conjured up half a dozen equally depressing scenarios to explain it.

⟞⟝

On Christmas Day, Martha woke up almost two hours later than usual. She sat up, bleary eyed, wondering why the sunlight was shining into her eyes. The other beds were empty, and she could hear her roommates moving around downstairs. She groaned as she put one foot on the floor. Clearly, they could hold their drink better than her. Father Josef had been right about the celebrations: the party had started soon after midday on Christmas Eve and gone late into the night.

In the kitchen, Delphine was cutting up onions. The acrid smell filled the room.

"Merry Christmas," Martha mumbled. "What are you making?"

"Onion soup." Delphine looked up, smiling. "It's a traditional French hangover cure. We always used to have it on Christmas morning."

Martha wasn't sure she could face eating anything—let alone onion soup.

"Merry Christmas!" Kitty came into the room, a mug of coffee in her hand.

"You look nice," Martha said. "Is that the dress the sewing ladies made from those sketches you did?"

Kitty nodded. "It turned out better than I thought. I wasn't sure whether the material would drape properly—but it looks okay, doesn't it?"

"It's more than okay," Martha said. "You look like you've stepped off the pages of *Vogue*."

"You don't think it's too much?" Kitty glanced down at the scarlet fabric.

Delphine shook her head. "It's Christmas! And that color really suits you."

"And everyone's going to be dressed up today," Martha added. "I saw some of the costumes hanging up in the blockhouses. Goodness knows how they got hold of ribbons and hats and fancy vests—probably best not to ask."

"Same with the alcohol," Delphine said. "I don't like to think where that's come from—but there seems to be an endless supply of it."

"I suppose I should have gone into that basement under blockhouse five." Martha shrugged. "I wouldn't be surprised if they've got stills down there. But it would feel so mean, taking them away. They deserve a good Christmas after what they've been through."

"So long as it doesn't put them in the hospital." Delphine tossed a pile of onions into the pan on the gas ring. The hot fat hissed. "We don't want anyone going blind."

"I shouldn't worry," Kitty said. "Sergeant Lewis has a secret weapon: he came across two boxes of Scotch whisky in the warehouse."

"What?" Martha gaped at her. "How did they get there?"

"The boxes were marked 'Gherkins.' He reckons they must have been delivered here by mistake when the army was in charge."

"How many bottles?"

"Sixty."

"And they say Santa Claus is make-believe," Martha murmured.

<hr>

It was impossible not to get caught up in the festive atmosphere, even though Martha had intended to make her excuses and slip away before the dancing started. She'd never heard of the mazurka, but by Christmas afternoon she knew all the moves. Her teacher was the leader of block-house three—a sprightly gentleman with a white beard, who told her he had been a ballet dancer for Victoria. After politely turning down his offer to teach her the polka next, she made a beeline for Delphine, who had found a seat in a corner of the mess hall.

"Has he worn you out?" Delphine said, as Martha flopped down beside her.

"I didn't realize I was so unfit," Martha groaned. "He said he'd danced for Queen Victoria—which must make him about a hundred years old!"

Delphine laughed. "Well, he doesn't seem tired at all. It looks like he's asking one of the sewing ladies. Oh, look out—here come the lovebirds!"

Kitty's cheeks were almost as red as her dress as she sat down to recover from dancing. Martha thought Charlie looked uncomfortable standing beside her, as if he were embarrassed at them knowing he and Kitty were an item.

"I've asked him to take a photo of the three of us," Kitty said. She delved into her bag and pulled out Charlie's camera.

"If we're going to pose, we'd better all have some of this." Delphine poured out generous measures of whiskey. "Come on, girls—raise your glasses."

"Merry Christmas!"

"Joyeux Noël!"

"Frohe Weihnachten!"

The flash left red blobs in front of Martha's eyes. Charlie took another, just to be sure. Then he said he'd better check that everything was okay at the warehouse. He shot a look at Kitty, which she returned with the almost imperceptible arch of an eyebrow. Martha tried not to smile. They were trying so hard to hide the fact that they were crazy about each other—and doing a terrible job of it. She hoped that Kitty knew enough about men to be sensible. She'd never hinted to Martha at how far things had gone with Fred. Growing up without anyone to guide her, she must have learned about sex from the factory girls she worked with. Charlie seemed like a nice guy. But Martha had thought the same about Arnie in the early days. Should she take her to one side and have a word with her about men?

Glancing across the table at Kitty, it seemed a ridiculous notion. She looked so glamorous and self-assured: a young woman who knew how to take care of herself and would probably burst out laughing if anyone tried to warn her about the risks of falling head over heels in love. But there was a brittleness about her smile. She never complained, but the snow stopping the mail from coming in must have been driving her crazy. Today of all days, her parents would have to be on her mind. Martha hoped that she wouldn't go overboard with the drinking as a way of blotting out the heartache. It would be all too easy for a man to take advantage of her in that state.

"You need a top-up." Delphine was reaching over with the bottle. "What shall we drink to this time?"

Martha put her hand over the rim. She was already starting to feel a bit woozy.

"To . . . life!" Kitty raised her glass.

"To life!" Delphine clinked her glass against each of the others. "A year ago, I couldn't have drunk a toast to that. There seemed no point in going on living." She took a sip of her drink. "It's not the *same* life—but it's a meaningful life. Thank you both, for helping me get there."

It was still light when Martha and Delphine went outside for some fresh air. There was a path through the trees where the snow had been trodden down when the DPs had gone out collecting branches to decorate the camp.

"I'm getting wet feet." Delphine giggled. "I forgot I was wearing these shoes!"

Martha glanced down at her own feet. She was so used to wearing the stout army-issue boots that had come with her uniform. It was the first time she'd put on a pair of her own shoes since the weddings last summer.

"Oh, look!" Delphine half walked, half slithered to a clearing in the trees. "The roses are still there!"

Martha made her way across to where Delphine was standing. There was part of a crumbling wall in the clearing—the remains of a building even more ruined than the one Stefan had taken her to. The vines growing against the wall consisted of little more than a tangle of gnarled branches dusted with snow, but a few withered roses were still attached.

"Wolf picked some of these for me in the first week we were here." Delphine reached out to pluck one of them. It was the color of old parchment, the edges tinged brown. She held it up to her nose. "Amazing!" She smiled as she held out her hand to Martha. "Can you believe it still has its scent?"

The petals were fragile. A couple fell away in Martha's fingers. She brought what was left up to her face. "Mmm . . . it smells lovely: like . . . vanilla . . . and honey."

"Isn't it strange, that it's still there? I think it's even more intense than when it was in full bloom."

Martha stared at the papery petals in her hand. Yes, she thought, it *was* strange that something that had flowered and died could still smell so magical.

"I kept one of those roses Wolf gave me," Delphine said. "I put it in a book and pressed it under the mattress. I told myself I'd take it out and look at it when I felt really low." She reached out, running her finger along the contours of one of the remaining flowers. "But I haven't had to. Maybe it's because we've been so busy."

"Maybe," Martha replied. She thought it was more than that: having Wolf and the other children under her wing had given Delphine a new family. But to suggest that anyone could replace a cherished husband and beloved son would have sounded insensitive. "Perhaps you're just stronger than you think," she said.

"That's what Father Josef told me when we went to Dachau. I don't *feel* strong, though."

"Nor does this." Martha traced the outline of the faded rose. "But it still has power. It's just hidden inside its heart."

CHAPTER 24

Three weeks after Christmas, the supplies in the warehouse were almost exhausted. With no idea how much longer the freezing weather was going to last, Martha had no option but to cut the daily ration. Now there was not even one meatball floating in the cabbage soup. The Spam and canned fish had run out. Watery porridge was the only thing available for breakfast when the last sack of flour had been used up.

Kitty found Martha crouched over the desk in the office, crying, two days after the announcement was made.

"It feels like this is never going to end," Martha mumbled. "A woman from blockhouse four was just in here. She says her little boy is anemic. Dr. Jankaukas told her to give him raw liver. We don't even have any of the paste left—let alone fresh meat." She fumbled in her pocket for a handkerchief and blew her nose. "I feel like telling the men to go out and take whatever they can: steal cows, sheep, anything they can lay their hands on. But then I think about the local people, living on God-knows-what after all the food we've taken from them. It wouldn't be fair, would it?"

"I think things are probably even worse outside the camp," Kitty said. "Before Christmas, Charlie told me that some of the boys at the base were trading food for sex with the local girls. They call cakes and chocolate Frau bait."

Martha shook her head. "It all seems hopeless. And I feel absolutely useless." It was so bleak, so dark. The lack of food, the short, bitter days, the wall of snow outside the gates. As if everything were closing in.

"You're doing your best. You didn't start this war. None of this is your fault."

Martha felt a hand on her shoulder. It was the first time Kitty had ever reached out and touched her. It felt like a pinprick of light in a dark, dark tunnel.

<hr>

It was not until the last day of January that the thaw finally set in. The first inkling of a change in the weather was the steady drip, drip of the blanket of snow on the roof of the cabin beginning to melt. Martha jumped out of bed and rubbed a hole in the condensation coating the window. The trees had lost their mantle of white. She could see the gravel path that had been concealed for weeks beneath compacted snow.

Then she heard the throaty rumble of an engine and caught sight of an army jeep. She threw on her clothes and ran for the stairs, taking them two at a time. She had to get to the warehouse before the jeep, so she could get Kitty out of Charlie's room before the relief detail came banging on the door.

She took the shortcut through the trees, splashing her trousers in the puddles of melted snow. With a bit of luck, the jeep would stop off at one of the kitchens to cadge some breakfast.

"Kitty!" She banged on the door of the guardroom attached to the warehouse. "Wake up! The army's here!"

There was no response. She went to the window and rapped as hard as she could without breaking the glass. A corner of the net curtain shifted and Kitty's startled face appeared.

"Quick!" Martha jabbed her thumb toward the kitchens. "They'll be here any minute!"

The door opened and Martha caught sight of Charlie in nothing but boxer shorts, his hair sticking up in a black spiky halo.

"What's happening?" He grabbed his trousers and tried to put them on, almost falling over as he missed the leg hole.

"There's an army jeep headed this way." Martha glanced back over her shoulder.

"What? How?" Charlie pulled on his shirt as Kitty darted past him, through the door. Her blouse was buttoned up crooked and her trouser zip was undone.

"There's been a thaw overnight—the roads must be open." Martha made a grab for Kitty. "Come here—you look as if you've wandered off of skid row!"

By the time the jeep came careening around the corner of the building, Kitty looked just about respectable.

"Good morning, Mrs. Radford, Miss Bloom. Long time no see!" It was Corporal Brody who jumped out of the driver's seat.

"Good morning! Are we glad to see you!" Martha stepped forward, blocking the view through the open door. "Poor Sergeant Lewis must be sick of the sight of this place. We were just dropping off some clean laundry for him—he only had the one uniform when the snow cut us off."

"Hey, Sarge!" Corporal Brody yelled. "You can come out of your hidey-hole! You're due about three weeks' R and R!" He shot them a sideways grin as Charlie appeared in the doorway.

"Wasn't expecting you." Charlie raked his hair with his hands.

Whatever Brody thought of his rumpled appearance, he kept it to himself.

"We'll leave you to it," Martha said. "I'll be in the office if you need anything."

"Thank you," Kitty breathed when they were far enough away to be out of earshot. "It would have been awful if you hadn't come—we'd never have heard the last of it."

"Let's not dwell on that," Martha said. "Just get yourself tidied up and come help me sort things out. There's going to be a mountain of stuff to catch up on now that the roads are open."

"You're not cross?"

"Why would I be? I mean, it's not the first time, is it?"

"You knew?"

"What was I supposed to think when I saw that your bed was empty? That you'd gotten up early for a bit of bird-watching?"

"I'm sorry. I should have asked you if it was okay."

"Listen, you're an adult—it's none of my business what you get up to in your free time. I just hope you and Charlie have been . . . sensible."

Kitty clicked her tongue against her teeth. "No need to worry about that. I take it you don't know about the ten boxes of French letters in the warehouse?"

"French letters?"

"It's what they call them in England. Charlie calls them jimmy hats."

"Why on earth do we have *those* in the warehouse?" Martha was trying not to smile.

"He said the army brought them here before we took over. They wanted to give them out to the DPs, but no one was interested."

"Well, that explains the continuing baby boom, I guess."

"He says they all want babies because they've lost their families. It gives them a reason to go on living."

"Well, that's understandable," Martha said.

"It's not how *I* feel."

Martha kept walking. For Kitty, this was a sensitive subject. She was still in the grim no-man's-land of not knowing if her family was lost. If she wanted to explain why she felt that way, it would have to come out without any prompting.

"It was having all those babies living next door when we first got here." Kitty turned to Martha with a rueful smile. "It was the best advert for birth control. I think it's probably put me off for life!"

———

The day after the snow melted, a heap of mail arrived at the camp. There was too much for Martha to carry on foot. She had to drive down to the gates and pile it all into the car. Kitty came out of the office to help her unload it. She didn't say anything, but Martha could see the tension in her face.

They started sorting the mail into piles. Most of the letters were marked with the insignia of UNRRA or the US Army. But there was the odd one with foreign stamps in the top right corner. Martha's heart skipped a beat with each one she spotted, but none were from Poland. There were three from France, addressed to Delphine, and one from America—a Christmas card from her cousin in New Orleans.

"Oh!" Kitty was staring at an envelope with her name on it, which had the words "International Settlement of Shanghai" stamped across the top. She glanced up at Martha, then ripped open the flap.

"It's from someone called Ruth Medavoy." Kitty's hand trembled as she held the letter. "She says the rabbi passed my letter on to her. She's the wife of the silk merchant my parents did business with."

"What does she say?"

Kitty's eyes darted across the page. She drew in a breath and closed her eyes. "She says they *did* get to Shanghai." Her eyes snapped open, brimming with tears. "They lived with her until the Japanese forced the Jews to move into the ghetto."

"Oh, Kitty!" Martha searched her face, half-afraid of what was coming next.

"They didn't go to the ghetto." Kitty drew the back of her hand across her eyes and read aloud: "'Many people went into hiding at that time. We left Shanghai and went to live in the north, but your parents went to another place. We have only just returned to the city. Everything is in disarray. I'm afraid I can't give you an address to write to because I don't know where your parents might be. I have heard that people are still in hiding.'"

Kitty looked up. "I . . . I can't believe it." Her teeth were rattling as she spoke. "Th . . . they m . . . m . . . made it. B . . . b . . . but now they . . ."

Martha shot around the desk as Kitty collapsed into the chair. She cradled Kitty's head in her arms and hugged her tight. There was no resistance, no attempt to pull away. "It's going to be all right," she murmured, stroking Kitty's hair. "It won't be long. You'll find them."

Kitty mumbled something Martha couldn't quite make out.

Martha glanced at the ceiling, willing what she'd said to be true. It would be so cruel, to have gotten this far, only for the trail to go cold.

<hr/>

Kitty had to wait a whole week to share the news about her parents with Charlie. He'd been given leave with immediate effect and had gone skiing in the Bavarian Alps. On his first day back, he rang through to the office to tell her—and she ran all the way there.

"Hey! What's this?" He stroked her face with his fingers when she broke away from kissing him.

"I'm sorry—I promised myself I wouldn't." She swallowed back the tears brimming her eyes. In a few staccato sentences she told him about the letter and what it contained.

"That's fantastic news!" He gathered her up in his arms and held her tight. "I wish I'd been here when it came. You must have been blown away!"

"I was," she murmured. "I couldn't believe that they'd made it—all that way across Europe and Russia. But I can hardly bear it, knowing that but not knowing where they are."

"It's only a matter of time, though, isn't it? They'll soon get things organized, like they did here when the war ended. Your parents could be in a camp already—and if they are, it won't be long until lists are sent out."

"I keep hoping that's what's happened," Kitty said. "Mrs. Medavoy wrote the letter at the end of November—more than two months ago."

"So, you could get news any day."

"But what if they . . ." She broke off, burying her face in the folds of his jacket.

"Try not to think that way." He rubbed his hands across her shoulders.

She raised her head. "I *do* try. But there's this voice in my head that tells me not to get my hopes up, that I'm stupid for allowing myself to get excited."

"Don't ever believe that." He kissed her forehead, nuzzling her hair. She felt his hand move off her shoulder. There was a rustle of fabric. Then he said, "I hope you won't be mad at me. I know what you said, about not being able to commit until you found out for sure about your mom and dad, but . . ." He released her, took a step back, and held out his hand. "I saw this in a little shop in the Alps. I couldn't resist it."

She stared at the small black box cupped in his fingers.

"Can I show you?" He opened the lid to reveal a ruby ring encircled with tiny diamonds. "It reminded me of that night we had before Christmas," he said. "Do you remember? The fire with the snow glistening all around it? And you looking up at the stars, watching the northern lights turn red?" He searched her face. "It doesn't have to mean anything. You can wear it on any finger you want. I just wanted you to have it."

Kitty was gazing at the ruby. She was suddenly transported back to the Christmas market in Vienna, to the glitter of falling snow against the jewel-colored lanterns strung across the stalls. She could smell the sweet, earthy scent of roasting chestnuts and hear the wheezing notes of an accordion. She felt the tickle of fur on her cheek as her mother guided her across the square. And there was a glimpse of something else—something that she had tried so hard to picture but had always evaded her: her mother's eyes, the pale, clear blue of a mountain lake, smiling as she broke off a chunk of gingerbread and popped it into Kitty's mouth.

"Oh, honey, don't cry!" Charlie snapped the box shut. "I never meant to upset you!"

She shook her head. "It's beautiful," she whispered. "I . . . I'm not crying. I'm just . . . remembering."

"*Good* memories?"

"Yes." She smiled. "Can I try it on?"

"Which hand?"

"That depends."

"Well, it's not the most romantic place, but here goes." He dropped down onto one knee. "Will you marry me, Kitty?"

⚬

"You said yes?" Delphine took Kitty's outstretched hand, angling it to the light. The diamonds cast rainbow beams across the wall of the cabin.

"I said I would marry him, but not yet," Kitty said.

"Wouldn't it be lovely to get married in our little chapel." Delphine was gazing out the window, a wistful look on her face.

"I don't think that's going to happen." Kitty twisted her ring around on her finger. "Charlie's Welsh Presbyterian and I'm Jewish. I know Father Josef's pretty liberal minded, but I think even he would have to draw the line at that. I think we'd have to ask the army chaplain at the base. If he says no, it'd have to be the town hall in Fürstenfeldbruck."

"That doesn't sound very romantic," Delphine said.

"Well, there's no point even thinking about it yet." Kitty smiled.

Martha sensed that Kitty's mask was back on. There was a defensive quality about her smile—a brittleness that hid a depth of feeling Kitty was reluctant to reveal. Martha wondered if she was secretly hoping her parents would be able to attend the wedding.

From the little news available, the situation in China sounded even worse than Kitty's letter had suggested. Now that the Japanese had been defeated, there were rumblings about a Communist takeover— like what had happened in Poland.

Martha hadn't breathed a word of any of this to Kitty. But it was more than likely she'd heard it herself. Charlie would be alert to any talk of that kind at the base—especially as his own family was part Chinese. What would they do if Kitty got the news she was longing for, but her parents were unable to get back? Would she risk her own future to go to them?

CHAPTER 25

Signs of spring appeared in Seidenmühle less than a month after the last of the snow had disappeared. Clumps of wild narcissus sprouted among the trees, and the hawthorn bushes along the river burst into blossom. But the change of seasons also brought the unwelcome news that another transport would be leaving for Poland in the first week of April.

If the DPs had been hesitant back in September, they were now outright scared of what awaited them if they returned to their homeland. The newspapers carried headlines of Churchill's speech, delivered in Fulton, Missouri, warning of the menace of Soviet Communism and an iron curtain descending on Eastern Europe.

Some of the DPs had acquired radios, which were continuously tuned to Radio Moscow. They heard Stalin denounce Churchill's warning as warmongering. There was a sinister sense of battle lines being drawn.

To make matters worse, reports came through that food prices in Poland had skyrocketed. According to the latest information, a pound of lard cost two hundred zlotys—the equivalent of twenty dollars, more than a man could expect to earn for a day's labor.

Martha read the major's memorandum about the transport to Kitty and Delphine as they gathered for their evening meal.

"Did I hear right?" Delphine frowned. "He's offering *sixty* days' worth of extra rations to anyone who volunteers for the transport?"

Martha nodded. "The army's calling it Operation Carrot. It's the equivalent of ninety-four pounds of food per person—distributed on arrival in Poland. When I spoke to him on the phone, he suggested that we put up a display of what they'd get and have them file through the mess hall to take a good look at it."

"That's a horrible idea." Kitty blew out a breath. "Like temptation on a plate."

"I know. But we're going to have to do it," Martha said. "He's sending someone to inspect it."

⟡

Kitty was put in charge of creating the display of food. "Because you're the artistic one," Martha had said.

A sense of shame crept over her as she began arranging the assortment of cans and loose goods. Ordinarily, she would have taken pride in making such everyday commodities into a three-dimensional work of art. But there was no escaping the feeling that what she was doing was baiting a trap.

She shaped the flour into a snowy mountain, flanked by a forest of dried peas. The lard was fashioned into a glistening glacier with salt sprinkled on its surface. Rolled oats formed undulating fields around the flour mountain, while cans of fish and evaporated milk formed something resembling a village nestled at its base.

Martha came to join Kitty when it was finished. "Smile," Martha whispered. "We *have* to smile."

They stood and watched as people filed past the display. The expressions on the faces of the DPs intensified the guilt Kitty felt. Their eyes glittered with terrible fascination at the sight of so much food piled up in front of them. It felt like a betrayal. The effort of maintaining a smiling mask almost paralyzed her.

To the women's surprise, Major McMahon himself arrived at the camp as the last of the DPs were leaving the dining room.

"Good job!" He beamed at the edible landscape. "I hope it does the trick!"

"*I* don't," Kitty murmured under her breath.

"What's that?"

"We're just worried about the news coming out of Eastern Europe," Martha said. "We don't feel good about trying to persuade people to go somewhere they might actually be worse off than they are here."

"Pardon me, ma'am, but did you really expect to feel *good* about any of this?" He waved his hand toward the open door. Some of the DPs were still standing outside, casting furtive glances at the food mountain. "As I said before, your job is to keep them alive—simple as that. They might not have a ball when they get back home, but the Russkies probably won't kill 'em."

"*Probably?*" Kitty shot him a look of incredulity.

"Is it so wrong for them to want something better?" Martha's eyes flashed. "If they had the choice, they'd go to America or Australia or Great Britain—anywhere but Poland."

"But that's the point. They *don't* have the choice. Every other door out of here is slammed shut. They're talking about letting a handful of Kraut war brides into the States, is all. No sign of things loosening up anytime soon." He dipped his hand into the floury mound on the table, sifting it through his fingers. "That's why it's so important to play up the positives. There are jobs in reconstruction work available, as well as all this food." He rubbed his hands together as if he wished he were going there himself. "And no one has to go back to the villages on the Russian side of the line. If their homes are there, they can apply for resettlement. They'll be given a piece of land in one of the places we took off the Germans: Silesia—that's good farmland. You can make a living there, no problem."

Martha tried to imagine how she would feel if America were to be divided up in this way, if she were told that New York and every state on the East Coast were suddenly out of bounds. How would she react to being told that, instead, she could become an orange farmer in Mexico?

"What about the people who live in Silesia?" Kitty said. "How are they going to feel about being thrown off their land?"

"They lost the war." He shrugged. "Now, ladies, I need a list by the end of this week: a minimum of four hundred this time." With a nod to each of them, he bustled out of the room.

"*Four hundred*—that's almost twice as many as last time." Kitty glanced at the landslide the major had caused in her carefully sculpted landscape. The lard glacier had shifted halfway down the flour mountain, toppling some of the sardine-tin houses. "I suppose I'd better clear all this up now everyone's seen it."

"I just don't understand why President Truman won't let them in." Martha's eyes narrowed as she watched more cans fall like dominoes. "America is a nation of displaced people. How can you close a border that's been open to the whole world for hundreds of years?"

Martha's dreams that night were invaded by hordes of soldiers. They wore scarlet uniforms with the gold hammer and sickle emblazoned on their chests, and they streamed up the road toward the camp like a river of blood. When they reached the gates, they started hurling rocks. One gate broke loose and flew into the air. It came hurtling down like a guillotine, straight toward a man who was lying facedown in the snow. She raced to catch it before it landed, but she was too late. Instead of catching the gate, she caught the man's severed head. When she turned it over, she saw that it was Stefan.

She must have cried out in her sleep, because she opened her eyes to find Delphine leaning over her. It wasn't properly light, but she could see that her friend's face was creased with concern.

"Are you okay?" Delphine whispered. "Bad dream?"

Martha nodded.

"What about?"

Martha didn't want to let on that the nightmare had been about Stefan. "Russian soldiers," she whispered back. "They were trying to smash their way into the camp. One of the gates went up in the air and nearly landed on me."

Delphine grunted. "Well, you don't have to be Sigmund Freud to work that one out: it's all that iron curtain stuff in the news preying on your mind."

"I suppose it is. I'm sorry I woke you up."

"You didn't." Delphine gave her a wry look. "I've been awake half the night, worrying about the auxiliaries. They haven't stopped talking about that food, you know. Two of the girls are ready to sign up."

"But they've got no home to go back to."

"I know. I'm trying to talk them out of it, but they think they've had enough experience at the hospital to get jobs in Warsaw. And the idea of getting two months' worth of rations in one go—when you think what it was like before the snow melted, well, you can understand it, can't you?"

"What about Wolf?" Martha held her breath. She couldn't bear to think of what it would do to Delphine if the apple of her eye up and left the camp.

"I asked him what he thought about it. He's . . ." She hesitated. Her eyes were glassy. "*Mon petit chou.* My little cabbage. It doesn't sound so good in English, does it?" She sniffed. "He said: 'I only go where you go.' I just wanted to weep when he came out with that. I mean, what kind of future does he have if he stays here?"

"Remember what you said to me?" Martha took her hand. "This place won't be here forever."

"But when it closes down, I'll have to go back to France, and as things stand, he wouldn't be allowed to come with me."

"There's a way he could. If you wanted him to." Martha hardly dared to say what had come into her mind.

"How?"

"You could adopt him. Legally, I mean. Both of his parents are known to be dead, so there's nothing to stand in the way of that."

Delphine was staring at the patch of gray light filtering through the window. "Do you really think I could?"

Later that morning, when she had finished doing the ward rounds with Dr. Jankaukas, Delphine went to find Wolf. He was in the side room, putting away sheets and pillowcases that had come back from the laundry. In the ten months she had known him, he had grown taller than her. He no longer needed to stand on a chair to reach the top shelf. As he worked, he chatted with one of the girls, who sat in a corner of the room, winding clean bandages.

"Wolf, can I have a word with you?"

He looked around at the sound of his name.

Delphine cocked her head toward the entrance to the hospital. She needed to talk to him outside, where no one would overhear.

There was a worried expression on his face when he sat down beside her on the wall in front of the hospital. "I do something wrong?"

"No." She patted his arm. "I just wanted to tell you something." She saw his face relax. "You know that one day this place will close down. And I will have to go back to France."

He nodded, staring at the ground. "You come to tell me I cannot go with you. That I will be alone again."

"No, Wolf, I didn't come to say that." Tears prickled her eyes. "At the moment, you wouldn't be allowed into France. But there's a way you could come with me. There's a word you won't know—*adoption*. It's when someone signs papers to say they will look after a child who is not their son or daughter. That's what I would like to do: adopt you."

His dark eyes widened as he looked up. "You will be my mama?"

She nodded. "If you want me to." She tried to swallow the lump in her throat.

"You can do this? Tomorrow?"

"Not tomorrow. I must write letters first. But soon, I hope."

He wrapped his arms around her, holding her tight, as if he never wanted to let go. She could feel his tears in her hair. She was crying, too.

CHAPTER 26

Operation Carrot had an immediate impact on morale in the camp. Within a couple of days, Martha was only a handful of people short of the target the major had given her. The names on the list were mainly young single men. There was almost no one over the age of forty. On the last transport there had been many older people—all of them desperate to be reunited with relatives in Poland, but the older DPs who remained at Seidenmühle knew there was no one waiting for them. Whatever nostalgia they had for the place they once called home, they didn't have the heart to return to a place inhabited by ghosts—and no amount of extra food was going to change that. But staying behind was only a temporary solution. The DP camps would have to close eventually, and no one, including Martha, had any idea how or when that would be accomplished.

She was relieved to see that Aleksandra and Marek had not volunteered for the transport. She hadn't sought them out, because she felt it was wrong to try to influence them. But the thought of them taking little Rodek to Poland was chilling. She knew that one day, she would have to wave goodbye to her little godson. But she wanted him to grow up in a place of hope, not fear.

She took the list to show to Father Josef. She wanted to know what he thought of the bribery the army was resorting to. He was in the chapel, clearing the altar table after Mass.

"It feels all wrong," she said, as he scanned the names. "I wonder how many of them would have signed up *without* the extra rations?"

"Probably no more than a few dozen," the priest replied. "Everybody's worried about what life will be like when they get back there, but the thought of having two months' worth of food gives them courage."

"Do *you* think it's wrong?"

He hesitated before replying, rubbing his beard with his fingers. "It's not a simple matter of what's right and what's wrong. There are thousands of DPs across the occupied territories. They all need feeding and housing. It can't go on indefinitely. And with other countries refusing to take them . . ." He trailed off, shaking his head. "I'm not saying I like what the army is doing—but I understand why they're doing it." He glanced at the list in his hand. "These people have made their choice. No one is being forced to get on that train."

"But it feels like I've failed them, sending them to a place where they could be worse off than they are here."

"That's understandable. The trouble is there's no way of knowing what daily life is like there now. It's almost impossible to get firsthand information. I've written countless letters to the bishop's office in Warsaw, but I never get a reply."

Martha's insides clenched. Was that why she'd heard nothing from Stefan? Was it possible that he had written to her, but his letters had never arrived? The thought of that was unbearable. "Do you think letters to the West are being intercepted? Censored?"

"Yes—both, I should think. And the Communists want to crush religion. I don't even know if the bishop's office still exists. I don't suppose the government would want a person like me knowing what was going on." He shrugged. "I'm probably on some blacklist."

Martha nodded. No doubt he would be seen as a troublemaker, this priest who had been sent to Dachau for his outspoken views about the Nazis.

"So, *you* can't go back?"

"Well, I could, of course. But it's likely I'd be arrested the moment I stepped off the train." He pressed his lips together, the tuft of gray above his chin coming up to meet his mustache. "Don't misunderstand me—I'm not afraid of going to prison. But I think God would rather I was here, doing what I can for the people who are still in the camp."

"Does it worry you to think of there being no church for the DPs to go to back in Poland?"

"I think of little else. When I listen to the radio, I get a sense of real evil coming from the mouths of men like Stalin. I've been trying to prepare people for what it might be like when they go back, encouraging them to meet in each other's homes for secret fellowship if the churches are closed." His eyes ran over the altar table, where the empty chalice sat, along with the plate scattered with bread crumbs. "It's all too easy to lose your faith if you're trying to practice it alone. It's like a coal falling out of the fire: it soon goes cold."

Martha thought about how quickly she had lost habits that had seemed like second nature when she and her grandmother had stopped going to their neighborhood church in New Orleans. "You don't think it's possible to go on believing unless you're with others who share those beliefs?"

"It's possible, yes. But it's not easy." He grunted. "Not even if you're a priest. That's one thing I learned in Dachau: if I had just one or two others to talk to, to pray with, it built me up. The times when I was all alone were the hardest. But the other thing Dachau taught me was that they can take everything away from you except what's in here." He raised his hand to his chest. "It's like the memory of someone you love: you carry that inside yourself always—even if you can't be with them."

He must have seen the expression that flitted across her face. She wondered if Stefan had spoken to the priest about her, in the confessional perhaps. Because the look he gave her was one of such compassion—as if he knew her pain.

"You know, I pray for you every day: for all of you."

"Well . . . thank you." *God knows we need it.* She'd almost said the words out loud. But that would have sounded flippant. "I did go to church when I was a little girl: to a Catholic church. I thought it was so beautiful—the candles and the statues and all of that." There was no need to tell him that, at the age of twelve, she'd started to think of religion as being like believing in fairies and Santa Claus.

"Do you still pray?"

The directness of his question caught her by surprise. There had been many times—especially since coming to Germany—when she had shot silent, fervent requests like arrows into the sky. Why? She couldn't answer that. "I suppose I do, in a way," she murmured.

"God hears those prayers."

"Even from people who don't know what they believe?"

"You believe in love, don't you? You spend all day, every day, caring for people in need. You didn't have to take that path—you chose to. And that kind of love is the essence of what God is."

As he handed back the list, she wondered if the people whose names it contained thought of her in the same way he did. She hoped they realized that it hadn't been her idea to try to get rid of them with the lure of food.

And if striving every day to provide for them was a kind of love, then yes, she did love them. Her mistake, in Stefan's case, had been to allow that sort of love to turn into a different kind.

As she was walking out of the chapel, his face filled her mind's eye. Without even realizing it, she fired off another silent plea. Not for him this time, but for herself: for inner peace and acceptance of what she couldn't change—qualities she'd tried and failed to nurture since the day she'd said goodbye to him. Like the people on the list in her hand, she had to let him go.

⟶⟶

Two days after the Poland-bound train pulled out of Fürstenfeldbruck station, Kitty received a telegram from the American Jewish Joint Distribution Committee.

"Oh, Martha . . ." She looked up. Her face had gone ghostly white. Her lips were trembling. "They've found them. They're alive!"

They ran all the way to the hospital to tell Delphine. Father Josef was there, too. After many hugs and tears, Kitty passed the telegram around for them all to see:

HERMANN AND ELSA BLUMENTHAL.
LEOPOLDSTADT VIENNA. ALIVE AND WELL
SHANGHAI. EXPECT LETTER.

"Twelve words," Delphine said. "Isn't it incredible: that your life can be transformed by just *twelve* words."

⟶⟶

The letter came three weeks later. Kitty stared at her name on the envelope, momentarily paralyzed by the sight of her mother's handwriting. She opened it very slowly and carefully, as if it were a delicate relic from some bygone age.

Martha and Delphine were there with her, listening eagerly as she translated from the German:

"Darling—what utter joy to know that you are alive! We had given up hope when our letters to you in London were returned to us. Papa and I thought we might die of happiness when we were given the news that you have been searching for us.

"For two years we have been living with a Chinese family in the countryside south of the city. They sheltered us in their home, and in return, we worked for them, making clothes. We didn't find out until last month that hostilities with the Japanese were at an end."

Kitty looked up, open-mouthed. "They didn't know the war was over. All those months, they just carried on hiding." She turned back to the letter: "We are now living with the Medavoys, who helped us when we first arrived in Shanghai. Thank God, we are both in good health and able to work until such time as we can leave China. We long for the moment when we will be reunited with you, my darling—but we have been told that there is no prospect of getting passage out of the country until the political situation here eases . . ." She trailed off, staring at the piece of paper in her hand.

"It can't be long," Delphine said. "If relief work is already underway, they'll be getting people out of there—just like we're doing here."

Martha nodded, wishing she felt as certain as Delphine sounded. What if, as in Poland, the Communists took control of China? Would anyone be allowed to get on a boat out of Shanghai in those circumstances? She tried to push those thoughts out of her mind. "You'll want to tell Charlie. He's not on duty today, is he? You can call him if you'd like to."

They left Kitty alone to make the call. It took a few minutes of waiting before the operator at the base managed to locate him and connect her.

"Sorry, honey—I was in the major's office." He sounded flustered. "What is it? Are you okay?"

"Yes, I'm fine. I got a letter from my parents! I couldn't wait to tell you!"

There was silence at the end of the phone.

"Charlie? Are you still there?"

"Yes . . . that's wonderful . . . I . . ." His voice faded away.

"Charlie?"

"I . . . I'm sorry. It's the *best* news—you must be . . ." She heard him blow out a breath. "It's just that . . . I've had some news, and it's not good. They're shipping me out next week."

"Shipping you out?" She stared at the phone.

"The army's winding things down here. They don't need as many troops. They're sending a bunch of us back to the States."

"But . . ."

"I know, honey. We can still do it, though. There's enough time—just about . . ." His words hung in the air between them. "I don't want it to feel like I'm rushing you. God knows it couldn't be a worse time. But if we don't do it now . . ."

She didn't need him to spell it out. "It would be all over for us, wouldn't it? They wouldn't let me into America."

"Well, they *might*, but right now, it's anybody's guess when that could be."

"It could be years from now." She felt as though someone else's voice was coming out of her mouth—a calm, rational voice, weighing it all up—while hers was trapped inside, screaming at the unfairness of it all.

———

Martha and Delphine had been to the warehouse to see what they could find for an impromptu celebration. They went back to the office clutching a bottle of Coke.

"Sorry it's not champagne," Delphine said, as they came through the door. "Oh, Kitty, what's the matter? What's happened?"

The two women listened in horrified silence as Kitty told them.

"I don't know what to do. He says the army chaplain at the base could marry us, but it would have to be the day after tomorrow. Charlie's due to catch a train to the coast the next day, and he sails the following morning." She buried her face in her hands.

"You still want to marry him, don't you?" Martha's hand was on Kitty's shoulder.

"Yes," she mumbled. "But how can I?" She lifted her head. "He says it would be a while before I'd get official permission to join him—a few months, maybe. But what if my parents managed to get out of China during that time? Where would they go?"

"Do you think they'll want to return to Vienna?" Delphine bit her lip.

"I don't think so. I saw what it was like."

"Would they want to live in America," Martha said, "if you settled there with Charlie?"

"I think they'd be happy anywhere, so long as we were together. But would they be allowed in? It's not as if they're *his* parents—it might be different if they were. In the eyes of the immigration people, they'd be foreign refugees, just like our DPs. They're banned from entering the States, and who knows if that ban will ever be lifted?"

"What does Charlie say about your parents?" Delphine reached across the desk for Kitty's hand.

"He says they'd be welcome to come and live with us whenever they get out of China." She shook her head. "He even offered to get his mother to write to the authorities in Shanghai—she speaks Chinese, and he said it might speed things up. But . . ." She heaved out a sigh that made her lips quiver.

"The problem is, at this moment, you have no control over what happens in China. You don't have time to wait for any letter to Shanghai."

"I know. So, what do I do?"

Martha glanced at Delphine over Kitty's head. "My advice would be to do the one thing you *do* have control over—which is to go ahead and marry the man you love."

———

There was no time for a wedding dress to be made, so Kitty wore the outfit she had designed for the Christmas party.

"Do you think it's a bit shocking, getting married in red?" she asked Martha.

"Well, it's unusual." Martha smiled. "But it's not a church service, so I'd say anything goes. And it's such a gorgeous dress."

"Charlie hasn't had a chance to buy a ring. I'm going to see if I can find anything in the weaving shed that we could use."

"Have mine." With some difficulty, Martha twisted the ring off her finger.

"Oh, I couldn't!"

"Why not? I don't need it anymore."

"But it's . . . it's gold. It must be worth . . ."

"It's not worth that much." Martha waved away her protests. "Arnie won it in a game of cards. If it fits you, you're welcome to it."

"Well, if you're really sure . . ." Kitty slipped the ring on and held out her hand for Martha to see.

"It goes really well with your engagement ring. You have such lovely hands—those long, slim fingers! I have to say, it looks much better on you than it ever did on me." It was strange, the sense of relief that parting with the ring gave her. She hadn't felt able to relinquish it before now: to put it away in a drawer would have been a depressing thing to do. But to give it away to someone who really needed it made her heart feel light.

———

Kitty and Charlie had just one night together as a married couple before he left for Bremen. Martha had offered Kitty the chance to travel with him as far as the coast, but she turned it down.

"I don't think I could have borne it, standing on the quayside, waving him off," she said when she arrived back at Seidenmühle the day after the wedding.

"It must feel strange, coming back to all this," Delphine said. "Probably makes it all seem a bit unreal?"

"It does." Kitty opened her bag and fished out a folded piece of paper. "All I've got to prove it happened is this. I have to apply to the army for a new identity card: Mrs. Katya Lewis—doesn't that sound strange?"

"Where will Charlie go when he gets back to the States?" Martha asked.

"His family live in San Francisco," Kitty said. "But he's not sure how long he'll stay there. He wants to go to college on the East Coast. There's a business course he's interested in at a university in New York. It begins with C—I can't remember the name."

"Columbia?"

"That's it."

It was a strange thought, Kitty in the not-too-distant future, walking streets that had once been so familiar to Martha. Perhaps they would be near neighbors one day, when the relief work was over and Martha's job came to an end.

It was something she tried not to think about—what would happen when that time came. The idea of going back to New York filled her with dread. She didn't know what she would do, where she would live. The truth was, she found it almost impossible to imagine a future beyond the gates of the camp.

CHAPTER 27

In the first week of May, four hundred new DPs arrived to replace those who had boarded the train for Poland in April. They had been living in a camp in another sector of the American zone. As more DPs returned to Poland, some camps were closing and the remaining inmates were sent to those that, for the time being, would remain active. Seidenmühle, it seemed, was in it for the long haul.

It wasn't easy, settling the newcomers in. They had neither wanted nor expected to move camps. Like all the DPs in the occupied territories, they nurtured dreams of a better life, and it was a depressing business to find themselves tacking up blankets and piling up suitcases to create makeshift living spaces.

Two days after the new DPs arrived, Martha was collecting the mail from the guardhouse when she saw a farmer's cart pull up outside the gates.

"I didn't think we were expecting a food delivery today." She glanced at Corporal Brody, who was already tucking into the bread and marmalade she had brought him.

"We're not." Reluctantly he put down the food and stepped outside to ask what the farmer wanted. The reply came from a voice she recognized. Her heart almost burst through her ribs as she darted outside. When she called out his name, all that emerged was a rasping whisper.

"Good morning!" He greeted her with a wary smile.

"G . . . good morning." She forced the words out, her body electrified with shock.

"Mr. Dombrowski, isn't it." Brody tilted his head as he looked at him. "Thought you went back to Poland."

"I came back." The muscles of his jaw clenched. "I am not asking to come into the camp. I know that is not possible."

Brody glanced at Martha. She hoped the corporal couldn't see how close she was to tears. She was staring straight through the gates, mesmerized by the face she thought she'd never see again.

Stefan met her eyes, searing her with his hot blue gaze. "I came only to show you . . ." He went over to the cart and said something in Polish that Martha didn't catch. Then two heads appeared over the side. Two little girls with their hair in braids—one dark, one fair—were peering shyly at Martha.

"This is my daughter, Lubya." Stefan lifted the blond child down and set her on the ground. "And this is her friend, Halina."

"Will you open the gates, please?" Martha had difficulty controlling her voice as she turned to Brody. "Mr. Dombrowski has had a long journey. I'm sure there's nothing in the rules to say we can't offer him some refreshment."

"Yes ma'am."

Martha turned back, smiling to cover her bewilderment, her eyes moving from Stefan and the girls to the cart, expecting another figure to emerge from among the crates of onions.

Stefan took both children by the hand and crouched down, murmuring words of reassurance. This time he was close enough for Martha to hear what he said, despite the blood pounding in her ears. He was telling them not to be afraid, that the lady was kind and would give them something nice to eat.

The dark-haired girl, Halina, looked doubtful. *"Wygląda jak żołnierz."* She looks like a soldier.

Stefan said that no, she wasn't a soldier—her name was Martha.

The girls looked at each other. Then his daughter said: *"Czy ona będzie moją nową mamą?"* Will she be my new mama?

When they were out of sight of the guardhouse, Stefan's hand brushed Martha's arm. It was the briefest touch—unseen by the girls, who were a few steps ahead, skipping along the path—but the look that came with it was intense.

"I'm sorry. I shocked you—I can see from your face. You didn't get my letters?" He paused, his eyes fixed on hers. "I wrote to tell you what happened when I got back to Warsaw. I . . ."

"Papa!" Lubya turned around. She was pointing to a squirrel darting about beneath the trees.

He stepped away, his hand dropping to his side, as if his fingers had touched an electric fence.

"It's okay," she whispered. "You go to her. We can talk later."

When they reached the office, Kitty did a good job of covering her amazement at the sight of Stefan coming through the door.

"It's a shame you didn't come back last week," she said. "We had lots of room then. But we can probably squeeze you into the stable block."

"They can't stay." Martha shot her a desperate look. "The army won't allow people back once they've left. But if we could rustle up something to eat . . ."

"Of course." Kitty dropped down in front of the girls, her head level with theirs. *"Czy jadłyście kiedyś amerykańską czekoladę?"*

Their eyes widened. She was offering them one of the precious Hershey bars Charlie had given her.

"Is that okay?" She glanced up at Stefan, who smiled. Turning to Martha, she said: "I'll meet you in the mess hall in about half an hour."

Martha nodded. Her throat was so tight she didn't trust herself to speak.

When they'd gone, she and Stefan stood in the room like a couple of strangers. She felt paralyzed, unable to run to him and wrap her arms around him because she didn't know what he was going to tell her. And he looked as uneasy as she felt.

"Will you walk with me?" He tilted his head toward the window.

Outside, stepping into the shadow of the trees, Martha found it easier to breathe. "Did you really write to me?" The question sounded foolish, the sort of thing a lovestruck teen might say, but it felt better than asking him outright what had happened to his wife.

"Three days after I left the train, I wrote. One week later, I had a visit from the police." He stopped, taking a breath, as if the images in his head were too painful to put into words. "They wanted to know why I sent a letter to an army camp in the West. They told me that if I did it again, they would arrest me." He cleared his throat. "So, I tried a different way: I gave American cigarettes to the captain of a ship. He said he would post my letter in Germany." Another pause; a shake of the head. "I don't know what he did with it. Maybe he just lied to me."

They were still walking. Martha kept silent. She hated the thought of him parting with precious cigarettes—very likely the only currency he had—in a vain attempt to get a letter to her. She sensed from the staccato sentences and frequent pauses that he was bracing himself to reveal what that letter had contained.

"I slept in the warehouse next to the river, where I stored timber before the war. My house . . ." He drew in a long breath and blew it out again. "Is gone. The Nazis destroyed the city. They hate the Polish way of life. They burned schools, universities, churches, castles . . . everything."

For a while, he went quiet. Their feet crushed pine needles as they trudged deeper into the woods. "My wife, she worked in a library: the Zaluski Library—the oldest in Poland." His voice was hoarse with emotion. "I went to find out what happened to her. But there was nothing there. They said German soldiers made a fire with all the books." He stopped and leaned against a tree, pressing his forehead against the bark.

Instinctively she reached for him, clasping her arms around his back. She could feel his body shaking. "Don't try to talk anymore," she whispered. "Just let me hold you." He turned around, knocking her cap to the ground as he buried his head in her hair. The only sound was the rustling of the breeze in the branches overhead. She closed her eyes, rocking him like a child.

She had no idea how long they stood there. She became vaguely aware of a cold, wet sensation on the side of her face. She thought it was his tears. It was only when she opened her eyes that she saw the raindrops pattering onto the pine needles. She guided him into the shelter of the nearest tree, taking off her jacket to hold over their heads.

"Lubya will worry where I've gone," he murmured. "When I found her, I told her I would never leave her again."

The rain eased as they began to walk back. Stefan helped her back into the jacket and brushed off the needles that had stuck into her cap. She was careful not to look at him, pressing her lips tight to contain the questions buzzing inside her head.

⟞⟡⟝

Kitty had a plate of bread and sausage waiting for Stefan in the dining room. Lubya and Halina were already eating theirs. When she caught sight of her father, Lubya rushed from her seat and hurled herself into his arms.

"They've been very well behaved," Kitty said, as he sat down. She glanced at Martha. It was a wary, quizzical look. Martha's face couldn't convey the maelstrom of emotion the walk in the woods had brought on.

"Father Josef is on his way." Kitty turned to Stefan. "He's had to go to the hospital, but he's longing to see you. He said that if you need somewhere to sleep, you're welcome to use the chapel."

Stefan looked at Martha. "I don't want to make trouble for you."

"He said it doesn't count as army property because it's a church," Kitty said. "So, you wouldn't be breaking the rules."

Martha wondered if Stefan had some other plan, whether he'd simply called at the camp to draw a line under things before moving on to some other place. "Do you have somewhere to stay?" she asked him.

"I asked the farmer who gave me a ride here. He said we could sleep in his barn if I worked for him."

"What about the girls?" Martha said. "Who would look after them?"

He shrugged. "I haven't worked it out yet."

"They need to go to school," Kitty said. "They could come to lessons at the camp, couldn't they?"

"They could have their meals here, too." Martha nodded. "There's nothing in the rules to prevent that: they're DPs and they've never lived here." She fixed her eyes on the table to hide the sense of helpless frustration rising inside her. "It's inhuman, that they *could* live here but Stefan is barred."

"Well, the chapel might be the answer—just until you decide what you want to do." Kitty leaned across the table to pour water into Stefan's glass. Martha looked up, catching her eyes as she lifted the jug. There was a glint of conspiracy in Kitty's expression. She seemed to understand the complexity of the situation without knowing any of the details. She had grasped that what Stefan needed was time and space, a sanctuary in which he could begin to unburden himself. It was something Martha would never have thought of—offering the chapel as a temporary home. *Thank you,* she mouthed, as Kitty moved back across the table.

That night, when the girls were asleep, Stefan came to find Martha, who was sitting on the log pile outside the chapel. It was a still, clear night. A crescent moon hung over the trees, and the scent of the wild garlic growing by the river was in the air.

For a while, after he'd sat down beside her, he didn't speak. He was close enough for her to feel the warmth of his skin through the thin cotton of his shirtsleeve. This was something she had conjured a hundred times, the memory of them sitting side by side like this last summer. She had been in turmoil then, too—torturing herself about breaking the boundary between professional duty and personal feelings. Now the torture was of a different kind. The devastation of Stefan's loss was tangible. She felt like someone blindfolded, about to blunder into a wall or trip over some unseen obstacle. She didn't know how to begin the conversation they had to have.

"Are they okay?" she whispered. "Not frightened of sleeping in there?"

"They don't worry when they are together." His voice was soft and low.

"Halina is an orphan?"

"Yes. She and Lubya, they were hiding with ladies of the church . . ." He paused. "What word is it in English? For a lady with a long dress, white hat, no husband?"

"A nun?" Martha glanced sideways. She could see the silhouette of his chin against the indigo sky.

"Yes. I found a letter in a box in the ground—where I lived before the Nazis smashed the house down. It said Lubya was with nuns down-river, in Płock." He let out a long breath. "She was five years old when she went there. I thought she wouldn't remember me, but she had a photograph. The nuns said that when her mama . . ." His voice splintered. He swallowed and tried again. "My wife took Lubya there when the killing started. They said the library burnt down one month after. Everyone who didn't die, they shot."

"Oh, Stefan," Martha whispered.

"Lubya started to cry when I said I was taking her away. She didn't want to leave her friend. So, I told her we can take Halina, too."

"How did you get back to Germany?"

"In the same box with the letter was a watch and some rings. We made a plan, before the Nazis took me, that she would hide them in the garden. I sold those things to get money for the train."

"You didn't want to stay there? In Poland?" She was thinking about the relatives he had told her about—the nephew and niece he was god-father to.

"There is nothing there for me now. No family." She heard the catch in his voice as he struggled to stop it from breaking again. "My brother, he lived in Grodno. When the Russians came at the start of the war, they took all of them to Siberia. They . . . did not come back."

She reached for his hand, wanting desperately to take him in her arms and kiss away his pain. But that would feel so wrong. Somewhere in the trees behind them, she heard the call of an owl. The melancholy sound echoed Stefan's words. He had chosen to return to this no-man's-land, this place of zero opportunity. What she longed to know was *why* he had come back. Was it because of her, or simply because there was nowhere else to go?

Kitty and Delphine were waiting up for Martha when she got back to the cabin. They listened, grim-faced, as she described what Stefan had been through in Poland.

"Poor man," Delphine murmured. "It's so unfair that he's not allowed to live here—especially with those little girls to look after. Where will he go? How is he going to feed the children?"

"He talked about getting a job on one of the farms," Martha said. "But I don't see how that would work. The girls are too young to be left alone."

"He speaks quite good German, doesn't he?" Kitty was staring at something invisible on the wall above Martha's head.

"Yes, he does." Martha's eyes narrowed. "What are you thinking?"

"Charlie told me the army needs translators. Now things are winding down, they're having to put more resources into making sure things don't collapse when they pull out."

"You think they'd give Stefan a job at the base?"

"I don't see why not," Kitty said. "He proved himself when he was living here before. You could vouch for that."

Martha nodded. "But where would he live? And what about Lubya and Halina?"

"He built the chapel," Delphine said. "What if he built himself a cabin in the woods, beyond the boundary of the camp? The girls could come here when he was working. We could feed them, and they could have lessons with the other children."

"I'm sure he *could* build a cabin. But . . ." Martha hesitated, thinking aloud. "Would he be allowed to? I don't even know who owns that land."

"Does *anybody* own it?" Kitty shrugged. "Seems to me it's just abandoned. Like that ruined house where you got the tiles for the stables."

"I don't think anyone would come asking questions," Delphine said. "In all the time we've been here, I don't think any of us has ever encountered another human being in those woods."

"Well, I suppose it could work, in the short term." Martha was picturing the little house among the trees. Having Stefan so close would be the perfect solution. But it would require considerable diplomacy on her part. If the DPs felt that he was getting special treatment—that he was being allowed to live in a way denied to any of them—because there was something going on . . .

"The short term is all any of us can plan for." Delphine's voice cut across her thoughts. "No one knows how much longer we'll be here for."

"Things have to change soon," Kitty said. "Charlie says there's a protest movement underway in the States. All kinds of people are speaking out, saying what a disgrace it is that the government is moving so slowly."

"Do you think that's what Stefan is hoping for, long term, to get to America?" Delphine glanced at Martha. There was a hint of a smile in the look she gave—a well-meaning smile, no doubt—but it triggered a horrible possibility in Martha's mind: that Stefan had come back to Seidenmühle with the sole intention of emigrating to the States, with her as his passport out of Germany. He would know that short of a sudden U-turn by President Truman, marriage to a US citizen was his only way into America. And she had never told him she was still married to Arnie. Was that why he had been so desperate to get a letter to her the moment he knew that his wife was dead?

She despised herself for harboring such thoughts. The heartache and the sense of loss he conveyed were entirely genuine; she was certain of that. There was something else as well—an act that spoke volumes in defense of his character: he had taken on the care of an orphaned child. And he had done it despite being in the desperate position of having to sell the few possessions he had left just to get out of Poland. It was a selfless decision that echoed the qualities that had drawn Martha to him from the outset. Nothing he had done while living at Seidenmühle had been anything other than decent.

"I don't know what he's hoping for." Martha couldn't look Delphine in the eye. If he *had* come back because of his feelings for her, she needed to step back, take a breath, allow him the time he needed to grieve.

CHAPTER 28

Martha went in person to ask Major McMahon to give Stefan a job. As she had anticipated, he wasn't thrilled to learn that a DP who had been repatriated had come back.

"His wife is dead and his home and business were destroyed," she said. "His child was living in a convent. You can understand why he might want a fresh start."

"He should have gone to Silesia." The major grunted. "Plenty of opportunity for a fresh start there."

"But I thought that was only for people who came from the Russian side of the line; he's from Warsaw, so he wouldn't qualify."

"Maybe not. But it's not something we want to encourage—people drifting back like ghosts. They'll be spreading stories that'll put others off going."

"With respect, I think Radio Moscow is doing a good job of that already. And Mr. Dombrowski isn't mixing with people in the camp; he's building himself a cabin in the forest."

"You say he speaks good German?"

"He was my right-hand man when I first came here. I couldn't have negotiated with the mayor's office without him."

"Well, we could use him." The major rubbed his chin. "But there'd better not be any more DPs coming back. If anyone else comes banging on the gates, you send 'em packing—got that?"

———

Delphine opened one eye as Martha tiptoed past her bed. It was light outside, but she guessed that it was only about six o'clock. Martha had always been an early riser, but the past couple of weeks, she had been creeping out of the cabin at least an hour before anyone else was up. Most mornings, Delphine would be woken by the chug of the car's engine as it headed back into camp. That was her signal to get up. It meant that Martha had collected Stefan and the girls, dropped him at the base, and was bringing Lubya and Halina back for breakfast.

"It's only until he gets a car," Martha had said on the day Stefan started his job. "He's looking for something he can fix up—and as soon as he gets paid, he'll be able to do it." She'd worn the same matter-of-fact expression she always adopted when she spoke of him, doing her best to create the illusion that all she cared about was giving him a helping hand. Delphine could see that she was only trying to protect herself. But she wished Martha would talk to her instead of pretending everything was okay.

It was just before eight when Martha popped her head around the door of the cabin. "Want some coffee?" Delphine called out.

"Yes, please."

"How are they all this morning?" Delphine came out of the kitchen with a mug in her hand.

"Fine." Martha took a sip of coffee. "The girls are playing with some of the children from blockhouse five. They're not as shy as they were when they first came here."

"And Stefan? How's he getting on?"

"Okay, I think."

"You think? You haven't asked him?"

"There's not much chance to talk." Martha cradled the mug in her hands, looking down at it. "I don't like to ask how things are, with the girls in the car."

Kitty came down the stairs, still in her pajamas. "I don't mind babysitting one evening, if you and Stefan want to spend some time together."

"That's kind of you—but . . ." Martha trailed off with a shrug.

"You're worried about what people will think?" Delphine said. "No one needs to know."

"It's not just that. I . . ." She hesitated. "I'm not sure if Stefan would want to."

"Has something happened?" Kitty sat down next to Martha.

"No, not really." Martha sighed. "I guess I'm just afraid to push things."

"You can't go tiptoeing around each other forever," Delphine said. "He's probably as nervous as you are."

"Have you told him you're getting a divorce?" Kitty asked.

"That would sound as if I was expecting something, wouldn't it? And anyway, I can't, can I? Because I've got no chance of getting one unless I can track Arnie down."

Delphine frowned. "You haven't told Stefan how you feel?"

"It didn't seem right. I think it has to come from him."

"You'll end up going round in circles, then, won't you?" Delphine sighed.

It was nearly a week later when Kitty came up with the idea of inviting Lubya and Halina to join in her art class. So, on that day, Martha didn't take them with her when she went to pick Stefan up from the base. He'd agreed to Kitty's suggestion, but Martha felt awkward when he got into the car. It was the first time they had been alone together since the day he'd come back from Poland.

She pulled onto the side of the road a little more than a mile from the camp. His cabin was inaccessible by car. Usually, she would let him and the girls out at this point, then drive off. Now that it was just the two of them, she didn't know what to do. She kept the engine running, not wanting him to think she was expecting to be invited to his new home.

"Will you come see what I've done?" He turned to her and smiled. "You haven't come for a long time."

It was true—she hadn't seen it since it was just a pile of logs stacked in a clearing. Some of the men who had worked with Stefan on the lumber detail in the early days had helped him build the cabin. Martha had kept away during the construction, aware of what the men might think if she was hovering around.

As they made their way along the path, she caught a glimpse of it through the trees. "Oh, look at that!" It was like a woodcutter's hut out of a fairy tale. It had a shingle roof and shutters at the windows. There was even a little porch with a rustic wooden bench.

He opened the door. "It's dark in here." He went in ahead of her. "No glass in the windows." He opened the shutters while she stood in the doorway. "You can come in now," he said.

The dappled sunlight shining in from outside revealed two beds like the ones in the blockhouses, made of sacking stuffed with straw. Army-issue blankets were neatly folded across them, and on the pillows of the larger bed sat the two rag dolls Martha had commissioned from the camp sewing class: one with plaits of yellow wool and the other dark brown. Hanging from hooks on the wall were the dresses and cardigans Martha had helped the girls choose from the clothing storeroom.

Apart from the beds, the only other furniture in the room was a table made of wooden planks. On it were a camping stove, a kettle, three tin cups, and three plates. Beneath the table was the suitcase

Stefan had brought back from Poland and an apple crate containing an assortment of tins and jars.

"Shall I make coffee?"

"That would be good," she said.

Martha watched him light the camping stove and place the kettle over the flame. She wondered where he was getting water. There were streams in the forest that fed into the river. Or perhaps he filled a container at the army base?

"We can sit outside." He followed her through the door. She took a seat at one end of the bench, and he settled down at the other end.

For a while they sat in silence. Martha thought how peaceful it was. No sounds apart from the occasional rustle of a bird in the branches and the low hum of the kettle as it heated up. But the tension in the space between them was palpable. She had to find a way in, some topic of conversation that would encourage him to reveal what was really on his mind. The safest subject, she thought, was the children.

"Lubya and Halina are settling in really well," she began. "Have they told you about their new friends?"

"The girls from blockhouse five?"

"They were all playing a game of baseball when I left the camp."

"It's good that they play with other children." He nodded. "And they told me about the game you play in the car—what do you call it? My little eye?"

"I Spy." She smiled. "It's what we do after we drop you off: they see something out the window, and I have to guess what it is. They teach me the Polish word, and I tell them how to say it in English."

"They like you very much," he said.

"Well, I like them, too. They're lovely girls." She stopped herself from saying what she would have said to Delphine or Kitty: that they were remarkably happy and well adjusted considering what they had endured in their short lives. "Do you know anything about Halina's parents—what happened to them?" She held her breath. She hoped she wasn't jumping in too quickly.

"They are *Żydami*."

"Jewish?"

"The nuns said they died in Auschwitz. They gave Halina to a neighbor to hide."

Martha felt as though an icy hand had squeezed her insides. "Does she know that the Nazis killed them?"

He shook his head. "She doesn't ask. I will tell her one day. She knows many people died in the war—the nuns told her that."

"They never talk about the past when they're with me." Martha was looking straight ahead, her eyes fixed on a tree stump beyond the porch. "And I try not to say anything that might upset them. That's why I started playing that game with them: it makes it easier to avoid difficult conversations."

"It is hard when they ask me questions," he said. "When we came to the camp, they saw children with a mama and papa. They wanted to know why. Then Lubya asked me where her mama had gone."

"What did you say?" Martha whispered.

"I told her she has gone to be an angel." She could hear the tremor in his voice. In one swift movement she slid across the bench and wrapped her arms around him. She felt the thud of a stifled sob rising from his chest.

"Sorry, sorry." He mumbled the words into the side of her face.

"Don't be," she murmured. "It's good for you to let it out."

"I want to tell you all of it. But . . ."

"It's okay."

The shrill whistle of the kettle took him away from her. It was a few minutes before he came back with the coffee. He set the cups down on the planks in front of the bench, then pulled something from his pocket.

"This is the photo Lubya had by her bed when she lived with the nuns."

Martha took the black-and-white snapshot from his outstretched hand. It was a wedding photograph. Stefan and his bride were wearing the type of traditional embroidered clothes she had seen at the camp weddings. A circlet of flowers framed the pretty smiling face of a girl who looked about the same age as Kitty.

"Her name is Krystyna."

Martha wondered if he was using the present tense because his wife still felt like a part of his life. Looking at the picture, she couldn't help being reminded of the image that had been on her bedside table throughout her childhood. Like Lubya, it had been her only link with her parents. But unlike Stefan's daughter, Martha had always known that there was no chance of either of them coming back.

"She's beautiful," Martha said, handing the photo back. "How old were you when you got married?"

"I was twenty-four. She was twenty." He sat down beside her and bent to pick up his coffee. "I didn't see her face for four years—until Lubya showed me this picture."

"You've been through so much. These past few months must have been agony."

He was staring across his cup. A curl of steam clouded his chin. "First, when I got back to Warsaw, I thought they had both gone to Auschwitz, like so many Polish people. Then I found out what happened at the Zaluski Library. I asked myself, where was Lubya when this happened? I tried to find people who lived where we lived. I thought maybe she went to some house nearby. But no one knew. Then I remembered the plan of the box. I went back in the night, so nobody would see me, and I dug in the ground."

"I can't imagine how you must have felt, finding out that Lubya was alive."

"First time, I didn't find anything. I went back and tried again. The ground was so hard. It started to snow. I lay down. Thought maybe I would die. Then I felt like Krystyna came to me. She pointed to a tree. I started to dig—then I found the box. I shone a torch on the letter . . ." He closed his eyes as he let out a breath.

"That sounds like a miracle," Martha said.

"It seemed like that to me. And when I went to Płock, to the nuns, and they fetched her, and she knew who I was . . ." He broke off, staring at his hands. "When she showed me the photograph from the wedding, I had to turn away from her, so she wouldn't see me cry."

Martha felt tears prickle the backs of her eyes. The raw emotion in his voice tugged at her heart. It brought back what Delphine had said to her, months ago, before he'd boarded the train for Poland: *His heart is split in two.* That might have been true once, when he didn't know what had happened to Krystyna. But now . . .

"Stefan," she whispered, "I have to ask you, why did you come back here?"

He didn't answer at first. She could hear him breathe in and out, as if he were weighing what to say. "I want to be with you." He didn't look at her when the words came out. He was staring at the trees beyond the porch, as if someone were hiding there, listening. "But when I heard Lubya ask if you were going to be her new mama, I thought I'd done wrong. It was like I was trying to replace Krystyna. I was putting what I want before what Lubya thinks and how she feels." He turned his face to her. "And I don't know how *you* feel. I shocked you when I came back. I asked myself, why would she want someone like you? I have nothing—and I brought two children with me."

"You really think material possessions matter to me? Or the idea of looking after someone else's children?" She bit her lip. "I thought you knew me better than that."

His eyes searched her face. "But I think maybe you have somebody else. You don't wear your ring anymore."

"Oh, Stefan!" She shook her head. "I gave my ring to Kitty when she married Sergeant Lewis." She took his hand in both of hers. "There is no one else."

"What happened to your husband?" He held her gaze.

"I don't know where he is. I should have told you—I've been trying to get a divorce. But he hasn't answered my letters."

He ran his finger along the scar on her cheek. "He is a bad man?"

"Not always. I think he was just . . . lost. He drank too much. It changed him."

Stefan rubbed his chin. "You ran away from him? Came here?"

"Yes, I did run away. I was too afraid to face up to him. I never thought I'd . . ." She hesitated. "I didn't do it with the intention of falling in love with someone else." There. She had said it. The words hung in the air like smoke from an explosion.

"It is not possible to choose—who you love." He slipped his hand from her grasp, lifting his arm to encircle her shoulders. When they kissed, it felt as if the forest had closed in around them, cocooning them, just for that moment, from the world outside.

"I don't want to make things worse for you," she murmured, as she broke away. "It's too soon for you—I understand that."

He cupped her face in his hands. "You waited all this time for me. You don't mind waiting a little more?"

"No," she whispered. "I don't mind."

They stayed there, just holding each other, as the sun slowly sank behind the trees and, all around, twilight flowed like dark smoky water.

PART THREE

CHAPTER 29

Kitty had been married for more than six months when she finally received the documents that would allow her to join Charlie in America. Martha was in the office with her when she opened the envelope.

"It says I can travel on any army ship leaving Germany from the end of this month." Kitty looked up. Her face was drained of color.

"What's the matter? Don't you want to go?" Martha had the telephone receiver in her hand. She had been about to call the base, but she put the phone down. Kitty should have been dancing around the room. Was she having second thoughts now that the plan to go to the States had become a reality? Did she regret getting married in such a hurry?

"I'm desperate to see Charlie," she said. "I miss him like mad. But I can't leave, can I? Not yet. I couldn't do that to you."

"Why not?" Martha looked at her, perplexed. "This is your future, Kitty. You mustn't jeopardize it by worrying about us."

"But I *do* worry. Every time people leave, more DPs arrive. It's never-ending. You and Delphine can't carry on like this. It's been well over a year since we got here, and neither of you has had a proper break. It just doesn't seem fair for me to go swanning off to America."

"We'll manage." Martha tried to smile. "You deserve this chance to be happy. This place certainly won't be the same without you, but that's no reason to hang around when you could be on a boat to the States."

"What will you do? Will UNRRA send someone to replace me?"

"Probably." Martha avoided her eyes. She didn't want to lie to Kitty; she hadn't told the others that the latest communication from Munich had relayed that the organization would cease to exist in a few months' time. The UNRRA was to become the International Refugee Organization. Their work was winding down; the camps would soon be empty. But as Kitty had rightly pointed out, that was not the case at Seidenmühle.

"You think they'll deploy someone from a camp that's closing down?" Kitty wasn't going to let her get away with such an evasive answer.

"I expect so." Martha knew that this was unlikely. It was what she'd thought would happen, but so far there had been no hint of it. It seemed that when a camp closed, the people who had been running it simply melted away to wherever they had come from. She suspected it came down to money. The cost of running the camps was a burden the Allies were obviously keen to shake off as soon as possible.

"I don't know how they can keep on closing camps, though," Kitty said. "No one wants to go back to Poland now. Not even the food bribe is working anymore."

Martha nodded. Stalin's grip on Poland was tightening by the day. Soon there would be no place for the DPs to go.

"I'll write to Charlie," Kitty said. "He's just moved to New York to start his college course. I need to check that it'll be okay for me to be on campus with him."

"What about your parents?" Martha said. "Will they be able to join you there?"

"In theory, yes. Once I'm living in America, I can sponsor them to immigrate." Kitty was looking out the window at the DPs filing past on their way to the mess hall. "I wish I'd heard from them. I haven't had a letter in weeks. Charlie's mother gets a newspaper called the *Chinese Pacific Weekly*. She told him there's civil war there now: the Communists fighting the Nationalists. I just don't know how they're going to get out of Shanghai."

Martha wished there were something she could say to ease Kitty's mind. She had so much to contend with. The troubled, lonely girl Martha had first encountered on the ship from England had transformed into a confident woman forging a future not just for herself and her husband but for her parents, too. If only the people she loved were not on opposite sides of the world, separated by oceans from one another; if only the end of the war had brought peace to China as well as to Europe. *If only . . .* They had to be two of the saddest words in the English language.

A few days later, Delphine got the news that her application for adoption had been approved. It had required months of letter writing and phone calls to get hold of all the documents she needed—copies of her birth and marriage certificates, financial details from her bank, references from the hospital where she'd worked—but finally it had all come through. In the cabin that evening, she passed the letter around for the others to see.

"Oh, this is wonderful news!" Martha angled the paper to the light. "Wait a minute . . ." She broke off, staring at Delphine in astonishment. "There are *three* names here."

"That's right." Delphine beamed at her across the table. "I didn't want to say anything until I was sure it would all go through."

Kitty grabbed the letter from Martha's hand. "Wolf Adamicz, Pawel Bednarz, and Agata Krawiec," she read aloud. "You're adopting *all* of them?"

"How could I not?" Delphine spread her hands, palms up, on the table. "I would have taken on the others, too, if they hadn't been so set on going to work in Warsaw."

"Have you told them yet?" Martha said.

"I thought I'd wait till the weekend. Maybe take them for a picnic in the forest and tell them then."

"They'll be ecstatic." Kitty's eyes were bright. She looked as if she was struggling to hold back tears.

"So will I," Delphine murmured.

"Have you thought about where you'll all live when the work's finished here?" Martha asked.

"Not really. Paris would be the obvious place, and I'm sure they'd pick up the language quite quickly. And in the meantime, they could all get work in the American Hospital." She paused, picking up a spoon and examining it, as if it held the answer to an intractable question. "I'm not sure I could go back there, though. Too many memories."

"That's understandable," Kitty said. "My parents said they feel the same about Vienna. They said it's the last place they'd want to go back to."

"You don't have to go back to France," Martha said. "With your experience, there'd be other countries that would snap you up."

"Only the French colonies," Delphine replied. "I wouldn't be allowed to emigrate to any other place."

"Well, not *yet*," Kitty said. "But things have to loosen up sooner or later. With your language skills, you could work in any English-speaking country."

Her optimism was uplifting. Martha desperately wanted to believe it—not just for Delphine's sake, but for the hundreds of DPs who dreamed of the chance to do what Kitty was suggesting. For Stefan, it was the only solution. Warsaw to him was like Paris to Delphine: a place full of ghosts.

"Maybe I could." Delphine nodded. "Or should I say, *we* could—I'm going to have to get used to saying that, aren't I?"

—————

The following morning Martha and Kitty were catching up on paperwork in the office when the blockhouse leaders came to the door in a state of panic. When Martha let them inside, they were talking so fast she couldn't understand what they were saying.

"There's a rumor flying round that soldiers from the Russian zone are on their way here," Kitty said.

"What?" Martha scanned the anxious faces. The Russian zone of Germany was only thirty miles away. "Why would they be coming here?"

"They say the camp is about to be closed down. The Russians are going to force them to go back to Poland."

"But that's nonsense!" Martha shook her head. "They can't force anyone here to do anything. We're outside of Russian jurisdiction."

"Well, I'll tell them that," Kitty said. "But I'm not sure they'll believe it. They're saying the timber detail is getting ready to fight them off with axes."

"Good grief! We'd better get . . ." The telephone rang out before Martha finished the sentence. She snatched it up, fearing more bad news. It was Major McMahon. What he had to say wasn't good, but it had nothing to do with an imminent invasion by the Russians.

When she replaced the receiver, Martha addressed the blockhouse leaders slowly and calmly, in their own language. "Go back to your people," she said, "and tell them that the US Army is sending us three hundred more Polish DPs. Ask them if the army would do that if the camp was going to be shut down."

The leaders glanced at one another. One by one, they filed out of the office.

"Is it true?" Kitty said when they'd all gone.

Martha nodded. "They're coming in three days' time—from a camp at Wiesbaden that's being closed. Not because of anything the Russians are doing," she added. "It's part of the army's plan to combine the camps so there are less to run."

"They're so scared." Kitty went over to the window. There were knots of people standing around, talking. Even from a distance they looked anxious.

Martha came over to where she was standing. "It's hardly surpris-ing. They devour every word that comes out of Radio Moscow."

"They can't keep sending us more DPs," Kitty murmured. "No one wants to go back to Poland. We're bursting at the seams as it is."

That evening, when Stefan drove into the camp to collect Lubya and Halina, he wasn't driving the old Volkswagen he'd fixed up—he was at the wheel of a sleek black Mercedes sedan. Martha didn't recognize him at first. He was wearing an officer's hat with gold braid and a handsome greatcoat. On his feet were calf-high leather boots.

"Stefan!" She stared at him, amazed at the transformation. "Where did you get that car, and the uniform?"

"They gave it to me this morning." He wasn't smiling. "I have a new job. I am . . ." He hesitated, pronouncing the next words slowly and carefully: "Polish liaison officer for repatriation."

"You're what?"

He leaned back into the car and pulled out a briefcase. He opened it to reveal a set of stamp pads and seals bearing the insignia of his new position. "They say I must go to all the camps in sector twen-ty-three of the American zone. I have to talk to every Polish person. Take names and see the papers that prove they come from Poland. I start here—tomorrow morning." He glanced over his shoulder. The car had attracted interest. People were coming to look at it. He climbed back inside and started the engine. Martha could see how uneasy he was. He wanted to get away before the DPs started asking questions.

Later in the evening, she drove to his cabin. The girls were already asleep, and he was sitting on the edge of the porch tending a fire over which a cooking pot was suspended. He looked like his normal self now—a white collarless shirt had replaced the stiff military-style jacket. He kissed her when she sat down beside him.

"You have had food already? This will be ready to eat soon."

"If I'd known, I would have waited." She smiled. "It smells delicious. What is it?"

"Rabbit. I made a trap." He cocked his head sideways, toward where the trees grew close together. "Lubya and Halina don't like me to do it. I have to say this meat is from the army shop."

"What did the army say this morning," she asked, "when they gave you the uniform and the car?"

"They say I do . . . what do they call it?" He paused, searching for the words. "Nationality screening."

"Did they say what would happen once you'd taken all the names and details?"

He shook his head. "But I don't like what they have asked me to do. When they took me on to work as a translator, I think they only did it because they needed a Polish man to make the DPs go home."

His words made Martha go cold. When she'd asked to see Major McMahon about translation work for Stefan, she hadn't held out much hope. She had been pleasantly surprised when the major had agreed to offer him a job at the base. Now it seemed there may have been a hidden agenda.

"I don't want a shiny car or fancy boots." Stefan poked the fire with a stick, sending a shower of sparks into the night sky. "They say they will give me more money. I didn't ask for that."

"But if you refuse to do what they want, you'll have no job at all?"

"They didn't *say* that, but I think it is true."

"What will you do?"

He stared silently into the flames. "What would you do? If you were me?"

She hesitated, trying to weigh it all. "Actually, all they're asking you to do right now is to gather information that already exists. It could simply be that with all the movement in and out of the camps, they need to clarify exactly who is living where." She sounded as if she was trying to convince herself as well as him. But he needed a job. And they had no proof that the information would be used to force DPs to return to Poland. If he were to quit now, the army would just find someone else to fill the post. "I think you should try it out. Go to a couple of camps and see how people react. And when you hand over the information, ask how they're going to use it."

The next morning, Martha looked down at the shawled women waiting in line outside the kitchen, pails in hand, for their morning coffee brew. She and Kitty were in the mess hall, where the nationality screening was to take place. They were sorting sheaves of birth certificates and baptismal records into alphabetical order for when Stefan arrived to register everyone.

"Do you think he'll come?" Kitty frowned. "I wouldn't blame him if he didn't."

"He doesn't have much choice," Martha said. "He can't exist on fresh air. Much as I'd love to have him living here, I'd have a riot on my hands if I did that."

"Well, you might have one anyway," Kitty said. "You should hear what they're saying out there." She tilted her head sideways. "They're not stupid. They know something's up."

"What are they saying?"

"That if the Russians aren't coming to force them to go back, the army will do the job instead. I've seen people packing suitcases, ready to run if the trucks arrive to take them away."

"But did you explain that the national screening is just a way of keeping track of everyone in the zone?"

"I've been trying to, but they don't believe it. I suppose you can't blame them, given what they went through in the war."

When Martha and Kitty stepped outside the mess hall, the main road through the camp was deserted. The occupants of the first five blockhouses were supposed to be lining up outside, but it seemed that everyone had vanished. The women went to blockhouse one and knocked on the door. There was no response. They knocked again. Eventually the door was opened a couple of inches. The leader peered out at them, a wary look on his face. Martha asked him why he and the others hadn't come to the mess hall.

"Bo boimy się Rosjan." Because we're frightened of the Russians.

It was the same story at the other blockhouses. The glimpse of Stefan's uniform and the insignia on his car had confirmed their worst fears. In their minds, the US Army was hellbent on delivering them up to Stalin's henchmen.

Stefan arrived at the camp half an hour later. He was driving the old Volkswagen, not the sleek Mercedes. The cap, boots, and jacket were missing, too.

"I couldn't sleep," he said when Martha came to greet him. "I've come to tell them I've quit the army job. I don't want them to hate me."

When she told him what had happened, he looked relieved. "I will go back to the army and tell them the DPs refused to show me their papers. Then I will leave." Seeing the look on her face, he took her hands in his. "Don't worry. I can find a new job."

She watched him walk toward the blockhouses. She felt proud of his courage—but fearful for the future. Winter was just weeks away. How would he and the girls get through it if there was no money coming in? The only other job he was likely to get was farm work, and there was precious little of that available at this time of year.

She trudged back to the office with a heavy heart. Kitty had coffee ready for her. She listened in thoughtful silence as Martha told her what Stefan had said.

"Why don't you offer him a job here?" Kitty raised her mug to her lips.

"*Here?*"

"Why not? He could do my job when I leave. UNRRA haven't offered a replacement yet, have they?"

"Well, no but . . ." Martha frowned. "I couldn't, could I? What would the army say?"

"There's nothing in the rules about *employing* an ex-DP—just that they can't live here."

Martha considered this, her mug of coffee suspended halfway between the desk and her mouth. "But how would I pay him?"

"Hmm. I hadn't thought of that." Kitty cocked her head to one side. "What about cigarettes? We've never taken our ration, have we? Between the three of us, we're probably owed hundreds of packs."

Martha's eyes widened. "You mean he'd get his wages by selling them on the black market?"

"He'd probably have to do it somewhere other than here," Kitty said. "He could drive to Fürstenfeldbruck, or some other town, couldn't he?"

"I suppose he could." Martha stared into her mug. It was a wild idea. The major would probably burst a blood vessel if he found out. But it was within the rules. She and Kitty and Delphine were entitled to those cigarettes. What they chose to do with them was no one else's business.

Martha had anticipated a standoff with Major McMahon over the DPs' refusal to register with the national screening program and Stefan's decision to quit his job. But when he called her the following day, it was for a different reason.

"Operation Carrot is off," he informed her gruffly. "No more food incentives."

"Can I ask why?"

"Too many Poles cheating on us. They get to the border, pick up their rations, then jump off the train. They sell the food and sneak back to Germany like stray cats."

Martha closed her eyes, a surge of relief rising from her stomach. "So, what happens to our DPs now?"

"We wait. There are some hopeful signs. Belgium and Britain need men to work in their mines. Canada, too. Nothing official yet, but by spring there should be some movement."

When she put the phone down, Martha had to go and open the window. It was late October and only five degrees outside, but she felt faint and a little dizzy. After all these months of anguish—trying to cajole the DPs into returning to a place that held little hope of a good life—the pressure was suddenly off. Working in the mines didn't sound like a picnic, but it was something. And the countries the major had mentioned were far from the iron curtain creaking ominously over Eastern Europe. With luck, this talk of a need for miners would be just the start. Perhaps it wouldn't be long before nurses, tailors, builders, and carpenters were invited as well.

But the major hadn't named America in his message of hope. An image flashed into Martha's mind—of her standing at the gates of the camp, waving off the last of the DPs, her suitcase in her hand and Stefan and the girls standing forlornly behind her. If they were to have a future together, America was the only possibility. She glanced at the photograph of President Truman pinned to the wall above the desk. *How much longer?* The words echoed inside her head.

CHAPTER 30

The ship that would take Kitty to the United States was due to sail ten days before Christmas.

"Charlie's going to meet me in New York and then we'll fly to San Francisco to spend the holidays with his family," she said when she broke the news to Martha and Delphine. "He says that when the next semester starts, we'll be getting a room in the residence on campus reserved for married students."

"You must be so excited!" Delphine reached out to give her a hug.

"I am." Kitty's eyes were shining. "But I'm nervous, too. And I'm going to be lost without you two."

"You will not!" Martha gave her a wry look. "You won't miss us half as much as we'll miss you."

Later, in the office, Martha asked Kitty what she was planning to do when she was living in New York.

"I'll try to find a job," Kitty said. "I thought I might be able to get something in an office. But what I'd really like to do is study art. Charlie says there's a school of art at Columbia. But I'm not sure I'm good enough to get into a university."

"Kitty!" Martha rolled her eyes. "You're so talented. Your drawings are beautiful."

"I don't know if we'd be able to afford it, though—not with Charlie studying as well."

"I think there are scholarships available at Columbia."

"Even for foreign students?"

"You'd count as an American citizen now that you're married, so that wouldn't be a problem." Martha smiled. "I want you to promise me you'll apply."

"Okay, I promise." Kitty smiled back, but Martha could see that it was an effort. She looked as if she were about to burst into tears. "We will see each other again, won't we? You are going back to New York when the camp closes?"

"That's the plan, but I've got a few mountains to climb to get there."

"Because of Stefan?"

Martha nodded. "I can't imagine my life without him. I'd marry him tomorrow if I could."

"It seems so unfair that you can't get a divorce. I wish there was something I could do to help. Do you think I could try to find Arnie for you?"

"That's sweet of you, but it'd be like looking for a needle in a haystack. New York is a huge city. And I don't even know if he's still there. He could've gone back to Louisiana, for all I know."

"Is that far from New York?"

"About fifteen hundred miles."

Kitty's eyes widened.

"I think you'll be amazed when you see what a vast country America is," Martha said. "You'll get an idea when you fly to San Francisco." She huffed out a sigh. "Makes it all the more senseless, when you think of how much space there is, that the government's so dead set against letting DPs in."

On the day Kitty boarded the train for the coast, Martha and Delphine tried to cheer each other up with plans for Christmas. They were wrapping presents for all the children in the camp in remnants of pretty, shiny fabric from the weaving shed. Each little bundle, tied with string, contained a packet of gum, a bar of chocolate, and a box of Sun-Maid raisins—all taken from the Red Cross delivery that had arrived earlier in the week.

"It's not much, really, is it?" Martha said. "But at least we have something to give them this year."

"Are you going to invite Stefan and the girls over for Christmas?" Delphine glanced up from the table.

"Well, I've been thinking about that," Martha said. "I thought it would be okay to invite him for a meal with us."

"I think it would be better for the girls if they stayed the night. Great fun for them, waking up with all the other kids on Christmas morning."

"I suppose so. But I doubt they'd want to be parted from Stefan. And it would be miserable for him, being alone in the cabin on Christmas Eve."

"I didn't mean the girls should come without him," Delphine replied. "He could stay here, couldn't he? As a guest, for a couple of nights. I'm sure there's nothing in the rules about that."

"Here? You mean . . ." Martha glanced toward the staircase.

"Why not? I could take the girls to sleep next door. They'd love that. You know how they idolize Wolf and the others."

Martha felt a blush rise up to her cheeks. From the sound of it, Delphine had been planning this for a while. The chance of spending a whole night alone with Stefan would be the best Christmas present she could wish for. But she didn't know if he would want it. Was it still too soon for him? And what if people found out that they'd spent the night together? "That's really thoughtful." She reached across the table and squeezed Delphine's hand. "But how would it look to everyone else?"

"No one needs to know." Delphine shrugged. "I'm pretty sure they'll all be too drunk to notice where he sleeps."

Martha nodded. If last year was anything to go by, memories of the three days of Christmas would be at best hazy. "I suppose I could ask him," she murmured.

———

The next day, Stefan arrived with the girls to start his new job as Kitty's replacement. It was strange having him working alongside her in the office. Like turning the clock back to those first days in the camp, when he had been her shadow. She couldn't remember exactly when the easy companionship between them had developed an edge of tension brought on by suppressed desire. Now he was behaving as if he were treading on eggshells. He was being so polite, so careful in everything he said and did. It made her nervous about broaching the subject of Christmas. She rehearsed what she might say, but every time she ran it through her head, it sounded as if she were trying to corner him into sleeping with her.

It was only when they went out into the woods together a few days later to gather foliage to decorate the mess hall that she plucked up the courage. Something about being outside among the trees seemed to free her mind in a way that rarely happened in the confines of the office. She put her hand on his arm as he reached to cut a pine bough. "Stefan, would you and the girls like to come and stay here for a couple of nights over Christmas?"

His forehead furrowed as he turned to her. "I don't want to make a problem for you."

"It wouldn't be a problem," she said. "There's no rule against you staying here for a short time as my guest."

"Where would we sleep? The camp is full."

313

"Delphine suggested that the girls could sleep in the cabin next door, with her and the auxiliaries. She thought they'd enjoy being with the older children." Martha hesitated. She couldn't meet his eyes. She was too afraid of seeing disapproval in them.

"We would be alone? No one else in your house?"

"If you want. But you don't have to. There's the room in the chapel, if you'd feel more comfortable there."

"What do you want?" His voice was soft and low. He didn't sound offended or disconcerted. She raised her head, daring herself to look at him.

"Well . . . I . . . I can't think of anything I'd like better than being alone with you." She searched his face. Nothing in his eyes gave away what he was thinking. "But we don't have to decide now. Why not just see how you feel?"

⟿

Christmas Eve at the camp followed the same pattern as the previous year: Martha was required to raise a glass and dance a sequence of polkas and mazurkas until the celebrations reached a pitch when no one would notice her slipping away.

Stefan remained in the office until it got dark. He hadn't wanted to advertise his presence until the party was well underway.

"It's even wilder than I remember!" Martha groaned as she flopped onto the chair behind the desk. "I'd ask you for a dance, but I don't think I have the energy."

"It's okay." He smiled. "I don't care to dance."

"Oh." Her face fell. She should have been more careful. He hadn't said how or where he had spent last Christmas. She imagined him holed up, alone and freezing cold, in the timber warehouse in Warsaw, mourning his wife. "I'm sorry," she said. "I can understand that this is all a bit much for you."

He tilted his head as he looked at her. There was still a smile in his eyes. "I have a present for you." Bending down, he took something from the bag at his feet. It was a little box, its chestnut-brown surface inlaid with a delicate tracery of paler wood.

"That's beautiful." She angled it to the light when he passed it to her. "Did you make it?"

He nodded. "There is something inside."

She lifted the lid to reveal a nest of blue velvet. Inside the folds was a ring. It was made of three delicate circles of wood, each intricately carved, all interlocking.

"I hope it fits you." He came around the desk and took her hand. He tried the ring on the third finger of her right hand. It fit perfectly. She stared at it, then at him, unable to voice what was in her mind. In Poland, this was the wedding finger.

"Oh, Stefan . . ." Tears stung the corners of her eyes.

"Shhh." He put his finger to his lips. "I know it's not possible right now. But we make believe, yes?"

———

Later, when they made love, it was Stefan who cried.

Martha cradled his head in the crook of her shoulder, feeling the tears seep into her skin. She didn't ask the reason. For him, there was so much to grieve, and he had allowed so little of it out up to now.

In the morning, waking up beside him, she lay for a few moments just looking at his sleeping face. Above the ruffle of blond hair, on the bedside table, she could see the photo of herself with Kitty and Delphine, taken on Christmas Day a year ago by Charlie. They were all smiling, their glasses raised in a toast. What would they have thought if, in that moment, they could have seen into the future? Kitty married and living in America, Delphine the adoptive mother of three children. And herself . . . She turned her gaze back to Stefan, whose eyelids fluttered momentarily in his sleep. A year ago, she'd thought she would never see him again. Like the feather she'd seen floating along the river the day he left her, he'd disappeared from view, entered choppy water, and been pulled under. But he had emerged, bedraggled but intact, farther downstream. There would be more turbulence ahead—that much was certain. But now they would face it together.

CHAPTER 31

The first months of the new year brought no new prospects for the DPs. Martha began to wonder if Major McMahon's conviction that other countries would soon open their doors was nothing more than speculation.

At the end of February, a letter came from Kitty. She was now settled in New York. She'd gotten a job as a typist in an attorney's office, and she had applied to study art at Columbia in the fall. She was still worried about her parents, who were trying desperately to get out of China. The letter said that the Communists were advancing ever closer to Shanghai. Anyone with money was getting out while they still could, but the price of a boat ticket was astronomical. Charlie's parents were trying to work out a way to wire money to them.

Martha's eye traveled down the page. She caught sight of a name that made her catch her breath. *Arnie.* Kitty had found him.

"We have all the New York telephone directories in the office," the letter explained. "I found nine people called Radford with the initial *A* in the Manhattan one. I hope you won't be cross with me—I just had to know if one of them was him. I worked my way through the list, pretending to be an old school friend of yours, newly arrived in New York. The seventh one I tried was Arnie. He called you a name I won't repeat and said he had no idea where you were. Then he slammed the phone down."

Martha stared at the address Kitty had written at the bottom of the page. Arnie was living in the Bowery. No wonder he hadn't replied to any of the letters she'd sent to Williamsburg. She grabbed the pad of airmail paper from the desk drawer and started writing.

———

"Did you tell him that you'd met someone else?" Delphine asked when Martha told her all about it over their evening meal.

"No. I thought that if he knew that, he might refuse—out of spite."

"What will you do if he agrees to a divorce? Could you do it from here?"

"I don't know," Martha replied. "Kitty might be able to help. Now that she's working in an attorney's office, she could probably find out. I might be able to hire someone to act for me, without me actually being there."

Delphine nodded. "What did you say in the letter? Did you give some other reason why you wanted to break up?"

"I just said that I'd be returning to the US before the end of the year, and I wanted to be able to lead an independent life." She glanced at her plate, digging her fork into what remained of the cabbage. "When I met Arnie, I thought that following him to New York would give me the confidence to make a new start. I guess I learned the hard way that marriage isn't really the way to achieve independence." She pushed the morsel of cabbage around her plate, her mind thousands of miles away, imagining Arnie in the kitchen of the apartment in Williamsburg, opening the letter, screwing it into a ball, throwing it across the room, then reaching for the bottle of Jack Daniel's. Of course, he was no longer in that apartment. But it made no difference. Unless he had changed his whole way of life as well as his address, he was unlikely to react favorably to her letter. She was clinging to the hope that he had met someone else and wanted a divorce as much as she did.

"Do you think he'll agree?" Delphine put down her knife and fork and pushed her plate aside.

"I don't know," Martha murmured. "I hope so. I don't know what I'll do if he refuses."

⟡

The following month brought the first real ray of hope for the DPs: Belgium put in an official offer to take twenty thousand coal miners. When the news came through, she and Stefan danced around the office. He went to pass it on to the blockhouse leaders, while she ran to the hospital to tell Delphine.

Delphine clapped her hands together when she heard. "Twenty thousand! That's a big number!"

"They're only taking men under the age of forty," Martha explained. "But there are hundreds here who could qualify."

"What about wives and children? Are they allowed to go?"

"They have to leave their families behind for three months until they've proved themselves in the mines."

"And what about the money? Do they say how much they'll be paid?"

"It's between five and seven dollars a day. If they can stick with it for the two years of the contract, they're allowed to look for other jobs. After five years they're eligible for Belgian citizenship."

Delphine's eyes widened. "There'll be a stampede."

"I know. Stefan's already gone to tell them."

⟡

There was a constant stream of applicants throughout the day. Martha had to tell them that it wasn't going to be her decision who would be chosen. The Belgian government was sending officials to each camp to screen potential recruits. Medical examinations would be required, as well as all the paperwork.

Among the applicants was Marek, the father of Martha's godson. She could hardly speak when he sat down in front of her to answer the questions required on the form. She had always known that a time would come when little Rodek would disappear from her life. But the reality of it was like a fist squeezing her heart.

If that wasn't upsetting enough, Delphine came to the office halfway through the afternoon, grim-faced. She said she'd found Dr. Jankaukas weeping in the side room at the hospital.

"What's happened?" Martha jumped up from the chair. "It's not Anka? Or Mikolaj?"

Delphine shook her head. "They're both fine. It's this." She tilted her head toward the pile of forms lying on the desk. "He wanted to apply."

"To be a *miner*?" Martha gasped.

"He said he'd do anything to get a proper home for Anka and Mikolaj. But he knows he wouldn't even get an interview—because of his missing fingers."

There was no time for Martha to dwell on the wretchedness of what Delphine had described. Part of her was glad that the doctor was debarred from applying. It would be such a terrible waste for a man of his talent to spend his days hewing coal. But there were other men waiting in line who were vastly overqualified for such a job: men who had been architects, bank managers, teachers in their former lives.

It wasn't until the office closed its doors for the day that she had a chance to talk to Stefan. It had occurred to her that he might want to apply himself. Would the prospect of an assured job in Belgium be more tempting than an uncertain future with her?

He shook his head when she asked him. "If it was a coal mine in America, I would say yes."

Martha's eyes went to the floor. Was it selfish of her to hold out this hope that he would be able to go with her to the US when the camp was closed? Could she sit back and watch him miss chances like this, with no real certainty of being able to take him there as her husband? With no response yet from Arnie, she could only hope and pray that America would soon follow Belgium in opening its doors to DPs.

⬥

More than 1,500 of the men living at Seidenmühle met the age criterion for selection to go to Belgium—but only 250 were chosen. The medical tests were the undoing of some applicants. They were checked for everything from venereal disease to TB. Others were rejected because they had too many children or had elderly dependents. It seemed that the shortage of housing in postwar Belgium precluded the admission of any man with a large or extended family.

It was Martha's first experience of selective immigration. There had been no such restrictions on the transports to Poland. She wondered what would happen to the middle aged and elderly, those left disabled by injuries sustained during the war, and those deemed medically unsuitable for admission.

Five weeks later, the selected men prepared to leave the camp. They were the cream of the crop: strong young men whose eyes were alight with eager anticipation as they stood clutching the contracts that were their passports to a new life. Such elation was a rare sight at Seidenmühle.

At dawn on the day of departure, a service was held outdoors. Father Josef stood in front of the trucks that had arrived to take the men to the train. The silver thread in his embroidered stole caught the pink glow in the sky as he raised a tall wooden cross.

"*W imię Ojca i Syna, i Ducha Świętego . . .*" In the name of the Father, Son, and Holy Spirit . . . This was the last blessing the men

321

would receive in their native tongue for a long time. The priest moved along the line of trucks, sprinkling holy water on each one. The men on board bowed their heads and crossed themselves as he passed by. Many had bunches of flowers in their hands, given to them by their wives and girlfriends. As the service ended, Aleksandra passed little Rodek into Marek's outstretched arms. She ran off to wait for him at the camp gates as the engines of the trucks grumbled to life. She wanted her husband to be able to hold his son until the last possible moment.

Martha followed her. Together they watched the procession head onto the road. The tires had left tracks in the dusty ground outside the guardhouse. To Martha, they were more than marks in the earth: they were hieroglyphs spelling out the beginning of the end of what she had come to Germany to do.

CHAPTER 32

Within weeks, offers started coming in from other countries. Canada wanted hard-rock miners and lumbermen. Australia required common laborers. Textile workers were being recruited for Britain and Holland, while domestic workers were needed in France. The tears Dr. Jankaukas had shed at being rejected by the Belgian recruiters were replaced by unbridled joy when he discovered that doctors were wanted in Venezuela.

As spring turned into summer, it seemed that there was no place on earth that was not opening its borders to refugees. Except the United States of America.

Every morning, when Martha went to collect the mail, she would search through the pile for a letter from Arnie. But nothing came. His lack of response was a daily torture. Almost worse than an outright refusal to start divorce proceedings. She didn't know if he'd moved on from the address listed in the telephone directory or was just being bullheaded.

⟺

The mood of hope and expectation that had overtaken the camp was marred by tragedy one morning in May. After watching a convoy of trucks depart with DPs bound for Holland, an elderly man went off into the woods and hanged himself.

Stefan was the one who went to cut down the body and carry it to the mortuary. He came back to Martha with the documents he had found in the man's pockets. Martha's eyes blurred with tears as she stared at the dog-eared papers lined up on the desk. The dead man was "Displaced Person No. 235,452," Georgi Konrad, born in Kraków in 1877. A former plant-breeding expert with a degree from the University of Warsaw. "It's as if he wanted to save us the trouble of identifying him," she murmured. "Why did he take his life?"

"He was seventy years old," Stefan replied. "He had no son or daughter to take him to a new country."

Martha had to call zone headquarters in Munich to inform them of the death. She was told that she must file an incident report. There was a particular form, which she found after a search through the filing cabinets. When she started to write in the details, she saw that there was a box in which she was required to specify the motive for the suicide. After pausing for a moment to consider, she wrote, "Despair."

The following afternoon, Martha sat alone in the chapel when the funeral service was over. Stefan had stayed by the graveside to help shovel the earth back in after the coffin had been lowered into it. She couldn't face returning to the office. She needed to be alone for a while.

As she gazed at the flowers on the altar table, the word she had written on the incident report hung over her like a thundercloud. It was all too easy to understand why Georgi Konrad had taken his own life. For him, there had been no hope. To the emigration officials, he was less a person, more a burden. For him, the future would have consisted of shifting from one dwindling camp to another until the last one closed and he was turned loose to survive in Germany as best he could.

Despair.

She had seen it on so many faces in the two years that she had been in Germany. How naïve she had been to think that, in coming here, she would be able to make everything right. It was like fighting with your arms tied behind your back: a constant battle against red tape and the decisions of faceless politicians in countries thousands of miles away. How could she go back to America, leaving people like Georgi destitute and without hope?

The quiet of the chapel was broken by the sound of footsteps. She turned to see Father Josef walking toward her. Without saying anything, he sat down beside her.

"He was in Dachau," the priest murmured. "He survived all that. And now . . ."

"Why didn't he come to you or me? If we'd known . . ." Her head dropped. "But what could we have said? What could we have offered him?"

"You shouldn't blame yourself. You're not the one who makes these callous rules."

"What about all the others? The old people with no families, the cripples, the TB cases . . . What's going to happen to them when this place closes down?" She snapped her eyes shut, furious with herself for welling up. What use were tears? She should have seen this coming, spoken to someone higher up, demanded to know what was to be done for those who would never make it to another country. "I'm sorry." She fumbled for a handkerchief.

"No need to apologize. It's good to let it out. I wonder how you keep going, with all you have to deal with." He paused. "These people will not be abandoned. The Church is aware of the problem. I'm hoping to stay on in Germany, to help with that work."

Martha screwed her handkerchief into a tight ball. His words shamed her. She'd given just two years to the DPs—but he was giving them his whole future. You had to be a special kind of person to put aside your own hopes and dreams for the sake of others. It hadn't occurred to her, as a child going to church in New Orleans, that this was what being a priest really meant.

"It's not what I imagined I'd be doing," he said. "I always hoped I'd go back to Poland. But I guess none of us could have seen what was coming." He shifted his weight, stretching out his bad leg. "What will you do when the camp closes?"

"You know about Stefan and me? That we'd like to be married, but . . ."

He nodded. "He does talk to me."

"I don't know what we're going to do." Each week that passed brought a creeping sense of hopelessness for a future with Stefan. Seidenmühle was to be closed and amalgamated by the end of October. Her job would no longer exist. What would happen then? "Stefan has passed up every chance to emigrate to the countries that would take him," she went on. "I've asked my husband for a divorce, but he doesn't reply to my letters. Our only hope is for Stefan to be able to emigrate to America with the girls in his own right."

"You think you might have to go back to America alone?"

"I can't bear the thought of that. I keep telling myself that it can't be long before America follows the example of Canada. The newspapers say there's a bill going through Congress." She tried to inject a note of optimism into her voice. But there was no guarantee that the bill would be passed. The wheels of government turned so slowly. How was anything going to change in time for Stefan to join her on a boat to New York?

"As long as you're alive, and you love each other, you'll find a way to get through this." He tapped the side of his head. "What goes on in here makes you despair. But in here . . ." His hand moved to his chest. "Love is hope."

CHAPTER 33

At the end of June, Martha received a call from Major McMahon. The Displaced Persons Act was now set to become law in the USA.

"You need to get moving right away," he barked down the phone. "They're going to let two hundred and two thousand DPs in. They can apply in advance of the act being passed, so the sooner those forms are filled in, the better."

Martha had to suppress the whoop of joy she was dying to let out. "That's such good news. I'll get the word out right away."

"There are discriminatory clauses," the major said. "In fact, there's a whole bunch of 'em. I'll send over all the details."

Martha ran to find Stefan, who had gone across to one of the kitchens to get coffee. When she saw him coming toward her, she grabbed the pot of hot liquid from his hand, laid it on the ground, and threw her arms around him, not caring if anyone saw.

"Hey . . . what happened?" He gave her a bewildered smile.

"America!" She beamed back at him. "You're going to America!"

The elation of that warm summer morning was short lived. The details of the new DP Act arrived with the afternoon guard detail. The major hadn't exaggerated the number of discriminatory clauses. There was just one that applied to Stefan. Martha's insides curled like burnt paper as she read it out to him: "'No adopted children or stepchildren to be allowed entry. No child under the age of sixteen who is not the son or daughter of the named applicant shall be granted the legal right to residence in the United States of America.'"

The color drained from Stefan's face. "That means Halina? They say she can't go?"

"This can't be right." Martha riffled through the pages of the document, desperate to find some qualifying statement, some subclause to take into account people like Stefan, who had taken on children whose parents were dead. But there was no mention of orphans. Those two stark sentences were the death knell for Stefan's hopes. How could he break his daughter's heart by leaving her best friend behind in Germany?

———

That evening, Delphine came back to the cabin to find Martha sitting outside, staring into space.

"I thought you might have gone back with Stefan and the girls," Delphine said. "It's such a lovely evening. Wolf wants us all to go into the woods and make a fire to cook our sausages on."

Martha's head didn't move. She looked as though she hadn't heard a word that Delphine had said. Delphine smiled. "Dreaming about America? Everyone's talking about it. I think Dr. Jankaukas is wishing he hadn't already been accepted for Venezuela."

"Well, it's a good thing he has." Martha's voice sounded strangely quiet. There was an unexpectedly somber quality to it. "They wouldn't let him into the States."

"What? Why not?"

"Mikolaj is not his son." Martha was staring at the ground in front of her feet. "They're not allowing anyone with a child who is adopted."

It took Delphine a moment to grasp the significance of these words. "Oh, Martha . . ." In a single, swift movement, she was beside her, crouching next to the chair. "Stefan . . ."

Martha nodded. When she spoke again her voice was hoarse. "He can't take Halina. I . . . I don't know what we're going to do." She shook her head. "I'm going to have to go back without him. Go to Arnie and beg him for a divorce. Then I'll have to find some way of getting back here so we can get married."

"Couldn't Kitty do something? Could she go to Arnie's place with a lawyer?"

"She already suggested it. But I'd have to be there to sign the papers—*if* he agreed to a divorce. And I'm so afraid that he won't." She raked her hair with her fingers. Delphine could see that her hand was shaking.

"There has to be another way." Delphine slid her arm around Martha's shoulders. "It's not as if Halina would be any kind of burden on the US taxpayer; she'd have you and Stefan to support her."

"I went over and over it," Martha murmured. "There's no loophole in those discriminatory clauses."

"What exactly does it say?"

"That no adopted child or stepchild is to be allowed entry. No child who is not the son or daughter of an applicant will be granted the legal right to residence in the USA."

"Hmm."

"What?" Martha tilted her head toward Delphine.

"No adopted child of an *applicant*?"

Martha nodded, a frown creasing her forehead.

"But there's nothing in the rules to stop *you* taking her to America."

"Me?"

"You could adopt Halina yourself. As an American citizen, there'd be no problem with you taking her home when you leave Germany. I take it Stefan hasn't formally adopted her yet?"

Martha was gazing at her, open-mouthed. "No . . . he . . . I . . . Oh my God, you're amazing!" The last few words were muffled by the folds of Delphine's uniform as Martha grabbed her in a bear hug.

Martha jumped in the car and headed off to find Stefan.

As he spotted her coming along the path through the trees, he put his finger to his lips. The girls were already asleep inside the cabin.

He searched her face as she whispered the solution Delphine had come up with.

"I don't know why I didn't think of it myself," she said.

"You really believe they will allow this?" His eyes were shining.

"There's no reason why not." She glanced across at the door of the cabin. She could see the girls, lying side by side in bed. "I wish we could tell them—they'll be so excited."

"Tomorrow." He smiled as he bent to kiss her.

She pulled him to her. His skin was warm. His lips breathed the hope her words had rekindled in his heart. She took that breath into herself. He was life. And he was hers.

CHAPTER 34

B y the end of September, the camp was beginning to look empty. The biggest single exodus came on the day when the families of the men who had left to work in the mines in Belgium were permitted to go and join them. Martha and Delphine followed the convoy of trucks to the station at Fürstenfeldbruck. When everyone was on board the train, they went from carriage to carriage, kissing and hugging the women and children.

The hardest goodbye was to Aleksandra and Rodek. The little boy who had been born in the back of Martha's car was now two years old. His mother had dressed him in an adorable sailor suit made at the Seidenmühle sewing class. Martha wished Kitty could have seen him. How amazed she would be at the change in him.

"Our godson," Delphine murmured, as Aleksandra held Rodek up to the window. She squeezed Martha's arm as the train began to pull away. "I don't suppose there's much chance of us ever seeing him again. But we gave him a good start in life, didn't we?"

Martha nodded, too choked up to reply. She made herself smile as the happy faces receded into the distance. She pictured the scenes of joy that would follow the arrival of the train in Belgium. So many families about to be reunited at what would be the start of a new and, hopefully, better life. This, she reminded herself, was why she had come to Germany.

As the train disappeared from view, Martha had a sudden vision of Kitty, not much older than some of the children bound for Belgium, waving goodbye at a station in Vienna. It was almost impossible to imagine how Kitty's parents must have felt, sending their only child off to an unknown land, wondering if they would ever set eyes on her again.

Kitty's last letter had contained worrying news about the situation in Shanghai. The Communists were advancing on the city and there was total chaos. She wrote that the docks were crammed with evacuation ships—some so overloaded that one had capsized in the Huangpu River with thousands drowning. Pan Am had sent extra DC-4s to meet the demand from departing Americans, but other foreign nationals like Kitty's parents couldn't get a seat. How terrible for them, to be trapped in China while the daughter they thought they had lost forever was there waiting for them on the other side of the ocean. And what a nightmare for Kitty, desperate to get them back before it was too late.

Martha thought of Kitty's face the night after the Victory Dance at the base, the way her eyes had shone with all the fun, excitement, and romance that evening had held. It had been a wild celebration—an eruption of joy that the world war was over, carrying with it the belief that this would not, could not, ever happen again. But the world was not at peace. The families bound for Belgium were so afraid of what was going on in Poland, they would probably never set foot in their homeland again. And in China, people like Kitty's parents were, once again, fearing for their lives.

When would it ever end?

⊷

A week later, Martha was back in Fürstenfeldbruck to sign the adoption papers for Halina. It had taken less time than she'd anticipated—thanks to Kitty's help getting the documents she needed from America.

"Can I see?" Delphine was waiting with celebratory glasses of vodka when Martha arrived back at the camp.

Martha fished the documents out of her bag. Halina's new name appeared in bold type at the top of each page.

"Halina Radford! It has a ring to it, doesn't it?" Delphine beamed.

"It ought to be Halina Dombrowski." Martha sighed. "I hope it will be, one day."

"I'm sure it will. Once you get back to America, you'll be able to sort things out with Arnie." Delphine put her hand into her pocket. "I had some exciting news while you were out." She handed a sheet of paper to Martha.

"New Zealand!" Martha looked up from the letter, open-mouthed.

"I never thought, in my wildest dreams, I'd be going there." Delphine laughed.

"So, you'll be escorting two hundred orphans from camps across the American zone . . ." Martha read aloud, "'to be placed with families waiting to adopt children of all ages.'"

"And they're providing me and my children with a rented house in Auckland. It couldn't be better, could it?" Delphine handed Martha a glass of vodka. "I think that deserves a toast, don't you? To New Zealand!" She clinked her glass against Martha's. "And to the future Mr. and Mrs. Dombrowski!"

Martha raised the vodka to her lips, but the smell of the alcohol made her feel nauseous. She ran to the bathroom.

"Martha! Are you okay?" Delphine was calling from the other side of the door.

"I . . . I'm fine." She felt her jaw tremble as she spoke.

"You don't look fine. Was it something you ate?"

"I . . . no . . . it's just . . ."

"Oh my God." Delphine's hand went to her mouth. "Is it what I think it is?"

"I . . . I'm not sure. I . . ." She sat down, holding the table for support. "Oh, Delphine," she whispered, "I'm so afraid."

"Afraid?" Delphine was beside her in an instant. "Why? It doesn't matter that you're not married. Stefan loves you. He'll be there for you—you mustn't worry about that."

Martha shook her head. "It's not that."

"What is it, then?"

"I lost a baby. When I was with Arnie. She was born prematurely— at five months. She was so tiny, so perfect . . ."

"Oh, Martha. I knew there must be something. I remember your face when Jadzia's baby was found in the river. There was something in your eyes—beyond the shock of what had happened."

"I never thought I could get pregnant again. I'm so scared I'll lose this one, too."

"You mustn't think like that." Delphine took both of Martha's hands in hers. "In my experience, it's quite common for women to lose a first pregnancy but go on to have healthy babies."

"I didn't know that," Martha murmured.

"That's because no one talks about it. It's kept hidden—a private pain."

"Arnie never wanted to talk about it. That's when things started to go really wrong between us. His drinking got a lot worse after it happened. I blamed myself for that. I thought that if I could have given him a child, he would have been a different person. But he didn't even want to try. He used to look at me as if I was . . ."

"Don't dwell on that." Delphine pulled Martha to her. "How about we get you properly examined? How far on do you think you are?"

"A couple of months. Maybe more."

"Have you told Stefan?"

"Not yet."

Delphine nodded. "Maybe better to wait until you're sure. He's going to be so excited."

"I'm terrified of telling him. I won't breathe a word until I absolutely have to."

"I can understand that. But listen to me: you're a fit, healthy woman. I've never known you to have a day's illness, the whole time we've been here. Just remember that—and try not to worry."

Martha gave her a wan smile. She so wanted to believe what Delphine had implied: that her good health was likely to mean a successful pregnancy. But it wasn't going to stop her from worrying. Because somewhere deep inside, she didn't feel she deserved this undreamed-of happiness.

CHAPTER 35

On a cold, crisp day in October, the Fürstenfeldbruck train reached its final destination. It had been a long time since Martha had smelled sea air. As she stepped onto the platform at Bremen, gulls wheeled overhead. In the distance she could see the funnels of enormous ships anchored in the docks.

Delphine was in the next carriage with her group of orphans. Martha caught a glimpse of Wolf, so tall now, jumping down from the train and catching one of the smaller children in his arms. Delphine followed. She wagged her finger at Wolf, but Martha could see that she was smiling as she looked up at him.

"Mama? Are we there now?" Halina, who had been asleep for the last part of the journey, was standing beside her.

"Yes, darling." Martha would have held her up to see the ships, but Delphine had warned her against lifting anything.

"Papa says when we get to America, we can have ice cream. Is that America?" She pointed to the ticket office at the far end of the platform.

"We're not there yet." Martha ruffled Halina's dark curls. "We have to go on the ship first. It'll be so exciting: you and Lubya will have special beds with a ladder to climb up."

Stefan appeared in the doorway, a suitcase in each hand, with Lubya peeping out behind him. Without thinking, Martha reached up to take the luggage from him. He smiled, shaking his head. "You go and say goodbye to Delphine," he said.

Martha had known there wouldn't be much time once they arrived at the port. After they got through the ticket barrier, they were unlikely to see each other again. They had said their goodbyes at the camp, at a farewell dinner made from the random selection of canned food remaining in the warehouse.

Delphine looked around as Martha touched her shoulder. The smile didn't leave her face, but the muscles around her mouth tightened. "This is it, then." She held out her arms for one last hug.

"You'll write to me, won't you?" Martha felt her throat swell as tears filled her eyes.

"Of course." Delphine's words were muffled by the collar of Martha's coat. "And I want you to promise to let me know the moment that baby is born."

"I promise."

They broke away as a whistle blew farther along the platform. A man was holding up a cardboard sign with "New Zealand" scrawled across it.

"That's us." Wolf tugged at Delphine's sleeve. "We better get these kids moving."

Through a blur of tears, Martha watched them walk away. Wolf and Agata and Pawel, still children themselves, but looking so grown up as they helped Delphine shepherd the group of little ones to the ship that would take them to their new lives.

"Mama! Hurry up!" two voices called out in unison. Lubya and Halina ran up to her, each grabbing her hand.

"I'm coming." She bent to kiss them both. When she looked up, Delphine had gone.

CHAPTER 36

On a bright New Zealand morning in March, Delphine kissed each of her children as they made for the door. Wolf was now almost a foot taller than she was. He and Agata and Pawel were beginning to develop Kiwi accents. It made her smile to see them with their school friends, speaking English as if they'd known it all their lives.

A few minutes after they'd gone, the mail arrived. Delphine's heart skipped a beat when she caught sight of an airmail envelope with a row of red US postage stamps. She tore open the flap and pulled out the thin sheets of paper.

> *Dear Delphine,*
> *We have a new daughter! She cleverly arrived on Stefan's birthday, March 2, and weighed 6 lb. 10 oz. Her name is Joanna—chosen by Lubya and Halina in honor of their favorite nun at the convent in Poland.*
>
> *Kitty came to visit me in the hospital. Her parents have just arrived in New York after a long journey via San Francisco. They weren't allowed to go anywhere when they got off the boat; they were put on a sealed train that brought them all the way to Ellis Island. Stefan was there when they arrived—he has a job at the embarkation*

center now—and he told me all about it. I wish I could have been there to see their faces.

Kitty has found an apartment for them in Queens, not far from where she and Charlie are living. She's loving the art course at Columbia. Did I tell you she was awarded a scholarship? It means that she and Charlie don't have to worry too much about money. It's wonderful to see her so happy.

I was so pleased to hear that your three are all settling into their new school. I wouldn't be surprised if Agata and Pawel followed Wolf's plan to go to medical school. You must be so proud of them.

I have one more bit of news to tell you before the nurse brings Joanna back for her next feeding: I managed to find Arnie. He'd moved from the apartment listed in the telephone directory—within days of Kitty calling him—which explained why I never got a reply to my letters. The amazing thing is that he has recently become a father, and it has made him turn his life around. He's as eager as I am for a divorce. So, Stefan and I are planning a summer wedding. The girls can't wait to be bridesmaids . . .

The writing blurred as Delphine read on. She was smiling and crying as she laid the letter down. There was something else inside the envelope. A copy of the snap Charlie had taken that first Christmas at Seidenmühle of the three of them, all smiling as they raised their glasses in a toast.

There was something on the back of it. Turning it over, Delphine saw what Martha had written: "To life—wherever it takes us."

AUTHOR'S NOTE

The idea for *A Feather on the Water* came from a photograph I found by chance. I was searching for an image of Marie Louise Habets, the former nun who inspired my earlier novel *The House at Mermaid's Cove*. I came across a black-and-white shot of her with another woman, both wearing military-style uniforms with the symbol of the United Nations Relief and Rehabilitation Administration on their caps. The other woman was Kathryn Hulme, the American journalist who wrote a book based on Marie Louise's life, *The Nun's Story* (which became a film starring Audrey Hepburn). I discovered that the women had met while working in a DP camp in Bavaria at the end of WWII, and that Kathryn had written about their experiences in another book, called *The Wild Place*. While the protagonists in my novel are purely fictional, many of the challenges they face reflect what Kathryn and Marie Louise encountered when they became aid workers.

Some of the characters in *A Feather on the Water* are not imaginary but real. Mr. Ho, the Chinese diplomat, is one of these. Feng Shan Ho helped thousands of Austrian Jews escape the Nazis by issuing them transit visas. In trying to discover why he did so, when other embassies in Vienna refused to help, I found out that Mr. Ho was born into poverty and lost his parents at a young age but was helped by Norwegian missionaries based in the Hunan Province of China. They gave him an education and taught him to give back to society in return for the gifts he had been given. In issuing the visas, he disobeyed the instructions of his superiors. Two years into the war, he was removed from his diplomatic post and sent back to China. In 2000 he was posthumously awarded the title of Righteous Among the Nations by Yad Vashem in Jerusalem for his humanitarian courage.

Another character who really existed is Laura Margolis, the representative of the American Jewish Joint Distribution Committee. She arrived in Shanghai in 1941, and of the approximately twenty thousand German and Austrian refugees then living in the city, eight thousand received at least one meal a day from the Joint's soup kitchens. Despite being interned for a time by the Japanese, she managed to keep the soup kitchens running.

I have used some literary license in the dates of certain historical events outlined in the novel. The evacuation of Shanghai began in October 1948 (not 1947, as I suggested). The sinking of the steamer *Kiangya* during the evacuation happened in December 1948. An estimated two thousand to three thousand passengers drowned—a higher death toll than that of the *Titanic*.

The DP Act allowing refugees into America wasn't passed until June 1948 (a year later than in my story). In October that year, the ship *General Black* arrived in New York Harbor—the first to bring DPs to the USA after WWII. Soon after, other ships arrived in Boston and New Orleans. It wasn't until February 1949 that the first Jewish refugees from Shanghai arrived in San Francisco, to be transferred to sealed trains that took them to Ellis Island in New York.

It took a long time for the millions of people displaced by WWII to find new homes. There were still camps operating in Germany in the 1950s. The last one closed in 1959, fourteen years after the fighting had ended.

ACKNOWLEDGMENTS

In addition to Kathryn Hulme's *The Wild Place*, Ben Shephard's book about the aftermath of the Second World War, *The Long Road Home*, was an invaluable source of information about Displaced Persons camps and the people who ran them. When researching the Kindertransport, I learned much about how it felt to be a child taken away from Nazi-occupied Vienna by reading Lore Segal's *Other People's Houses*. I also gathered vital information for the creation of the character Delphine from Anne Sebba's fascinating book *Les Parisiennes: How the Women of Paris Lived, Loved, and Died*.

Thank you to Jodi Warshaw and everyone at Lake Union Publishing for the great job they do. I'm also grateful to Christina Henry de Tessan for her perceptive suggestions during the editing process.

Huge thanks to my family for their unwavering support—particularly my daughter, Ruth, who made exploring Brooklyn so much fun, and Steve, my husband, for all the early-morning coffees and his unfailing good humor. Finally, thank you to my mum, my champion and my number-one fan: I'm heartbroken that you passed away before you got to read this.

ABOUT THE AUTHOR

Photo © 2017 Isabella Ashford

Lindsay Jayne Ashford is the author of *The House at Mermaid's Cove*, *The Snow Gypsy*, *Whisper of the Moon Moth*, *The Color of Secrets*, and *The Woman on the Orient Express*, which blend fiction with real events of the early twentieth century. Lindsay began her career as a novelist with a contemporary crime series featuring forensic psychologist Megan Rhys, followed by the historical mystery *The Mysterious Death of Miss Jane Austen*. Raised in Wolverhampton in the United Kingdom, Lindsay was the first woman to graduate from Queens' College, Cambridge, in its 550-year history. She earned a degree in criminology and was a reporter for the BBC before becoming a freelance journalist. She has four children and divides her time between a seaside home on the west coast of Wales and a farmhouse in Spain's Sierra de Los Filabres. Lindsay enjoys kayaking, bodyboarding, and walking her dogs, Milly and Pablo. Visit the author at http://lindsay-jayne-ashford.com.